I0699571

PHOENIX

PHOENIX, Volume 1

George A. Maxim

Published by George A. Maxim, 2024

Phoenix: Born of Ruin
Copyright © 2024 by George A. Maxim
All rights reserved.

No part of this publication may be reproduced, distributed, or transmitted in any form or by any means, including photocopying, recording, or other electronic or mechanical methods, without the prior written permission of the publisher, except in the case of brief quotations embodied in critical reviews and certain other noncommercial uses permitted by copyright law.

For permission requests, write to the author at:

info@georgemaximauthor.com

Contents

To my incredible wife and best friend Amanda, whose unwavering support, endless patience, and loving nudges kept me going when I needed it most. Your feedback and belief in me made this journey possible.

To my two amazing boys Zach and Vinny, whose excitement for this story inspired me every step of the way - this adventure is for you!

(1)

Out of the Ashes

The wind howled through the crumbling remnants of the old world. Shattered buildings jutted out of the earth like broken teeth, their edges softened by decades of erosion and decay.

Phoenix stood at the edge of what used to be a city, its name long forgotten, buried beneath years of dust and ruin. She gripped the handle of her knife, her knuckles white. Beside her, Edward's breathing was shallow, his eyes wide with fear and exhaustion.

They had been running for hours, maybe days, since the raid. The memory of it was still fresh, an image of fire and screaming seared into her mind. It had come out of nowhere, just like everything did in this world. One moment they were a tribe, a family. The next, they were two.

"Are we safe here?" Edward whispered, his voice barely audible over the wind.

Phoenix glanced at him, her heart heavy with the weight of this responsibility. But there was no choice. There hadn't been a choice for years.

"For now," she assured him, though she didn't believe it. Nowhere was safe.

She scanned the horizon. The sky was a muted gray, as it had been for as long as she could remember. They told stories, back when there were elders to tell them, about how the sky used to be blue, and the ground used to be green. That world was gone now, swallowed by the collapse seventy-eight years ago. A catastrophe no one understood anymore.

She didn't know what had caused it, or why it had taken everything. She only knew the world they had been left with: a place where every day was a battle for survival.

"We need to move," she prompted, nudging Edward to his feet. "We can't stay here."

"But where are we going?"

Phoenix didn't answer right away. She didn't know. All she had was the last words their mother had said before the raid, whispered into her ear as she bled out on the cold ground.

"Find the Haven."

What that meant, or where it was, Phoenix had no idea. It was the only thread she had left. She would follow it for Edward's sake.

"We're going to find home," she said, her voice falsely confident.

They began to walk, the knife clutched tight in Phoenix's hand, the ruins of the world looming largely around them.

They walked in silence, their footsteps muffled by the thick layer of ash and dirt that coated the ground. The world's silence was oppressive, broken only by the occasional, distant rumbling of something shifting in the landscape.

Phoenix kept her senses sharp. Her ears strained for any sign of movement. In this world anything could be lurking: raiders, wild animals, or things far worse-creatures that should have never existed but did, shaped by the collapse and the chaos that followed.

Edward kept close behind her. His hand brushed the hem of her worn jacket as if to find reassurance. He hadn't spoken much since the raid, and Phoenix couldn't blame him. What was there to say when everything they had ever known had been taken from them?

After hours of walking, they reached the outskirts of an old city. What lay ahead was a wasteland of broken streets, collapsed buildings, and twisted metal. Some structures still stood, but they leaned dangerously, ready to crumble with the slightest push. Nature had long since reclaimed much of the land, but even the plants were strange here, their leaves grayish and brittle.

"We should find somewhere to rest," Edward suggested, his voice small.

Phoenix nodded, scanning the area for anything that could serve as shelter. Her body ached. Fatigue gnawed at her bones, but she couldn't let her guard down. Not yet. She spotted a half-collapsed building up ahead. Its entrance was dark but intact.

"There," she said, pointing. "We can stay in there. But only for a few hours."

Edward hesitated, staring at the shadowed opening of the building.

"Do you think it's safe?"

Safe. The word felt foreign, almost meaningless in a world where safety was a myth. But Phoenix couldn't show fear, not to him.

"It'll do for now. Come on."

They approached the building cautiously. Phoenix's grip tightened on the knife. Inside, the air was damp, and the floor was littered with debris. A long-abandoned fire pit sat in the center of what might have been a room. The faint outline of graffiti clung to the walls, the colors long faded beyond recognition.

Phoenix led Edward to a corner, where they could sit with their backs against the wall. She dug into a small pack she had scavenged after the raid and pulled out a few scrapes of dried food. It wasn't much, but it would keep them going.

"Here," she said, handing a piece to Edward.
He took it, chewing slowly, his eyes far away.

Phoenix barely tasted the food. Her mind was elsewhere, drifting back to the raid, the fires, the screams…

The strange creatures that had attacked. They weren't like any animal she had seen before. They were bigger, and faster. Their eyes gleamed unnaturally in the darkness. They moved with a purpose, but Phoenix couldn't understand what drove them. Their sudden and vicious assault seemed almost orchestrated, a brutal force that had torn through her tribe with terrifying efficiency.

What were they? Why had they come now, after all these years of barely surviving?

"Do you think we'll find it?" Edwards' voice broke through her thoughts.

Phoenix blinked, turning to him. "Find what?"

"The Haven," he whispered. "Mom said it was real."

For a moment, Phoenix didn't know what to say. Did she believe in the Haven? Or was it just a story their mother told to give them hope in a world that had none?

"I don't know," she admitted quietly. "But we'll try. We'll keep moving until we find something."

Edward nodded, his face serious. "I believe you."

Phoenix wished she could believe herself.

They settled into an uneasy silence as the weight of the world pressed down on them. Tomorrow, they would have to keep moving. Tonight, they would rest – if only for a little while.

Phoenix couldn't sleep. Her eyes fluttered open every time a distant noise echoed through the broken walls. She clutched her knife tightly, the handle rough in her palm. Edward had dozed off, curled against her side. His breathing was steady and calm.

She glanced down at him, taking in his small, delicate form. He had always been fragile—sickly, with bouts of weakness that left him bedridden for days when they were younger.

Even then, Phoenix had felt like she was holding her breath, watching over him as though the slightest gust of wind could carry him away. The collapse of their world hadn't changed that. If anything, it made her even more aware of how vulnerable he was, especially in a place as harsh as this.

The journey ahead would be long and filled with dangers she couldn't predict. She knew Edward's strength would be tested. She could see the toll it had already taken on him; the shadows under his eyes, the faint tremor in his hands when he was cold or frightened. Somehow, he found the resolve to keep moving. It was a quiet courage she had never expected of him, and she cherished it deeply.

For a moment she envied him – his ability to find peace in the fractured world, even if only for a few hours.

Phoenix couldn't let her guard down. The creatures that attacked their tribe haunted her thoughts. Their glowing eyes, their unnatural speed nothing the elders told them prepared her for creatures like that. It was as though the collapse had twisted the world into something new and monstrous.

Her mother's words once again echoed in her mind. "Find the Haven."

She closed her eyes, trying to summon an image of it. In the stories, the Haven was a place untouched by the collapse. It was a sanctuary hidden somewhere far from the chaos and destruction. It had always sounded like a myth, a fairy tale told to children to help them sleep at night. Was it real, or was she leading Edward on a hopeless journey?

A soft sound snapped her out of her thoughts – a faint scratching noise from outside. Phoenix's heart skipped a beat. She sat up slowly, trying not to wake Edward, and strained her ears.

There it was again, a low scraping sound like nails against the stone.

Her grip tightened on the knife. She slid out from under Edward, moving silently across the room towards the crumbling doorway. The darkened city was still but the noise continued.

Her pulse quickened. If something had tracked them here, they wouldn't stand a chance. She glanced back at Edward's small figure huddled against the wall, and her resolve hardened. No matter what, she wouldn't let anything happen to him.

She pressed herself against the wall next to the doorway. Her knife was poised. The scraping sound grew louder, followed by shuffling and heavy breathing.

Phoenix's heart pounded in her ears. She took a slow, deep breath, trying to steady her shaking hands. Whatever it was, it was just outside now. She could feel it.

Without warning, the shape appeared in the doorway – a shadowy figure, hunched and massive. Its breathing was ragged and uneven.

Phoenix's instincts kicked in. She lunged, slashing out with the knife. But the figure was faster than she expected. It sidestepped her attack, a low growl escaping its throat as it turned to face her.

In the dim light, she caught a glimpse of its face – human, but not. Its skin was pale, stretched tight over its bones. Its eyes glowed faintly in the darkness. A mutant; one of the twisted remains of humanity.

She scrambled backwards and her back hit the wall. The creature stepped toward her, its movements jerky and unnatural. She raised her knife again, but she knew she was outmatched.

Before the creature could close the distance, a sudden voice rang out.

"Stop!"

Edward. He was awake, standing just behind her. His voice was strong despite the fear in his eyes.

The creature paused, tilting its head as if considering the command. For a long, tense moment, no one moved.

To Phoenix's astonishment, the creature then turned around and slinked back into the shadows, disappearing into the ruins.

Phoenix's breath came in ragged gasps. She lowered the knife, her hands trembling.

"W-What just happened?" She asked her voice barely above a whisper.

Edward didn't answer right away. He stared after the creature with an unreadable expression. Finally, he spoke with a low voice.

"I think it understood me."

Phoenix stared at Edward, disbelief written across her face.

"What do you mean it understood you?"

Edward Shook his head, rubbing his arms as if trying to warm himself from an invisible chill. "I don't know, Phen. I just felt like it would listen if I spoke. Like it knew what I was saying."

Phoenix tried to process what had just happened. The creature – mutant, whatever it was – had been ready to attack. Yet, Edward, with just one word, had stopped it. It didn't make any sense to her.

She stood next to him, placing a hand on his shoulder.

"Are you ok?" She asked, her voice softening.

Edward nodded. He looked shaken, but there was something else in his eyes now too - something Phoenix couldn't quite place. He was afraid, yes, but he seemed curious. It was as if he wondered what else he could do, or if that strange connection meant something more. He was trying to understand what he had just done.

She glanced warily towards the doorway. The night outside was heavy with uncertainty. "We need to leave at first light. Whatever that thing was, we are not safe here."

They settled back against the wall, neither of them able to sleep now. The remnants of the old world loomed outside, watching over them in silence.

As the hours passed, Phoenix found herself thinking about the mutant, the raiders, and everything that had come since the collapse. None of it made sense. The elders talked about the fall of society as if it had been swift – like a series of dominoes collapsing one after the other. Governments failed, resources dwindled, and eventually, the world fell apart. But the stories didn't explain why everything had changed, why creatures and people become twisted versions of themselves.

Seventy-eight years was long enough for the world to adapt, but what if something deeper had caused the collapse? Something had altered more than just the cities and the land. Something had changed the very people themselves.

"Do you think the Haven is real?" Edward's voice broke through her thoughts.

Phoenix sighed. She had been avoiding that question for days.

"I want to believe it is," she said. "But I don't know. Mom believed in it, though. That has to mean something."

Edward nodded, his expression thoughtful. "I don't think we're the only ones looking for it."

Phoenix frowned, turning to him.

"What do you mean?" She asked.

"Those creatures, and the raiders. I think they're all trying to survive just like us. If the Haven is real, maybe they're all trying to find it too," he said.

The thought sent a chill down Phoenix's spine.

"If that is true, then we need to find it first," she said.

Edward nodded slowly, determination settling into his features. "We will."

As the sky began to lighten with the first hint of dawn, Phoenix stood up. Her body ached from the sleepless night. She reached for her knife, the familiar weight of it felt comforting in her hand.

She nudged Edward gently, saying, "It's time to move."

They slipped out of the crumbled building, leaving behind the ruins and whatever had been lurking in the shadows. The road ahead was long and dangerous, but Phoenix's grip on her knife remained. She wasn't fighting just fighting for survival anymore. She was fighting for something more – hope. And that was a dangerous thing in this world.

The sun had barely risen. The sky remained a dull, oppressive gray, casting a muted light over the wasteland. The air was thick with the scent of dust and decay, but there was no time to take in the desolation. Every second in the open was a risk, and Phoenix knew it.

The road ahead was more a path of rubble than a proper street. Whatever city this had once been was unrecognizable now, overgrown and broken beyond repair. They moved quickly. Phoenix took the lead, and Edward stayed a step behind her.

After the encounter with the mutant, Phoenix's senses were heightened. She found herself scanning every shadow for movement; every whisper of wind from the shadows made her feel tense.

"We need to get out of the open," Phoenix muttered, glancing over her shoulder at Edward.

He nodded, his face still pale from the night before. "Where are we heading?"

Phoenix stopped for a moment, her eyes scanning the horizon. In the distance, she could see the crumbling skeletons of what had once been tall buildings. They leaned against each other like ancient giants, barely standing after years of neglect.

"Those buildings might provide some cover," she said, pointing towards them. "We can move through them and maybe find something useful."

Edward didn't argue. They pressed on; the silence between them was thick with unspoken fear. Phoenix knew that despite his calm exterior, Edward was just as scared as she was. Maybe even more so. But there was no room for fear if they wanted to survive.

As they reached the outer edge of the collapsed buildings, Phoenix slowed. The structures groaned under their weight. Now and then, chunks of debris would fall from one of the rooftops, crashing into the ground with a dull thud. It was risky, but they needed to find shelter before nightfall.

"Stay close," Phoenix whispered, leading Edward into the maze of broken concrete and twisted metal.

The air was cooler here. The shadows between the buildings were deep and long. Phoenix scanned the area, searching for any sign of movement. But the silence was unnerving. Too quiet.

"We should look for supplies," Edward suggested, his voice a soft murmur.

Phoenix agreed. "If there's anything left."

They chose a building and entered into it.

The inside of the building had been looted long ago, the shelves bare and the walls covered in layers of dirt and graffiti. Broken glass crunched under their feet as they moved through what looked like an old office or apartment complex, the remnants of desks and chairs scattered about in pieces.

"Look over there," Edward said, pointing to a small cabinet half buried under debris.

Phoenix nodded and began to clear the rubble away. They hadn't found much on their journey – enough food to survive, but nothing more. Every discovery was a chance, slim as it might be, to live another day.

After a few minutes, they managed to pull the cabinet open. Inside was a small stash – canned food, dusty but intact, and a couple of old blankets. Phoenix's heart leaped.

"This'll help." She said, handing a can to Edward. "We'll make this last."

Edward smiled, but the smile didn't quite reach his eyes. "We're lucky."

Luck, Phoenix wasn't sure what it was anymore. Everything felt like a gamble. One wrong move and they would lose everything. But today, they found something. That was enough for now. They each finished a can of food gratefully, setting the cans aside.

Before they could settle in further, a sound echoed through the hollow building. A faint shuffle, the clink of metal against stone.

Phoenix froze. Her hand shot out, motioning for Edward to be still.

Her heart pounded in her chest as she listened, straining to make out the direction of the sound. They were not alone.

And then, from the shadows, a figure emerged. It was a man. He was thin and ragged, wearing tattered clothes. His eyes were wild and darting, visibly in survival mode. He held a makeshift spear in one hand, his body tense as he spotted them.

"Who are you?" The man rasped, his voice hoarse. "What are you doing here?"

Phoenix's grip tightened on the knife. She stood up in front of Edward, her body ready to defend him if it came to that.

"We don't want any trouble," she replied, her voice steady. "We're just passing through."

The man's eyes flickered between them, his gaze settling on the small stash of supplies they had uncovered. His lips curled into a hungry smile.

"Well, it looks like you've found something worth keeping," he smirked, taking a step closer.

Phoenix's heart sank. She could feel the tension building in the air, the threat looming over them. She knew that this man was going to fight them for what they had.

Suddenly, the ground beneath them trembled. An ominous rumble echoed through the building. The man hesitated, his spear lowering slightly as his eyes darted nervously toward the ceiling. Dust and debris rained down upon them, and all three of them covered their heads with their hands.

"What's happening?" Edward yelled, the fear evident in his voice.

Phoenix's mind raced, realizing the structure might collapse on top of them.

A shrill alarm pierced the air—loud, mechanical, and unrelenting.

The man's eyes widened in panic. "His fear was palpable, but it wasn't the alarm that had shaken him.

No... no, not now," he muttered, backing away slightly.

From somewhere deep within the ruins, a familiar growl echoed — a sound Phoenix and Edward knew all too well. The creatures. They were back. Phoenix's blood turned to ice.

The man's desperation for food was now overshadowed by a shared terror between the three of them. He turned his head, scanning the shadows towards the sound of the creatures.

Phoenix seized the moment. "We need to leave, now!" She shouted over the alarm.

The man didn't listen to her. His gaze was fixed on the darkness beyond the crumbling walls, his knuckles white as he gripped his spear. "They're coming," he cautioned, almost to himself. "They always come when the alarm goes off."

In the distance, the growls grew louder, more frantic. The creatures were headed toward them.
"Let's go!" Phoenix yelled, grabbing Edward's arm and pulling him toward the door.

The man stood frozen, paralyzed by the fear.

As Phoenix and Edward bolted for the exit, the building began to shake more violently. Larger chunks of debris started to fall around them. The alarm blared louder, drowned by the snarls of the approaching creatures.

They didn't look back to see if the man followed — his fate was not their concern.

Bursting into the open air, they didn't stop running until the ruins were a distant silhouette behind them. Only then did Phoenix allow herself to breathe again.

Edward panted beside her, his face pale. "That was close," he gasped.

Phoenix nodded, her heart still pounding. She glanced back toward the ruins, the alarm now a faint echo in the distance. "We need to keep moving. They'll be out here soon."

Without another word, they continued, leaving the collapsing building—and whatever horrors still lurked within—behind.

As they moved farther from the crumbling buildings, Phoenix cast one last glance over her shoulder, her grip tightening on the hilt of her knife. The road ahead was long, but she would protect Edward, no matter what it took.

(2)
Shelter of secrets

The sun was setting, casting long shadows across the barren landscape. Phoenix and Edward walked in silence, their earlier tension replaced by exhaustion. The desolate stretches of land seemed endless, a stark contrast to the vibrant world that it once was.

Phoenix had chosen a sheltered alcove between two large boulders for their rest. The space was small, but it offered some protection from the wind. They set their meager supplies inside and took a moment to rest, both eager for the comfort of a reprieve.

The storm hit unexpectedly. Dark clouds gathered on the horizon, and within minutes, the sky was a roiling mass of gray, thick with the promise of rain and lightning. The wind howled, and the temperature dropped, sending a chill through the air.

"We need to find a better cover!" Phoenix shouted over the roar of the storm.

Edward nodded, shivering as he followed her lead. They dashed through the rain, their visibility reduced to mere feet. The wind whipped around them, making every step a struggle.

Through the curtain of rain ahead, Phoenix spotted a faint glow. She pushed forward, guiding Edward toward it. The outline of a hidden entrance became visible as they neared — a set of heavy metal doors, partially obscured by debris. The glow was coming from beneath the doors; a warm, inviting light amid the storm.

"Help me with this!" Phoenix shouted.

Together, they heaved the doors open, revealing a dimly lit underground bunker. The space was surprisingly warm and dry. It was a stark contrast to the tempest outside. They stumbled in, soaked and shivering. The doors closed behind them with a resounding thud.

The bunker's interior was cluttered with old technology and mechanical parts. The soft hum of machinery filled the air, a comforting background to the howling storm above. Phoenix and Edward glanced around, trying to get their bearings.

Before they could take in much, a figure emerged from the shadows. She was a rugged woman, perhaps in her early forties. She had piercing eyes that seemed to hold a depth of unspoken secrets. Her clothes were functional but worn. She moved toward Phoenix and Edward warily.

"Who are you?" The woman demanded, her voice sharp and devoid of warmth. "This is my home."

Phoenix took a cautious step forward, her relief tempered by wariness. "We were caught in the storm. We didn't mean to intrude."

The woman's gaze was icy.

"This place isn't a refuge for the lost." She paused, her eyes flickering over them with a calculating intensity. After brief consideration, she said to Phoenix, "You can stay until the storm passes, but don't mistake that for an invitation. Don't touch anything. Don't ask questions. And be gone by morning."

Phoenix and Edward exchanged a glance but nodded, understanding the tension in her voice. This wasn't a warm welcome at all, but they needed somewhere to rest. The woman had said they could stay, so they didn't argue.

"Thank you," Phoenix replied carefully, keeping her voice neutral. "We'll stay out of your way."

The woman didn't respond immediately. Her lips twitched with something that might have been disdain.

Finally, she reiterated, "My hospitality doesn't come with warmth. You're here because you've got nowhere else to go. That's all."

As Phoenix and Edward tried to settle in, the woman remained close to them. She moved about with deliberate efficiency. Her gaze never strayed too far from them; it was as though she was calculating whether they would become a threat to her.

Edward, ever the curious one, glanced around the bunker with wide eyes. "Do you really live down here? What is this place?"

She shot him a sharp look. "I already told you not to ask any questions."

Edward's mouth tightened, and Phoenix quickly placed a hand on his arm to keep him from pushing further.

"We understand," Phoenix said quietly, though her unease only grew. The woman's cold and guarded nature made her wish they had found a different place to stay tonight.

Nevertheless, they were here now. The woman cast a cold glance at them and retreated into the other room. It was understood that they would be allowed to rest now, so they did. The siblings rested against the cold metal wall, huddled together, and drifted off to sleep.

A few hours later, a sudden noise interrupted the tense silence, waking Phoenix from her sleep. It was faint, rhythmic thumping, like footsteps reverberating through the bunker's metallic walls. Phoenix sat up straight, instinctively putting her hand on Edward ready to wake him.

The woman stiffened, moving closer to the siblings. Her earlier indifference gave way to urgency.

"Someone is coming," she warned, her voice low and commanding. "Stay hidden. And do not make a sound."

Phoenix's pulse quickened, the weight of a new threat pressing down on her. She shook Edward awake, motioning for him to remain quiet. He sat up next to her in silence, taking in the threat that he had awoken to. Phoenix and Edward pressed themselves against the cold metal wall, trying to become as invisible as possible.

The woman moved swiftly, her expression hardening as she grabbed a small device from a nearby table. She clicked a button, and the hum of the machinery softened as though she had powered down parts of the bunker. She glanced at Phoenix and Edward one last time before moving toward the door.

"Stay quiet," she hissed, her voice low and sharp. "Don't move until I tell you."

The rhythmic footsteps grew louder, stopping just outside the heavy doors. Phoenix's breath caught, and she could feel Edward's fingers clutching her arm, trembling slightly. The tension in the air was thick, almost suffocating.

A loud, deliberate knock echoed through the bunker.

"Open up!" A rough voice called from outside. "I know you're in there."

The woman's expression darkened as she threw a quick, warning glance at Phoenix and Edward before slowly moving toward the door. She paused, her hand resting on the latch.

"What do you want?" She snapped through the door, not bothering to hide her irritation towards him. "I told you I don't deal with you anymore, Jax."

There was a chuckle from the other side, cold and humorless. "Just thought I'd check in. Call it intuition, if you will. But I'm guessing you aren't alone in there."

Phoenix's blood ran cold at the implication. She glanced at Edward, who stared wide-eyed at the door, his face pale.

Mira's jaw clenched. "Nobody is here. Get lost."

"If there is someone in there with you, you're making a grave mistake, Mira." The voice warned her threateningly.

"I'll take my chances," she spat back at him.

There was silence for a moment, and Phoenix could hear the man pacing outside, his boots scraping against the ground. After a tense pause, he spoke again, his voice dripping with menace. "I'm warning you, Mira. If you have someone in there with you… You know how that will end for them."

Phoenix and Edward held their breaths, fearing how that sounded.

The man gave one final knock on the outer wall of the bunker.

"I'm never too far away, Mira. I'm always watching you."

They heard his footsteps fading into the distance, but his threats lingered heavily in the air, surrounding them like a dark cloud.

The woman let out a sharp breath and turned to face Phoenix and Edward. Her face was a mask of cold indifference, but there was tension in her eyes that hadn't been there before.

"Get some more rest while you can," she whispered to them, walking away from the door. "But you are not safe here. It's not good that Jax knows about you here.
I'll need to take you somewhere else in the morning."

With that, she disappeared into the dimly lit corner of the bunker, leaving Phoenix and Edward to sit in the heavy silence.

Phoenix, shaken to her core, exchanged a glance with Edward. Something about this whole situation felt wrong. Mira was hiding more than just secrets about the bunker. Whoever this Jax was, clearly wasn't someone they could afford to cross paths with.

The siblings lay on the hard floor of the bunker, staring up at the dim, flickering lights overhead. Despite the raging storm outside, the sound of rain and wind had become a distant hum compared to the weight of Jax's threats. Her mind churned with questions—about Mira, about Jax, and about what in the world they had stumbled into.

Beside her, Edward fidgeted, unable to find a comfortable position. "Do you think Jax will come back?" He whispered, his voice barely audible.

Phoenix turned her head toward him. "I don't know," she admitted. "But we'll have to be ready if he does."

Edward's brow furrowed, his usual bravado cracking under the pressure of the situation. "Why does everyone have to be so angry all the time? It's like no one remembers how to be decent anymore."

Phoenix didn't have an answer for him. The world they were navigating now was full of distrust, hostility, and survival at all costs. Kindness felt like a relic of a forgotten past, one that had little value in this new, fractured reality.

"You still have me," she said quietly. "We have each other. That's all that matters."

Edward gave her a small nod, but the worry in his eyes lingered. Phoenix wished she could reassure him, but how could she, when she felt just as lost?

Across the room, Mira busied herself with some old machinery, tinkering with parts and adjusting dials. Phoenix watched her from the corner of her eye, noticing the tension in the way Mira moved. There was a lot more going on beneath the surface—more than Mira was willing to admit.

Phoenix sat up, deciding to break the silence. "Who's Jax?" She asked.

Mira didn't look up from her work. "He's a scavenger," she replied flatly. "He deals in trades, mostly weapons and supplies. But he's not someone you want to owe favors to."

"He seems… dangerous," Phoenix pressed, trying to glean more from Mira's clipped responses.

Mira finally glanced up, her eyes narrowing.

"Dangerous is an understatement," she warned, her tone colder than before. "People like Jax don't care about anything but power and control. And right now, he wants something from me. Something I'm unwilling to give him."

"What does he want?" Edward asked, curiosity getting the better of him.

Mira's lips thinned into a hard line. "It's none of your business."

Phoenix frowned at Mira's harshness but didn't push further. Mira clearly wasn't in the mood to share, and the last thing they needed was to get on her bad side.

The bunker suddenly felt smaller, the air thick with unspoken tension. Phoenix couldn't shake the feeling that Mira was hiding something. Something interesting enough to have Jax's full attention. The more they stayed here, the more likely they were to get caught in the crossfire. Again, Phoenix couldn't help but feel regret that they had chosen this place tonight.

"Thank you for hiding us here," Phoenix said finally.

Mira gave a non-committal shrug and returned to her work. Her silence spoke volumes. Mira had a lot of secrets here.

Phoenix moved to check their gear, to ready herself for their morning departure. As she checked her gear, her thoughts drifted back to the world they had left behind—their tribe, their home, everything that had been ripped away in a single, brutal moment. She felt the weight of loss settle on her chest, but she pushed it down. There would be time to grieve later. Right now, survival comes first.

Edward was staring at the walls of the bunker, tracing the lines of faded paint and worn metal. "Do you think we'll ever find a real home again?" He asked quietly.

Phoenix's heart clenched at his words. She wished she could give him an answer, a glimmer of hope. But the truth was, she didn't know. All they could do was keep moving forward, one step at a time.

"I don't know," she said softly, placing a hand on his shoulder. "But I promise we won't stop looking."

Edward looked up at her, a flicker of something hopeful in his eyes. It wasn't much, but it was enough for now.

The storm outside raged on, relentless and fierce, as the minutes bled into hours. The heavy weight of exhaustion tugged at Phoenix, but sleep felt like a distant luxury. Every creak, every faint noise in the bunker sent a jolt of anxiety through her body. Edward, on the other hand, had finally managed to fall into a fitful sleep, curled up beside her with his head resting on his pack.

Mira still hadn't said much since Jax left. She worked tirelessly on the machinery, her movements precise and deliberate, but there was something restless about the way she moved—like a predator too long in a cage.

Phoenix had been watching her for a while now, trying to figure out who she was beneath the cold exterior. The storm may have forced them together, but it was clear Mira wasn't about to let her guard down.

Unable to stand the silence any longer, Phoenix stood up and approached her. "You don't seem like the type to trust easily," she observed, keeping her voice neutral.

Mira didn't look up, but there was a flicker of something in her eyes. "Trust is earned," she muttered, adjusting a dial on the control panel. "And right now, you haven't done anything to earn it."

Phoenix folded her arms, leaning against the wall. "Fair enough. I didn't mean to cause you any trouble by coming here tonight."

Mira finally turned to face her, her expression hard. "Everyone's here to make trouble," she said bluntly. "Whether they mean to or not."

Phoenix frowned. "And what about you? Why live down here all alone? What are you hiding?"

Mira's eyes narrowed, and for a second, Phoenix thought she might lash out. Instead, she smirked—a cold, bitter smile. "You ask too many questions."

"I'm not asking to pry," Phoenix said, holding her hands up defensively. "I'm asking because you're obviously in over your head with this Jax guy. And if you need help, we could—"

"I don't need your help," Mira cut her off, her voice sharp and final.

Phoenix clenched her jaw, resisting the urge to snap back. She had tried to offer a branch, but Mira had slapped it away. It was clear that whatever secrets she kept about this place—or herself—she wasn't going to share them willingly.

"Fine," Phoenix muttered, turning to leave.

But before she could take another step, Mira's voice stopped her in her tracks. "Wait."
Phoenix turned, surprised by the sudden shift in Mira's tone. The hostility was still there, but now it was tempered with something else—reluctance, maybe even a hint of vulnerability.

Mira looked away, her fingers tapping against the metal of the control panel. "There's something you should know about Jax," she said quietly. "He's not just a scavenger. He runs a network of people who trade in… information. Secrets."

Phoenix felt a chill run down her spine. "What kind of secrets?"

Mira didn't turn around, but Phoenix saw her shoulders stiffen slightly.

Phoenix pressed, "You said Jax deals in information. He's after something from you—something important enough to threaten you. Now he knows about Edward and me. If we're going to make it out of here, I need to know what we're up against. We're involved in this now."

Mira finally stopped tinkering with the controls and slowly turned to face Phoenix. There was a long, tense pause as their eyes met. For a moment, Phoenix saw a flash of something unrecognizable in Mira's eyes. But it was gone as quickly as it had appeared.

Mira pursed her lips, refusing to volunteer any more information.

Phoenix felt her frustration rise, but she bit her tongue. Mira's walls were thick, built over years of surviving in a world that had no place for kindness or vulnerability. Still, Phoenix wasn't willing to back down so easily.

"Jax knows we're here." Phoenix pressed. "Whether you like it or not, we're a part of this. So if you don't trust me, fine. But at least give me something to work with. I need to protect Edward, and I can't do that if I don't know what we're walking into."

Mira stared at her for a long moment, as if weighing her options. Finally, with a heavy sigh, she leaned against the control panel and crossed her arms. "Jax wants access to my bunker," she admitted reluctantly. "But not just for the supplies. There's something else down here. Something that he wants for himself."

Phoenix raised an eyebrow. "What's that?"

Mira's gaze flicked toward a large, rusted door at the far end of the bunker—the one she had kept locked since they arrived.

"Technology," she admitted after a pause. "Old-world technology. Most of it doesn't work anymore, but some of it could change things. That's what Jax wants for himself."

Phoenix's heart skipped a beat. She had heard stories about old-world technology—remnants of the time before the collapse. Most of it had been destroyed or scavenged long ago, but rumors persisted of hidden caches that could alter the balance of power in this new world. Weapons, data, and even systems that could control entire regions if activated.

"You've got some of that tech down here?" Phoenix asked, her voice barely above a whisper.

Mira nodded grimly. "Jax knows it. If he gets his hands on it, it'll be the end."

Phoenix felt a cold knot of fear tighten in her chest. She glanced toward the door Mira had indicated, her mind racing. "Why haven't you destroyed it then?" she asked, incredulous.
"If it's so dangerous-"

"It's not that simple," Mira interrupted, her tone harsher than before. "The tech is embedded in systems that run parts of this bunker. If I disable it, I lose everything. Power, security, protection." She gestured vaguely to the storm outside, "Out there is a death sentence."

Phoenix took a step back, the weight of the situation settling over her like a heavy shroud. They weren't just dealing with a dangerous scavenger—they were caught in the middle of something much bigger, something that could reshape the world as they knew it.

"So, what do we do?" Phoenix asked, her voice steady despite the turmoil inside her.

Mira's expression hardened once more. "You do nothing," she replied flatly. "Once the storm clears, we leave. I need to get you away from Jax. And I need to get you out of here. You know too much already."

Before Phoenix could respond, a sudden clang echoed through the bunker, followed by the unmistakable sound of metal scraping against metal. Both women froze, their eyes snapping toward the rusted door Mira had pointed out earlier.

"What was that?" Phoenix whispered, her pulse quickening.

Mira's face went pale, and for the first time since they had arrived, Phoenix saw real fear in her eyes.

"Something's wrong," Mira muttered under her breath, grabbing a nearby tool and moving quickly toward the door. "Stay here."

Phoenix had a sinking feeling that whatever was on the other side of that door wouldn't be so easily contained.

The clang echoed again, louder this time. It reverberated through the walls, sending a cold shiver down Phoenix's spine. Edward stirred beside her, mumbling in his sleep, still unaware of the tension rising in the room.

Mira stood frozen by the door, her hand hovering over the control panel that locked it shut. The rusted metal creaked ominously as if something, or someone, was trying to force its way through.

Phoenix's heart pounded in her chest. "What's behind there?" She asked, her voice low but urgent.

Mira shot her a glance, eyes dark with a warning. "Stay out of this," she muttered through clenched teeth.

Another sound—a deep, metallic groan—echoed from the door, as though something massive was straining against it.

Mira took a step back, her jaw set, and grabbed a rusty crowbar from a nearby shelf. She held it tightly, her knuckles white. Phoenix knew she had no intention of opening the door, but the fear radiating from her told a different story.

"Mira," Phoenix whispered, her voice anxious despite her effort to stay calm.

"Quiet," Mira snapped, her eyes never leaving the door. Her breath came in quick, shallow bursts, as though she were preparing for something bad.

Phoenix took a step closer, her mind racing. What had Mira been hiding all this time? The longer she stayed here, the more secrets Mira seemed to have hidden in this bunker.

Without warning, the sound of metal grinding against metal stopped. The silence that followed was suffocating, almost worse than the noise itself. The storm outside still roared, but inside the bunker, everything went still.

Phoenix's pulse quickened. She exchanged a glance with Mira, whose face had gone pale.

"What is it?" Phoenix whispered. "What's in there?"

For a moment, Mira didn't answer. She just stared at the door, as if trying to will it to stay closed. But then, after what felt like an eternity, she spoke.

"It's not just technology," she said quietly, her voice barely audible over the storm. "There are remnants from before. Things that shouldn't have survived."

Phoenix's blood ran cold. "What do you mean 'things'?"

Mira clenched her jaw, eyes flicking between Phoenix and the door. "Experiments. Mutations. Leftovers from before the collapse."

The realization hit Phoenix like a punch to the gut. She had heard stories—fragments of the old world where scientists and governments had played with forces they didn't understand.

"As in, creatures? You have them locked down here?" Phoenix asked, her voice rising slightly. "Why? Why didn't you destroy them?"

Mira's face darkened. "Because they're part of the system. They power parts of the bunker. Without them, everything shuts down—including the defense systems."

Another metallic creak echoed from the door, and Phoenix felt the hairs on the back of her neck stand on end.

"What happens if they get out?" Phoenix asked. Her voice was tight with fear.

Mira didn't answer right away. When she did, her voice was hard and cold. "If they get out, none of us are making it through the night."

The silence stretched, heavy and suffocating. Phoenix could hear nothing but the storm outside and the hammering of her heartbeat. Mira's words hung in the air like a threat, filling every corner of the bunker with an oppressive dread.

Phoenix's throat went dry. She glanced toward the rusted door again, half expecting it to buckle under the strain of whatever lay behind it. Edward stirred in his sleep, starting to wake because of the noise. Phoenix knew that every second they stayed here was a gamble with their lives.

She swallowed hard and forced herself to speak. "We can't stay here. We need to go."

Mira's eyes snapped to hers, dark and unyielding. "There's nowhere else to go. The storm's still raging. If you step outside now, Jax will find you before the rain stops."

"We can't stay here," Phoenix repeated, her voice firmer this time. She could feel the walls closing in, the invisible presence behind the door gnawing at her nerves. "You said yourself if they get out, we're dead. Why take that chance?"

Mira clenched her jaw, the muscles in her neck tensing as she gripped the crowbar tighter. "I've kept them locked in here for years. They've never gotten out before."

"Maybe they haven't tried hard enough before," Phoenix shot back. "Or maybe they're getting stronger. I don't know, but sitting here hoping they'll stop doesn't sound like a plan to me."

For the first time, a flicker of uncertainty crossed Mira's face, and Phoenix seized on it. She stepped closer, lowering her voice so only Mira could hear. "If whatever's behind that door breaks free, we're all dead. You, me, Edward. I'm not willing to risk his life because of your secrets."

Mira's eyes flashed, and for a moment, Phoenix thought she would snap. But instead, Mira closed her eyes, her grip on the crowbar loosening slightly. The tension in the air was thick enough to cut with a knife.

Finally, Mira spoke, her voice rough. "There's a failsafe. Something I installed in case things went south. It's old and risky, but if it works, it'll fry everything in this bunker—door locks included."

Phoenix's pulse quickened. "And the creatures behind that door?"

"They'd be trapped permanently."

Phoenix stared at her, trying to read between the lines. "Why haven't you used it already?"

Mira's eyes narrowed. "Because if I activate the failsafe, the bunker goes dark. No power, no heat, no defenses. I lose everything I've been working on. I'll lose all of this. And then we're sitting ducks out there for worse to come."

Phoenix felt her frustration boiling up again. It was always a trade-off in this world—safety for danger, survival for sacrifice. But this time, the cost felt too high.

Before she could respond, a loud thud echoed from the door, followed by a deep, guttural growl that reverberated through the bunker. The noise was unlike anything Phoenix had ever heard—inhuman, primal, and filled with a kind of rage that sent a chill racing down her spine.

Mira's face went pale, and Phoenix's stomach twisted into knots. Whatever was behind that door wasn't just an experiment. It was something much worse.

"We need to go," Phoenix urged, her voice barely a whisper. "Now."

Mira looked torn, her eyes darting between the door and the control panel.

The growl came again, louder this time, followed by another violent thud. The door rattled in its frame, the metal groaning under pressure.

Phoenix didn't care about Jax anymore. Whatever was coming for them now felt far more immediate and deadly. She grabbed Edward's pack and slung it over her shoulder, shaking him gently awake.

"Edward, we need to go," she told him.

Mira remained by the door, gripping the crowbar so tightly her knuckles had turned white. Phoenix could see the battle playing out in her mind—the decision that could seal their fate one way or another.

"Mira!" Phoenix snapped. "Are you coming or not?"

For a moment, Mira didn't move. Then, with a sharp intake of breath, she dropped the crowbar to the floor with a clatter.

"There's an exit in the back," she said.

Phoenix didn't hesitate. "Lead the way."

Phoenix's pulse raced as another heavy thud rattled the metal door, followed by the unmistakable sound of claws scraping against the steel. She could feel the tension in the room rising like the pressure before a storm.

This was no ordinary danger. Whatever was on the other side was relentless, driven by something primal, something far more dangerous than anything they had encountered yet.

She grabbed Edward's arm, pulling him upwards. His sleepy eyes had widened in fear, now fully awake and aware of the danger.

Phoenix's eyes were locked on Mira, who was staring at the door with an intensity that bordered on panic. The hardened survivor who had been so guarded and calculating just moments ago now seemed fragile like she was on the edge of something she'd kept hidden for far too long.

The silence between thuds was unbearable.

Finally, Mira moved. Her hand hovered over a hidden panel on the wall, hesitating as if she were considering an option she hadn't used in years.

"I swore I'd never open it again," she muttered, half to herself. "I locked it away for a reason."

"What is it?" Phoenix demanded, her voice sharp with fear. "What's behind that door, Mira?"

Mira's eyes flicked to hers, dark and filled with a mixture of regret and dread. "I told you—leftovers from before the collapse. Things that should have been destroyed. Things that the world forgot."

The door buckled again, a deep, guttural snarl reverberating through the room, filling the space with a fit of raw, animalistic anger. It was hungry, violent—and intelligent.

Mira took a step toward the control panel. "They were experiments," she said, her voice low and hurried. "Part of some government project before everything went to hell. They wanted to create super-soldiers, creatures that could survive in this new world they knew was coming."

Phoenix's stomach twisted. She had heard whispers of the old world's experiments—half-forgotten stories passed around campfires. But they had always seemed like myths, like cautionary tales. Now, faced with the harsh reality of what was pounding on that door, she realized just how real those nightmares had been.

"They made them too strong," Mira continued, her voice hoarse with tension. "They weren't just enhanced—they were changed. Mutated. Turned into something else. When the collapse happened, they were left behind in these bunkers, forgotten. But they didn't die. When I found this place, they were already here—barely alive, but enough to power the system. I didn't have a choice. If I destroyed them, I'd lose everything."

The growling from behind the door intensified, the scraping of claws becoming more frantic, more insistent. The metal groaned under the pressure, as though it could break at any second.

Mira's eyes flickered with something like desperation. "Something's changed. They've gotten stronger. I've tried to keep them dormant, but now they've woken up."

Phoenix's heart raced, her mind spinning with the horrifying reality of what Mira was telling her.

"What happens if they get out?" It was Edward's turn to ask this question. His voice was filled with fear.

Mira didn't answer at first. Her hand hovered over the control panel, her face a mask of conflicting emotions. When she finally spoke, her voice was a mixture of fear and determination.

"If they get out, they'll tear through everything. They're programmed for one thing. Survival. At any cost."

Phoenix swallowed hard. The storm outside, Jax, none of it mattered now. The real threat was here, clawing its way through the bunker door, and it was only a matter of time before it broke free.

The door rattled again, and this time, Phoenix heard the unmistakable sound of metal bending, warping under the pressure. Time was running out. She looked to Edward, his face pale with fear, and then back to Mira.

"Do it," Phoenix commanded, her voice firm despite the terror rising in her chest. "Shut it down. Do what you can to stop them, Mira."

Mira hesitated for a split second, then her hand slammed down on the control panel. The lights in the bunker flickered, and for a moment, everything went still. Phoenix held her breath, the silence deafening as the air seemed to hum with energy.

Then, with a final flicker, the lights went out.

Phoenix's eyes strained against the sudden blackness, her breath catching in her throat. For a moment, all she could hear was the pounding of her heartbeat in her ears, and then the soft, deliberate sound of something moving behind the door.

The door creaked open, and the air filled with the sound of breathing—heavy, ragged, and hungry.

She tightened her grip on Edward's hand, pulling him close. The air felt heavier, and colder, as if the very walls of the bunker were closing in around them. Her skin prickled with the sensation that something unseen was watching them, something primal and unforgiving.

Mira's voice came out in a harsh whisper. "We move now. Slowly. No noise."

Phoenix barely nodded, every muscle in her body tensing as she tried to stay calm. Her mind raced with questions. What were these creatures? How had Mira survived this long with them locked away? But there was no time for answers. Not yet.

A low, guttural growl came from the doorway, followed by the soft, unmistakable sound of claws dragging across the floor. Phoenix's stomach twisted. The creature was moving towards them.

Mira moved first, her footsteps light but purposeful as she led them through the dimly lit corridor toward the back exit. The only illumination came from the occasional flash of lightning filtering through the narrow windows above, casting long, eerie shadows across the walls. The bunker groaned under the weight of the storm outside, but the sounds from within were far more unsettling.

She could feel Edward shrinking beside her. "Phoenix," he whispered, his voice barely audible. "What if…"

"Shhh," She wanted to stay calm, to reassure her brother that everything was going to be okay in this moment. "Just stay close to me."

Mira shot them a sharp look, her eyes flashing with warning. "Quiet," she hissed. "They can hear better than you think."

Phoenix's heart pounded as they continued down the corridor. Every sound, every creak of the floor, seemed amplified in the silence. The storm raged outside, but the real storm was in here, lurking just beyond the door. Then it happened.

A loud, metallic creak echoed from behind them, followed by the unmistakable sound of the door shifting—slowly, but undeniably. Phoenix froze, her blood running cold as the realization hit her. The sound of many creatures trying to get out.

Mira spun around, her face pale. "Run," she whispered, the fear in her voice unmistakable.

Without hesitation, Phoenix grabbed Edward's hand and bolted down the corridor. The darkness closed in around them as they ran, the sound of the door screeching open behind them filling her ears. She didn't dare look back, but she could feel it—the presence of something massive and deadly crawling out of the darkness and into the bunker.

They reached the back exit, Mira fumbling with the locks in the dim light. "Come on," Phoenix urged, her voice breathless, the panic rising in her chest.

The door gave a low, groaning sound as Mira finally pulled it open, the cold, wet air of the storm rushing in. Phoenix shoved Edward through first, then followed, her legs shaking with adrenaline. Mira was the last out, slamming the door behind her with a force that echoed in the narrow alley outside.

For a moment, they stood in the rain, panting, drenched, the wind whipping at their faces. Even through the storm, Phoenix could hear it—the sound of many claws on metal, growing louder, trapped within the bunker.

Mira turned to them, her face set in a grim expression. "We have to keep moving."

Edward asked, "What were those things?"

Mira shook her head. "They were men, once. Soldiers. But now they're something else. Something the world wasn't meant to see."

A chill ran down Phoenix's spine. She didn't press for more. Whatever these creatures were, she had a feeling they hadn't seen the last of them.

Mira wiped the rain from her face and turned toward the distant mountains, where the storm raged on. "There's a place we can go. But it's a long way from here, and if Jax finds us first, all of this is over."

Phoenix looked at Edward, whose face was pale and drawn with fear. She squeezed his hand, trying to muster some strength.

They followed Mira, once again on the hunt for safety.

(3)
The Watchtower's Refuge

After a short while the storm had finally passed, leaving behind a damp chill in the air as Phoenix and Edward trudged through the forest. Mira led the way, her steps confident and precise, though her silence hung like a heavy cloud between them. Phoenix stole a glance at her brother. Edward was walking a little slower, but his eyes were focused, sharp. She knew they needed to rest soon.

"There's a place, not far from here. But we must move fast," Mira told them.

Before Phoenix could question further, Mira was already moving again. Her determination sparked something in Phoenix—frustration. She'd trusted her to help them, but Mira seemed to have her own agenda. There were secrets she was keeping.

After a short but grueling trek, they reached the mouth of a cave, concealed behind a thick layer of overgrown vines and moss. The entrance was barely visible unless you knew exactly where to look. Mira peeled back the vines, revealing a narrow opening. It was just big enough for them to squeeze through.

"This is it?" Edward asked, his brow furrowed in confusion.

Mira didn't answer, instead stepping inside without a second thought.

Phoenix hesitated, exchanging a glance with Edward. The cave didn't exactly scream safety, but at least it wasn't the bunker. The lingering distrust toward Mira gnawed at her, but right now, they didn't have many options.

Inside, the air was cool and damp, the darkness broken only by the faint light filtering through the entrance. The walls of the cave were uneven, carved by years of erosion, but it was spacious enough for them to take refuge.

Mira had found it long ago—Phoenix could tell by the way she moved, navigating the shadows without hesitation. She had been here before, and not by accident.

As they settled, Phoenix found a flat stone to sit on, her body aching from the ordeal.

"Is this where you hide when things get bad?"
Edward asked, his voice softer, more trusting than Phoenix liked.

Mira paused, her eyes flickering toward him before she returned to her work. "I made sure no one else knows about this place," she said, evading the question. "Not even Jax."

At the mention of his name, a cold shiver ran down Phoenix's spine. Jax.

"You've been hiding things from us," Phoenix said quietly, trying to keep her voice steady. "What else aren't you telling us, Mira?"

Mira glanced up, her expression guarded. "You're not the only ones running."

Phoenix glared at Mira, her suspicion growing with every word. "Running from what? Jax?"

Mira's jaw tightened, and she stood up, pacing a few steps away. "It's more complicated than you think," she muttered, her voice low but filled with frustration. "You wouldn't understand."

Phoenix stood, fists clenched at her sides. "Then help us understand! You're leading us around like we're pawns in some game you're playing. How do you know so much about Jax? What aren't you telling us?"

Edward shifted uncomfortably, caught in the tension between the two. He looked up at Mira, eyes wide but cautious. "You said Jax wouldn't find this place. How can we be sure?"

Mira's gaze softened for a moment as she looked at Edward. "He won't. I made sure of it. I've been hiding it from him for years."

Phoenix felt a sharp pang in her chest. There was so much she didn't know about Mira—so much she'd held back. But the way Mira spoke about Jax now… there was more to their connection than just betrayal.

"Who is he to you?" Phoenix demanded, her voice trembling with a mixture of anger and fear.

Mira's expression darkened. "He was family once."

The word "family" hung in the air like a bomb waiting to go off. Phoenix blinked, her anger momentarily overshadowed by confusion.

"Family? You mean he's your—"

"My brother," Mira cut in sharply. "He's my brother. Or at least, he was."

The revelation hit Phoenix like a punch to the gut. Jax, the man that had threatened them, was Mira's brother? She looked at Edward, whose face mirrored the same shock she felt.

"I haven't worked with him, or his gang, in years," Mira continued, "Not since the world fell apart for good. He changed."

Phoenix shook her head, her pulse quickening. "How do we know you're not still working with him? Maybe all of this is just part of some sick game between you two."

Mira's eyes flashed with anger. "I'm not like him. You know nothing."

The weight of her words settled into the silence that followed. Phoenix could see the pain in Mira's eyes, the anger that masked deeper emotions—regret, guilt, maybe even fear. It wasn't just about survival anymore; it was about the bonds that had been broken long before any of them had met.

"He's been wanting me back," Mira volunteered after a pause, her voice quieter now. "He always has. I knew one day he'd come for me. But it's not what you think. He doesn't want me dead. He wants something else…"

Phoenix didn't miss the way Mira's voice faltered at the end. There was more to the story, something Mira wasn't telling them. And for the first time, Phoenix wasn't sure if she wanted to know.

Before she could press further, Edward suddenly stiffened. His eyes darted toward the cave entrance, and a strange look crossed his face.

"Something's out there," he whispered, his voice barely audible.

Phoenix immediately grabbed the knife from her belt, her body tensing. Mira straightened, pulling a small, sleek weapon from her bag.

"What do you mean?" Phoenix asked, her heart pounding in her ears.

Edward's eyes were wide, his breathing shallow. "I don't know. I feel it, though."

The air in the cave seemed to grow heavier as if something was closing in around them. Mira took a step toward the entrance, her eyes narrowing as she peered into the darkness.

"We need to stay quiet," she whispered.

What could Edward possibly be sensing? And why did it send such a chill down her spine?

Suddenly a low growl echoed from the trees outside. It was faint, almost imperceptible, but it was enough to send a wave of fear through Phoenix's body.

What he said next troubled her to her core.

"The creatures. They followed us here."

The Hunter in the Shadows I

Jax stood at the edge of a jagged cliff, his dark silhouette stark against the fading light. The wind tore through his hair, but he barely noticed.

His eyes remained fixed on the dense forest below, where restless shadows moved—creatures drawn to an unseen force that seemed to ripple through the trees, a force he could sense but never command.

They were evolving. The collapse had changed them, twisted them. He couldn't control them—no one could—but he knew their ways better than anyone. He had spent days studying them, their patterns, their responses. In understanding them, he could anticipate their moves.

A faint smirk pulled at his lips, a flash of grim satisfaction in the chaos society had left behind. Here he was, steady, unyielding, an edge in a world dulled by desperation.

But this time, it was personal.

Mira.

Her name lingered in his mind like a splinter, sharp and unrelenting. His sister—his blood, his responsibility. He had given her everything she needed to survive: protection, knowledge, power. He'd shielded her from threats she couldn't even begin to imagine. And still, she feared him. She didn't understand.

Yes, he had changed. The collapse had carved away weakness, reshaping him into something relentless. But everything he had done—every calculated step—was for her.

He would keep her safe, even from herself. Mira's ambition was a volatile force, one he had witnessed countless times before. He knew exactly what she was capable of—and how easily her thirst for control could spiral into disaster.

If it came to it, he'd do whatever was necessary to stop her from going too far, from shattering the balance he'd struggled to hold together in a world that barely clung to it. Even if it meant standing against her.

Jax's jaw tightened as his thoughts shifted to the two who had crossed Mira's path. Phoenix and Edward. He knew their names well, names whispered from the past like a warning. The siblings… the children of those he'd once worked alongside. He understood what they were capable of, especially Edward.

The boy's power was no surprise to him. Jax had sensed it even then, a potential as unpredictable as it was dangerous. But the collapse had altered things. Edward's abilities had grown, twisted alongside the creatures he could influence. It was as if something within him called to them. And if there was one thing Jax could not allow, it was a threat he could neither predict nor contain.

He watched as the creatures moved restlessly through the trees, a ripple of dark energy pulsing through them. Whatever Edward was, whatever power he wielded, had shifted to something fundamental. Jax could feel it, the balance of power teetering on the edge of ruin.

He turned, his gaze hardening as he began to descend the cliffside, his movements as silent as the shadows he commanded. He knew the game was already in motion, each piece falling into place, but he had always been one step ahead. Always prepared.

Phoenix, Edward, Mira… They didn't know he was there. Watching. Waiting.

But they would.

And by then, it would be too late.

Back in the cave, Phoenix's senses were on high alert. The distant growls from outside were a grim reminder of the danger they faced. Mira was pacing, her face set in a worried frown.

"They're getting closer," Mira said, her voice tight with anxiety. "We need to secure this cave and prepare for anything."

Phoenix nodded, her heart racing. "We need to figure out what's drawing them here and how to keep them at bay."

Edward was visibly shaken, his eyes watching the cave's entrance. "It's like they're drawn to us. Like they're following us."

The storm's fury was a distant echo of their immediate threat. The lantern's flickering light cast eerie shadows, making the cave feel even more ominous. They had little time to plan their next move before the creatures converged on their position.

Mira had started fortifying the entrance with whatever she could find—rocks, old wood, anything that could provide some semblance of protection. Phoenix and Edward, seeing what Mira was doing, quickly moved to help her.

Phoenix's nerves were on edge as the three of them closed off the cave's entrance. The growls from outside had faded but not disappeared, leaving an uneasy silence that seemed to amplify every sound.

Edward moved closer to Phoenix, his face pale and eyes wide with fear. "Do you think they'll get in?"

Phoenix shook her head, trying to keep her voice steady. "We have to hope they don't. Mira's right—we need to figure out how to handle this situation."

Mira worked with determined efficiency, her hands moving quickly as she adjusted the makeshift barricade. "We can't stay here forever. We need to find out why they're so close and what's drawing them here. If they're this close, Jax and his gang might be too."

Phoenix glanced at Mira, her frustration boiling over. "You promised us answers. Now's the time."

Mira's face was a mask of frustration and resolve. "I know you're scared and angry, but right now, our priority has to be survival. I'll explain everything once we're out of immediate danger."

Phoenix's eyes narrowed. "We're risking our lives on your plan. You owe us more than just vague promises."

Mira's expression softened slightly, but her voice was firm. "I understand. But I need you to trust me for a little longer. We have to be smart about this. If we stay here and the creatures get in, it'll be too late for explanations."

The cave's entrance was now pretty secure, but Phoenix could still hear the occasional growl from outside. The noise was unsettling, a reminder of the threat lurking just beyond their refuge.

Mira took a deep breath and pulled out a small, weathered notebook from her pack. She spread it open on the ground, revealing a map of the surrounding area. "We need to figure out our next move. The storm's making it hard for anyone to track us, but we need to stay ahead of Jax and the creatures."

Phoenix and Edward gathered around the map, their fear simmering as they tried to focus on the immediate challenge. The lantern's flickering light cast shadows on the cave walls, adding to the tense atmosphere.

Mira traced a route on the map with her finger. "We'll head for higher ground. It's a long shot, but it might give us a better vantage point to avoid Jax and the creatures."

Phoenix looked at Mira, trying to gauge her sincerity. "And what if the creatures find us before we can get to higher ground?"

Mira's face was a mixture of worry and determination. "Then we'll have to be prepared to fight. We have some weapons, and we'll use them. But our priority must be getting away from here and finding a more secure location."

Phoenix and Edward exchanged uneasy glances. Their trust in Mira was strained but not entirely broken.

Mira's resolve was unwavering as she prepared them for the next leg of their journey. "Get some rest if you can, I'll stand guard. We'll need our strength for what's coming."

Phoenix nodded, though sleep was elusive with the danger looming so close. The cave offered a brief respite from the chaos, but it also felt like a fragile shield against the overwhelming threat outside.

As Phoenix settled into a corner of the cave, she couldn't shake the feeling that the storm was just beginning. The secrets Mira held, the threat of her brother Jax, and the looming danger of the creatures all combined into a tumultuous storm of their own. The road ahead was uncertain, but Phoenix knew they had no choice but to press on.

The hours in the cave felt like days, each minute stretching into an eternity. Phoenix's thoughts were a chaotic swirl of fear and frustration. She tried to rest, but every sound from outside made her heart race. The growls had subsided to an eerie quiet, but the silence was just as unnerving.

As dawn's light began to filter through the cave's entrance, Mira stirred. She glanced around at the group, her face etched with exhaustion but also determination. "It's time. We need to move."

Phoenix and Edward gathered their things, their nerves on edge as they prepared to leave their temporary sanctuary. Mira led the way, carefully dismantling the barricades and peering out cautiously. The storm had left the forest in a soaked, muddy mess, but the rain had eased to a drizzle.

"Stay close and keep quiet," Mira instructed. "We don't know if the creatures are still around, and we can't afford to take any chances."

Phoenix, her knife at the ready, followed Mira with Edward close behind. The forest was eerily quiet, the usual sounds of wildlife silenced by the storm's aftermath.

As they made their way through the dense forest, Phoenix couldn't shake the feeling of being watched. The sense of foreboding was almost palpable, and the recent growls seemed to echo in her mind.

Edward, too, was on edge. His senses still tingled with the remnants of his encounter with the creatures.

After a few hours of trudging through the soggy underbrush, Mira led them to a small clearing that overlooked a ridge. The view from the ridge provided a better vantage point, and Phoenix hoped it would also offer a clearer path away from their pursuers.

Mira pulled out her map again and spread it on the ground. "The higher ground should give us a better chance. We'll head east to the old watchtower. It's abandoned but might provide some shelter."

Phoenix glanced at the map and then at Mira. "Are we just hoping the creatures won't find us, given that they followed us here in the first place?"

Mira's expression was serious. "I've never seen them venture this far from their usual territory. It's a risk, but we must take it. We can't stay here."

Edward looked at Phoenix, his face showing determination. "We can do this, right? We've already survived a lot."

Phoenix nodded, trying to be reassuring. "We have to. We'll make it through this."

They set off toward the watchtower, moving cautiously and keeping an eye out for any signs of the creatures or Jax's gang. The muddy ground and fallen branches added to the difficulty of their hike, but they pushed forward with a sense of urgency.

As they neared the watchtower, the tension was palpable. The old structure loomed ahead, a relic of a bygone era. Weathered but tall, it offered potential refuge from the dangers they faced.

Mira led them to the base of the watchtower, where they found an old ladder leading up to a platform. She carefully climbed up first, checking for any immediate threats before signaling for Phoenix and Edward to follow.

As the siblings reached the top, they were greeted with a panoramic view of the surrounding area. Phoenix scanned the horizon for any sign of movement.

Mira turned to them. "This should give us some time to regroup and plan our next move. We need to figure out how to stay ahead of Jax and the creatures."

Phoenix nodded, feeling a sense of cautious relief. The watchtower, though battered, offered a brief respite. The three of them took a moment to catch their breath and assess their surroundings.

Phoenix looked out over the forest, her thoughts racing. Sure, they had found temporary refuge in this watchtower. But the journey ahead was uncertain, and the threats they faced were ever-present. The road to safety was still long, and the challenges they faced were far from over.

The sky was still dark and ominous with the remnants of the passing storm. Phoenix, gazing at it, noticed a faint flickering red light on the horizon, moving erratically. The light seemed to pulse with an unnatural rhythm, casting an eerie glow over the landscape.

Edward, noticing Phoenix's gaze, whispered, "What is that?"

The watchtower's radio crackled to life, filling the silence with static. A distorted, unidentifiable voice came through. "They are coming… closer… the master's shadow grows."

Mira quickly turned off the radio.

Phoenix felt a shiver run down her spine. The red light, the ominous message from the radio, and the growing sense of unease all pointed to something far more sinister than they had anticipated. The watchtower offered temporary safety, but the secrets it held were dark and unsettling.

As Phoenix and the others settled in for the night, the sense of impending doom grew stronger. They had found refuge, but the real danger was still looming, just beyond the edge of their understanding. The watchtower, a seeming haven, was a silent witness to the darkness that awaited them.

(4)

Shadows of the Past

The radio crackled with static, the eerie message still echoing in the silence that followed: "They are coming… closer… the master's shadow grows."

Phoenix sat frozen as the words replayed in her mind. Edward shifted uneasily beside her, his fingers gripping the worn edge of the table in the small, dark room. The dim light flickered, casting long shadows on the walls of the dilapidated watchtower they had stumbled upon.

"Well, what did that mean?" Edward asked, his eyes fixed on Mira.

Mira stood by the window, staring out at the dark landscape beyond, her expression cold and distant. She didn't turn to face them, her silence gnawing at Phoenix. There was something about the way she stood there, her shoulders tense, like she was trying to ignore the weight of the question.

"Mira?" Phoenix pressed with apprehension. "What was that?"

Mira finally exhaled, but when she spoke, her tone was dismissive. "It's just old radio chatter. Signals like that have been bouncing around for years. You shouldn't pay attention to it."

"It sounded like…" Phoenix began, but Mira cut her off.

"Like nonsense." Mira turned away from the window with a hardened gaze. "People used to make up stories to scare others. Don't let it get into your head."

Edward scoffed, standing up suddenly. "You expect us to believe that? You're lying again."

Mira's lips tightened, but she didn't respond.

Phoenix could sense the tension rising, and the uncertainty only fed into the knot of fear twisting inside her. The cryptic message, the watchtower's unsettling atmosphere, and Mira's refusal to explain felt overwhelming. It felt like something dark was closing in on them; something they couldn't understand.

"Edward, stop," Phoenix whispered, trying to calm her brother, but his frustration was mounting.

"No, Phoenix!" Edward snapped. "She's hiding things from us. That message— 'the master's shadow'? What does that even mean? Why do you keep acting like we're not in danger, when we are?"

Mira turned to face him, her face cold and unyielding. "Because knowing more will get you killed," she said flatly. "That's all you need to understand. You need to trust me, or we're not going to survive the night."

Edward's eyes narrowed. "Trust you? We have trusted you, Mira, but you've barely told us anything."

The tension between them was palpable. Phoenix felt the weight of their collective fear and frustration, a pressure that seemed to seep into the walls of the watchtower. She glanced at Mira, searching for any sign of genuine concern or empathy.

"I'm not trying to deceive you," Mira said, her voice softer but still firm. "I'm trying to protect you from what I know. Some things are better left undisturbed."

Edward's face flushed with anger. "What about the creatures? What about Jax? We need to know what's happening."

Mira's eyes flickered with a hint of something—guilt, perhaps, or a fleeting moment of vulnerability.

"I know it's hard," she replied quietly. "But you don't have the full picture. There are things out there that are far beyond what you can imagine. If you knew everything, you'd only be more afraid."

Phoenix felt tears welling up in her eyes. The pressure of their situation, the loss of everything they knew, and the constant threat of danger were becoming too much. She tried to hold back her emotions, but the strain was too great. She began to cry, her sobs escaping in shaky breaths.

Edward rushed to her side, wrapping his arms around her. "It's going to be okay, Phoenix," he whispered, though his own voice was thick with emotion. "We'll figure this out."

The siblings' shared moment of vulnerability seemed to break through Mira's defenses. She looked at them with a mixture of sympathy and resignation.

"I'll tell you what I can," she offered quietly. "But you have to understand that some things are too dangerous to reveal all at once."

With a deep breath, Phoenix composed herself.

"We need to trust each other," she requested, her voice shaky but determined. "We need to share everything we know if we're going to survive."

Mira nodded, her expression softening before she spoke.

"We had a safe place once. It was a community that thrived when the world fell apart. We had resources, technology, and a plan to rebuild. But not everyone was on board. The collapse turned everyone against each other. Those who wanted power took it. Those who wanted to help... made sacrifices."

Phoenix and Edward listened intently as she confided in them.

"We didn't just lose the world. We lost ourselves as well. The group that I was part of was betrayed." She stopped there, her tone icy as she remembered the betrayal she spoke of.

Phoenix prompted her to keep talking. "And Jax? What's his role in all of this?"

Mira's iciness continued at the mention of Jax's name. "He was important to the group. He had access to things that could have changed everything, but he chose his path. His choices led to many of our downfalls."

The conversation grew heavy as Mira's revelations hung in the air. The siblings were left with more questions than answers, but the sense of shared vulnerability created a fragile bond between them. They needed to understand more about Mira, but it seemed like she was still holding back crucial pieces of the puzzle.

Her confessions came to a halt, however, as she went to the small kitchen area and started rummaging through supplies.

"We should eat something before we rest," she announced, her voice taking on a practical tone. "There's enough food here to last us a few days. I'll make us something."

As night fell, the reality of their situation began to weigh heavily. They needed to rest, but sleep was elusive. The watchtower was cold, and the wind howled outside, creating a constant, unnerving soundtrack.

As Mira cooked, Phoenix and Edward set up a corner of the room with whatever blankets and cushions they could find. They made a rough, but comfortable, sleeping area. The watchtower's creaky floorboards and the howling wind outside provided a constant reminder of the dangers that still lurked beyond their temporary shelter.

As Phoenix arranged the final touches on their makeshift bed, she noticed something partially obscure in a dusty corner. She nudged Edward and pointed to the leather-bound notebook partially hidden under a toppled crate. Edward picked it up, brushing off the grime to reveal its worn cover. Before they could examine it further, Mira called them over to the metal table where she was setting out their meal.

The aroma of beans and dried meat filled the air, a simple luxury in their dire situation. Edward reluctantly placed the notebook on a nearby shelf and joined Phoenix at the table.

Mira moved with practiced efficiency, her hands working quickly to prepare the food.

"How did you find this place?" Phoenix asked as Mira handed her a bowl of beans and joined them at the table.

Mira hesitated, then shrugged. "I stumbled upon it years ago. It was abandoned, but it had everything I needed. It's been a refuge of mine since then."

As they ate, the siblings took turns sharing with Mira about their past. Phoenix talked about their parents and their tribe. Her voice softened as she spoke of their father, a skilled hunter who had taught them how to survive in the harsh world. Edward shared memories of their mother, who had been a healer, always ready with a comforting word or a remedy for their ailments.

"I remember when we first came to the tribe," Phoenix recounted, her voice tinged with nostalgia. "It was a small community, but it felt safe. We had a routine, a sense of normalcy. We played games, told stories…"

Edward nodded, his eyes distant. "It was a good life, despite the dangers. Our parents did everything they could to keep us safe. They were strong, even when things started to go wrong."

Mira listened, her face reflecting the emotions of their stories. She seemed to be processing the information, her eyes revealing a hint of empathy for the two.

"Do you have any family left?" Phoenix asked Mira, her curiosity piqued.

Mira's expression hardened. "I had a family once. But they're gone now. It's just me."

The room fell silent for a moment as each person dealt with their thoughts and feelings. The shared meal had provided a brief respite from their worries, but the reality of their situation remained.

As the night wore on, the conversation drifted into more personal territory. Phoenix and Edward spoke about their hopes and fears, their dreams of finding a safer place where they could start anew. Mira listened, her gaze softening with each shared story.

"It's hard to imagine a place where it's safe," Edward said, his voice low. "Every time we think we've found something, it turns out to be more dangerous than the last. How do we even know if this watchtower is safe?"

Mira looked at him thoughtfully. "Safety is a relative concept now. What you can do is make the best of what you have and be prepared for the worst. That's how survival works."

The siblings exchanged glances, their weariness evident. The food had helped, but the weight of their situation was ever-present. They had to come to terms with their new reality, understanding that their journey was far from over.

"How long have you been out here, Mira?" Phoenix asked, breaking the silence.

"Too long," Mira replied, her tone tinged with bitterness. "I lost track of time a long time ago. It's been just survival since then."

Edward finished his meal and leaned back, staring into the shadows. "Is there anyone else out there? Any other survivors?"

Mira shook her head. "Not many. Most people you encounter out here are dangerous or desperate. Trust me, you don't want to run into them."

Phoenix felt a pang of sadness. "We've seen that for ourselves. It's like the world is falling apart even more."

"That's one way to look at it," Mira agreed. "But it's also a chance to start over, to rebuild. If we can get through this, there's always hope for a better future."

The night grew colder, and the wind howled outside, sending shivers through the watchtower. Mira, noticing the growing discomfort, moved to the corner and retrieved some extra blankets. She handed them out, her gestures gentle despite her earlier sternness.

"Here," she offered. "You'll need these to stay warm."

The siblings took the blankets, their gratitude evident. They arranged their makeshift bedding and settled in, the blankets providing a small comfort against the chill. The watchtower's creaky floorboards seemed to groan in protest as they shifted, trying to find a comfortable position.

Mira remained near the window, her gaze fixed on the dark landscape outside. Phoenix noticed her contemplation but decided not to disturb her. Instead, she focused on her brother, who was already drifting off to sleep.

The night filled with uneasy dreams and restless sleep. Phoenix often woke up, her thoughts racing with worry about what lay ahead. Edward slept fitfully beside her, occasionally muttering in his sleep, his face creased with concern.

In the early hours of the morning, the first light of dawn began to filter through the cracks in the watchtower walls. The cold seemed to retreat slightly, replaced by the soft glow of morning.

Mira stirred as the light brightened the room. She moved with a sense of purpose, preparing another simple meal. The siblings woke to the smell of cooking, their bodies aching from the uncomfortable night.

"Morning," Mira said as she served the food. "I've got some more of the same. It's not gourmet, but it'll keep us going."

Phoenix and Edward accepted the food gratefully. The warmth of the meal was a small comfort after the long night. They ate in silence, the only sound being the soft crackle of the fire Mira had started on the small stove.

As they ate, Mira continued her story, filling in more details about her past.

"After the collapse, I joined a group of survivors who were trying to maintain some form of order. We had technology and knowledge that could have helped us rebuild, but power struggles and betrayal led to our downfall. I had a mentor, someone who believed in our cause. He was like a father to me. When he died, it left a void. I've been on my own since then, trying to survive and avoid making the same mistakes."

Phoenix and Edward listened intently, absorbing the gravity of Mira's experiences. It became clear why she was so guarded, why she seemed to have walls built around her heart. They realized that, despite her tough exterior, she had endured her share of pain and loss.

"We lost our family in the raid," Phoenix offered sympathetically, with sadness in her voice. "It feels like we're carrying their memory with us. Every step we take, we're trying to honor them by finding something better."

Mira nodded, her expression softening. "I understand that feeling. Carrying the memory of loved ones can be both a burden and a source of strength."

Edward looked at Mira, his eyes filled with a mix of understanding and determination. "I wish we knew more about what we're up against. If we had more information, maybe we could better prepare ourselves."

Mira took a deep breath. "There are things I haven't shared, not out of malice, but because I'm trying to protect you. But I'll tell you more, as much as I can, when the time is right. We will face this together."

Phoenix and Edward exchanged glances, their resolve strengthening. They knew that the road ahead would be challenging, but they were determined to face it together.

After their meal, the siblings helped Mira clean up and reorganize the watchtower. They took the opportunity to rest and plan their next move. The watchtower, though still cold and stark, was a temporary haven, offering them a brief respite from their relentless journey.

Mira shared more about the watchtower and its features, pointing out potential dangers and hiding spots. She emphasized the importance of vigilance, especially with the strange radio transmission still fresh in their minds.

When evening fell again, Phoenix and Edward settled into their sleeping area, their bodies exhausted but their minds restless. Mira remained vigilant, keeping watch from her perch near the window. The night was filled with the sounds of the wind and the occasional creak of the watchtower, a constant reminder of the world's fragility. Her gaze kept drifting to the horizon, where that same faint red light pulsed in the distance. The static-filled transmission from earlier echoed in her memory.

"They are coming... closer... the master's shadow grows..."

A soft rustling broke her thoughts. She turned to see Phoenix slipping quietly from her makeshift bed, leaving Edward fast asleep. The girl moved carefully, her eyes scanning the room before they met Mira's.

"Couldn't sleep," Phoenix whispered as she approached. "I'll take the watch. You should get some rest."

Mira hesitated, then shook her head. "I'm fine," she said quietly, though the tension in her voice was clear.

Phoenix settled beside her anyway, gazing out the window toward the red glow. For a moment, they sat in silence, the quiet of the night wrapping around them.

"That light," Phoenix mentioned with a low voice, "it's been there since last night. What do you think it is?"

Mira's eyes stayed fixed on the distant pulse. "I don't know," she said, her usual guarded tone slipping for just a moment. "But whatever it is, it's not good."

Phoenix swallowed hard, her gaze flicking to the red light. "It feels like it's watching us," she whispered.

Mira nodded. "I've been thinking the same thing."

They fell silent again, the wind's hollow whistle filling the gaps between their thoughts. Finally, Mira exhaled softly, exhaustion creeping into her bones.

"Alright," she murmured, standing up and stretching her stiff limbs. "You win. I'll get some rest."

Phoenix gave a nod, watching as Mira settled into her sleeping area, casting one last wary glance at the faint red light blinking in the corner. Phoenix adjusted her position, shifting to stay warm as she took up Mira's night watch. Her eyes scanned the quiet surroundings, every shadow and whisper of movement holding her attention.

Hours slipped by in the quiet of the night, and Phoenix's thoughts wandered, but her focus never faltered. The weight of everything they had faced clung to her, yet she remained vigilant, determined to keep them safe through the final hours of darkness.

As dawn's first light began to filter through the cracks of the old watchtower, Phoenix glanced over to see Mira stirring. The early light cast long shadows, and the chill of the morning crept into the room, stirring Mira from her sleep. She rose slowly, her movements careful and quiet, avoiding any creaks in the floor as she moved toward the window.

Phoenix, still alert, gave Mira a nod as she relinquished the night watch, the last traces of darkness lingering in her gaze. Mira returned the nod, moving to the small kitchen area in the corner. She began preparing breakfast in silence, the scent of cooking beans gradually filling the air.

The aroma soon roused Edward, who rubbed his eyes and stretched as he sat up, still wrapped in his blanket. Phoenix and Edward exchanged tired but grateful glances, offering Mira murmured thanks as she served the modest meal.

For a while, they ate in silence, the warmth of the food chasing away the morning chill. Finally, Mira's gaze softened, and she spoke in a low, reflective tone.

"You know," she began, her voice barely above a whisper, "there was a time when my brother, Jax, and I had dreams. We were close once, working together to build something better out of the ruins of the old world."

Phoenix looked up, curiosity piqued. "You mentioned Jax before, but you didn't say much. What happened between you two?"

Mira's gaze turned distant, as if she were looking through the walls of the watchtower and into the past. "Jax and I were part of the same group that aimed to restore some semblance of order. He was always driven, always wanted to control the chaos around us. We had different visions for the future. Where I saw rebuilding, he saw domination."

Edward listened intently, his interest growing. "So, he turned against you?"

"Yes," Mira replied quietly. "When the collapse came, and our group fell apart, Jax saw it as an opportunity to seize power. He made choices that led to our downfall. I had to distance myself from him to survive. Our paths diverged, and he became someone I couldn't recognize."

Phoenix's heart ached for Mira. "It must have been hard to lose someone you were so close to."

Mira nodded, her eyes reflecting a mixture of sorrow and anger. "It was. He became ruthless, driven by his own ambitions. I had to make a choice to protect myself and the remnants of what I once believed in. It's a decision I live with every day."

Edward's face softened with understanding. "Our family was everything to us. Losing them in the raid felt like losing a part of ourselves."

Mira looked at the siblings with newfound empathy. "I understand that pain. I lost my family in different ways, but the hurt is similar. It's a burden we carry."

As they ate, the conversation shifted to more personal stories. Phoenix and Edward shared more about their parents, recounting their lives before the collapse. They talked about their father's skills as a hunter, his dedication to keeping the tribe safe, and their mother's nurturing presence, which had been a source of comfort and strength.

"Our mother was incredible," Phoenix lauded, her voice tinged with nostalgia. "She had this way of making everything seem okay, even when things were falling apart. She'd always know just what to say to make us feel better."

Edward nodded. "And our father—he taught us everything we know about surviving out there. His lessons were harsh but necessary. He wanted us to be strong, to face the world head-on."

Mira listened, her expression softening. "It sounds like they were remarkable people. Their influence has shaped who you are today. It's a testament to their love and their dedication."

The siblings nodded, their eyes reflecting their shared memories. The conversation brought them closer, creating a sense of connection that had been lacking in their journey.

After breakfast, Mira suggested they take some time to explore the watchtower and its surroundings. The siblings agreed, feeling the need to stretch their legs and familiarize themselves with their temporary refuge.

They spent the morning inspecting the watchtower's various rooms and the surrounding area. Mira showed them the different features of the watchtower, including its defensive positions and potential hiding spots. She pointed out the locations of old supplies and the best vantage points for observing their surroundings.

As they explored, Phoenix noticed Mira's attention to detail and the careful way she moved through the space. It was clear that Mira had made the watchtower her own, adapting it to her needs and ensuring its security.

By midday, the group had covered the majority of the watchtower and its surroundings. They gathered back in the main room, where Mira sat down, her expression thoughtful.

"There's something else I need to tell you," Mira forewarned, her voice serious. "The radio transmission we heard—there's a possibility it was a warning. There are groups out there that are far more dangerous than what we've encountered. They have their own agendas, and they won't hesitate to use any means necessary to achieve their goals."

Phoenix and Edward exchanged uneasy glances, sensing the gravity of her words.

Mira continued, her gaze focused as if recalling distant memories. "The world's a lot more complicated now. Some groups are ruthless— like the raiders who attacked your tribe. They take what they want, killing anyone in their path, and their only goal is to survive through violence and control. Then there are others…" She hesitated, choosing her words carefully. "Not all are like that. Some just want to live in peace, like the trading settlements scattered across the wastelands. They've managed to carve out small territories where they can grow crops or craft goods, trading with whoever passes by. They don't seek power, just a quiet life."

Edward leaned forward, his curiosity piqued. "So, we could find safe places? Settlements where people won't try to kill us?"

Mira nodded slowly. "Yes, but it's not always that simple. Even the peaceful groups have to defend themselves, and trust is in short supply. Some of these settlements have built strong walls to keep others out. They trade, but they do it cautiously—always with one hand on a weapon."

Phoenix's brows furrowed. "And the others? The more dangerous ones?"

"There are groups out there who aren't interested in peace or trade," Mira responded with a low voice. "They see themselves as the new rulers of this broken world. They call themselves things like 'The Sovereigns' or 'The Legion.' They move in, take over settlements, and impose their own twisted rules. People are forced to swear loyalty, and those who don't… well, they don't last long."

Edward frowned, trying to process the complexity of it all. "So, we'll have to be careful. But there's hope, right? Not everyone out there is trying to kill us."
Mira's expression softened a little. "That's right. There are places where you can find safety, even friendship. But it won't be easy. The trick is knowing who to trust and who to avoid. It's a delicate balance, and one wrong move could cost you everything."

Mira looked at them with a mixture of determination and concern. "We stay vigilant. We keep our wits about us and be prepared for anything. I'll share everything I know, but we have to work together and stay on guard."

The siblings nodded, understanding the gravity of Mira's words. They knew that their journey was fraught with dangers and uncertainties, but they were more resolved than ever to face whatever lay ahead. As the day turned to evening, they settled back into their routine.

The watchtower, though still cold and stark, had become a place of temporary respite and newfound camaraderie. The shared experiences and stories had forged a fragile but meaningful bond between them.

When night fell again, they gathered around a small fire Mira had started. The warmth of the fire provided a small comfort against the encroaching cold. They talked and laughed, their spirits lifted by the companionship and the promise of a new day.

As they prepared for another night of rest, Phoenix felt a sense of hope. Despite the challenges and uncertainties, they had each other—a support system in a world that seemed increasingly hostile.

The night passed with a sense of calm, the watchtower serving as a temporary haven in their tumultuous journey. The promise of a new day brought with it a renewed sense of determination and hope. As they drifted off to sleep, the flickering firelight cast warm shadows on the walls, a symbol of their shared strength and resilience.

(5)

Lights in the Darkness

The late morning sun crept through the broken shutters of the watchtower, casting long, fractured shadows across the room. Phoenix was already awake, her eyes heavy with exhaustion, watching Edward roll up his makeshift bed. Mira had finally fallen asleep after her long night on watch, curled up in the corner of the room. Phoenix had taken over the last few hours. She let them both sleep longer than usual, hoping to give them a little more rest before their next move.

Everyone was awake. Mira stretched and rubbed her eyes, her expression tense as she glanced out the window. The quiet of the watchtower was now laced with an underlying sense of urgency.

"We need to move quickly," Mira warned, her voice sharper than usual.

Phoenix, who had been methodically packing her belongings, looked up in confusion.

"What's wrong?" She asked, noting Mira's sudden change in demeanor.

Mira hesitated, then exhaled sharply. "I've been hearing strange noises at night—rustling, distant voices. I spotted some unusual tracks near the base of the tower. It might be nothing, but we can't afford to take chances. If someone or something is out there, we need to be prepared."

Phoenix nodded, her face reflecting a mix of concern and resolve. She checked her pack again, her movements more urgent now. It was only when she reached for her knife that Edward's voice broke through her thoughts.

"Hey, wait—what about this?" Edward inquired as he held up the notebook. The worn leather cover looked even more fragile in the light of day, its pages brittle with age and secrets. He turned it over in his hands, as though seeing it for the first time since they'd found it.

Phoenix had nearly forgotten about the notebook in the chaos of the last day. She walked over, taking it from Edward's hands, her fingers brushing over the surface. "We never got a chance to really look at it," she muttered, flipping it open.

Mira's gaze snapped to the notebook, her eyes narrowing. "You think that's going to help us now? We need to keep moving. Jax's men or worse could be nearby."

Phoenix paused, feeling the weight of the notebook in her hands. Something about it tugged at her—a gut instinct telling her that it was more important than they realized. She opened to the first few pages, scrawled with strange, hurried handwriting. Diagrams. Maps. Words she couldn't quite decipher.

"There's something here," she mused, more to herself than anyone else. Her fingers traced a small, nearly faded sketch of what looked like an old radio tower. Beneath it, a series of coordinates were scribbled, barely legible but clear enough to make out.

Edward leaned over her shoulder. "It's a map," he observed softly. "Look… it matches the areas around here." He glanced at Mira.

Mira exhaled sharply, folding her arms. "If that notebook belonged to someone connected to Jax, we're walking into another trap."

"But what if it's not?" Phoenix countered, looking up at her. "What if this is where we need to go? What if it leads to something we can use?"

Mira frowned, silent for a moment before she pulled out her own map. "Fine. But if we're going to follow this, we need to move fast and stay quiet. We're exposed here."

Phoenix glanced back at Edward, who gave her a firm nod. It wasn't much, but it was enough. They had a direction now, a clue that might lead them closer to understanding not only Jax's plans but the larger mystery of this fractured world.

As they packed up and stepped out of the watchtower, the morning air felt cooler, heavier with strange anticipation. The tower loomed behind them, a relic of a world long gone. Its once-gleaming metal was now a patchwork of rust and decay. The remains of old equipment scattered around its base gave it a forsaken, haunted feel.

Phoenix led the way as they approached the tower, its skeletal frame casting long shadows across the barren ground. The entrance was partially obscured by debris—a jumble of broken metal and overgrown vegetation. As they squeezed through, Phoenix noticed how the walls inside were lined with peeling paint and fading posters, remnants of a time before the collapse.

Inside, the air was musty and thick with dust. Old equipment lay strewn about: rusted radios, tangled wires, and remnants of machinery. The silence was punctuated only by the occasional drip of water from a leaky pipe above. The floor was littered with debris, making each step a cautious endeavor.

Phoenix and Edward moved carefully through the clutter. Phoenix's flashlight beam swept over an old control panel, its surface covered in grime. Edward's eyes lit up with recognition as he approached. "This looks like it could still work. Maybe we can find something useful here."

Mira nodded but remained wary, her eyes darting around. "Be quick. We don't know what could be lurking in this place."

Phoenix crouched beside the control panel, carefully brushing away the dust. She noticed a few wires still connected and some gauges that looked intact. She began fiddling with the panel, connecting and disconnecting wires in hopes of reviving the old equipment.

Meanwhile, Edward sifted through a pile of scattered documents and old maps. His fingers came across a faded journal. Its cover was cracked and fragile. He opened it gingerly, revealing pages filled with hurried scribbles and diagrams.

"These might be more clues," he said, holding up the journal.

Phoenix glanced over and saw that the journal had a few pages that matched the sketches in the notebook. "This might be part of the same set of documents," she suggested.

As Phoenix worked on the control panel, she noticed a faint humming sound as the equipment began to come to life. The static from the old radios filled the room, crackling with intermittent bursts of sound. Phoenix adjusted the frequency, hoping to catch something useful.

Suddenly, the radio sputtered, and the familiar distorted voice came through, barely audible. "...They're coming... closer... the master's shadow... growing stronger."

The message cut off abruptly, leaving an unsettling silence. Phoenix's heart raced as she and Edward exchanged uneasy glances. Mira's face tightened.

"We need to figure out what this means," Mira said. "But we also need to be cautious. This place is full of old tech, and we don't know what else might be in here."

The group began to gather what they could from the tower—useful equipment, old maps, and anything that might help them on their journey.

As they prepared to leave, Phoenix couldn't help but feel a bit of hope. She felt a strong connection to the abandoned technology, a faint echo of the world that once was.

Phoenix's thoughts drifted back to her family. They had once discussed the history of these old structures, marveling at their complexity and the lives that once thrived around them.

She remembered her father's stories. Communication networks connected people across vast distances, a stark contrast to the isolated world they now lived in. The tower symbolized both a past filled with possibilities and a present overshadowed by fear and uncertainty.

Edward's voice broke through her reverie. "Are you okay, Phen?"

She looked up to see Edward's concerned face. "Yeah," she replied, forcing a smile. "Just thinking about how different things used to be."

Mira, who had been silently observing, spoke up. "We all have memories of the past. It's what keeps us going sometimes. But right now, we need to focus on surviving and figuring out what this new information means for us."

Phoenix nodded, grateful for Mira's understanding, even if it was begrudging. She knew Mira had her burdens, hidden behind her guarded demeanor. The tension between them was palpable, a reminder of the trust that still needed to be built.

As they exited the tower, the harsh sunlight felt like a jarring contrast to the darkness they had just left. Phoenix's thoughts were consumed by the implications of what they had found.

The radio message, the notebook, and the clues they had discovered were all pieces of a larger puzzle. The journey ahead promised to be filled with uncertainty and danger, but with each step, she felt a growing resolve to face whatever challenges lay ahead.

The group moved on, the landscape stretching out before them with its jagged cliffs and barren fields. Phoenix walked beside Edward, his earlier enthusiasm now tempered with the weight of their discoveries. Mira led the way, her expression unreadable but her pace determined.

As the sun climbed higher in the sky, Phoenix realized that their quest was not just about finding answers but also about understanding each other. Their shared experiences and the secrets they harbored would shape their path forward.

For now, all they could do was press on, driven by the hope that the next clue might bring them closer to the truth—and to a future where the echoes of the past might finally make sense.

As they moved through the desolate landscape, the weight of their findings settled heavily on their shoulders. Phoenix, Edward, and Mira walked in a tight-knit formation, their footsteps crunching over the rough terrain. The sun blazed overhead, casting stark shadows that made the world seem even more alien and unwelcoming.

Phoenix glanced over at Edward, who had taken to trailing slightly behind her. His usual enthusiasm was replaced by a contemplative silence, and she could see the strain in his eyes. She reached out and placed a reassuring hand on his shoulder.

"Hey, Ed," she said softly. "I know this is a lot to take in. We're all in this together, okay?"

Edward looked up, meeting her gaze with a small, grateful smile. "Thanks, Phen. I guess I'm just trying to wrap my head around everything. It's like we're piecing together a huge, complicated puzzle."

Phoenix nodded, squeezing his shoulder gently. "We are. But we'll figure it out. One piece at a time."

Mira, walking ahead, kept a watchful eye on their surroundings. Her silence spoke volumes, and Phoenix could sense the inner turmoil she was trying to hide. The tension between Mira and the siblings was palpable. Phoenix could only imagine the secrets Mira was keeping.

As they approached a small ridge, Mira stopped and turned to them. "We need to rest for a moment. This terrain is rough, and we need to stay alert."

Phoenix nodded, finding a spot near a rocky outcrop where they could sit and catch their breath. Edward pulled out some of the rations they had left and began to distribute them. The simple act of sharing food felt oddly comforting amid their grim journey.

While they were eating, Mira finally broke her silence.

"I know this is a lot to process. I can't tell you everything as I don't know it all. But I can tell you that the notebook and radio tower are pieces of a much larger puzzle. Running into the wrong people, especially Jax and his gang, would end this journey for us. So, we need to stay sharp, never letting our guard down. Not even for a moment. Always be on the lookout."

Phoenix studied Mira, noting the weariness in her eyes. "You've already told us about your past with Jax. Is there anything else you can share? Maybe something that could help us understand what we're up against?"

Mira's face darkened. "I've told you what I can for now. The full story is tangled and painful, and some things are better left unsaid for the moment. What matters is that Jax is dangerous, and we need to be on guard. Running into him would be our absolute demise."

Edward, sensing the gravity of the conversation, added, "We're just trying to figure out who we can trust. The more we know, the better we can protect ourselves."

Mira sighed, her shoulders sagging slightly. "I understand. But trust takes time. For now, we need to focus on the immediate threats."

As they finished their meal, Phoenix observed Mira's guarded demeanor. Despite the tough exterior, there was a vulnerability in her that hinted at a deeper story. Phoenix wondered if Mira's past was as painful and complex as her own.

The conversation shifted to their next steps. Phoenix took out the notebook and began discussing the coordinates they had found.

"According to this, we should be heading towards an area marked on the map. It looks like it's not too far from here."

Edward looked at the map and frowned. "It's in the direction of those old ruins. We'll need to be extra cautious."

Mira agreed, her face set in determination. "We'll move as quietly as possible. The last thing we need is to attract unwanted attention."

As they packed up and resumed their journey, the sky began to darken, casting long shadows across the land. Phoenix couldn't shake the feeling that they were being watched, though there was no sign of immediate danger.

The conversation between the three grew quieter as they walked, each lost in their thoughts. Phoenix's mind wandered to the stories she had heard about the old world—tales from her parents and elders. She remembered the descriptions of towering cities, bustling with people, and the advanced technology that had connected their lives. Those stories felt almost mythical now, a glimpse into a world she had never known.

Coincidentally, Edward broke the silence. "Phoenix, what do you know about the old world? What was it like before all this?"

Phoenix hesitated, smiling that they were having the same thought, then began to speak.

"From what I've been told, the old world was full of life and technology. People lived in huge cities, and there were machines and gadgets that made life easier and more connected. But it also sounds like it was complicated and chaotic, with so many things happening all at once."

Edward listened intently, clearly intrigued. "I wish I could understand it better. Sometimes it feels like the past is just a story we've heard, rather than something real."

Mira, who had been walking ahead, glanced back. "It's important to remember the past but don't let it hold you back. We need to focus on the present and what lies ahead."

Phoenix nodded, understanding the truth in Mira's words. The past was a part of them, but the future was where their focus needed to be.

As night fell, they reached the outskirts of the old ruins marked on the map. The area was eerie. Remnants of buildings and structures cast ghostly silhouettes in the moonlight. The once-bustling area was now a silent testament to the world's fall.

Mira led the way, her flashlight cutting through the darkness. "We'll need to be careful here. There's a lot of debris and potentially dangerous traps."

Phoenix and Edward followed closely, their senses heightened. The ruins were a maze of broken walls and crumbling buildings. Every sound seemed amplified in the stillness, and the occasional rustle of wind through the ruins added to the tension.

As they explored, Phoenix found herself drawn to a partially intact building. The structure looked more stable than the others, and she sensed that it might hold something important.

"Mira, can we check this building?" Phoenix asked, her voice low but insistent.

Mira hesitated, then nodded. "Alright, but let's be quick."

They entered the building, which had surprisingly well-preserved walls and a few intact shelves. Phoenix's flashlight beam revealed old files and documents scattered around. She began to sift through them delicately, ensuring they remained intact.

Edward found a small safe embedded in the wall. "This could be worth checking out," he suggested, his voice tinged with curiosity.

With a few moments of effort, Edward managed to pry the safe open. Inside, they discovered a collection of old documents and a small metal box. The documents, yellowed with age, were stacked in neat piles. Some were official records with faded text. Their headers suggested they were once important administrative files. Others were detailed maps, their edges crinkled and stained, showing various locations and coordinates that hinted at once-critical sites and safe zones.

Among these, there was a folded letter that caught Edward's attention. It was written in neat cursive, the ink smudged but still legible. The letter seemed to be a personal note, possibly from one family member to another, filled with words of reassurance and love. The paper was fragile and had a distinct, musty smell.

Phoenix turned her attention to the small metal box and picked it up. Inside the box was a locket, its surface engraved with intricate patterns that had faded over time but were still visible. The locket was worn but intact. Phoenix's fingers traced the delicate engravings as she carefully opened it.

Inside was a small photograph, protected by a thin glass cover. The photograph was slightly curled at the edges but still clear. It depicted a family standing together in front of what looked like a small, well-kept house.

The parents were in their mid-thirties, smiling warmly at the camera. The mother had shoulder-length dark hair and a gentle, caring expression. The father had a strong, reassuring presence with a broad smile. Between them stood two children, a boy and a girl, both around ten years old. The boy had tousled hair and a cheeky grin. The girl, with her hair in pigtails, looked directly at the camera with wide, curious eyes.

The background was lush and green, suggesting a garden or a park. The sunlight caught the edges of their clothes and the happy expressions on their faces. It gave the photograph a sense of warmth and normalcy that seemed starkly out of place in their current world.

"This must be someone's family," Phoenix mused softly, her voice sad with emotion. Her eyes lingered on the picture, feeling a profound sense of loss for the happiness captured in the photo. It was a vivid reminder of the world that it once was, and the personal connections that had been lost in the collapse.

Mira approached, her expression softening as she saw the locket. "It looks like it was important to someone. Sometimes these small, personal items can mean a lot more than we realize."

Phoenix nodded, her eyes misting. "It's a reminder that there were real people who lived through this. We're not just surviving; we're part of something much bigger."

As they gathered the documents and the locket, the weight of their discoveries felt heavier. They knew that their journey was far from over. The road ahead would be fraught with challenges. But for now, they had glimpsed into the past and gained a renewed sense of purpose.

The group made their way back to the open ruins, their spirits lifted despite the grim circumstances. The night air was cool, and the stars above seemed to offer a small comfort in the vast emptiness around them.

As they settled in for the night, Phoenix looked around at her companions. Edward was already dozing off, exhausted from the day's events. Mira was busy organizing their finds, her face illuminated by the soft glow of her flashlight.

Phoenix lay back, staring up at the stars. She thought about her family, the past, and the uncertain future that lay ahead. For a moment, she allowed herself to hope. She hoped that their journey would lead them to answers, and that, somehow, they might find a way to rebuild what was lost.

The night was quiet, and the ruins held their secrets close. As Phoenix drifted off to sleep, a distant glow caught her eye. She blinked and sat up, focusing on the flickering light that cut through the darkness. It was steady and distinct against the backdrop of the starry sky.

"Hey, Mira," Phoenix whispered, nudging her awake. "Look over there. Do you see that light?"

Mira's gaze followed Phoenix's finger, and her expression hardened. "It looks like a fire. There might be a settlement or camp over there."

Phoenix and Mira exchanged a glance, a mix of curiosity and caution shared between them. Edward stirred awake, drawn by the conversation.

"What's going on?" Edward asked groggily.

"There's a firelight in the distance," Phoenix explained. "It might be a settlement."

Edward's eyes widened with a blend of hope and apprehension. "Should we check it out?"

Mira's face was apprehensive as she considered their options. "It's a risk. If it's a settlement, we need to approach it carefully. It could also be a trap."

Phoenix nodded in agreement. "Let's observe from a distance first. We need to be sure about what we're dealing with."

The trio packed their belongings quietly and moved to a higher vantage point, where they could see the source of the light more clearly. The settlement was nestled in a small valley, partially obscured by the terrain. The firelight flickered in the distance, casting long shadows over the structures below.

They crouched behind a rocky outcrop, watching the settlement. Figures moved around the fire, their shapes and activities faint but discernible. Occasionally, the murmur of voices and the occasional burst of laughter reached their ears, adding to the atmosphere of uncertainty.

Were these people potential allies or dangerous foes?

Phoenix glanced at Edward, considering their options.

"We should decide. Do we approach the settlement, or find another place to camp for the night?"

After a while, Mira broke the silence. "If we're going to make contact, we need to do it before nightfall."

Hunted Shadows

Phoenix crouched behind the rocks, watching the distant firelight flicker against the twilight. Mira's words hung in the air, tense and heavy. There wasn't much time left before nightfall, and the decision to approach or stay hidden felt like a line they couldn't cross back over once it was made.

Edward shifted beside her, glancing nervously between the settlement and his sister. "What if they aren't friendly?"

Phoenix bit her lip, her mind cycling through the possibilities. The figures moving around the fire seemed ordinary enough—just shadows cast by the flames—but that didn't mean anything. They had learned the hard way that appearances could be deceiving.

"We'll never know unless we get closer," Phoenix said quietly, her gaze still fixed on the settlement. "But we can't stay out here all night either. If we camp in the open, we risk being spotted by whoever or whatever lives here. It's better to take the initiative."

Staying hidden might buy them time, but it wouldn't provide answers—or safety. The longer they waited, the more likely they'd be discovered.

Mira took a deep breath. Her eyes flicked toward Phoenix, something unreadable behind them. "We go in, but carefully. We observe first and keep our distance. If we think there's any sign of trouble, we leave."

Phoenix stood, adjusting her pack, her eyes narrowing as she tried to shake off the nagging sense of dread in the pit of her stomach. "Ed, stay close to me. No wandering."

Edward nodded, gripping the small knife he carried more for comfort than for any real protection. "I'll stay right behind you."

With that, the trio began their descent toward the settlement, moving with deliberate caution. The path down was uneven, littered with loose rocks and patches of dry grass that crunched underfoot. Phoenix's muscles were taut, each step calculated, her senses on high alert.

As they neared the edge of the settlement, the murmur of voices became clearer. Phoenix could hear laughter now - jarring in the quiet of the wasteland. It should have been comforting, the sound of normalcy in a broken world. Instead, it only set her more on edge.

Mira held up a hand, signaling for them to stop. She crouched lower, her eyes scanning the area ahead. Phoenix followed suit, pulling Edward down beside her.

"What do you think?" Phoenix whispered.

Mira didn't answer right away. Her expression was hard to read, her face a mask of focus. "It's strange. They don't seem to have sentries. No guards posted, no one watching the perimeter."

"That could mean they don't expect trouble," Phoenix offered.

"Or," Mira countered, her voice tight, "they don't need to."

The sun was sinking faster now, and the settlement was only a short distance away. It could offer shelter, food, and protection. It was worth the investigation.

Phoenix swallowed, trying to keep her breathing steady. They had to make a move soon.

"We get closer," she opted, her voice firmer this time. "We'll keep out of sight until we know more."

Mira nodded in agreement.

Without another word, they crept toward the settlement, the final stretch ahead of them filled with the uncertainty of what they might find inside. The settlement loomed closer, the firelight casting long, flickering shadows across the crumbling buildings.

Phoenix kept low, mirroring Mira's precision. The voices from the fire were louder now, and clearer—but there was something off about the sound. The causality of the place seemed staged, and it didn't seem right. Even so, they needed to figure out what kind of people lived there.

Mira motioned for them to stop again, crouching behind a pile of debris that had once been part of a house. She turned to Phoenix, her voice a careful whisper. "There are fewer people than I expected. We need to get closer but stay out of sight. I'll go ahead."

Phoenix frowned. "Why you?"

"Because I know how to handle them," Mira said, her tone offering no room for debate. "Trust me."

Trust. It was a word that lingered too long between them. Phoenix swallowed her doubt, forcing herself to nod. "Fine. But be careful."

Mira gave a small, humorless smile before slipping off into the shadows. She moved with the grace of someone who had done this many times before, her figure almost disappearing into the landscape.

Edward sidled closer to Phoenix, his voice dubious. "Do you think she's coming back?"

Phoenix hesitated. Mira had saved their lives more than once, but that didn't mean she was entirely trustworthy.

"She'll come back," Phoenix said quietly, more to reassure herself than Edward. "But we need to stay ready."

They huddled behind the debris, the minutes stretching out like hours. The sun had almost completely disappeared, and the night was taking over. Phoenix's mind raced with possibilities—were the people by the fire dangerous? Trustworthy? She clenched her fists, centering herself. She had to stay focused. For Edward. For herself.

Suddenly they heard a rustling sound beyond the shadows. Phoenix stiffened, her knife raised. Edward's hand tightened around her arm.

"Mira?" She whispered, her eyes scanning the dark.

No response.

Phoenix's heartbeat quickened. They couldn't be seen, not now. If it wasn't Mira, then who—or what—was moving out there?

Another rustle, closer this time.

Edward's grip on her arm was so tight it hurt, but Phoenix didn't flinch. She needed to focus, needed to be ready. The firelight flickered in the distance, casting distorted shadows across the buildings. Whatever was approaching wasn't Mira.

The shape moved again, and this time Phoenix saw it. It was a figure, cloaked in shadow, slowly stepping forward. Her heart pounded in her chest. She shifted her position, angling the knife in front of her, ready to defend Edward no matter what came at them.

But then the figure stopped.

It wasn't coming toward them. It wasn't even looking in their direction. Instead, it seemed to be observing the settlement, watching the fire just as they had been. This person wasn't part of the group around the fire, either.

She lowered her knife slightly, her eyes fixed on the stranger. Edward shifted beside her, leaning forward to get a better look. The person's features were obscured, indiscernible. Whomever it was moved slowly and deliberately, studying the scene below with careful intent.

Phoenix exchanged an uncertain glance with Edward. Who was this person? What were they doing here? Was it just a coincidence, or was this settlement attracting more than just them?

The figure stood still for another moment, then turned—slipping back into the shadows just as silently as they had come.

Phoenix let out a breath she hadn't realized she was holding.

"Who was that?" Edward whispered.

"I don't know," Phoenix muttered. "But we need to be careful. There's more going on here than we thought."

Before Edward could respond, Mira reappeared, her steps quiet but determined. She crouched beside them. Her face was ashen, and her eyes looked darker than usual.

"They're not what they seem," she whispered. "We need to leave. Now."

Phoenix's curiosity peaked at Mira's urgency. "What do you mean? What did you find?"

"There's something wrong with them," Mira whispered, glancing over her shoulder as if expecting someone—or something—to be watching. "They aren't just settlers trying to survive. They're hiding something, and it's dangerous."

Edward shifted uncomfortably beside Phoenix. "But they were laughing. They sounded normal."

Mira shook her head. "That's what they want you to think. But it's too perfect. Too staged. Too careless. They're hiding something big."

Phoenix frowned. "Did you see who they are?" She asked.

Mira nodded, but her expression remained grim. "They're well-armed, well-fed. Too much for what should be a struggling settlement.

They've got supplies that don't add up. Someone's giving them those things, and they aren't doing it out of charity."

Phoenix's mind raced. Who would give a small, hidden settlement that much firepower and food? Nothing came for free in this world—not without strings attached. A pit formed in her stomach as her thoughts turned to Jax, the shadow that seemed to loom behind everything, even when he wasn't directly involved.

"Jax?" She whispered.

Mira's face darkened further, "It could be related to him!" She agreed. "I wouldn't discount it."

Phoenix swallowed. If Jax was tied to this place, or even just supplying it, then they were already in deeper trouble than they'd realized. The people in the settlement could be working for him and preparing for something bigger. Phoenix didn't want to imagine what that could mean.

"We need to go now," Mira urged them. "They're distracted by their fire for the moment, but that won't last. We have our answer; we aren't staying here tonight."

Phoenix remained deep in thought. If Jax was involved, that information could be valuable for their survival. If they left now, they might escape unnoticed, but they'd lose the chance to know what was going on here.

"We can't just leave," Phoenix protested, surprising herself with her own words. "We need to know more. If Jax is here, we have to find out."

Mira's expression hardened. "Information won't matter if you're dead. There's nothing we need to know, other than to stay away from him and his people."

Phoenix met her gaze, her resolve growing. "Then we'll be careful. But I need to know for myself what we're dealing with. He made threats towards us, and I want to know why."

Mira stared at her for a long moment in obvious conflict. Finally, she exhaled sharply. "Alright. We'll stay. But not for long. If anything goes wrong, it's on you!"

Phoenix nodded resolutely. She knew they were playing a dangerous game, but if she could find out answers about Jax, it was worth the risk.

Edward, who had been silent for most of the exchange, finally spoke up, his voice quiet but steady. "I think there's something else here."

Phoenix turned to him, frowning. "What do you mean?"

Edward's gaze dropped to the ground, his voice quiet. "I felt something when we got close to the settlement. It was faint, but it was there. The creatures, or something like them. I don't know how to explain it."

Phoenix's heart skipped a beat. Edward's connection with the creatures had been growing stronger, and she wondered how. The creatures weren't anywhere in sight, and yet Edward had sensed them—or something related to them. Could it mean that this settlement had some kind of link to the creatures?

Mira looked between them, her eyes narrowing. "You felt the creatures? Here?"

Edward nodded. "I didn't hear them, but it was like a pull. Like they're close but hidden."

Phoenix felt the weight of his words sink into her. Hidden. That was what the settlement felt like, too—a mask for something darker, more dangerous. If the creatures were somehow connected to this place, then they couldn't afford to leave without understanding why.

Edward's warning had only deepened the mystery. If they stayed, they could uncover the truth, but the danger grew by the second. They had to decide now what they were going to do.

Phoenix glanced at Edward, then back at Mira. "I say we stay, but only until we find out what's going on. Then, we're out."

Mira gave a sharp nod, noting Phoenix's tenacity. "Fine. But let's make this quick."

With that, the three of them slipped back into the shadows, edging closer to the heart of the settlement—toward whatever secrets it was hiding.

The night deepened as the three crept closer to the heart of the settlement. Their footsteps were nearly silent on the rough ground. The flickering firelight ahead cast strange shadows, distorting the broken buildings and making it harder to gauge just how many people were there.

Phoenix could feel the weight of every step, her heart pounding in her chest. She glanced back at Edward, whose face was pale but determined. His earlier warning about the creatures still rang in her mind.

If there was a connection between this settlement and the creatures, or Jax, they had to figure it out. The fear gnawing at her was growing stronger with each passing moment.

They moved toward a low wall at the edge of the settlement, crouching behind it as they scanned the scene ahead. From their new vantage point, the fire came into full view, along with the figures gathered around it. Phoenix squinted, trying to make out more details.

There were six people inside, all seated casually as if they didn't have a care in the world. They were eating and drinking jovially. A woman with a sharp, angular face, laughed loudly at something one of the men had said.

They looked almost relaxed. But there was something off about this arrangement. Phoenix couldn't shake the feeling that they were putting on a show—like their ease was rehearsed, staged for some unseen audience.

"What are they waiting for?" Edward whispered, catching on quickly to their ruse.

Phoenix shook her head. "I don't know."

As soon as she spoke, something caught Phoenix's eye. A slight movement at the edge of the firelight. A shine of something metallic held in someone's hand.

The same figure they had seen before was standing in the shadows, holding a long, silver blade. A better look showed the form of a man, tall with squared shoulders, though his face was hard to see in the darkness. He was watching them and didn't want to be seen.

"Mira," Phoenix whispered urgently. "We saw him earlier, while you were gone."

Mira's eyes shifted toward the spot Phoenix had indicated. For a moment, they watched, waiting for the figure to move again. But he didn't. He remained perfectly still, just outside the fire's reach, keeping his distance from them.

"He's watching the group," Mira observed quietly. "He's not watching us. He's waiting for something."

Phoenix's mind raced. Another player in the game, another piece of the puzzle that didn't fit. Whoever this person was, they weren't part of the settlement, but they weren't exactly an outsider either.

"We need to get out of here," Mira said firmly, urgency rising in her voice.

Phoenix nodded. The last thing they needed was to get caught between this hidden figure and whatever connection he had with the people by the fire. She turned to Edward, noticing that he had distanced himself. He was looking at the ground. She touched his shoulder to get his attention.

Edward looked up at her, his eyes unfocused. "The creatures are very close. They're closer than before."

Phoenix felt an overwhelming sense of trepidation at what Edward was saying to her. Edward's connection to the creatures was becoming stronger. With the creatures nearing towards them, they were in more danger than they realized. There wasn't time for answers anymore. Phoenix nodded to Mira, who nodded back. It was time to leave.

They started to back away, careful not to make any sudden movements that would draw attention to their position. They slipped through the shadows, each step bringing them further from the fire and closer to safety. Phoenix looked back, noticing that the figure in the shadows had disappeared.

As they neared the outskirts of the area, a loud sound of movement stopped them in their tracks. The three of them stood still, terrified at the closeness of the sound. Edward held his breath, squeezing Phoenix's hand to warn her. They were here.

From the direction of the fire, came a voice—sharp and commanding, cutting through the night like a knife.

"Who's there?" The voice was deep and authoritative, used to being obeyed.

The people around the fire had stopped talking, their laughter cut off as if by a blade. They stood now, tense and alert, their eyes searching for what had made the sound.

"Who's there?" The voice called again, sharper this time, filled with suspicion.

Edward grabbed Phoenix's arm, his grip tight and urgent. He started to pull, signaling the creatures' presence near them. The siblings and Mira began to retreat further into the shadows, moving as quietly as they could.

Phoenix's heart pounded in her chest. They had to get out of sight, but there was nowhere to hide—just crumbling buildings and piles of debris. She cast a glance at Mira, who was already scanning the area with her usual sharp, calculating eyes.

"There!" Mira hissed, pointing toward a narrow alley between two half-collapsed structures.

Phoenix didn't hesitate. She grabbed Edward's hand and darted toward the alley, Mira close behind. The walls pressed in on them from both sides. Phoenix held her breath, praying they hadn't been spotted.

Then, the sound came. The familiar growl of the creatures, loud and clear in the darkness. More than one of them, chiming together in unison. The most terrifying sound to ever hear.

Phoenix's breath caught in her throat. She turned slowly, her eyes scanning the darkness for the source of the sound.

She saw a mass of shadows moving just beyond the edge of the firelight, huddled together in unison. Each shadow of the group was larger than any human, and too grotesque to resemble any animal. Each with long limbs and long, gnarled, fingers. Dead, yet alive, through corrupt science. The creatures that Edward was somehow connected to.

Waiting here meant certain death, as the creatures would surely find them here. But running blindly into the night would get them seen – and caught, inevitably. They were in desperate need of a plan that worked if they were going to survive at this moment.

"Mira, do you know a way out? Somewhere they won't track us?" Phoenix asked despairingly, pulling Edward close to her.

Mira's expression remained grim, her eyes scanning their surroundings. "There's a path back through the hills. It's narrow and very steep. If we take it, the creatures can't follow easily."

Phoenix glanced at the settlement, where the men by the fire had resumed talking. They were unaware of the danger lurking just beyond the light. If they didn't notice the creatures soon, they'd be slaughtered.

Part of her wanted to warn them—to give them a chance to run—but she knew it would be suicide. The creatures were too close, and there wasn't time anymore.

Mira was already on the move, hastening through the shadows toward the edge of the settlement. She motioned for Phoenix and Edward to follow her. Phoenix grabbed Edward's hand, pulling him along as they crept through the darkness, staying low to avoid detection.

Phoenix's breath caught as she noticed one of the creatures prowling near the fire. The flames flickered, casting long shadows across its grotesque form. Its limbs were long and sinewy, its eyes glowed wickedly in the dark. Its swarm gathered near, many eyes glowing in the darkness. Her stomach twisted as she realized just how dangerous these things had become.

The group by the fire still hadn't noticed, their laughter echoing loudly into the night. The creatures were closing in upon them, slowly surrounding the settlement like giant predators stalking small prey. How had the creatures crept so close without anyone noticing?

"We have to go faster," Edward whispered, his voice trembling.

Phoenix nodded, her legs burning as she pushed forward. She made sure never to let go of Edward's hand, scared to lose him. They followed Mira through the jagged ruins.

As they reached the outskirts of the vicinity, a bloodcurdling scream pierced the night.

Phoenix whipped around, her eyes wide with horror. One of the settlers had finally seen the creatures. The group scattered by the fire, their weapons drawn, but it was too late.

The creatures lunged, their movements swift and brutal, tearing into the fleeing figures with a savage efficiency that made Phoenix's blood run cold.

The scene unfolded in front of her like a nightmare—blood, screams, and the brutal sounds of bones breaking. Phoenix wanted to look away, to keep running, but she was momentarily paralyzed in horror. Her eyes were glued to the scene, engrossed in the tragedy that was unfolding.

This was the reality of their world, the reality she had been running from for so long. There was no escaping it, no matter how far they went. This is what the creatures were. This was the fate that followed them.

"Phoenix, come on!" Mira's voice snapped her out of her trance.

Phoenix shook her head, forcing herself to move, to keep going. This time, Edward pulled her forward. Her legs felt numb as they pushed past the last of the rubble and into the open expanse beyond the settlement. The sounds of the slaughter echoed behind them, growing faint as they sprinted toward the hills.

The night was dark, and the path ahead was barely visible, but Mira led the way to safety. Phoenix followed close behind and Edward's grip on her never loosened. Every breath felt like fire in their lungs, but they didn't dare slow down. Not now.

The growls of the creatures faded into the distance, but the terror lingered. They had been too close. Too close to death, to the end of everything.

After what felt like an eternity, they reached the base of the hills. Mira slowed, her breath heavy but controlled, her eyes scanning the narrow path ahead. "This is it. It's steep, but we can make it."

Phoenix nodded, her legs shaking with exhaustion.

Edward was pale, his face drenched in sweat, but he was still standing, still alive. That was all that mattered.

As they prepared to ascend the path, a low growl rumbled from the shadows behind them. Phoenix's heart stopped. Her muscles tensed and she was chilled to the bone. Her breath caught in her throat as she instinctively tightened her grip on Edward's hand. His hand felt as cold as hers did.

Not all the creatures were behind at the camp. A few had managed to keep up with them, sneaking alongside the three in the darkness. The stench of the creatures permeated their nostrils, the sickening smell of decay and rot. Their shadows towered high as they drew nearer to their location.

Phoenix dreadfully remembered the sound of bones ripping at the fire but disregarded that memory as quickly as it came. Not Edward, she vowed. This wasn't going to end for him.

Mira had already turned to face the sound, but she didn't break her focus. "Phoenix, go!"

Phoenix, determined to save her brother, pushed Edward ahead of her. He needed to be ahead of her. She would sacrifice herself for him if she needed to.

The ground was uneven as they started up the steep path. Rocks jutted out at odd angles, making every step a precarious balance between speed and caution. They couldn't afford a misstep, as the growls continued behind them.

The creatures moved through the rubble, but their speed was slowing as Mira had predicted.

"Keep going, Ed!" Phoenix urged, her voice strained as she pushed him forward.

Edward stumbled, his breath ragged, but he didn't stop. His small body moved with desperation, every step a fight against the exhaustion weighing down his limbs.

Mira was ahead of them, scaling the steep path with the agility of someone who had climbed this terrain before. Phoenix could see her silhouette against the dark sky, moving swiftly and vigorously.

Phoenix's legs burned, the strain of the climb pulled at every muscle, but she forced herself to keep moving. The creatures lagged, their large bodies struggled to climb the jagged structures. Nonetheless, they pressed forward with animalistic resilience.

Suddenly, Edward tripped, his foot catching on a loose rock. He fell hard, hitting the ground with a gasp of pain. Phoenix skidded to a stop, kneeling to his side.

"I'm fine," Edward lied, holding the wrist that had broken his fall.

Phoenix could see the fear in his eyes, the terror that had built since they'd first seen the settlement. She helped Edward to his feet, careful of his injured wrist. She ignored the sharp pain in her legs as she pushed him forward again.

Mira had stopped farther up the path, noticing that they had fallen behind. She delayed herself, waiting for the siblings to gain traction.

Phoenix and Edward scrambled up the rocky incline. The path was narrow and steep, making every step treacherous. The rocks shifted beneath their feet, threatening to send them tumbling back down. They pressed on, fueled by the sheer terror of what was chasing them.

The creatures were closing in, their guttural snarls echoing off the hillside. Phoenix could feel the ground quaking beneath her feet, as though the creatures' presence was warping the very earth around them. She risked another glance back, her heart sinking as she saw their grotesque forms bounding up the hill. Their glowing eyes locked on them as their prey.

"We're not going to make it," Edward gasped, his voice faltering.

"Yes, we are!" Phoenix snapped, refusing to let the fear take over. "Just keep moving!"

But she knew the truth. They were out of time. The creatures were too strong, and she and Edward were too weak. They couldn't outrun them much longer.

Again, Mira stopped ahead of them. This time, she turned sharply to face the creatures. Phoenix's heart skipped a beat as she watched Mira reach for something strapped to her back—a small, cylindrical device she had never seen before.

"Mira, what are you—"

"Keep going!" Mira shouted, her voice commanding. "I'll handle them!"

Phoenix's eyes widened. Handle them? Was she insane?

But there was no time to argue. The creatures were nearly upon them, and if they didn't keep moving, they'd all be dead.

"Mira, you can't—" Phoenix began, but Mira cut her off with a sharp glare.

"Go, Phoenix! Protect your brother! I'll buy you time!"

Phoenix hesitated, her mind racing. She didn't want to leave Mira behind, but she knew Mira was right. Edward was her priority. Keeping him safe was all that mattered to her.

With a heavy heart, she grabbed Edward's arm, pulling him forward. "Come on, Ed. We need to go."

Edward looked back at Mira, his eyes wide with fear. "But what about—"

"She knows what she's doing," Phoenix assured him, though she wasn't sure if she believed it herself.

They ran, the sounds of the creatures growing more frantic as they neared Mira. Phoenix's chest tightened, her legs burning with every step, but she didn't look back. She couldn't. Not now.

Behind them, there was a sudden flash of light, followed by a loud, high-pitched screech that echoed through the night. Phoenix stumbled, nearly losing her footing as the sound reverberated through her skull.

Edward gasped, clutching his ears.

"What was that?" He yelled, unable to gauge the volume of his voice.

"I don't know!" Phoenix yelled back at him, though she couldn't hear herself speak. She dared to glance back, afraid of what she was about to see.

Mira stood alone on the path, the small cylindrical device in her hand glowing faintly. The creatures had stopped, their grotesque forms twitching and writhing as if they were in pain. For a moment, it looked like they might retreat, their glowing eyes flickering in the dark.

One of the creatures let out a furious roar, shaking off whatever had stunned them. It lunged forward, faster than before.

"Mira!" Phoenix shouted, her voice hoarse.

But Mira didn't move. She stood her ground, the device glowing brighter in her hand.

"Go!" Mira shouted, her voice barely audible to Phoenix. "Don't stop!"

Phoenix's heart pounded as she turned away, pulling Edward up the path. They had to keep moving. Mira was buying them time but they couldn't waste it.

With every step, the sounds of the creatures faded into the distance, but the terror lingered. They had escaped, for now—but at what cost?

Phoenix's legs felt like lead as she and Edward pushed up the steep, rocky path. The night was dark and oppressive, with only the faint light of the moon to guide them. Phoenix didn't dare slow down. The sound of the creatures' roars still echoed in her mind, even as the distance between them grew.

Edward stumbled again, his breath ragged and labored. Phoenix pulled him back to his feet, her muscles screaming in protest, but she forced herself to keep going. They couldn't stop. Not now.

"Mira…" Edward panted, his voice weak. "She's still back there."

Phoenix swallowed hard, her throat dry. "She'll catch up," she lied, not knowing if it was true. She wanted to believe it. Mira had always been the strong one, the one who knew what to do when things got bad. Phoenix couldn't shake the image of Mira standing alone, facing those monstrous creatures with only that strange device in her hand.

What had it been? Some kind of weapon? Phoenix didn't know, but it had worked—at least for a moment. The creatures had been stunned, even repelled by it, but she had no idea how long it would last. If Mira couldn't get away…

No. She couldn't think like that. Mira had survived worse, hadn't she? She had to believe that.

The path was getting steeper, and Phoenix's legs ached with every step. She could feel Edward slowing down, his exhaustion catching up to him. His frail body had pushed through the pain, driven solely by fear and instinct. But he had given it all he was capable of.

"Just a little further," Phoenix vowed to him. "We'll be safe soon."

As the words left her lips, she realized how hollow they sounded. Safe. What did that even mean anymore? There was no safe place—not in this world. Not with creatures hunting them, not with the mystery of Jax still unresolved.

Edward's hand slipped from hers, and Phoenix stopped, turning back just in time to see him collapse to his knees. His breath came in ragged gasps. His face was pale, his body strained with exhaustion. Phoenix's heart sank low. She had pushed him too far.

"I can't, Phoenix." Edward panted, letting defeat take over him. "I can't go anymore. I'm sorry."

Phoenix knelt beside him, tears brimming in her eyes as she recognized the defeat. She knew Edward couldn't keep going.

"We'll rest for a second," she said, trying to keep her voice calm, though panic clawed at her insides. "But just for a second. Then we need to keep moving."

Edward nodded weakly, his breath still coming in shallow bursts. Phoenix's mind whirled with possibilities, but none of them seemed like real solutions. They were exposed, and vulnerable, and the creatures weren't far behind.

A rustling sound to her left sent her heart racing again. She whipped around, her knife already in her hand, her muscles tensed for a fight. But it wasn't a creature.

Mira emerged from the shadows, her face drawn and pale. She moved quickly, closing the distance between them with a grim determination in her eyes.

"Mira!" Phoenix's voice was a mix of relief and shock. "How did you—"

"No time," Mira snapped, glancing over her shoulder as if expecting the creatures to appear at any moment. "They're still following."

Phoenix blinked, trying to process what she was seeing. Mira had made it. Somehow, she had escaped the creatures—but how? What had happened back there? The questions burned in her mind, but Mira's urgency left no room for answers.

Edward struggled to his feet, his body swaying with exhaustion. Phoenix quickly grabbed his arm, steadying him as they prepared to move again. "Mira, help me with him!" Mira grabbed his other arm, and the two pitched in to give him the strength he didn't have on his own.

As they started to move again, Edward was supported heavily by the other two. Phoenix glanced at Mira. Curiosity overcame her.

"What was that thing you used? That device?"

Mira's expression didn't change, but Phoenix saw the slight flicker of tension in her eyes.

"It's a tool I've kept for emergencies," Mira replied, her voice clipped. "It disrupts the creatures' attention spans for a short time, but it's not something I can rely on more than once. We need to put as much distance between us and them as possible."

Mira was still hiding something—Phoenix knew it. That device was no ordinary tool, and Mira had been far too prepared for creatures like these. There would be more time for discussion later, but first they needed to survive the night.

Edward stumbled again, but Phoenix leaned into him before he could fall, and she caught him.

"I've got you, Ed," she reassured him. "Just keep going."

The three made their way up the last stretch of the steep path, Mira's eyes constantly scanning for danger.

Phoenix couldn't help but admire how calm and focused she remained, even with the creatures on their heels. Mira's composure never wavered, and she rarely ever showed fear. Phoenix couldn't shake the feeling that Mira's calm wasn't just about survival—perhaps, it was about control. The thought was unnerving.

They reached the top of the ridge. The air was thinner and colder here. From their new vantage point, Phoenix could see the rugged landscape below. A mix of jagged rocks and darkened valleys stretched before them. Mira had been right, the terrain here would make it harder for the creatures to follow, but they couldn't be certain.

"We'll go down the far side," Mira decided, pointing to a narrow path that wound its way through the rocks. "We need to find shelter soon, but this will slow them down."

Phoenix nodded, though she wasn't sure how much longer Edward could keep moving. He was barely able to stand now. Phoenix's heart ached for him—he was trying so hard to be strong, but he was just a kid. A kid caught in a nightmare that felt like it would never end.

Mira glanced back at them, her face unreadable. "Can you make it?" She asked, her voice sharp but not unkind.

Phoenix looked down at Edward, who was leaning heavily against her. She didn't want to admit it, but they were running out of options. "I don't know."

For a moment, Mira's expression softened, but only for a second. "We don't have time for hesitation. I'll carry him."

Before Phoenix could respond, Mira knelt and scooped Edward into her arms with surprising ease. Edward gasped in surprise, but he didn't protest. He was too tired to argue, too weak to resist.

Phoenix opened her mouth to protest, but the words died on her lips. Mira wasn't asking for permission. She was making a decision. As much as Phoenix hated to admit it, she needed Mira's strength right now.

"Thank you," Phoenix said quietly, falling into step behind Mira as they began their descent.

The path was narrow and steep, forcing them to move slowly. Every step felt like a battle, the weight of exhaustion pressing down on Phoenix's shoulders like a physical force.

She kept her eyes on Mira and Edward. She watched Mira move with the same grim determination she always carried, with Edward cradled in her arms.

Phoenix's thoughts swirled as they made their way down the ridge. Mira had saved them again, but at what cost? What was she after? What secrets was she still hiding?

The further they descended, the quieter the night had become. The growls of the creatures had faded into the distance, but Phoenix knew better than to believe they were safe. The creatures might be slowed by the terrain, but they wouldn't stop. They never stopped.

As they neared the bottom of the ridge, Mira slowed, her eyes scanning the rocky landscape for any sign of shelter.

"We'll find a place to rest soon," she ensured, her voice calm but firm. "But we need to stay alert. They could still be tracking us."

Phoenix nodded, her heart heavy with the weight of uncertainty. She didn't know how much more they could take. For now, all she could do was keep moving—and hope that whatever came next, they would be ready for it.

As they descended into the valley, the landscape shifted from jagged rocks to more uneven terrain. Deep cracks and outcroppings provided some cover from the open sky. The ground was harder here, solid beneath their feet. It would be difficult to find any natural shelter here.

Mira kept moving ahead, scanning their surroundings with a sharpness that Phoenix had come to rely on, even if it unsettled her. Edward's breathing was steady, though he was drained. Every so often, Phoenix would glance at his pale face, hoping that the exhaustion wouldn't overtake him.

"We'll stop soon," Mira reiterated, her voice firm but low, almost as if she could sense the creatures' presence even when they couldn't hear them. "But we need a place that can hide us well enough for a few hours."

Phoenix swallowed her nerves, nodding in agreement. A few hours of rest sounded like a luxury they hadn't earned, but they needed it. Edward needed it.

Finally, Mira stopped near a formation of large, jagged rocks jutting up from the ground. Between them, there was a narrow crevice that formed a sort of cave. It was small, dark, and hidden from plain view. It wasn't perfect, but in this world, perfect didn't exist.

"This will have to do," Mira said, setting Edward down gently before crouching to inspect the space. "It's tight, but they won't be able to find us easily here."

Phoenix knelt beside Edward, brushing his hair back from his forehead. He looked up at her, his eyes glassy with fatigue. "Are we safe now?" He whispered.

Phoenix hesitated, glancing toward the entrance of the cave-like crevice. She could still feel the weight of the night pressing in on them. The threat of the creatures was just out of reach, but for now, they had a chance to catch their breath.

"For now," she answered softly. "Just rest, okay?"

Edward nodded weakly, closing his eyes as his body finally gave in to the exhaustion.

They settled into the crevice, each of them grateful for the small reprieve. Mira positioned herself near the entrance, her gaze sharp as she kept watch.
The stillness of their hiding place, far removed from the ever-present sounds of pursuit, offered a rare moment of calm.

Phoenix leaned back against the rock wall, feeling the sturdiness against her back as she held Edward close to her.

For the first time in days, he seemed to let go of the constant worry shadowing him. His breathing slowed as he drifted into a deep sleep, cradled in his sister's arms.

(7)
The Hunter in the Shadows II

Jax stood at the edge of the ridge, his silhouette blending with the shadows cast by the rising moon. Below, the remnants of the settlement smoldered, a few dying embers glowing faintly in the dark. He had watched the entire thing unfold from a distance, unseen, unnoticed—just as he always was.

Mira had been there, along with the girl and the boy. He clenched his fists as he thought of the siblings - the ones she was using to reach her twisted goal. He had tried to warn her, tried to stop her before it was too late. But Mira never listened.

She had changed.

Or maybe she had always been like this, and he had just refused to see it.

His eyes narrowed as he scanned the horizon, following the path Mira and the others had taken. He could still feel their presence, just beyond the ridge, moving cautiously, unaware that he was watching. Always watching.

His thoughts drifted to Edward. The boy was special. Jax had seen the signs, the way the creatures reacted to him. Edward didn't know the full extent of his power, but Jax did.

He had studied it for years, long before the collapse, long before everything had gone to hell. The power inside the boy was unique, designed for a specific purpose, and it was that purpose that terrified Jax more than anything else.

The wind picked up, rustling the leaves in the distance, and Jax took a deep breath, grounding himself in the moment. He had to stay focused. He couldn't afford to lose sight of the bigger picture.

Mira was leading them somewhere—he knew it. She always had a plan, even when she pretended not to.
And that plan was going to get them all killed.

One of his scouts approached from the shadows, his boots silent on the rocky ground.

"Jax," he whispered, "they've moved on. Should we follow?"

Jax didn't respond right away. His eyes remained locked on the distant horizon, his mind racing with possibilities. He had spent years preparing for this—tracking Mira, understanding her every move. Now it was all coming to a head.

"No," he answered at last, his voice low and deliberate. "We let them continue for now."

The scout hesitated, clearly unsure of Jax's reasoning.

"But… Jax, they're exposed. If we stop them now—"

"They're not the prey," Jax interrupted, turning to face him. "Mira is the one we're after. The others are just pawns in her game."

The scout shifted uncomfortably. "And if they lead us to the facility?"

Jax's expression hardened. The facility. That was the real prize—the place Mira had been so desperately trying to reach. Only Edward could unlock the place.

His lips curled into a grim smile. "Then we'll take it from them. But not yet."

He turned away from him, his eyes once again drawn to the horizon. He could feel the tension in the air, the sense that something far greater was about to unfold. He had been preparing for this moment his entire life.

Mira thought she was in control, but she had no idea what she was up
against. He would stop her no matter the cost.
"I'll keep tracking them," Jax ordered. "I want you to get back to your
family, but stay out of sight on your way back"

The scout nodded. He disappeared into the shadows, leaving Jax alone
with his thoughts. The wind picked up again, carrying the faint scent
of smoke from the settlement below. Jax took one last look at the
distant ridge where Mira and the others had disappeared, then began
to descend the rocky path, his movements smooth and practiced.

He knew what was coming. And when the time was right, he would
strike. But for now, he would wait. And watch.

(8)
Threads of Fate

Phoenix narrowed her eyes, watching Mira closely. Something had shifted in her behavior since they'd left the settlement behind. Mira was usually calm and collected but now seemed hurried and anxious.

Phoenix could feel the unspoken tension hanging in the air and was wondering what was on Mira's mind. When she was about to ask, Edward spoke up.

"It's like I can hear something, but not with my ears," he muttered, almost like he didn't want to say it out loud.

Phoenix turned to him. "What do you mean?"

"I don't know. It's weird. Ever since we left that place," he motioned back the way they'd come, "The creatures have been calling to me. But not a sound. More like a feeling." He gave her a nervous glance, as if unsure of his own words.

Phoenix opened her mouth to reply when a loud crack echoed through the trees. Her muscles tensed instinctively, and her hand flew to the knife at her side. "What was that?"

Mira stood up quickly, eyes scanning the trees. "Stay down," she hissed. She crouched low behind the fallen log, motioning for them to do the same.

Phoenix ducked beside her, her heart pounding in her chest. Edward followed, but his face was distant. His gaze was fixed somewhere beyond the tree line.

"Ed?" She whispered, nudging him to get his attention.

He blinked and finally crouched down, though he looked distracted. Phoenix clenched her jaw. "Stay focused," she muttered. She glanced at Mira, who had her eyes locked on the forest ahead.

Moments passed in silence, amplifying the sound of rustling leaves in the wind. Then, out of nowhere, a low growl echoed from the underbrush, sending a chill down Phoenix's spine. She tightened her grip on her knife, ready to spring into action.

Mira's hand twitched toward her weapon, but she didn't fire.

"It's close," she whispered, barely loud enough to hear.

Another growl came, this time from behind them. Phoenix's heart raced. They were surrounded.

Edward's breathing grew heavier, but his eyes were no longer wide with fear. Instead, there was something else in them — something Phoenix hadn't seen before. His hands clenched into fists, and for a moment, she thought she saw him close his eyes as if concentrating.

"Ed?" She called again, but his focus was elsewhere, and her voice was drowned out by another, louder growl. This time, it was right on top of them.

Without warning, something burst from the trees — a creature, but not like the ones they'd seen before. This one was bigger, faster, more aggressive. It charged toward them with terrifying speed, its eyes glowing with a strange light.

Phoenix's heart hammered in her chest. They were out of time. They made it this far, but this was it. The end of their journey.

Suddenly, Edward stood up, his face calm and focused.

"Stop," he ordered, his voice cutting through the noise.

To Phoenix's utter bewilderment, the creature skidded to a halt, its glowing eyes locking onto Edward. For a moment, everything froze. The growling stopped. The surroundings calmed.

"Go back," Edward commanded with authority.

The creature let out a low whine, its gaze fixed on Edward. To Phoenix's further disbelief, it backed away, disappearing into the shadows of the trees without another sound.

Phoenix stared at her brother, her heart racing. "What just happened?"

Edward didn't answer. He only looked at her, seeming unsure of what he'd just done himself.

The silence that followed was unnerving. Phoenix couldn't shake the image of that creature. The way it had stopped at Edward's command, the way it had listened to him. It felt wrong, unnatural.

She glanced at her brother. He was still standing, staring blankly at the spot where the creature had disappeared.

"Ed," she asked again, stepping toward him, "how did you—?"

"We don't have time," Mira interrupted, slinging her pack over her shoulder and starting to walk again, her pace brisk. "We need to get as far away from here as possible before it changes its mind or brings friends."

Phoenix shot a look at her. Mira's tone was clipped, but her eyes betrayed something else— fear. Phoenix's hand instinctively went to Edward's arm, pulling him gently as they began following Mira deeper into the forest.

Edward stayed silent, but Phoenix could see the strain on his face. He remained lost in thought, detached from their surroundings. Now and then, his eyes flicked to the treetops as if expecting something to appear again.

They walked for hours, tension building over time. Mira led them through unfamiliar territory. Finally, Phoenix broke the silence.

"What was that back there?" She asked, her voice low but firm. "Why did that thing listen to Ed?"

Mira didn't answer right away. She kept walking, her gaze forward, her jaw set.

"We don't have time for this right now, Phoenix," she muttered. Phoenix could hear an edge in her voice. There was more to it than just urgency. There was something Mira wasn't saying.

"I think we do have time," Phoenix shot back, her patience running thin with her. "You've been acting weird since we left the settlement. What's going on, Mira? What aren't you telling us?"

Mira finally stopped, turning to face them. Her eyes were hard, but Phoenix could see conflict beneath the surface.

"You wouldn't understand," she said, her voice almost bitter.

"Try me," Phoenix challenged with her eyebrows raised.

Edward remained silent, his gaze flicking between them. Phoenix could feel the shift in him—he was no longer confused, just tired. He hadn't said a word since the encounter with the creature, and that worried her even more.

Mira looked at Edward with a stony expression. "There are things you don't know. Things you can't know. Not yet."

Phoenix took a step forward, her frustration finally boiling over.

"We deserve to know what's going on! Especially after what just happened back there. Edward stopped that creature, and you didn't seem surprised. You didn't ask how he did it. It's like you already knew he could do that. You know things about Edward and his connection to the creatures. But you haven't told us one thing about it."

Mira sighed, rubbing her temples. "Look, it's not simple. There are forces at play here—things you can't possibly understand."

"You need to explain it to us!" Phoenix snapped, her voice rising. "Because right now, it feels like you're leading us into a trap."

Mira's eyes flashed with something—guilt, perhaps—but she quickly masked it.

"It's not a trap," she said firmly, her voice lowering.

Phoenix opened her mouth to argue, but Edward finally spoke up, his voice soft and strained.

"It's okay, Phen."

She turned to him, surprised. "What?"

Edward met her eyes, and she saw something new in his expression. He wasn't scared. He seemed resigned, no longer resisting what lay ahead.

"She's right. I don't know how, but I felt something back there. It wasn't just the creature. There's something else. Something bigger going on."

Phoenix stared at him, her mind racing. Edward had always been the sensitive one, the one with the strange intuition. This was different. She didn't know what to say.

Mira glanced between them, her expression softening slightly. "We're close," she said quietly, almost to herself. "Closer than you think."

Phoenix frowned, taking a step back. "Close to what?"

"You'll see soon enough," she murmured. Without another word, she turned and started to march ahead.

"Wait," Phoenix called out, her voice firmer now. "You can't keep leading us without telling us what's going on. If you don't start talking, we're not going anywhere."

Mira slowed but didn't turn to face them. The silence hung heavily in the air, thick with unspoken truths. Phoenix felt Edward shift beside her, his unease growing, but he didn't say anything.

Finally, Mira sighed and turned. The hardened mask she'd been wearing slipped for a fraction of a second. Her eyes lingered on Edward for a moment before she spoke, her voice quieter, almost regretful.

"This isn't just about survival," she began, her gaze flicking between them. "It's about control. Control over things much bigger than us."

Phoenix asked, her frustration spilling over. "Control over what?"

Mira hesitated.

"Your brother," she revealed, her voice barely above a whisper. "He's not like everyone else, Phoenix. He's different. Special, as you've seen for yourself. Where we're headed—what we're looking for—all of it is connected to him."

Phoenix's heart skipped a beat, and she instinctively moved closer to Edward. "What do you mean 'connected' to him? How does any of this involve him?"

Mira's gaze softened, but there was something dark in her eyes, something she was still holding back. "He's part of something big. Something that started long before either of you were born."

Edward's brow furrowed, his voice small but steady. "What are you talking about?"

Mira took a deep breath, her expression conflicted.

"There's a place not far from here. A facility. Your father knew about it, Edward. He was part of the project—before everything went to hell."

Phoenix's heart pounded in her ears. Their father? They hadn't spoken about him in so long. Hearing his name in this context didn't feel right.

"What project?" Phoenix asked, her voice shaking slightly.

Mira's eyes darkened further. "A project to control the mutations. To stop them from spreading. To harness them."

Phoenix's mind reeled. Their father had been involved in something like that? Why had they never known?

"What about Edward?" Phoenix asked, her voice tight. "What's his part in this?"

Mira swallowed hard, clearly struggling with how much to reveal.

"Your brother was born different, Phoenix. He's connected to these creatures in ways you can't imagine. The facility we're heading to holds the key to all of this. Edward is the only one who can unlock it."

The words hit Phoenix like a punch to the gut. She looked at Edward, who stared back at her, wide-eyed and pale. He looked just as shocked as she was, but there was something else in his expression. It was something deeper, like a distant memory he couldn't quite reach.

"I don't understand," Phoenix muttered, her voice thick with emotion. "Why Edward? What are you not telling us?"

Mira looked away, her lips pressed into a thin line.

"I've told you enough for now," she said with a hollow voice. "The rest you'll have to see for yourselves."

Without another word, Mira turned and continued walking. Phoenix and Edward stood in the clearing, the weight of the revelation sitting heavily on their shoulders.

Phoenix's mind spun with questions, anger, and fear.

"Ed?" She whispered, her voice unsteady. "Are you okay?"

Edward didn't respond immediately. His eyes were distant, lost in thought. After a moment, he nodded.

"I don't know what this means," he pondered, "but we have to find out."

(9)

The Key Within

Phoenix jolted awake, her breath shallow, her heart racing as the remnants of a fading dream clung to her thoughts like smoke.

In the dim light of the morning, she could make out Edward's shadow hunched near the edge of the camp. His back was to her, and beside him stood Mira, speaking in low, hurried tones. A knot of mistrust formed with each passing second as Phoenix tried to listen in to their conversation.

She sat up, brushing the dirt from her face, eyes fixed on the pair. What were they talking about? Ever since Mira's vague revelation the day before, something had changed noticeably about the situation.

Mira had always been guarded and secretive. Now it felt like more than secrets; it felt like manipulation. A cold chill ran through Phoenix at the thought.

Could Mira be trusted? Phoenix's gut twisted. Edward, for all his courage, was still only thirteen—too young to bear the weight of what was happening. Too young to understand the danger Mira might be leading them into. Especially, since whatever secrets they were about to discover, involved him. Phoenix knew she had to protect him, whatever it took. Even if it was the last thing she would ever do.

Mira, noticing that Phoenix had awakened, got up and stretched. She broke camp, putting out the fire and gathering her belongings.

Edward continued to gaze at the horizon, lost in thought after his conversation with Mira. He looked so much older at that moment, far removed from the boy he once was. It broke Phoenix's heart to see how much he had changed recently.

Unable to stay still any longer, Phoenix made her way over to Edward.

"You okay, Ed?" She asked softly, using the nickname she had called him since they were little. She hoped it would draw him back, ground him in something familiar.

He looked up at her distantly, remaining quiet. For a second, Phoenix thought he wouldn't respond. But then, he nodded slowly, though the motion seemed more out of obligation than anything else.

"I don't know, Phen…" The nickname he used for her sounded fragile. "It's just… everything's happening so fast. Mira… the creatures… this place we're going to… I don't even understand what's going on with me." His words tumbled out in a rush, the cracks in his armor showing.

Phoenix crouched down beside him, pulling him into a tight embrace. "I don't understand it all either," she admitted, her voice steady but filled with concern. "But whatever happens, we'll figure it out together. You don't have to carry this alone."

Edward leaned into her embrace. For a moment, Phoenix could feel the weight of his fear. He was trying to be strong, but the truth was, he was a kid born into a world that demanded too much of him. She wished she could shield him from it all.

"But what if…" Edward's voice cracked, pulling away from her to look directly into her eyes. "What if this thing inside me—this connection—is something I need to control? What if it's a bad thing?"

Phoenix swallowed hard, unsure of how to respond. She wanted to reassure him, to tell him that everything would be okay. But how could she when she wasn't sure about Mira's intentions? She wasn't ready to tell Edward her full doubts about Mira, not yet. He didn't need to hear about that right now.

"We'll figure it out," she said finally, trying to sound more certain than she felt. "But for now, we need to stay sharp. We need to keep our eyes open, and we need to stay together no matter what."

Edward nodded again, but the unease lingered in his eyes.

Just then, Mira reappeared, her movements deliberate, controlled. She glanced at them both, her face betraying no emotion.

"We leave in ten minutes," Mira announced, her voice cutting through the morning air. "We're getting close now, and the path ahead won't be easy. Make sure you're ready."

Phoenix gave Edward a final, comforting squeeze on the shoulder before standing up to face Mira. She met her gaze head-on, refusing to show the uncertainty that churned inside her. "We'll be ready."

Mira raised an eyebrow, something unreadable flickering behind her cold eyes. "Good. We can't afford any delay."

Phoenix watched as Mira moved back toward the small bundle of supplies she had gathered. Her movements were mechanical. There was no warmth in her, no hint of fear or doubt. It was like she had turned herself into a weapon—sharp, focused, and dangerous.

This was the woman who had saved them, whom they thought they could rely on. But her elusiveness, her coldness, and her secrets made it increasingly difficult to feel comfortable around her. With every passing hour, it became more difficult to tell who the real enemy was. Everything was becoming more uncertain.

Edward stood up beside her, his small frame straightening as he wiped the remnants of sleep from his face. He was doing his best to appear composed, but Phoenix knew him too well. She could see the tension in the set of his shoulders and the way his hands fidgeted at his sides. He wasn't okay, no matter how much he pretended to be.

Phoenix moved to pack her own belongings, glancing back at Mira every now and then. Each time, she saw the same cold expression. Mira was hiding something big, and they were about to find out what it was. Phoenix could almost feel the weight of it pressing down on them, like an invisible force drawing them closer to whatever lay ahead.

"Phen," Edward's voice broke through her thoughts, pulling her attention back to him. "What if we don't have a choice?"

Phoenix froze for a moment, her hands halfway through tying her pack shut. She turned to face him, her expression softening. "What do you mean?"

Edward hesitated, his brow furrowing as he searched for the right words. "What if Mira's not the enemy?" His voice was quiet, but there was a strange conviction in it. "I mean, I don't trust her either. But, what if going to the facility is the only way to stop all of this? What if I can actually do something?"

Phoenix's heart sank. She wanted to protect him from the weight of those thoughts—from the idea that it all depended on him. But she couldn't deny the gnawing fear that he might be right. If Mira was telling the truth—even half of it—it meant Edward's power was tied to something much bigger than either of them could understand. Something that could change everything.

"We'll figure it out," Phoenix repeated, her voice firmer this time. "But we can't trust anyone blindly. Not even Mira. You don't have to do anything you're not ready for."

Edward looked at her, his eyes filled with doubt. "But what if I don't have time to get ready? What if it happens whether I want it to or not?"

Before Phoenix could respond, Mira called out again, her tone impatient. "We need to move. Let's go."

Phoenix bit back her frustration, securing her pack and giving Edward a reassuring nod. He nodded back, affirming that he was ready.

They fell into step behind Mira, who led them through the dense, fog-covered terrain. The air was thick with moisture, making every breath feel heavier. The forest around them seemed to close in with unnerving silence.

Phoenix kept her senses sharp, her eyes scanning the shadows for any sign of movement. The creatures were always out there, lurking just beyond their reach. With every step, they were getting closer to whatever awaited them at the facility.

Mira moved with purpose, never looking back to check on them. Phoenix found it infuriating, the way Mira seemed so detached from everything now. She didn't share in their fear or uncertainty. She just pressed forward, as though this were all part of some plan only she understood.

After nearly an hour of walking, the trees began to thin. The ground sloped downward, revealing a narrow gorge. Mira paused at the edge, surveying the landscape below. Phoenix and Edward came to a stop beside her, both of them peering down into the mist-filled ravine.

"There it is," Mira said, her voice low and almost reverent.

She pointed toward the far side of the gorge, where the ruins of a large, weathered structure rose from the fog.

Its walls were cracked and overgrown with vines. Even from this distance, Phoenix could see the strange, angular design of the facility. It looked ancient, yet somehow out of place—like something from another world.

"This is it?" Edward asked, his voice barely above a whisper. He stepped closer to the edge, his eyes wide with a mixture of awe and fear.

Mira nodded, her eyes never leaving the facility. "That's where we need to go."

Phoenix's chest tightened as she stared at the structure. It loomed in the distance with a silent and menacing presence. The sight of it made her skin crawl. Yet, here they were, standing at the edge of a path that led straight into its heart.

Edward sat down on a nearby rock, his eyes still fixed on the distant facility. He hadn't said much since they arrived at the edge of the gorge, but Phoenix could tell his mind was racing. She sat down beside him, her shoulder brushing against his. The silence stretched between them, heavy with unspoken fears.

Behind them, Mira busied herself with checking supplies, her sharp eyes constantly scanning the surroundings. Phoenix could feel her presence looming over them, even from a distance. It was like Mira was always watching, waiting for the moment to make her move.

Mira finally broke the silence, her voice clipped. "We've rested enough. If we're going to do this, we need to move now."

Phoenix stood, pulling Edward up with her. She met Mira's gaze, her expression hard. "We'll move, but we're going in carefully. No surprises."

Mira arched an eyebrow, a hint of a smirk on her lips. "No promises."

Phoenix bristled, but she didn't push the issue. There would be time to deal with Mira later. Right now, they had a bigger problem—one that waited for them on the other side of the gorge.

They descended into the gorge cautiously, the rocky terrain making every step a potential hazard. The fog seemed thicker down here, clinging to the air like a ghostly veil, swallowing the ground beneath their feet. Phoenix's instincts screamed at her to turn back, to take Edward and run, but she pushed the thoughts away.

Mira led the way, moving with the same calculated precision she always did, but there was something different in her posture now— something Phoenix hadn't noticed before. Was it urgency? Or was it something darker? Phoenix couldn't be sure, but the air felt charged as if they were walking into something far bigger than any of them realized.

Edward was quiet, his eyes scanning the surroundings. He had been like this since they left camp earlier. Further distant and more withdrawn. Phoenix knew he was processing everything, but the change worried her. She wanted to reach out, to comfort him, but she didn't know how. Not when she herself was so uncertain.

They reached the bottom of the gorge, the walls towering over them like jagged teeth. The facility loomed just beyond, partially obscured by the swirling mist. Up close, it looked more imposing—its once-sleek metal exterior was now corroded and covered in layers of thick vines. The air around it seemed heavier and more oppressive as if the land itself rejected the structure's presence.

Mira came to a halt, her eyes locked on the facility's entrance. It was a massive metal door, half-buried in the rubble, and flanked by broken pillars that jutted out at odd angles. She didn't say a word, but Phoenix could see the tension in her shoulders, the way her fingers twitched with anticipation.

Phoenix exchanged a glance with Edward, her stomach twisting with unease. Something wasn't right. The whole place felt wrong, hiding something possibly terrible within its rusted walls.

Mira stepped forward, running her hand along the surface of the door. "This is where it all started."

Phoenix's eyes narrowed. "What do you mean? What started here?"

Mira glanced over her shoulder passively, too anxious to explain. "You'll see soon enough. But first, we need to get inside."

Edward stepped forward cautiously, his gaze fixed on the door. "How do we open it?"

Mira smiled—an unsettling, knowing smile that made Phoenix's skin crawl. "That's where you come in."

Phoenix felt a cold wave of dread wash over her. She moved to Edward's side, her protective instincts flaring up. "What are you talking about?"

Mira didn't answer right away. Instead, she knelt in front of the door, brushing away dirt and debris to reveal a small panel hidden beneath the vines. It was cracked and covered in grime, but there was something unmistakable about it—a faint, pulsing light at its center, as though it waited for something.

"For years, I've been trying to get into this facility," Mira divulged, almost reverently. "But it was sealed tight. Only someone with the right… connection… can unlock it."

Phoenix's heart raced. "You mean Edward."

Mira nodded. "He's the key."

Edward stared at the panel, his expression a mixture of fear and curiosity. "But… I don't know how to do this."

"You don't have to know," Mira coaxed him. "You just have to try. The facility will respond to you. It was built for people like you."

Phoenix's pulse pounded in her ears. People like him? What did that even mean? She stepped closer, her voice hopeful. "And if it doesn't work? What happens then?"

Mira's reply was offhanded. "It will."

It wasn't the answer Phoenix wanted to hear. She turned to Edward, her hand resting on his shoulder. "You don't have to do this if you're not ready."

Edward looked at her, his eyes wide with uncertainty. "What if this is the only way to stop everything? We need to go in there to figure out what's happening to me, Phen."

Phoenix's heart broke hearing him accept this truth, but she knew he was right. There were no easy answers here. No turning back.

With a deep breath, Edward bravely stepped forward. His hand raised, hovering over the panel. The soft glow seemed to pulse in time with his movements as if sensing his presence. For a moment, everything was still. The only sound was the faint hum of the facility, barely audible over the wind.

Whatever was inside, it had been waiting for Edward. And now, it was ready to let them in.

Shattered Truths

With a soft click, the door began to shift. It groaned as it slid open, revealing a dark, gaping entrance that led into the bowels of the facility. A faint, metallic scent hung in the air, mixed with the acrid staleness of decay.

Phoenix hesitated at the entrance, her fingers tightening around the strap of her bag. Something about this place felt wrong.

"Come on," Mira prompted, her voice steady but cold. She seemed too focused on what lay ahead to notice the unease creeping over Phoenix.

Edward stood at the threshold, his hand hovering near the panel that had responded to his touch. His face was a mixture of curiosity and fear, but something else flickered in his eyes. Something Phoenix couldn't place.

She stepped closer to him.

"Ed, you don't have to go in first," she whispered, not wanting Mira to overhear. "We can figure this out together."

Edward glanced at her, his brow furrowing. "I think it's waiting for me."

Phoenix's stomach tightened. She didn't like the way those words sounded. Before she could say anything more, a flickering light sputtered to life on the ceiling above them. Then another, as the long-dormant machinery within the facility began to hum. The sound echoed down the corridor, like a distant, rhythmic pulse.

A hologram stuttered into existence in front of them. The distorted image flickered for a moment before solidifying into a translucent figure.

"W-welcome to the H-Humanity's A-Alliance for V-vitality, E-empowerment, and N-navigation… F-facility," the voice stammered, its words broken and robotic. The hologram was glitching. "We hope y-your experience in HAVEN is s-safe and p-prosperous."

Phoenix froze. Her breath caught in her throat. HAVEN. The word hung in the air, sharp and undeniable. Her heart began to race. For a split second, the cold hallway around her faded. Her mother's voice echoed in her mind, clearer now than it had ever been since she died.

"Find the Haven…"

The words had haunted her for some time. The final whisper of her mother's lips left Phoenix with more questions than answers.

For so long, those words had meant little—just the dying breath of someone too far gone. Perhaps a better future for herself and her brother, somewhere they could start anew. Standing here in this dark, sterile facility, the meaning slammed into her like a wave.

This was it. It was something else entirely.

Phoenix staggered, the realization hitting her hard. Her hands trembled as confusion and grief washed over her at once. How had her mother known? Why did she want her to find this place?

Mira's voice cut through the haze.

"We should keep moving," she asserted, sensing Phoenix's hesitation.

Phoenix could barely hear her, lost in her memories. The pieces of this puzzle were snapping into place, and the weight of it was almost too much to bear. She swallowed hard, coming to her senses.

She started to follow as the other two trekked further into the facility. Whatever the truth was, it was waiting for them in this place. Now, she was sure of it.

The faint hum of old machinery echoed around them, creating an eerie and unsettling rhythm. Every step seemed to carry them further from the surface, deeper into the heart of something ancient and forgotten. The narrow corridors branched out in all directions, twisting in ways that made it easy to get lost.

Phoenix's eyes darted over the rusted metal walls, flickering lights above casting long, jittery shadows. The place felt alive as if the very walls were watching them. It unsettled her even more.

"What is this place?" Phoenix muttered under her breath, her voice barely more than a whisper.

Mira didn't slow her pace, her eyes forward as though she knew exactly where she was going. "Your father once called it Haven, but it was more than that. It was a research facility, one that your family was connected to—whether you knew it or not."

Phoenix's stomach twisted at the mention of her father. Mira had already revealed too much, and yet Phoenix could sense there were still layers of truth buried beneath the surface, secrets that Mira was holding back.

Phoenix narrowed her eyes at Mira, frustration bubbling up. "You keep acting like you know everything about us—about Edward, about me. But you never explain how. What aren't you telling us, Mira? What really happened here?"

Mira kept walking, her expression unreadable. "Some things are better left for later. Now's not the time to dwell on the past."

Phoenix clenched her fists, anger rising. "I think it's exactly the time."

Mira didn't respond. Instead, she turned sharply into another corridor, leaving Phoenix's question hanging in the air.

They reached a wider room, filled with broken consoles and decayed machinery. Dust-covered control panels lined the walls, their screens cracked and inactive. Phoenix's eyes scanned the room, taking in the remnants of what once might have been a bustling research center.

Edward moved silently beside her, his gaze distant. He had been quiet ever since they entered the facility, his focus entirely elsewhere. There was a pull—something deeper driving him forward—and Phoenix could sense it. She felt a flicker of worry but kept it at bay. They had to stay focused.

Mira moved toward a console at the far end of the room. "This place holds more than just broken-down tech. It holds answers, but only if you're willing to go far enough."

Phoenix's frustration boiled over. "Enough with the cryptic hints, Mira! What are you saying?"

Mira stopped, her hand hovering above one of the consoles. For a moment, there was silence, as if she were weighing her words carefully.

"There's something you need to see," she said finally, her voice cold.

Before Phoenix could respond, she noticed something out of the corner of her eye. A small, dusty frame lay on one of the consoles, almost hidden beneath a pile of scattered papers. Her breath caught in her throat as she stepped closer.

She wiped the grime off the glass, revealing the image beneath. It was a photograph—faded and worn with age. But she recognized the faces immediately.

Her father, standing tall with a serious expression, his arm wrapped protectively around her mother. Phoenix herself, just a toddler, stood beside them, wide-eyed and innocent. And there, cradled in her mother's arms, was Edward—just a baby.

But there was someone else.

In the background, almost blurred, stood Mira. Her eyes were locked on the family, her expression hard and cold, as if she didn't belong in the picture.

Phoenix's heart pounded. She clenched the frame, her pulse racing as anger surged through her. She held it up, waiting for Mira to see it.

Mira turned slowly, her eyes narrowing as she saw the picture in Phoenix's hands. For the first time, Phoenix saw a flicker of something—regret, perhaps, or maybe something darker.

"Where did you get that?" Mira's voice was low, but there was tension there.

Phoenix stepped forward, shoving the picture toward her. "You were there. You've been hiding things from us this whole time. What were you doing with my family?"

Mira hesitated, her face unreadable. "It's not what you think."

Phoenix's eyes blazed with fury. "Then explain it to me. Explain everything—now!"

Phoenix's grip tightened around the frame, her knuckles white with the force of her anger. She could feel her pulse in her ears, her heart pounding as she stared at Mira, waiting for an explanation.

Mira's eyes flicked between the photograph and Phoenix, her lips pressed into a thin line. "You wouldn't understand."

Phoenix's temper flared. "Try me."

Mira let out a slow breath, her gaze hardening. "Your father and I worked together. He trusted me once. Trusted me to help him with the project. But things changed."

Phoenix's heart twisted painfully at the mention of her father. "What project? What did you do?"

Mira looked down at the ground, her face darkening. "Project Genesis. It was meant to save us. To control the mutations that came after the collapse. But it went wrong. The people we experimented on didn't survive. Most of them."

Phoenix's stomach churned. She didn't want to hear this—didn't want to know the extent of what her father had been a part of. But she couldn't stop now.

"And Edward?" Phoenix's voice cracked. "What did he have to do with it?"

Mira hesitated, her eyes flickering with something Phoenix couldn't place. "Your brother Edward was special. He wasn't like the others. He was born after the project began, after we understood more about the mutations. Your father kept him a secret from the rest of us, but I knew."

Phoenix felt a cold chill running down her spine. "What do you mean?"

Mira's gaze softened slightly as if she were reliving something painful. "Your father wanted to protect him. He knew Edward to be different. He had some kind of connection to the mutations. But even then he didn't fully understand it."

Phoenix couldn't wrap her mind around what Mira was saying. She couldn't fathom how her father had kept all of this hidden from them. "Why didn't he tell us?"

Mira's eyes narrowed, her voice low and sharp. "Because he knew it would destroy you. He was trying to keep you both safe, even if it meant lying to you."

Phoenix felt her hands tremble, her grip loosening on the frame. She had always suspected her father had secrets, but this was too much. "So, what? You're telling me he experimented on Edward?"

Mira nodded her head. "Yes. He studied Edward's connection to the Lost, to the creatures. But before he could figure it out, everything went to hell. That's when Jax got involved."

Edward's eyes widened. "The Lost?"

Mira gave a small nod. "That's what we call them now. In the beginning, they were simply mutations—humans who had been affected by the collapse. But as time passed, they became something much worse. They've lost everything that made them human—memories, identity, reason. They are driven only by an instinct to survive, to consume, to destroy. People started calling them 'the Lost' because that's what they are—lost souls wandering a world that no longer remembers them."

Phoenix felt a shiver run down her spine. The Lost. It sounded so fitting, so tragic. She glanced at Edward, who looked equally disturbed by the name.

Mira's expression darkened. "Jax was working with your father. He was part of the original team "

Phoenix took a step back, her mind reeling. Everything was coming at her too fast—too many secrets, too many lies. Her father, Edward, and Jax, it was tangled together in ways she couldn't begin to unravel.

"And you?" Phoenix spat, her anger boiling over. "What's your role in all of this?"

Mira glanced back at her, her expression hard. "I was part of the original team as well. This facility—Haven—was built to study and control the mutations. Your father, Jax, and I… we all worked together. But things didn't go as planned. When the project failed, Jax went rogue. We all split ways, and the team disassembled. Now all that's left are the consequences of our failures."

Phoenix's fists clenched at her sides. "So, you dragged us into this? Knowing everything?"

Mira's eyes flashed with anger. "I dragged you here because it's the only place that has answers. Answers about your father, about Edward, about the creatures. I'm not the enemy, Phoenix. Jax is. He's always been."

Phoenix's chest tightened. Her rage and confusion bubbled into something uncontrollable. She couldn't trust Mira or anything she said. At the same time, she knew that the truth was buried here, in this place. Mira had brought them here to uncover it.

Before Phoenix could speak again, the ground beneath them shuddered, a low rumble reverberating through the facility.

Mira's eyes widened. "We need to move."

The dimly lit corridors twisted and stretched out before them, endless and cold. The deeper they went, the more Phoenix's mind raced. Every flicker of the overhead lights, every echo of their footsteps, felt like a warning, like the facility itself was alive and watching them. But what gnawed at Phoenix more than the eerie silence of the place was Mira.

Phoenix's eyes kept drifting toward her, catching the small, imperceptible moments when Mira would hesitate before turning down a corridor as if weighing her options.

Mira had known about this place all along. The way she had deflected, the evasive answers she gave. It all pointed to this.

As they passed yet another broken console, Phoenix's frustration boiled over. She was tired of walking through this maze of secrets, tired of being kept in the dark.

Edward's silence weighed heavily on her, too. He seemed distant, lost in his own world. Phoenix didn't know how much longer she could protect him without knowing the full truth.

Phoenix's heart raced. She had suspected Mira was more involved than she let on, but hearing it confirmed, hearing that her father and

Jax had been part of this place—it made everything feel even more dangerous.

Phoenix felt a wave of nausea as she asked, "Why didn't you tell us sooner? You've been keeping this from us this whole time, leading us around like we're just pawns in your game."

Mira's gaze darkened. "Because I didn't think you could handle the truth."

Phoenix's anger flared again. "You don't get to decide what I can handle, Mira. You've been lying to us from the start."

Mira stopped walking and turned to face her, her expression cold. "Lying? I've been keeping you alive, Phoenix. You don't understand what's at stake here."

Phoenix stepped forward, her fists clenched at her sides. "Then make me understand! Stop treating us like children and tell me what's really going on!"

Mira's eyes narrowed. "You want the truth? Fine. But once you hear it, you'll wish you hadn't."

Before Phoenix could respond, they stepped into a large room at the end of the corridor. It was different from the others—larger, more intact. Old computer terminals lined the walls, their screens dark but still functional. Dust-covered tables were scattered across the room, littered with old papers and notebooks. Remnants of the work that had been done here long ago.

Phoenix scanned the room, her breath catching as she spotted something on one of the tables. A pile of documents, yellowed with age but still legible. She stepped forward, picking up one of the papers. Her heart raced as she read the words printed at the top:

Project Genesis – Subject Profiles.

Her hands trembled as she flipped through the pages. Each document detailed different subjects and different experiments. Some of the profiles had pictures attached—faces of people who had once been part of something bigger, something darker. People who were now gone, erased by the collapse.

Phoenix's eyes landed on one profile in particular, and her blood ran cold.

Subject 002: Malakos [REDACTED] – Status: Critical. Secondary Connection: The Lost.

Her heart pounded as she scanned the details, her breath quickening with every word. This name—Malakos—meant nothing to her, but the sheer weight of what was described made her stomach twist. Whoever—or whatever—Malakos was, it was tied to Edward, tied to something bigger, something darker.

The word engineered stood out on the document like a warning. Malakos had been part of an experiment within this facility, part of Project Genesis, just like Edward. But whatever the experiment had been, something had gone wrong. The status listed for Malakos— Critical—suggested that the subject had transformed, perhaps something uncontrollable, something dangerous.

Phoenix glanced at Mira, her pulse racing. "Who is this? Malakos? What did you do here?"

Mira's face remained unmoved, cold as ever. Her gaze flicked toward the documents in Phoenix's hand, but she didn't flinch.

"Malakos," Mira disclosed, her voice chillingly detached, "was one of the first successful subjects of Project Genesis. We were tasked with creating organisms that could survive the mutations, that could withstand the collapse. And for a while, it worked."

Phoenix's heart pounded harder. "You mean, experiments?"

Mira's eyes darkened slightly, but her tone remained flat. "We engineered them. Fused them with bio-mechanical enhancements. It wasn't just about survival. It was about control. We needed to be sure we could direct and harness the mutations. Malakos was one of the most promising candidates."

Phoenix's stomach turned. She had known this place was full of horrors, but hearing Mira talk about it so casually, like it was just another failed project, made her blood boil. "And you just, what, created monsters?"

Mira's gaze was icy, her voice firm. "It wasn't supposed to turn out this way. Malakos was unique. His connection to the mutations went deeper than we anticipated. When the collapse accelerated, the subjects became uncontrollable. Malakos became something far worse than we intended."

Phoenix felt her vision blur with rage. "Worse? You created these things? You created him?"

Mira's lips thinned into a hard line. "It wasn't just me. Your father, Jax, the entire team—we all had a hand in it. Malakos wasn't supposed to survive, but he did. And now, he's out there."

Phoenix could barely process the words. Malakos wasn't just some random creature—they had engineered him, molded him into whatever he was now. And Edward, her brother, was somehow tied to all of this, part of the same twisted experiment.

Her hands trembled as she returned to the documents. Her anger burned hot in her chest, but she couldn't stop herself from reading more.

Project Genesis: Objective Overview

The goal of Project Genesis is to create a controllable, superior organism capable of surviving in post-collapse conditions. Using biomechanical technology, subjects are fused with advanced neural implants designed to enhance cognitive and physical functions while maintaining their humanity.

Phoenix's stomach twisted as she continued scrolling. The next file revealed something worse.

Subject List – Experiment Group Alpha

Subject 001: Edward [REDACTED] – Status: Active. Primary Connection: The Lost.

Subject 002: Malakos [REDACTED] – Status: Critical. Secondary Connection: The Lost.---

She held her breath as she read Edward's name next to Malakos's. The documents were linking them—connecting her brother to this horror. A sick feeling spread through her, and for a moment, she felt like the walls were closing in on her.

"You put Edward through this?" Phoenix's voice trembled with fury as she looked up at Mira, barely able to contain the raw emotion in her chest.

Mira's eyes flickered with something—a glimmer of regret, perhaps—but her face remained cold. "Edward was different. Your father tried to protect him, but even he couldn't sever Edward's connection to the creatures. Edward was born into the experiment, Phoenix. He was engineered from the very start."

Phoenix froze. "What are you talking about?"

"Edward is not your real brother. He was created—engineered in this facility. His connection to the Lost wasn't an accident. It was designed."

The words hit Phoenix like a punch to the gut. Her knees felt weak, her mind spinning as she tried to process what Mira was saying. Edward wasn't her brother? He had been… made? Brought into their lives by this twisted project?

"No… no, you're lying," Phoenix whispered, her voice faltering. "He's my brother. We grew up together. We—"

"He was placed with your family to protect him," Mira cut in, her tone cold and matter-of-fact. "Your father thought he could hide Edward from the consequences of Project Genesis. But he couldn't escape what was already in his blood. The bond with the Lost—the connection to Malakos—it was always there, waiting to be triggered."

Phoenix's heart raced as the weight of Mira's words settled in. Everything she had known, everything she had believed about Edward, about their family… it was all a lie. Tears welled in her eyes, but she refused to let them fall. Not now.

"You did this," Phoenix whispered, her voice shaking with emotion. "You and my father… you made Edward into this. You made Malakos. How could you? How could you destroy everything?"

Mira took a slow step forward, her expression softening ever so slightly. "We didn't know it would turn out like this. We thought we could control it, Phoenix. We thought we could protect the world from the mutations. Malakos changed everything. And Edward was the key."

Phoenix felt sick. Every word Mira spoke was like a dagger, twisting deeper into her heart. She wanted to scream, to cry, to lash out—but she stood frozen, the crushing weight of the truth suffocating her.

Phoenix's body trembled as she clenched the papers in her hands, her anger boiling over. "You did this to him. You did this to my family."

The room spun around her, her mind racing. The truth was suffocating her, the weight of what had been hidden for so long crashing down all at once.

Mira's voice was sharp but calm, almost as if Phoenix's anger didn't faze her. "It's too late to change the past. What matters now is what you choose to do next."

Phoenix felt herself teetering on the edge. Every word Mira said fed the fury that roared inside her. Her vision blurred with red-hot rage, and all she could think about was making Mira pay for what she had done—for the lies, the manipulation, the destruction of everything she had held dear.

In an instant, the tension snapped. Without thinking, Phoenix lunged at Mira, her fist connecting with her face. Mira staggered back, her hand flying to the gash on her cheek as blood seeped between her fingers.

Mira winced, her hand pressing against the cut Phoenix had opened on her cheek. Blood seeped through her fingers, but her eyes were cold, devoid of any warmth or remorse. She straightened herself, glaring at Phoenix as she spoke through gritted teeth.

"You think hitting me will change anything? You think your anger can erase what's been done?"

Phoenix stood her ground, her chest heaving with fury. "You've been lying to us from the start. You used us. You used Edward, and you manipulated everything!"

Mira's jaw tightened, but her voice remained eerily calm. "You think I wanted this? You think any of us had a choice in this?"

Phoenix's fists clenched, her whole body shaking with rage. "You experimented on my brother. You turned him into… into some kind of weapon! How could you?"

In the distance, she could hear a faint sound—footsteps.

Edward.

The thought jolted her from her paralysis. She looked around, realizing that while she and Mira had been locked in their confrontation, Edward had wandered off, slipping away into the dark corridors of the facility.

"Edward!" Phoenix called panic rising in her chest. She turned to Mira, her voice desperate. "Where did he go?"

Mira's face darkened. "He's already feeling the pull."

"What pull?" Phoenix's heart raced as she took a step toward her. "What are you talking about?"

Mira's eyes flickered with something dark, something she had been holding back. "The connection between Edward and Malakos. It's been there since the beginning, buried deep in his mind. But now that we're here, now that the facility has reactivated… it's calling to him."

Phoenix felt her blood run cold. "No… no, we have to stop it."

Mira shook her head. "You can't. Malakos is already taking him."

"No!" Phoenix shouted, her voice fraught with anger and fear. "I won't let that happen. He's still my brother!"

But even as she said the words, she could feel the truth slipping through her fingers. Edward was changing—he had been changing ever since they entered the facility. And now, whatever connection he had to Malakos was pulling him deeper into something she couldn't understand.

Phoenix's frustration boiled over, her chest tightening with a mixture of helplessness and fury. She clenched her fists, feeling the rage course through her veins, and then she screamed—a raw, desperate sound that echoed down the dark corridors.

"This is all your fault!" Phoenix turned on Mira, her voice shaking with anger. "You've lied to us, you've used us, and now Edward is paying the price! I don't care what you think you know or what you've done—I'm done with you!"

Mira's expression remained cold, her eyes hard as stone, but Phoenix wasn't finished.

"I'm doing this myself!" Phoenix's voice cracked with emotion, her heart racing as she spoke. "I'll find Edward, and I'll save him— without you! I don't ever want to see your face again!"

She didn't wait for Mira's response. Without looking back, Phoenix turned and sprinted down the corridor, her breath coming in ragged gasps as she fought back the rising panic inside her. She had to find Edward. She had to save him. And she would do it alone.

"Edward!" she called, her voice echoing through the cold, dark halls. But there was no answer.

(11)

The lost Brother

The deeper Edward ventured into the facility, the stronger the pull became. It wasn't a voice or a command—it was a feeling, deep in his bones, as though something was calling him, pulling him toward an unseen destination. His legs moved on their own, carrying him forward with a sense of purpose that terrified him.

Phoenix's voice echoed faintly in the distance behind him, but Edward couldn't respond. He couldn't even slow down. His heart raced, his breath coming in shallow gasps as he followed the twisting corridors, his body trembling with anticipation—and fear.

The lights overhead flickered erratically, casting long shadows that seemed to stretch and twist, warping the already cold and sterile environment. The air was thick with dust, and each breath felt heavier than the last like the facility itself was suffocating him.

And then, he found it—the core.

The corridor widened into a massive chamber, its walls lined with cables and ancient machinery. At the center of the room stood a large, cylindrical structure, glowing faintly with an eerie blue light. The core pulsed with energy, each pulse sending a tremor through the floor beneath his feet.

Edward's eyes widened as he stepped closer, his pulse quickening. He could feel it now, more clearly than ever—the pull. It was coming from this place, from the core.

But it wasn't just the core.

A shadow shifted in the far corner of the chamber, and Edward's heart lurched in his chest as a hulking figure stepped into view. Malakos.

The creature was larger than he remembered from his visions. Its twisted form was barely human, with glowing, molten eyes that burned with malevolent intent. Its movements were slow, and deliberate, as it approached the core, its presence dominating the space around them. Malakos looked different here, more powerful, more complete.

Edward's chest tightened, his breath catching in his throat as he took a step back. But there was nowhere to run—nowhere to hide.

Malakos' gaze locked onto him. At that moment, Edward felt something shift inside him. The pull became unbearable, like a thousand hooks lodged deep within him, dragging him closer, and forcing him to face the inevitable. His mind reeled, but his body moved forward, drawn toward Malakos—and toward the core.

And then, it began.

The fusion.

A surge of energy crashed through Edward's body, sending him to his knees as a guttural scream tore from his throat. His vision blurred, his muscles spasmed, and for a moment, he thought he might lose consciousness. But the pain kept him grounded, anchoring him to the horror that was unfolding.

Malakos stood still, watching, waiting, as Edward writhed on the cold metal floor, his hands clutching his head. The creature's eyes burned brighter as the core's energy seeped into Edward, wrapping itself around him like chains.

He could feel Malakos inside his mind now—the rage, the hatred, the endless hunger for power and destruction. It was like a flood, an unstoppable tide crashing into him, tearing down everything he was.

His mind fractured. Memories—his memories—started slipping away, dissolving into the darkness. His childhood, his family, Phoenix... everything was fading.

"No!" Edward gasped, his voice a whisper. He clawed at the floor, trying to pull himself away, but it was no use. Malakos' presence was too strong, too overwhelming. The fusion had already begun.

His body jerked violently, his muscles contorting, and twisting as the energy coursed through him. And then, with terrifying clarity, he understood.

His body was dying.

Edward could feel it—the slow, creeping numbness, the way his heart stuttered, each beat weaker than the last. His breath came in shallow, labored gasps, and he knew it wouldn't be long before his body gave out entirely.

He lifted his head, and through the haze of pain, he saw himself—his own body, crumpled on the floor, motionless. His skin had gone pale, his eyes dull and empty. He was dead.

And yet, he was still here.

His body was gone, but his consciousness—his mind—was inside of Malakos now. His mind was fusing with the creature, becoming part of the monster.

Edward loomed over his own body, staring into his own dead eyes. At that moment, Edward understood. He didn't become part of Malakos; he became Malakos.

A wave of despair crashed over him as he stared down at his lifeless body. His heart was pounding in his chest—or was it Malakos' chest? The line between them was blurring, and the horror of what he had become was suffocating him.

Edward's mind screamed, but no sound came out. He was lost, trapped inside the beast, staring at his lifeless body he no longer inhabited.

I'm still here, Edward reassured himself. The words felt hollow, and distant, as if they were already slipping away, drowned out by the overwhelming presence of Malakos in his mind.

Edward felt it then—Malakos' satisfaction. The creature had been waiting for this moment, for this fusion, and now it was complete.

He wanted to fight. He wanted to push Malakos out, to reclaim his body, his mind—his life. But the darkness was too strong, and he could feel it pulling him under, consuming everything he was.

In the distance, Phoenix's voice echoed faintly, calling out to him. But Edward—the Edward she knew—was gone.

The walls of the core room seemed to hum in tune with the fusion that was happening. Edward—no, Malakos—stood taller, more aware, more complete. Overwhelming power surged through him, binding them together as one. It wasn't just a merging of minds. It was a domination.

Malakos had taken control now.

Inside the darkness, Edward felt the growing rage, the fury that had been locked away inside Malakos for so long. Every ounce of Malakos' hatred for the world, for the humans who had abandoned him, poured into Edward's mind, drowning out his thoughts and memories.

He couldn't fight it. The pull was too strong. Every time he tried to think of Phoenix, their home, or their life before all of this, the image was swallowed by Malakos' burning desire for destruction.

Next came the pain. It wasn't physical—Edward's body had died, after all—but it was a deeper, more profound agony. It was the weight of Malakos' suffering, isolation, and betrayal. It filled Edward's mind until he thought he might break under the pressure.

But something held him back. Something kept him tethered, just at the edge of losing himself completely.

Phoenix.

Her voice, her face, her relentless hope. It cut through the darkness, a faint but unyielding presence in his mind. Edward clung to it, even as Malakos' influence swirled around him, threatening to tear it all away.

For the briefest moment, Edward found clarity. He was still here, trapped inside the body of this monster, but he hadn't disappeared completely. Somewhere, deep down, he was still Edward.

He glanced back at his own body again, lying lifeless on the cold floor. The sight twisted his stomach, a reminder of the finality of what had happened. He had died. Edward, the boy who had grown up with Phoenix, who had fought to survive in this broken world—he was gone.

And yet, part of him remained. His mind, his thoughts—they still lingered, tangled with Malakos' consciousness.

How long could he hold on?

The core pulsed again. Malakos—Edward's new form—took a step forward, his limbs moving with newfound strength. He could feel the power surging through him. The raw, unbridled force that made Malakos nearly invincible.

A voice echoed in his mind—Malakos' voice—twisted and dark. "You can't fight this," it whispered, taunting him. "You are mine now."

Edward's mind recoiled, but the voice grew louder and more insistent. "You are part of me. Together, we will tear this world apart."

No, Edward screamed inside his mind, his thoughts clashing against the dark presence. He couldn't let this happen. He couldn't let Malakos use him to destroy everything. But his resistance was weakening.

Phoenix's voice still called to him, faint but persistent. She was somewhere in the facility, searching for him, desperate to find her brother. But Edward knew the truth—he wasn't her brother anymore. Not fully. Not ever again.

With each passing moment, Malakos' influence grew stronger, pushing Edward further into the recesses of his own mind. The fusion was almost complete, and when it was, Edward feared that even the memory of who he was would be gone.

But he couldn't stop fighting—not yet. For now, there was a sliver of control. A small moment where Edward could still think and act on his own.

As Malakos' body turned toward the core, Edward felt a surge of power ripple through him. The creature was preparing, gathering its strength for whatever was to come next. He had to warn Phoenix. He had to tell her to stay away—to run, to escape before it was too late.

How could he, trapped inside this twisted, monstrous form, possibly reach her?

His mind raced, desperation clawing at him. If he could just reach out to her—if he could just make her hear him. He tried, focusing every ounce of his remaining will on one thought. *Phoenix, stay away.*

The core pulsed again, and with it came a wave of pain so intense that Edward nearly collapsed. Malakos laughed, a cruel, mocking sound inside his head. "You're too weak. She can't hear you."

Edward refused to give in. He clung to that one thought. One last desperate attempt to save her. *Phoenix, stay away.*

The darkness closed in around him again, and for a moment, he thought it was over. The fusion was complete. Malakos had won.

But then, in the distance, he heard it—Phoenix's voice.

She was calling for him, her voice trembling with fear, but strong and defiant. She was still searching, still fighting to find him.

"Edward!" Her voice echoed through the chamber, desperate and determined.

Malakos' laughter echoed through Edward's mind, a cruel mockery of his struggle. "You're too weak," the creature hissed, its voice a poisonous whisper in the dark. "You are mine, and you'll watch as I tear everything apart. Your sister. Your world. Everything."

Phoenix's voice still echoed faintly through the facility, her cries growing more desperate as she searched for him. At that moment, something inside Edward stirred. He wasn't just a passenger in Malakos' body. He was still here, still able to fight.

Malakos moved toward the core, his massive form hulking over the glowing structure as the energy rippled through the chamber. Edward could feel the power pulsing from the core, feeding Malakos, and making him stronger. But there was something else, something Edward hadn't noticed before.

The core wasn't just a source of power for Malakos—it was a weakness.

For the first time since the fusion began, Edward felt a flicker of hope. If he could just reach it—if he could disrupt the core's energy, maybe he could stop Malakos from fully taking over. Maybe he could end this.

Malakos' presence was suffocating, pressing down on him. He could feel over a decade's weight of rage and hatred coming from within him. Edward's mind fought to hold on, but it was like trying to hold back a tidal wave with his bare hands.

"You can't win," Malakos growled, his voice filling Edward's thoughts. "You're nothing but a shadow now. I am in control."

Edward focused every ounce of his remaining will on the core. He could feel its energy pulsing in time with Malakos' movements. He knew that this was his only chance. If he could just reach it, if he could just disrupt it…

With a surge of desperation, Edward pushed forward, his mind clashing with Malakos' in a violent struggle for control. His body—no, Malakos' body—jerked, the creature's movements faltering as Edward fought to break free.

You're not taking me.

Malakos roared, a deep, guttural sound that reverberated through the chamber, but Edward didn't stop. He pushed harder, forcing his way through the darkness, reaching for the core. His mind burned with the effort, but he couldn't stop. Not now.

With one final push, Edward felt the connection snap.

The core flared, its energy surging wildly as Edward's mind slammed into it. The pulse of power exploded through the room, and for a brief, shining moment, Edward was in control.

Malakos screamed, a sound of pure fury, as the creature's hold on Edward weakened. The fusion wasn't complete. Malakos hadn't won.

But Edward wasn't free, either. The core's disruption had stopped Malakos from fully taking over. Now, they were both trapped—two minds fighting for dominance inside one monstrous body.

Edward staggered back, his breath coming in ragged gasps as he tried to process what had just happened. He was still in control, but he could feel Malakos lurking just beneath the surface, waiting for any chance to take over again.

The core flickered, its energy dimming as the disruption took hold. The room around them trembled, the machinery groaning under the strain.

Edward's mind was still his own. For now.

He looked down at his monstrous hands—Malakos' hands—and felt a wave of nausea. His human body lay dead on the floor behind him, but his mind was still here, trapped inside the body of the very creature he had been trying to fight.

"I'm still here," Edward asserted, in control of the monstrous body. His heart was pounding in his chest. But he knew it wouldn't last. The struggle for control had only just begun, and Malakos wouldn't stay quiet for long. The fusion was incomplete, but the battle was far from over.

Phoenix's breath caught in her throat the moment she stepped into the chamber. The sight before her made the world tilt on its axis, her knees nearly giving way beneath her. Lying in a crumpled heap on the cold, metallic floor was Edward—her Edward. His body was still and lifeless. His skin was pale, drained of the warmth she had known her entire life.

"No…" She whispered despairingly, her heart shattering into pieces.

Her legs felt like lead as she staggered forward, falling to her knees beside him. The horror of it all crashed over her like a tidal wave, suffocating her, crushing her beneath its weight.

"Edward…" Phoenix's voice broke, then came the scream—a primal, anguished cry that tore from the depths of her soul. She clutched his body, her hands shaking as they pressed against his cold skin, desperate to feel some spark of life, something to tell her that this wasn't real. But there was nothing. He was gone.

"Edward!" She screamed again, tears streaming down her face as she shook his lifeless form, her sobs wracking her body. Her mind refused to accept what her eyes saw.

"Please, no. No, no, no! You can't—" Her voice broke, turning into a choked sob.

She was too late.

Her brother was dead.

Phoenix's sobs filled the chamber, her world crashing down around her. Her brother's dead body in her arms—how could this be happening? She couldn't breathe. It felt like the world was ending.

In her agony, she barely noticed the looming figure. The shadow moved slowly and deliberately towards her, relishing the sight of her pain. The sound of heavy, clawed feet scraped against the metal floor as Malakos approached her.

"It's a shame," Malakos' voice growled, cold and twisted. His form towered over them, monstrous and dark, his molten eyes burning with malevolent intent. "He was just a means to an end."

Phoenix froze. The voice—the presence—it was something otherworldly, vile. Slowly, she turned, her tear-filled eyes widening as they locked onto the creature looming above her.

Malakos. It hit her—this thing had taken her brother from her. It had killed him.

Malakos took another step forward, towering over Phoenix as his clawed hand reached out. "And now, little Phoenix," he hissed, a sick smile curling his grotesque lips, "you will—"

In mid-sentence, the creature faltered. Malakos' body jerked, his hand pausing mid-air.

"—Run!"

The word cut through the darkness like a flash of light. Phoenix blinked, confusion flooding her mind. The voice—it wasn't Malakos. It was Edward.

Malakos' glowing eyes flickered. His body twitched as if he were in pain. He let out a guttural growl, his monstrous form trembling.

"She's mine!" Malakos snarled, but his voice cracked, interrupted again.

"RUN!" Edward's voice broke through again, stronger this time, cutting Malakos off completely.

Phoenix's breath hitched, her heart pounding. She looked up at the creature—no, at her brother.

"Edward?" She whispered incredulously, taking a step back. Her eyes locked onto Malakos' twisted form, her mind unable to comprehend what was happening. Was Edward still in there? Was he fighting?

"RUN!" Edward's voice shouted, raw and desperate. Malakos' body twitched violently as Edward took control, fighting against the dark presence that held him captive.

"I can't hold him much longer!"

Phoenix stared, frozen in shock and disbelief. Tears still ran down her face, but her body refused to move. Her mind was unable to process the terror and confusion swirling around her.

"GO!" Edward's voice broke through again, his desperation clear. "Get out of here!"

Phoenix shook her head in denial. "No. I can't. I can't leave you. I won't."

Her heart shattered, the idea of abandoning Edward—leaving him in the clutches of this monster—it was too much.

Malakos growled, his body contorting as Edward fought for control. "She... will... not..." The creature's voice rumbled, but it was broken, fractured by Edward's presence.

"Go! Now!" Edward's voice screamed, his control slipping as Malakos began to regain dominance. The air around them seemed to tremble with the intensity of the struggle.

Phoenix took a step back, her heart racing, but her feet wouldn't move fast enough. She wanted to stay, to fight for her brother. But Edward was telling her to go. To run.

With tears blurring her vision, she turned and bolted toward the door. Her sobs echoed through the chamber, her feet stumbling over debris as she ran. She couldn't understand it. She couldn't accept it. Edward's dead body still lay on the floor, but his voice—it was still there, fighting, trying to protect her.

Behind her, she heard Malakos let out a roar of frustration. The walls of the facility trembled as the creature's rage shook the room.

The sound of collapsing metal filled the air. The entrance to the core room was coming down—Edward was making sure she couldn't come back.

Phoenix sobbed as she fled, her heart breaking with every step she took. Her brother was gone. She had lost him. Now there was nothing left but pain.

Phoenix's sobs echoed through the darkened corridors as she ran, her heart pounding in her chest. Each footfall felt heavier than the last like the weight of the world was pressing down on her. Her vision blurred, her body trembling with grief. She had to get away. Edward had told her to run, to escape—he had sacrificed himself to save her.

But how could she run from this?

The sound of crumbling metal and the thunderous collapse of the core room reverberated through the halls, shaking the facility with each passing second. Phoenix didn't dare look back. The fear of what was happening, of what Edward had become, gnawed at her insides.

She stumbled, catching herself against the cold wall as her legs buckled beneath her. Her breath came in ragged gasps, her chest tightening with each sob that tore from her throat.

"Edward…" She whispered, her voice broken, barely a breath.

The memory of his lifeless body burned in her mind. Yet, he had still found a way to reach her, to protect her. At what cost?

The facility continued to shake, groaning as the entrance to the core room collapsed entirely. Dust and debris rained down from the ceiling as Phoenix pressed herself against the wall, trying to make sense of what had just happened.

Her brother—her Edward—was trapped inside that monster. She had no idea if she would ever be able to save him.

But deep down, she knew. The boy she had grown up with, the brother she had loved and fought for, was gone. Malakos had him now. Even though Edward had fought for her, she could feel it—the darkness was winning.

A cold, suffocating silence settled over the facility as the final echoes of the collapse faded. Phoenix leaned against the wall, her body shaking with the weight of her grief. Her tears fell steadily now, her sobs turning into shallow gasps for air.

She wanted to scream and tear the world apart. But all she could do was stand there, helpless and broken.

Somewhere, in the back of her mind, a tiny spark of hope flickered. Edward had fought back. He had saved her. Maybe—just maybe— there was still a way to reach him, to bring him back.

But not now.

Now, all she could do was run.

The facility creaked and groaned around her, and Phoenix knew she couldn't stay. She had to keep moving. She had to escape before the entire place collapsed. Her legs trembled as she pushed herself away from the wall, forcing herself to take another step.

Her mind was numb, her heart shattered, but she couldn't stop. She wouldn't stop. Not until she found a way to save Edward. Not until she found a way to end this nightmare.

With one last, broken look toward the corridor she had come from, Phoenix wiped the tears from her face and stumbled forward, disappearing into the shadows of the facility.

(12)
Beneath the Weight

Phoenix's body felt like it was moving underwater. The world around her seemed distorted. Each sound was muffled. Each breath felt more difficult than the last, and her limbs moved heavily.

Edward was gone. The thought kept pounding inside her mind, refusing to settle. Her brother-her only family--was gone, taken from her by Malakos. There had been nothing she could do to stop it.

She stumbled forward, her vision blurred by tears. Her hands shook uncontrollably as she pressed them against the cold, hard ground. The walls of the facility loomed over her, their imposing shadows closing in with oppressive weight.

She had run, just like Edward had told her to do. She had left his body lying on that floor, abandoned to the monster that had consumed him.

Phoenix's legs gave way, and she crumpled to the ground, unable to hold herself up any longer. Her knees hit the cold surface with a thud, but she barely felt the pain. The scream that tore from her throat was raw, primal, and filled with a grief so deep it threatened to tear her apart.

"No... no, no, no," she choked out, her voice shaking. "I couldn't save you. I couldn't save you, Ed..."

The words echoed in the empty corridor, bouncing back to her, mocking her failure. Her fingers clawed at the floor, grasping for something--anything--to hold onto.

She couldn't stay here. She knew that. The weight of her guilt was suffocating, keeping her pinned in place.

She should have been stronger. She should have fought harder. Maybe there was something, some detail she had missed- something she could've done to stop this. Phoenix clenched her fists, nails biting into her palm. Every mistake, every misstep swirled inside her mind like a hurricane of regret.

How could she have trusted Mira? How could she have been so blind to her manipulation?!Phoenix's chest tightened as anger flared within her. It was Mira who had brought them here. Mira who had lied to them and manipulated them. In the end, it was Mira's games that had taken Edward away from her.

Her breath came in ragged gasps as she whispered through clenched teeth, "I'II kill her. I swear, I'll kill her."

But right now, Mira was gone like Edward. Phoenix was completely alone. The weight of that loneliness pressed down on her, making it hard to breathe or think. Her body shook with the effort of keeping herself together, but her mind was unraveling.

Suddenly, the ceiling groaned above her, metal grinding against metal. Phoenix froze, her eyes widening as the noise grew louder, and closer.

Before she could react, a section of the ceiling caved in with a deafening crash. A heavy beam slammed down on her, pinning her leg beneath it. Pain shot up through her body, sharp and excruciating,

Phoenix screamed, her hands clawing at the floor as she tried to free herself, but the weight of the beam was too much. It pressed down on her leg, waves of agony coursing through her. Her breaths came in short, ragged bursts as she struggled to stay conscious, the pain overwhelming her senses.

"No... no, not like this..." Phoenix gasped pleadingly.

She tried to push the beam off, but her strength was fading fast. The edges of her vision began to blur, darkness creeping in as the pain consumed her. Her leg throbbed, sharp pain radiating through her body, and her breath came in ragged bursts. She tried to focus, to stay conscious, but it was like fighting against a powerful current, pulling her under.

Her body gave in, and the darkness swallowed her whole.

Time passed in a haze, an endless void of numbness and fleeting dreams. Eventually, Phoenix stirred. Her eyelids fluttered, heavy and reluctant to open, her mind foggy with disorientation.

She groaned softly. Her hand instinctively reached for her leg, expecting to feel the sharp pain of the injury, but it wasn't as intense as before. Slowly, her eyes opened, adjusting to the dim light around her. She realized she wasn't in the corridor anymore.

(13)

Silent Reckoning

Phoenix's body swayed with each step Jax took, her consciousness drifting in and out. Her leg throbbed beneath the bandages, and her mind felt heavy, fogged by pain and exhaustion. When she finally opened her eyes, she blinked against the dim light of dusk. The trees above blurred together, their shadows long as the sun lowered in the sky.

It took her a moment to realize she wasn't lying still. She was moving—no, being carried. The soft but rigid support beneath her back told her she was on a stretcher, and the steady rhythm of footsteps alongside her confirmed she wasn't alone.

"You're awake," Jax's deep voice cut through the haze, calm but alert.

She sat up, the bandages on her leg pulling against her skin. A sharp pain shot through her, but she clenched her teeth, pushing through it. Phoenix sat frozen, staring up at Jax. The man she had spent so much time fearing, was now the reason she was alive.

"Where are we?" Her voice came out hoarse, barely a whisper. Her throat was dry, the words scraping like sandpaper.

"We're heading to my settlement," Jax replied, his tone as steady as his steps. "Your leg needs proper care. It's a two, maybe three-day walk from here, but we'll make it."

The words hit her like a blow. Three days? They were so far from everything—far from where she'd lost Edward. The ache in her chest grew tighter, the memories of those final moments with him flooding her mind. Her stomach clenched. Her brother, her only family, was gone. No matter how much pain she was in, nothing compared to the gaping hole his loss left behind. Now here she was, saved by someone she thought was the enemy.

"I couldn't leave you behind," Jax continued, glancing down at her. "Not like that."

Phoenix's heart tightened. The thought of being so far from Edward felt like a betrayal like she was abandoning him all over again. But her body was weak, broken, and her leg screamed in pain every time she shifted.

"I don't trust you," Phoenix whispered, her voice shaking with emotion.

Jax nodded as if he expected that. "I wouldn't, either."

They sat in silence for a moment, the air between them thick with unspoken tension. Phoenix's mind was swirling with questions—about Jax, about Edward, about what came next—but for now, all she could do was survive.

Phoenix found the courage to continue, despite the fear she felt toward him, "You're the reason Edward is dead! You're the reason we're in this mess in the first place! Mira told us everything about you—about what you've done."

Jax frowned, his brows knitting together. "Mira?" He leaned back in his chair, the confusion deepening in his eyes. "What exactly did Mira tell you?"

Phoenix glared at him, her fists clenching at her sides. "That you're dangerous. That you've been hunting us. That you were behind the experiments at the facility—that you helped create the Lost and everything else that's tearing this world apart."

For a moment, Jax said nothing. He stared at her, processing her words, and then something shifted in his expression. His eyes hardened, and he let out a low, humorless chuckle.

"So, that's what she's been telling you," he muttered, more to himself than to Phoenix.

He rubbed a hand over his face, his frustration evident. "I should've known," he murmured, shaking his head slightly. "Of course, she'd twist everything to make me the villain."

Phoenix narrowed her eyes, her anger still simmering. "You're saying she lied about you?"

Jax met her gaze, his expression sharp. "Mira's good at playing games, Phoenix. She's always been able to twist the truth to fit her agenda." He sighed, leaning forward, resting his elbows on his knees again. "I didn't create the Lost. I didn't follow you to harm you. I've been trying to stop her."

Phoenix's mind reeled, her body tense. "Stop her from what?"

Jax's gaze flickered with something darker - regret, perhaps, or maybe anger. "From finishing what she started. The experiments, the mutations… they weren't supposed to go this far. Mira kept pushing, kept taking things beyond what any of us wanted. Your father tried to stop her, but by then, it was too late."

Phoenix's breath caught in her throat. She had always known there was more to the story, that Mira was hiding things, but hearing it from Jax twisted everything she thought she knew.

"You're lying," she said, but her voice lacked conviction.

Jax shook his head. "Believe what you want. But I'm not the one who's been lying to you."

He paused, his gaze softening just slightly. "I didn't want this, Phoenix. I didn't want Edward to die. I've been trying to stop Mira - to stop the chaos she unleashed. But I couldn't do it alone."

Phoenix swallowed hard, her throat dry as the weight of Jax's words pressed down on her. She didn't want to believe him. She couldn't. Mira had been manipulative, sure, but she had also helped them survive—hadn't she? Could Jax be telling the truth?

Her mind raced, battling with everything she thought she knew. Anger and confusion bubbled beneath the surface as she tried to make sense of Jax's words.

"You expect me to just take your word for it?" "You expect me to believe that Mira's the real villain in all of this, but not you?"

Jax met her gaze, his expression unreadable.
"I don't expect you to believe anything," he responded calmly. "I'm just telling you the truth. What you do with it is up to you."

Phoenix clenched her fists, her heart pounding in her chest. She wanted to scream, to lash out, to make sense of the chaos in her mind. But she was too exhausted, too overwhelmed. Her leg still throbbed with pain, and the emotional weight of Edward's loss pressed down on her like a suffocating blanket.

She let out a frustrated breath, her eyes narrowing as she looked at Jax. "Why are you helping me now?" She asked, her voice suspicious. "Why didn't you come sooner? Why didn't you stop her before everything fell apart?"

Jax's jaw tightened, his gaze flickering with a hint of regret. "Because I was too late," he admitted, his voice gruff. "By the time I realized what Mira was doing, she had already gained too much control. The Lost, the mutations—they were her army, and I couldn't take her down alone. Your father tried to stop her, but he didn't make it in time either."

Phoenix felt a cold chill run down her spine. Her father had been trying to stop Mira? The man she thought had abandoned them, had kept so many secrets, had been fighting against her? It didn't make sense, and yet… it did.

She shook her head, her emotions a storm swirling inside her. "Why should I trust you?" she whispered, barely able to get the words out. "You could be lying just like she did."

"I don't care if you trust me, Phoenix. I'm not here to convince you. I'm here because we both have the same goal—to stop Mira from destroying what's left of this world." He paused, his gaze softening. "And because your brother wouldn't want you to die here."

The mention of Edward sent a fresh wave of pain through Phoenix's chest. She bit her lip, trying to hold back the tears that threatened to spill. "Don't talk about him," she whispered, her voice trembling. "You don't get to talk about him."

Jax held up his hands, his expression softening further. "I'm sorry," he sympathized quietly. "But I need you to understand that I'm not your enemy."

Phoenix's heart ached, her mind warring with itself. She didn't want to trust him—couldn't—but at the same time, she was alone. Edward was gone. Mira was gone. And now, all she had was this man, this stranger who had saved her life.

She clenched her fists, her body shaking with emotion. "If what you're saying is true," she began, her voice hoarse, "then how do we stop her? How do we stop Mira?"

Jax's eyes darkened, his jaw tightening again. "We find her. And we end this once and for all."

Phoenix's pulse quickened, her resolve hardening. She didn't know if she could trust Jax completely, but one thing was clear—Mira had to be stopped. And Phoenix was going to make sure it happened.
But first, she needed to get back on her feet.

Echoes of the Past

When she woke again, it was darker, and they had stopped. The air was cooler, and the flicker of firelight danced across her face. She was lying beside a small fire, the warmth cutting through the chill of the night air. Her leg still ached, but the pain had dulled somewhat, and she noticed that Jax had rewrapped the bandages—neat, tight, and secure.

Jax was seated across from her, tending to the fire. His expression was hard to read in the low light, but he seemed lost in thought. When he noticed her stirring, he reached for a canteen and held it out to her.

"Here. Drink. You'll need to stay hydrated. You'll be able to walk in a day or two," he said, his voice calm but firm. "It won't be pain-free, but you'll manage. Just rest, and let your leg heal. I'll take care of things in the meantime."

Phoenix propped herself up just enough to take the canteen. The cool water soothed her dry throat, though the relief was only temporary. She handed it back, her thoughts already turning back to the weight of everything that had happened.

Jax seemed to sense her turmoil. He looked at her for a long moment, his gaze steady but unreadable. "You've got questions," he said quietly. "I know."

Phoenix swallowed hard, her voice thick with exhaustion and emotion. "Why didn't anyone tell me? Why didn't my father tell me what was happening?"

Jax's expression tightened slightly. He leaned back, his voice lowering. "Your father thought he was protecting you. He didn't want you involved in any of this. He wanted you to be safe."

Phoenix shook her head, frustration flaring in her chest. "But I wasn't safe. Edward's gone. Everything's gone, and I had no idea why any of it was happening."

Jax nodded, his face shadowed in the firelight. "Your father underestimated the world. He didn't see how fast things were falling apart. By the time he realized what Mira was doing, it was already too late to stop it."

The name sent a fresh wave of anger through Phoenix. Mira. The one who had manipulated them, used them, and ultimately caused Edward's death. "What do you mean, 'too late'?" She asked, her voice sharp despite the fatigue.

Jax sighed, rubbing his hand over his face. "Your father was working on Project Genesis to heal the world after the collapse. He wanted to stop the mutations, to make things right. Edward was supposed to be the key, someone who could change things. But Mira saw potential in him that your father never did. She pushed him beyond what your father could've imagined."

Phoenix's chest tightened at the mention of Edward. "So he was just some experiment? That's all?"

Jax's eyes softened. "Not to your father. Edward was his son—just like you were his daughter. The connection between Edward and Malakos wasn't supposed to happen. Your father never intended for it to go that far."

Phoenix bit her lip, the grief for Edward fresh and raw. She wanted to ask more, to understand everything, but she didn't know if she could bear to hear it.

Jax's voice was quieter now, almost regretful. "Your father tried to stop it. He tried to stop her. But Mira was always a step ahead."

Phoenix stared at the fire, the crackling flames reflecting in her eyes. "He tried to stop her…" she echoed, her voice barely above a whisper. "But he failed."

Jax nodded solemnly, the firelight casting shadows over his weathered face. "Mira was relentless. She saw Edward as more than just a person. He was a tool, something she could manipulate to fulfill her goals. Your father didn't want any of this. He wanted to protect you and Edward. He just didn't realize how far Mira would go."

Phoenix's throat tightened, the betrayal stinging anew. All this time, she had thought she understood her father—understood the world he was trying to build for them. Now it felt like everything had been a lie, built on secrets and mistakes she never knew existed.

Her hands trembled as she wrapped her arms around her knees, trying to stave off the cold that seemed to seep into her bones.

"I don't know what to believe anymore," she confessed softly, her voice shaking. "He kept everything from me… and now I've lost Edward because of it."

Jax watched her carefully, his voice gentle but firm. "Your father made mistakes, Phoenix. But he loved both of you. He thought keeping you away from all of this would keep you safe. He was wrong about that, but his intentions were never to hurt you."

Phoenix shook her head, the tears welling up again despite her efforts to keep them at bay. "But he did hurt me. He kept me in the dark, and now I'm left picking up the pieces of a world I didn't even know existed."

The silence between them was heavy, the crackling of the fire the only sound filling the space. Jax didn't offer any more explanations and didn't try to fix the unfixable. He just sat there, his eyes fixed on the flames, as if he, too, was lost in the weight of the past.

After a long moment, Jax spoke again, his voice quieter than before. "Your father and I… we weren't just colleagues. We were friends. Close, even. I knew your mother too."

Phoenix glanced at him, surprised by the sudden shift. The pain in her leg still throbbed, but her focus was on Jax's words.

"You knew my mom? Tell me." Her voice was filled with a mixture of curiosity and hesitation. "Tell me about them."

Jax's eyes softened as he looked at her, his tone growing almost wistful. "Your mother, Leona, was a force of nature. Strong-willed, stubborn. She never backed down from a fight. I remember one time, she took on three guys twice her size in a bar because they wouldn't leave your father alone. She walked out without a scratch."

Phoenix felt a pang in her chest at the mention of her mother. Her memories of Leona were distant, blurred by the years and the chaos that followed the collapse. Hearing Jax talk about her brought warmth to the coldness that had settled inside her.

"She loved you both more than anything," Jax continued, his gaze distant as he recalled the past. "She fought for you, for your future. Even when things started to fall apart, she never stopped believing that there was a way to make things right."

Phoenix's chest tightened. "I barely remember her," she admitted, her voice small. "I was so young when they died."

Jax looked at her, his expression softening. "She was proud of you, Phoenix. Even when you were little, she used to say you had her fire and your father's mind. She believed you could change the world."

Phoenix listened, her heart aching as she pictured the parents she barely remembered. Their faces were a blur in her mind, their voices distant echoes. But hearing Jax talk about them made them feel real again like they were more than just memories.

"Your father, on the other hand, was quiet and methodical. He was always thinking, always planning. He was the one who kept us grounded. He saw the bigger picture when the rest of us couldn't."

Jax continued, his voice quieter now, almost reflective. "That's why he founded Project Genesis. It wasn't just something he got involved in—he started it. He believed in it. He believed it could change everything.

He created Edward as part of it… Edward was meant to be the answer, the hope for something greater."

Phoenix's throat tightened, her emotions swirling inside her. She wanted to ask more, to hear every detail Jax knew about her parents, but she also felt a sharp sting of betrayal. If Jax had known all of this, why hadn't he come sooner? Why hadn't he told her the truth before everything fell apart?

Phoenix swallowed hard, the tears finally spilling over. She wiped them away quickly, refusing to let herself break in front of Jax. But the ache in her heart only grew. Her parents had been taken from her, and now Edward was gone too. She felt so lost, so alone, and she didn't know how to move forward.

"I wish I could remember them better," she whispered. "I wish I had more time with them."

Jax didn't respond right away. He just watched her, his face unreadable. Then, after a long pause, he reached into his pack and pulled out a small, worn photograph. He held it out to her, his expression soft but guarded.

Phoenix hesitated for a moment before taking it, her hands trembling as she unfolded the edges. The image was faded, the colors dull with age, but it was unmistakable. Her father, her mother, and a much younger Phoenix, barely more than a toddler, all smiling together. The sight of it made her heart lurch. She had never seen this photo before. She hadn't even known it existed.

Jax's voice was quiet. "I kept it… after everything. I thought you might want to have it."

Phoenix stared at the photograph, her vision blurring with tears. It felt like a small piece of her family had been given back to her, even though they were gone. She didn't know what to say, her throat tight with emotion.

"Why now?" Phoenix asked, her voice thick with emotion. "Why tell me all of this now, after everything that's happened?"

Jax's expression darkened, his gaze meeting hers with a mixture of regret and determination.

"I stayed away because I didn't know how to stop Mira—not after your father died. I thought keeping my distance would keep you safe, but I was wrong. I should have told you sooner, but I thought if I showed up, Mira would find out and go after you even faster. I failed you, Phoenix. But now, we don't have the luxury of hiding."

Phoenix swallowed hard, her mind spinning with everything Jax had just revealed. She didn't know what to believe anymore, but one thing was clear—her parents had been involved in something far bigger than she ever realized. And now, it was her fight, too.

For a long time, they sat in silence, the weight of the past hanging between them. Phoenix clutched the photograph in her hands, her heart aching but grateful for the small reminder of who her parents had been.

The next day passed in a blur of movement and exhaustion. Jax pulled Phoenix on the makeshift stretcher, his pace steady but cautious, avoiding the rougher terrain where he could. The forest around them grew denser as they moved deeper into the wilderness. The sound of wild birds and rustling leaves was their only company.

Phoenix remained quiet for most of the day, her thoughts consumed by the photograph tucked safely in her pocket. Now and then, she'd pull it out and stare at it, her heart aching with the loss of her parents. She wanted to hold on to that memory, to the way they had looked at her, full of love and hope.

Jax had spoken little since the night before, only offering small reassurances as they traveled. He was focused, his attention on the path ahead, but Phoenix could tell he was giving her space to process everything.

As the afternoon wore on and the light began to fade, Jax finally spoke again, breaking the silence between them.

"We'll stop soon for the night," he assured, his voice low. "I need to check on your leg and make sure the bandages are holding."

Phoenix nodded, though her mind was elsewhere. She hadn't asked him about Mira again, about the raid that had destroyed her village and taken her parents. The conversation from the night before still lingered in her mind. There was so much pain and uncertainty in the truths she had uncovered.

When they finally stopped, Jax set her down carefully near a small clearing, the trees providing shelter from the cold wind. He crouched beside her, unwrapping the bandages around her leg with practiced hands. Phoenix winced at the sight of the swollen, bruised skin beneath. Jax's touch was gentle, his movements steady.

"It's healing," he said quietly. "But you need to keep off it as much as possible. It'll take time."

Phoenix watched him work, her mind still clouded with everything she had learned. When he finished rewrapping her leg, he stood and moved toward the fire he had started, sitting down across from her.

For a long moment, neither of them spoke. As the fire crackled between them, Jax leaned back, his expression thoughtful.

"I'll tell you more about your parents if you want," he offered kindly. "Stories from before everything fell apart. They weren't just scientists and leaders. They were people, like you and me."

Phoenix nodded, her heart aching for the family she had lost, but grateful for the chance to hear more about them. "I'd like that."

As the night stretched on, Jax shared stories of her parents—memories of their strength, their laughter, and their love for each other and for their children. Phoenix listened, her heart heavy but full of a new understanding of who they had been, who they had tried to be in a world that was crumbling around them.

As the fire burned low and sleep began to tug at the edges of her consciousness, Phoenix felt a strange sense of peace settle over her. The pain of her loss would never go away, but hearing Jax's stories had given her something she hadn't realized she needed.
A connection to her past. To her family.

The next morning, Phoenix awoke to the soft sounds of the forest. Birds chirped in the distance, their songs echoing through the stillness. The air was cool, damp from the previous night's rain, and the faint scent of earth filled her nostrils as she stirred.

Jax was already awake, crouched by the fire, stirring a small pot that emitted the scent of something warm and savory. He glanced over his shoulder as she shifted on the bedroll, his eyes tired but alert.

"Morning," he mumbled, his voice low. "How's the leg?"

Phoenix pushed herself up slightly, testing the weight of her body against the ache in her leg. It throbbed, but the pain wasn't as sharp as before.

"Better," she muttered, still groggy. "Thanks for everything."

Jax nodded, not making a big deal of her gratitude. He stood, handing her a small bowl of the stew he had made. "It's not much, but it'll keep you going."

She accepted the bowl, the warmth of it seeping into her cold hands. As she ate, they sat in silence. The only sound was the crackle of the fire and the occasional rustling of leaves in the breeze. Phoenix's thoughts, though, were anything but quiet.

Her mind kept circling back to Jax's words from the previous day, about her father and Project Genesis, about Mira and everything that had gone wrong. She still couldn't quite reconcile the image she had of her father—a quiet, gentle man—with the reality of what he had been involved in. The fact that he had kept it all from her, even as their world collapsed around them, stung.

As if sensing her thoughts, Jax broke the silence.

"I never asked for this, you know," he spoke dismally, staring into the fire. "When your father started Project Genesis, I wasn't supposed to be part of it. I was just a soldier back then, trying to survive like everyone else."

Phoenix looked up from her bowl, surprised by the admission. "Then why did you get involved?"

Jax sighed, rubbing a hand over his face. "Your father convinced me. He saw something in me, something I didn't even see in myself. He believed I could help him—protect him and the project. He was always thinking ahead, always planning for the worst."

Phoenix frowned, her brow furrowing. "But he never told us. He never told me or Edward what was really going on."

Jax's eyes softened. "He thought it was the only way to keep you safe. The more you knew, the more dangerous it became. Your father carried the weight of that decision every day. It wasn't easy for him."

Phoenix felt a pang of sympathy, though it was laced with anger. "Well look where that got us," she whispered, her voice thick with emotion. "Edward's gone. Our village is gone."

Jax didn't argue with her. He just nodded, his expression pained. "I know. I've had my regrets, too. We all thought we were doing the right thing, but things spiraled out of control faster than anyone could've predicted. Mira… she played us all."

Phoenix set the empty bowl aside, staring into the flames. "What was she like? Before all of this?"

Jax hesitated for a moment, as if unsure how to answer. "Mira wasn't always like this. Back when Project Genesis first started, she was different. Driven, yes, but not cruel. She believed in your father's vision. Somewhere along the way, something changed in her. She started pushing boundaries, doing things your father would've never allowed. And once the collapse happened, she saw an opportunity to take control. She became obsessed with power."

Phoenix clenched her fists. "She's the reason Edward's gone."

Jax's gaze hardened. "Yes, she is. And that's why we have to stop her."

The determination in his voice stirred something in Phoenix. She still wasn't sure how much she could trust Jax, but she knew one thing for certain: Mira had to be stopped. She had taken too much from them already.

They packed up camp in silence, Jax helping Phoenix onto the litter once again. The day stretched before them, and Phoenix's mind wandered as they continued their journey. She thought about her father, about what he had been trying to do, and about Mira's betrayal. But more than anything, she thought about Edward.

"Tell me more about the settlement," she requested after a while, trying to push the heavier thoughts away. "What's it like living there?"

Jax glanced over at her, his expression softening a little. "It's peaceful, for the most part. We've carved out a life there, a community. We're hidden deep enough that most people don't even know we exist. There are families there, kids. It's not perfect, but it's home."

Phoenix imagined it—people living together, protecting each other, building a life in a world that had been torn apart. It was so different from everything she had known. "And your family? They're there?"

Jax nodded, his gaze distant. "Elara—my wife—and our son, Luka. They're waiting for me. I've been gone too long already."

Phoenix felt a strange pang in her chest. Jax had a family, people who loved him, and who were waiting for him. She wondered what that must feel like, to know there was someone waiting for you, someone who cared whether you came back.

"Do they know about all of this?" she asked softly. "About Project Genesis, about everything?"

Jax hesitated, then nodded. "Elara knows. She's always known. She was there when it all started. Luka, though, he's just a kid. He doesn't need to know the details yet."

As they traveled through the woods, the silence stretched, broken only by the soft rustle of leaves and the rhythmic sound of their steps. Phoenix found herself thinking about the life Jax had described—the settlement, his family, and the sense of peace he hinted at. It seemed so far removed from the life she had known, from the chaos and violence that had torn everything apart.

After a long while, Phoenix spoke again, her voice hesitant. "What was it like? Before the collapse, I mean." She had grown up hearing bits and pieces of what the world used to be like, but most of it felt like stories, like another world entirely.

Jax slowed his pace, casting a glance at her as he considered the question. "It was… different. There was order and structure. People worked, lived in cities, and believed things would always stay the same. But it wasn't perfect. There were tensions and cracks in the foundation. Your father saw that. He knew something was coming—he just didn't know how bad it would be."

Phoenix frowned, her mind trying to picture it. A world with cities, jobs, and normal lives. It was hard to imagine, and the way Jax spoke about it, there was a wistfulness in his tone, but also a deep sense of loss.

"He was always trying to prepare for it," Jax continued, his gaze distant as he recalled those days. "Project Genesis was supposed to be a solution, a way to safeguard the future. But the collapse changed everything. The mutations, the creatures… it wasn't just about surviving anymore. It became about controlling what was left."

Phoenix's thoughts drifted to her father. She had spent so much time wondering why he had kept so much from her, why he had chosen to bear the weight of those secrets alone. But hearing Jax talk about him now, she began to understand—at least a little. He had been trying to save them all, trying to give her and Edward a future.

"And my mom?" Phoenix asked quietly. "Did she believe in it? In what my father was doing?"

Jax smiled faintly, though there was sadness in his eyes. "Leona supported your father, but she wasn't like him. She wasn't focused on the big picture the way he was. She cared more about the people around her, about protecting the ones she loved. She fought because she believed in her family. She believed in you and Edward."

Jax glanced at her, his voice softening. "She would have been proud of you, Phoenix. She was proud of both you and Edward. She saw something in you—a strength that she knew would carry you through, no matter what happened."

The weight of those words pressed down on her, and for a moment, Phoenix didn't know what to say. She had spent so much time feeling lost, feeling like everything had been taken from her. But hearing that her mother had believed in her, had seen something in her, stirred something deep inside—a spark of the strength she hadn't known she still had.

As they walked, the conversation shifted, and Phoenix found herself asking more about Jax's family. He spoke of Elara and Luka with a fondness that softened the edges of his usual hard demeanor, and for a brief moment, she saw him not as the hardened soldier, but as a man who had something to fight for, just like her father had.

"You must miss them," Phoenix empathized with sincerity.

Jax nodded, his gaze distant again. "I do. But I'll see them soon. And we'll figure out what comes next. Together."

Phoenix admired his certainty, the way he seemed so sure of his place in the world, even after everything that had happened. She wasn't sure if she'd ever feel that way again.

As the afternoon stretched on, they took a break beneath the canopy of a large tree. Jax checked her leg again, rewrapping the bandage with care, his hands steady and practiced. The pain had dulled somewhat, but it was still a constant reminder of everything that had happened—of how close she had come to losing everything.

"You're healing," Jax appraised cheerfully. "But you still need to take it easy. No rushing off into danger once we get to the settlement."

Phoenix managed a weak smile, though the weight of their journey still hung over her. "I'll try to stay out of trouble."

Jax chuckled softly, shaking his head. "I doubt that."

As they prepared to move again, the wind shifted, carrying with it the faint scent of rain. Jax glanced up at the sky, his expression tightening. "Storm's coming. We need to find shelter soon."

Phoenix nodded. Her body already ached from the day's travel. As much as she wanted to keep pushing forward, she knew Jax was right. They needed to rest and gather their strength for whatever lay ahead.

They pressed on for another hour before Jax found a small, sheltered cave nestled into the side of a hill. It wasn't much but it would keep them dry. He set up a small fire near the entrance while Phoenix settled in against the cool stone, her leg stretched out in front of her.

As the rain began to fall outside, tapping softly against the rocks, Phoenix stared into the fire, her thoughts a whirlwind of everything they had discussed. There was still so much left to uncover, so many questions that lingered in the back of her mind. But for now, she focused on the warmth of the fire, the safety of the cave, and the quiet presence of Jax beside her.

Tonight, for the first time in a long time, Phoenix felt like she could breathe. The steady rhythm of the rain lulled Phoenix into a rare moment of calm, but her thoughts still churned. She wasn't sure if it was the pain in her leg or the weight of everything Jax had told her, but sleep felt elusive.

The fire crackled softly, its glow flickering against the cave walls. Phoenix glanced at Jax, who sat across from her, staring into the flames. He seemed lost in his own thoughts, but she could see the same weariness in his eyes—the kind of weariness that came from years of fighting, of carrying burdens too heavy for one person to bear.

"Jax," she spoke quietly, breaking the silence.

He looked up, his gaze meeting hers, waiting.

"Do you ever wish things had been different? That none of this had happened?"

Jax's expression didn't change, but there was a brief pause before he answered. "Every day."

Phoenix nodded, not surprised by his response. She often found herself wondering what life would have been like if the world hadn't fallen apart—if her parents had lived if Edward was still with her. But the past was a closed door, one that she could never reopen.

For a while, they sat in silence, the rain providing a steady backdrop to their shared contemplation. Then Jax spoke again, his voice softer now. "There's a part of me that's always wondered what your father's plan really was. I trusted him, believed in him, but..."

He trailed off, his brow furrowing as he stared into the flames.

"But what?" Phoenix pressed.

Jax sighed. "But I don't think even he knew how it would all end. He had this vision, this hope that he could save humanity from the collapse, but the world had already changed too much. By the time

Mira twisted everything, it was beyond saving in the way your father imagined."

Phoenix swallowed hard, the ache in her chest growing as she thought of her father—of the choices he had made and the secrets he had kept. "Maybe he didn't want to admit that it was too late."

"Maybe," Jax agreed. "But even in the end, he was still fighting for you and Edward. He believed you two were the future."

Phoenix stared into the fire, the weight of those words pressing down on her. Her father had put everything into Project Genesis, into trying to create a better world for her and Edward. And now, she was the one left to pick up the pieces.

"I'm not sure I can live up to that," she admitted, her voice barely above a whisper.

Jax's gaze softened. "You don't have to be your father, Phoenix. You just have to be you. That's enough."

Phoenix wasn't sure if she believed that, but she appreciated the sentiment. She had spent so much time trying to figure out what her role was in all of this—trying to live up to the legacy her parents had left behind. But maybe Jax was right. Maybe it was enough just to keep fighting, in her own way.

She looked down at her leg, the bandage wrapped tightly around it and took a deep breath. "Do you really think we can stop Mira?"

Jax didn't hesitate. "Yes. But it won't be easy. She's more dangerous now than ever."

Phoenix nodded, knowing that the battle ahead was far from over. Hearing Jax's confidence gave her a sliver of hope, something to hold onto as they moved forward.

"I wish Edward was still here," she whispered, her voice cracking.

Jax's expression softened. "I know. And I'm sorry, Phoenix. Edward didn't deserve what happened to him."

Phoenix blinked back the tears that threatened to spill. She wasn't ready to talk about Edward's loss—not yet. But Jax's words, his quiet acknowledgment of her pain, brought her some comfort.

The soft crackle of the fire filled the cave with comforting warmth, though the steady patter of rain outside reminded Phoenix of the storm rolling in. She stared into the flames, her thoughts lingering on the life Jax had described at the settlement. The idea of families living together, children playing, and a sense of security felt like a distant dream—one that belonged to another world.

"You know," Jax's voice broke the silence, "the settlement… it's not perfect. We've had our share of problems. There's always the threat of raiders, and sometimes the Lost come too close for comfort. But we've survived."

Phoenix glanced at him, noticing the way his brow furrowed slightly. "What keeps you going?"

Jax stirred the fire, his gaze distant. "You find something to fight for. Whether it's family, friends, or just the hope that things can get better. Elara and Luka. Knowing they're waiting for me. It makes every fight, every sacrifice worth it."

He paused, his voice softening. "Luka's only eight. Too young to know the full weight of the world outside our walls, but old enough to sense when things aren't right. I want to give him a chance to grow up in a world where he doesn't have to worry about monsters lurking in the shadows."

Phoenix's heart tightened at his words. She thought of Edward. They had fought so hard to survive together. Now he was gone, and she wasn't sure if there was anything left for her to fight for. She looked away, blinking back the tears that threatened to spill.

Her parents were gone, Edward was gone, and now she was left in a world that felt colder and more dangerous with every passing day. As much as she wanted to shut down, to let the grief consume her, she knew she couldn't. Not if there was still a chance to stop Mira. Not if there was still something worth fighting for.

"I don't know if I can do this," Phoenix admitted, her voice barely above a whisper. "I don't know if I'm strong enough."

Jax was silent for a moment, then he spoke, his voice steady. "You're stronger than you think, Phoenix. You've survived this far, and that's more than most people can say. Your parents saw that strength in you, and I see it too."

She didn't respond right away, her mind too clouded with doubt and uncertainty. But there was a part of her, deep down, that wanted to believe him. She wanted to believe she was capable of more than just surviving.

As the fire crackled between them, Phoenix shifted the conversation to something lighter. "Tell me more about Luka," she said, hoping to push away the heavier thoughts for a moment.

Jax smiled, the tension in his shoulders easing slightly. "He's a handful, that's for sure. Smart kid, too. Always asking questions, and always wanting to know more about the world outside the settlement. Elara's always telling him to stay close, but he's got that same curiosity your father had. Wants to understand everything."

"He's strong-willed, too," Jax continued, a touch of pride in his voice. "Actually, he reminds me of you. Doesn't back down easily. Always ready to fight for what he believes in."

Phoenix smiled faintly, imagining a small boy with bright eyes and an insatiable curiosity. It sounded… normal. Like the kind of life she had always imagined but never quite had.

Jax's words echoed in her mind — about finding something to fight for, about carrying on the legacy her parents had left behind. Maybe she didn't have all the answers yet, and maybe the grief would never fully leave her. However, there was something inside her that refused to give up. Something that knew, deep down, that the fight wasn't over yet.

As the rain began to let up and the fire died down, Phoenix settled into the quiet, her mind calmer than it had been in days. Tomorrow they would reach the settlement, and with it, whatever new challenges awaited. But for now, she let herself rest, knowing that for the first time in a long time, she wasn't facing the darkness alone.

Her body grew heavy, her eyes drooping as sleep finally began to pull her under.

(15)

The Healing Flame

The next morning, they resumed their journey. The sun broke through the clouds, casting a golden light over the forest as they walked. Phoenix leaned heavily on her makeshift crutch, but the pain in her leg had dulled to a manageable ache.

Jax walked beside her in silence, but there was an unspoken understanding between them now—one forged by shared loss and a common goal.

As they neared the forest's edge, Phoenix could make out the faint outline of the settlement in the distance. A high wall surrounded it, with a watchtower peeking above the treetops. It was smaller than she had imagined, but there was a sense of security in how it was tucked away from the world.

Jax stopped and turned to her, his expression serious. "We're here. You'll get the help you need, and then we'll figure out our next move."

Phoenix nodded apprehensively. She wasn't sure what to expect from the settlement, but she knew one thing for certain—this was just the beginning. There was still so much left to do, so many battles left to fight. But for the first time in a long time, Phoenix felt like she was ready.
The structures were modest, resembling a small village hidden away from the chaos of the world. The sense of security it exuded was undeniable. The walls weren't just physical—they symbolized something she hadn't felt in a long time: safety.

They were close enough now to see movement on the walls, guards patrolling the perimeter. Jax raised his hand, signaling to the lookout in the tower. Moments later, the gates creaked open, revealing a narrow path lined with small wooden houses and tents. Smoke rose lazily from a few chimneys. The settlement felt alive in a way Phoenix hadn't experienced for years.

Jax glanced at her and said, "I'll take you to Elara. She'll want to look at your leg."

Phoenix nodded, gripping her crutch tighter as they passed through the gates. People turned to watch them as they entered, their eyes curious but not hostile. A few children ran by, their laughter echoing in the air. It felt strange to see such normalcy, like stepping into a different reality.

"This way," Jax murmured, leading her toward a larger building near the center of the settlement. The structure looked sturdier than the others, its roof reinforced with metal plates. As they approached, the door swung open, and a tall woman stepped out. Elara.

Her dark hair was tightly pulled back into a braid, eyes sharp with authority. She scanned Phoenix with a mixture of concern and authority. "Jax," she greeted him, her voice calm but tinged with relief. "You made it."

Jax nodded, his expression easing slightly. "We had an arduous journey, but we're here. This is Phoenix. She needs your help."

Elara's gaze shifted back to Phoenix. Her expression softened. "Come inside," she offered gently, stepping aside to let them enter.

Phoenix limped through the door, her body aching with exhaustion. The inside of the house was warm, the scent of herbs and something sweet filling the air. Elara guided her to a small cot near the fireplace, helping her sit down.

"Let me look at that leg," Elara said, already gathering supplies from a nearby shelf. Her movements were quick but gentle, her hands sure as she unwrapped the bandage around Phoenix's wound.

Phoenix watched her work silently, her mind still spinning from everything she had seen and heard over the past few days. It was comforting to be cared for, even if it was by a stranger. Elara's presence was steady as if she had done this a thousand times before.

"It's healing," Elara affirmed after a moment, her tone matter-of-fact. "But you need more rest, and I'm going to make you a poultice for the pain. We have a healer here, too. Her name is Serena. I'll have her look at it." She glanced at Jax. "How long are you planning to stay?"

Jax shifted slightly, his gaze flickering toward Phoenix before returning to Elara. "A few days, maybe. Long enough to regroup, figure out our next steps."

Elara nodded thoughtfully. "You'll want to talk to the others, then. They've been asking questions, wondering when you'd come back."

Jax sighed, rubbing the back of his neck. "I figured as much. I'll deal with it."

Phoenix glanced between them, feeling out of place amid their conversation. But something about how they spoke to each other, the familiarity in their voices, made her feel included.

Elara finished rewrapping Phoenix's leg, then stood, her hands on her hips.

"Rest for now," she instructed. "You've been through enough. Jax, get her something to eat. She looks like she hasn't had a decent meal in days."

Jax chuckled softly, giving Elara a mock salute. "Yes, ma'am."

As he left the room, Elara sat down in the chair beside Phoenix.

"You don't have to be strong all the time, you know," she said quietly, her eyes kind but direct. "It's okay to let yourself heal."

Phoenix didn't know how to respond to that. The idea of letting herself be vulnerable, of not having to fight every second, felt foreign. But she nodded anyway, grateful for the kindness.

After a few moments, Jax returned with a bowl of soup and a slice of bread. Phoenix accepted it gratefully, the warmth of the food soothing her tired body. As she ate, Jax and Elara spoke quietly in the corner, their voices too low for her to hear.

When she had finished, Elara helped her lie down on the cot, pulling a blanket over her. The warmth of the fire and the soft murmur of conversation lulled her into a sense of peace she hadn't felt in a long time.

For the first time in what felt like years, Phoenix let herself relax. There were still battles to be fought, still questions that needed answers. But for now, she was safe.

As her eyes drifted shut, she heard Elara's voice, soft and comforting. "Rest now. Tomorrow is another day."

The fire crackled softly in the hearth, casting a warm glow across the room. Phoenix lay still on the cot, her body sinking into the softness of the blankets. The steady murmur of Jax and Elara's conversation became a distant hum in the background, leaving her alone to process her thoughts.

Edward.

She closed her eyes, letting out a shaky breath as the memories flooded in. His laugh, the way he used to make her feel safe even when the world around them was crumbling. He was her constant, the one thing she could always rely on. Now he was gone.

Her heart clenched painfully. It still didn't feel real. How could he be gone? How could someone who had been such a massive part of her life disappear?

Phoenix curled in on herself, pulling the blankets tighter around her. She had been strong, or at least tried to be, ever since she lost him. But now, in the quiet of the room, with no one around to see, the weight of Edward's absence crashed over her.

Before she could stop herself, the tears came. They were quiet, slow, but profound. Her body trembled as she wept silently, the grief that she had been holding back for so long spilling out in the safety of the empty room.

"I'm so sorry, Edward," she whispered into the darkness, her voice broken. "I should have done more. I should have saved you."

Her words hung in the air, unanswered. The tears fell faster now, her chest tightening with every breath. It felt like her heart was breaking all over again, the pain as sharp as it had been the day she lost him.

She missed him so much it hurt. Every part of her ached with the longing to see him again, to hear his voice, to feel his presence beside her. But no matter how much she wished for it, she knew he wasn't coming back.

Phoenix wiped her eyes with the back of her hand, though the tears kept coming. She let herself cry, let herself grieve for the brother she had lost, for the life that would never be the same.

Eventually, the tears slowed, leaving her exhausted and hollow. Her eyes burned, and her body felt heavy with fatigue, but the tightness in her chest had loosened just a little. It was as though letting out the tears had given her a momentary reprieve from the weight of her grief.

She sniffed, pulling the blankets closer, her breath still hitching softly. The warmth of the fire wrapped around her like a comforting embrace, but it did little to fill the space beside her where Edward should have been.

"I miss you," she whispered into the stillness, her voice quiet so the others couldn't hear. "I miss you so much."

Her eyelids grew heavier as exhaustion crept in. The warmth of the fire and the softness of the bed finally lulled her into a restless sleep. Even in her dreams, Edward lingered in the corners of her mind, a shadow that would never entirely leave her.

As the night deepened and the settlement remained quiet around her, Phoenix found a small measure of peace. It wasn't enough to take away the pain, but it was enough to let her rest for now.

The darkness behind her eyelids began to change, softening into something brighter.

She found herself standing in a familiar clearing, surrounded by tall trees. The air was warm, and sunlight filtered through the canopy above, dappling the ground with golden light. It was peaceful here, serene in a way she hadn't felt in a long time.

Then she saw him.

He stood a few feet away, his face calm, a small smile playing on his lips. His presence was ethereal as if he were a part of the light surrounding him. He looked as he always had—her brother, her constant, but there was something more in his eyes now, something she hadn't seen before. Peace.

Phoenix stepped toward him, emotions welling up inside of her at the sight of him. "Edward?" She whispered. She couldn't believe he was here.

He nodded, his smile widening just slightly. "Phoenix," he said, his voice soft but steady. "It's okay."

Her breath caught in her chest. "I'm sorry," she choked out, the words spilling from her before she could stop them. "I'm so sorry. I should have saved you. I should have—"

Edward shook his head, stepping closer to her. "No, Phoenix. You did everything you could. You fought for me. You fought for both of us."

Tears welled in her eyes, blurring his image. "But, you're gone," she whispered despairingly, the pain of his loss hitting her all over again. "You're gone, and it's my fault."

Edward's hand reached out, brushing lightly against her cheek.

"It's not your fault," he said gently. "You couldn't have known. You couldn't have stopped what happened. But that doesn't mean you failed me."

Phoenix shook her head, the tears spilling over. "I don't know what to do without you," her voice broke as she said it. "I don't know how to keep going."

Edward smiled softly, his eyes full of wisdom and understanding. "You'll find your way," he said. "You're stronger than you think, Phoenix. You always have been."

The weight in her chest began to lift just a little as she looked into his eyes. There was no anger, no blame—only love, the same love he had always shown her.

"You have to keep going," Edward continued, his voice quiet but steady. "You have to keep fighting. For me. For Mom and Dad. For yourself."

Phoenix nodded, her heart aching but lighter now, as if his words were slowly mending the fractures inside her. "I'll try," she whispered. "I'll keep going."

Edward's smile grew. For a moment, its warmth filled her with a sense of peace she hadn't known was possible.

"I'll always be with you," he said, "no matter what."

The golden light around them grew brighter until it was all she could see as the dream started to come to an end. As Edward's image blurred and disappeared, Phoenix felt something inside her heal, just a little. The guilt and pain were still there—but so was the love. And that was enough.

When she woke, the fire had burned down to embers, and the room was still and quiet. But for the first time in a long time, Phoenix didn't feel the crushing weight of guilt pressing down on her chest.

Edward had forgiven her. And maybe, just maybe, she could start to forgive herself, too.

(16)
Restless Hearts

The following day, Phoenix woke with the sun filtering softly through the window. The light was gentle, but it still made her eyes sting. The sound of soft voices and the smell of something herbal filled the room.

She couldn't remember where she was for a moment, the dream still clinging to her mind like the remnants of mist in the early morning. As she blinked and looked around, the warmth of the fire, the wooden walls, and the muffled voices outside reminded her that she was in Jax's settlement.

She pushed herself up slightly on the cot, wincing as her leg throbbed beneath the blankets. The pain was a dull ache now, more manageable than it had been, but it was still a reminder of everything that had happened. Everything she had lost.

The door creaked open, and a woman entered, her hands carrying a small bowl of steaming liquid. She had a calm, steady presence. Her dark hair was tied back in a braid, her face lined with years of experience but softened by kindness.

"You're awake," the woman said gently, setting the bowl on a small table beside Phoenix. "I'm Serena, the healer here. How are you feeling?"

Phoenix blinked, still groggy from sleep and the lingering emotions from her dream. "Better," she muttered, her voice rough. "My leg still hurts, but it's not as bad as before."

Serena nodded, her sharp eyes assessing Phoenix as she sat on the edge of the bed.

"That's to be expected. You've been through a lot. I've rewrapped the bandages, but it'll take time to heal. Here," she handed Phoenix the bowl. "Drink this. It'll help with the pain."

Phoenix took the bowl, the warmth of the liquid seeping into her hands. She sipped it cautiously. The taste was bitter but soothing. Serena moved with quiet efficiency, checking the bandages on Phoenix's leg, her movements precise and practiced.

"Jax told me about what happened," Serena said after a moment, an admirable tone in her voice. "You've been through more than most. It's a wonder you're still standing."

Phoenix looked down at the bowl in her hands, the weight of Serena's words pressing on her. "I'm not sure if I'm still standing," she said half-jokingly, gesturing to her injured leg.

Serena smiled, placing a hand on Phoenix's shoulder. "You are, though. And that's what matters. Healing—physically and otherwise—takes time. You don't have to have all the answers right now."

Phoenix swallowed her throat tight and nodded. She didn't have the energy to argue.

Just then, the door creaked again. Jax appeared, his presence steady as always. He nodded to Serena in thanks before turning his attention to Phoenix.

"How are you feeling?" He asked, his tone stern but concerned.

Phoenix forced a small smile. "I've had worse."
Jax grunted in response, but his eyes showed a glimmer of amusement. "You'll be back on your feet soon enough," he said. "Serena will make sure of it."

Serena stood, gathering her things. "You're in good hands here, Phoenix. Rest for now. I'll be back to check on you later."

With that, she left the room, leaving Phoenix alone with Jax. The quiet between them wasn't uncomfortable, but it was heavy with unspoken words.

Finally, Phoenix broke the silence. "Jax. Thank you. For everything."

Jax shifted, clearly uncomfortable with the gratitude, but he nodded. "You don't have to thank me. We're not done yet."
The room fell into silence again, the crackling of the fire the only sound. Phoenix stared at the flames, letting their warmth chase away the chill that clung to her. Her body still ached, but it was her heart that felt the heaviest.

"I keep thinking about Edward," Phoenix admitted after a long pause. "I don't know how to move forward without him."

Jax sat in the chair near her bed, his usual stoic demeanor softening slightly. He didn't speak immediately, as if he chose his words carefully.

"Losing someone like that… it doesn't just go away. But you find a way to keep going because that's what they want. Edward wouldn't want you to give up."

Phoenix nodded, biting the inside of her cheek to keep her emotions at bay.

"He was always the one who kept me grounded. He made sure I didn't fall apart." She looked down at her hands, feeling the tears prick at the corners of her eyes. "I'm not sure I know how to do that on my own."

"You're stronger than you think, Phoenix," Jax said quietly. "You've survived things that would break most people. You're still here. That says something."

Phoenix didn't know how to respond. The idea of being strong, of surviving when so much had been lost, felt foreign. But hearing it from Jax, of all people, gave her pause. Maybe she wasn't as broken as she thought.

A soft knock on the door interrupted their conversation, and a moment later, a boy about seventeen stepped inside. His dark hair was tousled, and there was a mischievous gleam in his eyes as he strolled in, the hint of a smirk playing at the corner of his mouth.

"Interrupting something important, am I?" The boy teased. He looked between Phoenix and Jax with exaggerated curiosity.
Jax rolled his eyes but didn't seem surprised. "Phoenix, this is Rowan—Ro for short," Jax said, gesturing toward the boy. "He's one of the guards here. And he's also supposed to be on duty right now."

Ro gave a mock salute, his smirk widening. "Ah, but you see, I am. I'm just guarding the most important asset we have right now." He winked at Phoenix, clearly unbothered by Jax's disapproving glare.

Phoenix couldn't help but smile at his sarcasm, though she felt a little self-conscious under his playful gaze. "I don't think I'm that important," she muttered, but Ro was already shaking his head.

"Nonsense," Ro quipped, plopping down on the edge of a nearby table. "Word around here is you've survived more than half the people in this settlement ever have. I'd say that makes you plenty important. Besides," he added with a grin, "it's not often we get someone new around here. You're basically the star of the show."

Phoenix couldn't stop the small laugh that escaped her despite the weight still hanging over her. Ro's light-hearted nature was infectious, and for the first time since waking up, she felt a little less trapped in her grief.

Jax shot Ro a look but didn't stop him from talking. Instead, he stood, giving Phoenix a brief nod. "I'll check in with you later. Get some rest."

As Jax left the room, Ro leaned back, crossing his arms over his chest. "Don't mind him. He's all tough on the outside, but he's a softie when it comes to people he cares about."

Phoenix raised an eyebrow, amused by Ro's casual manner. "And you? Are you tough on the outside?"

Ro snorted, clearly entertained by the question. "Oh, I'm all tough, inside and out. But I can be fun too, as you'll see."

Phoenix shook her head, smiling despite herself. Something about Ro's energy was hard to resist. He was reckless, clearly, but there was a charm to it, a kind of carefree spirit she hadn't seen in a long time. "So, what's your story?" Phoenix asked him, making small talk. "How'd you end up here?"

Ro's expression shifted slightly, a flicker of something more serious passing through his eyes before he shrugged it off.

"Orphaned when I was a kid. I found my way to this place when I was about seven. Jax and the others took me in and trained me to fight. Been here ever since."

Phoenix's heart ached at his words, recognizing the pain that lay behind them. But Ro didn't seem to dwell on it. If anything, he used his sarcasm and humor as a shield.

"And now you're a guard?" Phoenix asked, her curiosity about him growing. "How does that work?"

Ro grinned, clearly enjoying her interest. "I keep this place safe. Or at least, that's what I'm supposed to do. The truth is, nothing much happens around here. It's too peaceful if you ask me. I'm itching for something more exciting."

Phoenix raised an eyebrow. "Exciting?"

"Yeah, you know. Adventure. Danger. Something to keep the blood pumping," Ro embellished, his grin widening. "Not that I'm complaining, but I didn't spend years training just to stand around guarding gates."

Phoenix shook her head, smiling. "And what would you do if you found that adventure?"

Ro leaned back, crossing his arms over his chest, his smirk never fading.

"I'd take it head-on, obviously. I've been waiting for something like that my whole life. A chance to prove myself. Not just to the people here, but to myself."

He paused for a moment, his eyes glinting with a mix of excitement and restlessness. "Don't you ever feel that way? Like you're meant for something more?"

Phoenix's smile faltered slightly as his question hit too close to home. She had spent most of her life trying to protect Edward, trying to survive in a world that was always teetering on the edge of chaos.

Before everything had gone wrong, she had always felt like there was something more—something she was supposed to do. With Edward gone, that sense of purpose felt more urgent and more elusive than ever.

"Yeah," she admitted quietly. "I guess I do."

Ro studied her momentarily, his teasing demeanor softening just a little.

"I can tell," he said after a beat. "You've got that look—like you're not done yet. Like you're still searching for whatever you're supposed to do."

Phoenix didn't know how to respond, so she didn't. Instead, she looked down at her leg, feeling the dull ache pulsing through the bandages.

"Well, right now, I'm just trying to get back on my feet," she said, her tone a little lighter.

Ro nodded, his grin softening. "Good. Because you wouldn't make it far with that leg of yours."

Phoenix rolled her eyes at his comment but found his presence comforting. She had spent so much time in darkness that his sarcasm was a welcome distraction.

"Well," Ro continued, plopping down into the chair by the door, "the real fun is just getting started around here. Serena's making a big dinner meal tonight. You should come."

Phoenix blinked, surprised by the invitation. "Dinner?"

"Yeah. Nothing fancy, but we all eat together in the main hall when possible. Serena cooks, Jax broods, and I keep everyone entertained." Ro winked, clearly proud of himself.

Phoenix felt her smile widen despite the heaviness that still clung to her. "I'm sure that's a sight."

"Oh, it is," Ro said with a mock-serious expression. "You should consider it your formal invitation."

She nodded, a part of her grateful for the chance to be around people again, even if the thought made her a little uneasy. "I'll think about it."

Ro stood, his usual energy buzzing through him. "Good. I'll see you there, then."

Before Phoenix could respond, he turned and left the room, leaving her with her thoughts again. This time, the silence wasn't as suffocating.

She could still feel the ache in her chest, the weight of everything she had lost, but the idea of dinner—of being surrounded by people who had survived just as she had—felt like a step forward, even if it was a small one.

She leaned back against the pillow, staring at the ceiling, and for the first time in a long time, she allowed herself to hope that things could get better.

That evening, Phoenix stood at the dining hall doorway, her hands gripping the crutches Serena had given her earlier in the day. Her leg still throbbed, but it was manageable now, and she could at least move around independently. The thought of walking into the hall—a room full of people she didn't know—made her stomach tense.

She couldn't hide forever.
Taking a deep breath, Phoenix stepped into the hall, her eyes immediately drawn to the long wooden table in the center of the room.

It was packed with people, most deep in conversation, their voices mingling with the clatter of dishes and the crackling of the hearth fire. The scent of roasted meat and fresh bread filled the air, and for the first time in days, Phoenix realized just how hungry she was.

She scanned the room, her eyes landing on Jax, seated at the head of the table, talking quietly with Serena and his son, Luka. His wife glanced up, catching sight of Phoenix and offering her a warm smile.

"There you are," Serena called out, waving her over. "Come, sit with us."

Phoenix hesitated momentarily before slowly making her way over, the crutches supporting her as she moved. She felt a few curious glances from the others at the table, but no one stared too long. It seemed they were used to strangers—used to people coming and going.

Serena scooted over to make room for her, and Phoenix gratefully lowered herself onto the bench, setting her crutches aside.

"I'm glad you came," Serena said, her voice soft as she placed a plate of food in front of Phoenix. "You need to eat."

Phoenix nodded, her stomach growling as she looked down at the plate. "Thank you," she murmured, picking up a piece of bread and taking a bite.

The conversation at the table flowed around her, and for a while, Phoenix listened, taking in the easy camaraderie of the people around her. It felt strange—almost surreal—to be surrounded by so much life after everything she had been through, but it was comforting.

As the meal progressed, Phoenix found herself growing more comfortable. The soft murmur of voices, the clinking of plates, and the warm light of the hearth created a sense of calm that she hadn't realized she needed. She didn't engage in much conversation, but she listened, letting laughter and light-hearted teasing fill the spaces that had been so quiet for too long.
Jax, sitting across from her, seemed more at ease as well. He spoke quietly with Serena, a faint smile tugging at his lips. Phoenix had never seen him like this—relaxed, almost normal. It was a side of him she hadn't known existed, and it made her wonder about the life he had built here, about the people he had sworn to protect.

Rowan, sitting a few seats down, was busy entertaining Luka with an exaggerated story about a battle that never happened. His hands gesturing wildly as he painted a picture of heroism, Luka, wide-eyed and grinning, hung on his every word.

"You should have seen it," Ro said, his voice rising excitedly. "The creatures were everywhere. It was just me, a stick, and my wits. But did I panic? No. I fought them off one by one until the ground was littered with their fallen bodies."

Luka gasped, his eyes shining with awe. "Wow! That's amazing, Ro! Did you do all that?"

Ro winked at Phoenix from across the table. "Well, you know, I'm not one to brag, but… yeah, pretty much."

Phoenix smirked, shaking her head. "I'm sure you didn't exaggerate any of that at all," she teased, her voice quiet but carrying enough to reach Ro.

Ro held up his hands in mock offense. "Hey, no need to ruin my heroic tale in front of the kid." He leaned closer to Luka, his voice lowering to a conspiratorial whisper. "She's just jealous she wasn't there to see it."

Phoenix rolled her eyes, but a small laugh escaped her. It was the first real laugh she had let out in days, and it felt strangely good. Ro's lightheartedness was infectious, and for a moment, the weight on her chest didn't feel so heavy.

Serena glanced over at Phoenix with a knowing smile. "It's nice to hear you laugh," she said softly. "You've been through so much, but moments like these—they're what keep us going."

Phoenix nodded, taking a deep breath as she glanced around the table. It was true. These people had all lost something but still found reasons to laugh, smile, and live. It was a lesson she needed to learn.

The rest of the evening passed in a blur of conversation and shared stories, and as the night wore on, the fire burned lower, casting long shadows across the walls. Phoenix felt a strange sense of belonging settle over her—a quiet acceptance of where she was, if only for the moment.

As the conversation continued around her, she found herself sinking into her thoughts, the sounds fading into the background. The loss of Edward was still raw, still something she hadn't fully processed. And sitting here, surrounded by life, only made his absence feel more profound.

She thought about the dream she'd had of him, his peaceful face, and the words he had spoken. It still didn't feel real that he was gone. That she would never see him again.

Phoenix's throat tightened, and she blinked rapidly, trying to hold back the tears that threatened to fall. She didn't want to cry here, in front of these people and Jax and his family.

She wiped her eyes quickly, hoping no one would notice. She was grateful for the distraction and kindness of the people here, but it didn't erase the pain.

After a while, Jax stood, signaling the end of the meal. People began to disperse, gathering plates and cups and murmuring goodnights to one another as they made their way out of the hall.

Serena gave Phoenix's shoulder a gentle squeeze.

"Get some rest tonight," she said warmly. "You're healing—inside and out. It'll take time, but you're not alone."

Phoenix offered her a small smile, grateful for Serena's understanding. She wished she believed the words more, but maybe she could with time.

(16)

Kindred Sparks

Phoenix had never been one to sit still for too long. Even in the days after her injuries, when the pain kept her from doing much more than lying on the cot, her mind had raced with thoughts of what came next. She needed to move, to feel like she was part of something again. Today, Serena seemed to have finally noticed that restless spark in her.

"You've been healing faster than I expected," Serena remarked as she entered the room, carrying an improved pair of makeshift crutches. "I think you're ready for these."

Phoenix's eyes widened as Serena handed her the crutches. They were sturdy, fashioned from solid wood, with padded grips. She tested them, feeling a new sense of freedom even as her leg throbbed beneath the bandages.

"Take it slow," Serena warned, her sharp gaze watching Phoenix carefully. "Your leg still needs time. But you should be able to get around the settlement now."

Phoenix nodded, grateful to have some measure of independence again. The thought of walking outside, of seeing more of the place Jax called home, gave her a sense of purpose she hadn't felt since the days before Edward was gone.

As she moved gingerly out of the small room she had been resting in, the crisp air hit her face, refreshing in a way that made her forget the ache in her leg.

The settlement was small but bustling with activity. People moved between homes, tending to gardens, repairing structures, and preparing food. It was peaceful, with none of the chaos that had consumed the world outside.

A few children ran past her, laughing as they played. Their carefree nature made Phoenix's chest tighten with envy and longing. She remembered what it had been like growing up in a place like this—a place where there was still hope, still a future—back when she and Edward were no older than these children.

As Phoenix made her way toward the center of the settlement, she caught sight of Elara, Jax's wife, helping some of the other women with what looked like preparing food for the evening meal. Elara glanced up and noticed Phoenix, a cheerful smile on her face.

"Phoenix!" Elara called, waving her over. "Come, sit with us for a bit."

Phoenix hesitated, unused to the friendliness of the people around her. She made her way over, carefully lowering herself onto a bench near the group. The warmth of the firepit in the center of the gathering spread toward her, making her feel comfortable.

Elara's presence was calming, much like Serena's, but with a maternal warmth that Phoenix found herself drawn to. "How are you feeling?" Elara asked, her eyes full of concern. "You look much better than when you first arrived."

"I'm getting there," Phoenix said with a small smile. "It helps to be able to move around."

Elara nodded. "Good. That's good to hear. Jax hasn't stopped worrying about you since you arrived." She chuckled fondly, her gaze flicking toward the path where Phoenix had come from. "He doesn't always show it, but you've got him looking after you like a hawk."

Phoenix felt a pang of gratitude and a bit of guilt. Jax had done so much for her already, and yet she was still unsure of where she fit in this place, in this new reality.

As she sat there, listening to the conversations around her, Phoenix couldn't help but wonder if she could ever belong in a place like this. The people here had carved out a stable life for themselves, something she had never known.

As she thought that, a small voice in the back of her mind reminded her that this peace was fragile. Mira was still out there, and everything that Phoenix had seen in the world outside these walls couldn't be forgotten so easily.

"You're welcome to stay as long as you need," Elara said as if sensing Phoenix's thoughts. "This place can be a home for you if you want it to be."

Phoenix's heart tightened. "Thank you," she murmured, unsure what else to say.

Phoenix turned to see Ro leaning against a nearby post, his ever-present smirk firmly in place. He sauntered to her, his arms crossing over his chest as if settling in for a long conversation.

"Well, look at you, walking around on crutches already. I knew you were tougher than you looked."

Phoenix rolled her eyes but couldn't suppress the small smile that tugged at her lips. "I thought you were supposed to guard the settlement, not harassing the injured."

"Ah, but I'm multitasking," Ro said with a wink. "I can guard and harass at the same time. It's a skill."

Phoenix chuckled, the lightness of Ro's banter a welcome distraction. "I'm sure Jax loves that."

Ro shrugged, stepping further into the room and plopping in the chair beside her bed. "Jax is too busy being stoic and brooding to care what I do half the time."

Phoenix shook her head, amused by his attitude. "So, what's the plan for today? More guarding and harassing?"

Ro leaned back, crossing his arms over his chest with an exaggerated sigh. "That's the thing—there's never a plan. It's always the same.

Guard the gates, make sure no one's sneaking around, and try not to die of boredom."

Phoenix raised an eyebrow. "I'm sure there's more to it than that."

Ro grinned. "Maybe, but not much. Don't get me wrong, this place is safe—safer than anywhere else I've seen—but sometimes I wonder if that's a good thing."

"What do you mean?" Phoenix asked, curious.

Ro's playful demeanor faded slightly, a more severe expression crossing his face. "It's just… we're all hidden away here, tucked safely behind these walls. But out there—out in the world—it's chaos. People are fighting to survive and to make a difference. And we're just hiding."

Phoenix frowned. She had felt that restlessness, too, even in the short time she had been here. It was easy to fall into a sense of security within the settlement, but the world outside was still dangerous and unpredictable.

"I think I get it," Phoenix said quietly. "I've been running, fighting, surviving for so long that now, being here, it almost feels like I don't know how to stop."

Ro nodded, his gaze thoughtful. "Exactly. It's like, we're surviving, but is that enough? Shouldn't we be doing something more?"

Phoenix looked at him, surprised by the depth of his words. Ro was reckless, sure, but she hadn't realized how much he had been thinking about the same things she was—about purpose, about what came next.

"So, what do you want to do?" She asked, genuinely curious.

Ro shrugged, but there was a spark in his eyes. "I want to leave, honestly. See what's out there. Make a difference, if I can."
Phoenix's heart tightened at his words. She understood that longing, that need to do something more, but the world out there was

dangerous, full of threats they couldn't even begin to predict. She had seen it firsthand, taking so much from her.

"You think you're ready for that?" Phoenix asked softly.

Ro leaned forward, his expression serious. "I don't know if anyone's ever ready. But I don't want to stay here forever, doing nothing while the world falls apart."

Phoenix was silent for a moment, thinking. Ro reminded her a bit of herself when she was younger—eager to fight, to prove herself. But the world had a way of changing you, showing you just how fragile survival was.

"You're braver than you look," Phoenix said with a small smile.

Ro smirked, his playful demeanor returning. "Don't let the sarcasm fool you. Underneath all this charm, I'm a warrior."

Phoenix shook her head, laughing despite herself. But something about Ro's determination, his restlessness, struck a chord with her. He was right about one thing—there had to be something more than just surviving.

 "So, what do you do for fun when you're not limping around or sleeping all day?" He teased her.

Phoenix blinked, surprised by the question.

"I don't know," she admitted. "I guess I haven't had time for fun lately." She sighed, wanting to change the subject. "So, what's the plan for today? Besides guarding and harassing?"

Ro leaned back, crossing his arms over his chest with an exaggerated sigh. "That's the thing—there's never a plan. It's always the same. Guard the gates, make sure no one's sneaking around, and try not to die of boredom."
Phoenix raised an eyebrow. "I'm sure there's more to it than that."

Ro grinned. "Maybe, but not much. Don't get me wrong, this place is safe—safer than anywhere else I've seen—but sometimes I wonder if that's a good thing."

"What do you mean?" Phoenix asked, curious.

Ro's playful demeanor faded slightly, a more severe expression crossing his face.

"It's just… we're all hidden away here, tucked safely behind these walls. But out there—out in the world—it's chaos. People are fighting to survive and to make a difference. And we're just… hiding."

Phoenix frowned. She had felt that restlessness, too, even in the short time she had been here. It was easy to fall into a sense of security within the settlement, but the world outside was still dangerous and unpredictable.

"I think I get it," Phoenix said quietly. "I've been running, fighting, surviving for so long that now, being here, it almost feels like I don't know how to stop."

Ro nodded, his gaze thoughtful. "Exactly. It's like, we're surviving, but is that enough? Shouldn't we be doing something more?"

Phoenix looked at him, surprised by the depth of his words. She hadn't realized how much he had been thinking about the same things she was—about purpose, about what came next.

"So, what do you want to do?" She asked, genuinely curious.

Ro shrugged, but there was a spark in his eyes. "I want to leave, honestly. See what's out there. Make a difference, if I can."

Phoenix's heart tightened at his words. She understood that longing, that need to do something more. But the world out there was dangerous, full of threats they couldn't even begin to predict. She had seen it firsthand, taking so much from her.

"You think you're ready for that?" Phoenix asked softly.

Ro leaned forward, his expression serious. "I don't know if anyone's ever really ready. But I don't want to stay here forever, doing nothing while the world falls apart."

Phoenix was silent for a moment, thinking. Ro reminded her a bit of herself—eager to fight, to prove herself. But the world had a way of changing you, showing you just how fragile survival was.

"You're braver than you look," Phoenix teased.

Ro smirked, his playful demeanor returning. "Don't let the sarcasm fool you. Underneath all this charm, I'm basically a warrior."

Something about Ro's determination, his restlessness, struck a chord with her. He was right about one thing—there had to be something more than just surviving.

"You need a tour guide?" Ro asked, raising an eyebrow. "I can show you the 'exciting' parts of this place. Not that there's much, but I can make it fun."

"I'm not sure I'm ready for all that excitement," she replied with a hint of amusement.

Ro grinned. "You'd be surprised. Come on, I'll walk with you."

Elara shot Phoenix a knowing look as Ro helped her up, his arm carefully guiding her as she adjusted her weight on the crutches. "Be careful," Elara warned, though a twinkle was in her eye. "Ro's got a talent for finding trouble."

"I'm not the one who brings trouble around here," Ro called back, his grin widening as he led Phoenix down the path toward the other end of the settlement.

As they walked, Phoenix felt the tension in her shoulders ease. Ro's easygoing nature made her feel more at ease than in days, and she found herself grateful for the distraction he provided.

In his company, she wasn't consumed by thoughts of Edward, loss, or the dangers that still loomed outside. For now, she could be. Even if it was only for a little while.

Ro kept up a light conversation as they walked, pointing out different parts of the settlement as if he were showing off a grand city rather than a small, hidden village. His humor was sharp, filled with a self-assuredness that Phoenix couldn't help but appreciate. He had a way of making the world seem less serious, of sparking adventure when there was none.

"This here," Ro said dramatically, gesturing to a small wooden structure that couldn't have been more than a shed, "is our most important building. The armory. It's where we keep our finest sticks and sharp rocks."

Phoenix chuckled, shaking her head. "Really? Sticks and rocks?"

"Don't let the modesty fool you," Ro replied a glint of mischief in his eyes. "We've got a few real weapons, too. Just not enough to win a war."

Phoenix glanced around, taking in the sights as Ro continued to narrate their walk. The settlement was peaceful—too peaceful, in some ways. The people here didn't seem to be preparing for the battles Phoenix knew were coming. They were surviving but not fighting.

"Is it always this quiet?" She asked after a while, her voice a bit more serious.

Ro's smirk faded slightly, and he glanced around to ensure no one else could hear them.

"Mostly, we've been lucky. Jax keeps things running smoothly, and we're far enough away from the bigger dangers that people feel safe here." He paused, his tone shifting. "It's not going to last forever. You know that, right?"

Phoenix nodded, her stomach twisting with the same foreboding she had felt since she arrived. "I know."

Ro sighed, his usual playful demeanor slipping for a moment. "That's why I want to get out of here. Go beyond the walls. Find something more. I know there's more out there than this."

Phoenix looked at him, seeing a reflection of herself in his restlessness. She had spent her entire life moving, fighting, surviving. The idea of settling down in one place and staying still while the world continued to crumble around her didn't sit right. Then again, this place held comfort, something she hadn't realized she wanted until now.

"You've never been outside the walls?" Phoenix asked, her curiosity piqued.

Ro shook his head. "Not since I was a kid. I've heard stories, though. From people who pass through or from Jax, back when he used to talk about the outside. It's different hearing about it and living it, you know?"

Phoenix nodded. She understood that feeling better than most. "It's dangerous out there. More dangerous than you can imagine."

Ro shrugged, though there was a flicker of doubt in his eyes. "Danger doesn't scare me. Being stuck here, doing nothing—that's what scares me the most."

Phoenix considered his words, the weight of them settling over her. She had spent so much of her life running from one danger to the next, never staying in one place long enough to feel the fear of stillness. Now that she was here, in this peaceful settlement, she understood the appeal of wanting more of wanting to fight for something bigger than just survival.

They continued walking, Ro pointing out more of the settlement's landmarks. But Phoenix's thoughts remained on what he had said, on the restlessness that seemed to infect both of them.

As they rounded a corner, Phoenix spotted a small garden nestled between two houses. It was modest but well-tended, with rows of vegetables and herbs growing in neat lines. A woman knelt in the dirt, her hands working carefully to pull weeds from the soil.

"That's Lena," Ro said, nodding toward the woman. "She's the one who keeps us fed, mostly. Works magic with the little we have."

Phoenix watched the woman momentarily, marveling at the quiet resilience it must take to tend to a garden in a world that was falling apart. It reminded her of her childhood, of the tiny bits of normalcy her family had tried to hold onto even as the world around them collapsed.

"She reminds me of my mom," Phoenix said quietly, surprising herself with the admission. "My mom used to tend to a garden like that. She always said it was her way of ensuring we had something to rely on when everything else felt uncertain."

Ro glanced at her, his expression softening. "Sounds like she was smart."

Phoenix nodded, her heart aching with the memory. "She was."

They continued walking silently for a while, the weight of the conversation hanging between them. Phoenix felt a strange sense of peace settle over her, even as the restlessness in her chest stirred. She didn't know how long she could stay here or be content with this quiet life. For now, it was enough just to be.

Eventually, they returned to the central part of the settlement. The sun began to dip lower in the sky, casting long shadows across the ground. The people of the settlement were winding down for the day, gathering around fires and preparing for the evening meal.

Ro stopped at the edge of the clearing. His arms crossed over his chest as he watched the people moving about their routines.

"It's not much," he said after a contemplative pause. "But it's home."

Phoenix looked at him, seeing the conflict in his eyes—the same one she felt in her heart. "Home isn't always a place," she said quietly. "Sometimes it's just the people you're with."

Ro glanced at her, a hint of a smile tugging at the corner of his mouth. "Maybe you're right." He shifted, his playful grin returning. "If you ever get bored of this place, you know where to find me."

Phoenix laughed, shaking her head. "I'll keep that in mind."

As Ro wandered off to check on his "guard duties," Phoenix stood momentarily, watching the people around her. The settlement was more peaceful than anywhere she had been in a long time. Even as she stood there, surrounded by the warmth of the firelight and the quiet hum of life, she knew this peace couldn't last.

Mira was still out there. Eventually, Phoenix would have to face her.

Even so, she let herself enjoy the moment of stillness for now. Phoenix took slow, steady steps toward the infirmary, each movement of the crutches sending a dull ache through her arms.

Phoenix leaned back against her pillows, closing her eyes and allowing herself to breathe. Ro's presence had been a reminder that the world hadn't completely fallen apart. There were still people in it who could make her smile and laugh, even when everything else felt broken.

A soft knock interrupted her thoughts. The door opened slowly, and Serena stepped inside, her calm expression instantly grounding Phoenix back into the reality of her recovery.

"How are you feeling?" Serena asked, her voice gentle as she approached the bed. Her hands reached again for the bandages on Phoenix's leg.
"Better," Phoenix replied, the words coming out easier than she expected. "A lot better."

Serena looked at her knowingly, her fingers deftly unwrapping the bandages to check the wound. "I saw Ro with you earlier. He has a way of lifting people's spirits, even when they don't realize they need it."

Phoenix smiled faintly. "He does. He's… different."

Serena nodded, her hands moving with precision as she rewrapped the bandages. "He's been through a lot, but he hides it well. His way of coping, I think. Sarcasm keeps the shadows at bay."

Phoenix watched Serena work, her thoughts drifting to what Ro had said earlier. About wanting adventure. About being restless. She understood that feeling all too well—the itch to do something, to prove something. It was the same feeling that had driven her for so long. In this settlement, she had time to reflect. She wondered if she had ever really stopped to breathe.

"He makes it seem easy," Phoenix said softly, her mind still on Ro. "Like nothing bothers him."

Serena smiled gently as she finished her work. "That's just his way. But even the strongest walls have cracks. You'll see in time."

Phoenix nodded, absorbing Serena's words. She knew all about walls and the cracks that hid beneath them. But for now, Ro's carefree nature was a gift—a reprieve from the weight she carried.

As Serena packed up her things and made to leave, Phoenix called out softly, "Serena … thank you. For everything."

Serena turned, offering Phoenix a sincere smile. "You're welcome. Get some rest. You'll need your strength for what's to come."

With that, she slipped out of the room, leaving Phoenix alone once again.
This time, the silence didn't feel so heavy. Phoenix closed her eyes, her thoughts drifting to Ro's smirk, jokes, and playful nature. She hadn't expected to meet someone like him here, in this place where the shadows of the past still loomed large. Perhaps he was the reminder she needed—that there was still more to the world than loss and pain.

(17)

Gathering Storm

The next morning, the first light of dawn filtered through the small window of Phoenix's room, casting a soft, golden glow across the walls. She stirred from her sleep, her body still heavy with exhaustion but her mind slightly clearer. For a moment, she lay still, taking in the quiet.

The settlement was beginning to wake up, the familiar sounds of life rising with the sun—the distant chatter of people starting their day, the clatter of tools, the occasional bark of a dog.

Phoenix sat up slowly, grimacing as her leg throbbed. It was healing, but the pain remained a constant reminder of everything she had been through.

Taking a deep breath, she pushed herself out of bed, her movements slower than usual as she made her way to the crutches. She was getting used to them, though the frustration of being slowed down gnawed at her. She wasn't used to being held back from needing help. But for now, she had no choice.

After a few minutes, she was dressed and ready to leave her room. The warmth of the fire still lingered in the hearth, but she didn't linger. Something about the day ahead made her restless—an undercurrent of anticipation that hummed beneath the surface.

When she stepped outside, the fresh, cool, crisp morning air hit her face. The settlement was already bustling with activity. People moved about purposefully, going about their routines. There were sounds of children laughing in the distance, the rhythmic clang of metal as someone repaired a tool nearby, and the quiet murmur of life continuing.

Being in such a peaceful place was strange, especially after everything she had been through. It starkly contrasted the quiet tension Phoenix had grown so accustomed to in her previous days of recovery.

Her mind was a whirl of thoughts—of Edward, the settlement, the fight she knew was still ahead. There was so much to figure out, so much that felt uncertain. She missed her brother with an almost physical ache, and the weight of his absence pressed down on her.

She wasn't sure where she was headed, but her feet carried her toward the main hall—the heart of the settlement, where Jax and the others often gathered. As she approached, she spotted Ro leaning against the wall near the entrance, his usual smirk firmly in place.

"Morning, sunshine," Ro greeted, leaning casually against the doorframe. "Serena sent me to ensure you're still in one piece."

Phoenix rolled her eyes, but the hint of a smile tugged at her lips. "I'm fine, Ro. You can tell Serena I'm not falling apart."

Ro grinned, stepping inside and closing the door behind him. "Good to hear. Let's go on another walk, shall we? Or, well, a slow hobble, I guess."

Phoenix raised an eyebrow. "A hobble?"

"Yeah, you know, on those fancy crutches of yours. Thought I'd take you out for some more fresh air."

"All right," she said, adjusting her grip on the crutches. "But only if you promise not to push me down a hill or something."

Ro's grin widened. "No promises, but I'll try to behave."

Phoenix hobbled beside Ro, the crutches supporting her weight as they made their way through the narrow paths between the tiny wooden homes. The sounds of life around them— the laughing children, the busy people—created a hum of normalcy that Phoenix hadn't felt in a long time.

Ro led her to a small clearing just outside the settlement's perimeter. It was a peaceful spot where the trees opened to reveal a view of the forest beyond. The sunlight filtered through the branches, dappling the ground with golden light.

Phoenix paused, leaning on her crutches as she took in the scene. It was beautiful, in its way—a stark contrast to the chaos and danger that lingered just beyond the trees.

Ro plopped down on the grass, leaning back on his elbows as he stared at the sky. "See? I told you this place wasn't so bad."

Phoenix smiled faintly, moving to sit beside him, though the effort with the crutches was more awkward. Once settled, she let out a small sigh of relief. "You were right. It's nice out here."

Ro tilted his head toward her, his expression softening just a little. "You doing okay?" He asked, his tone more serious now. "I know you've been through quite a lot."

Phoenix stared at the trees, the weight of Ro's question settling over her. She had been through hell. She still was, in a way. But being here, in this place, surrounded by people who had survived just like she had, made the weight a little easier to bear.

"I don't know," Phoenix admitted, her voice quiet. "Some days I feel like I'm holding it together, and others… not so much."

Ro nodded, his gaze thoughtful. "That's normal. It doesn't just go away, you know? Losing someone like that."

Phoenix swallowed, her throat tightening at the thought of Edward. "Yeah," she whispered. "I miss him every day."

Ro didn't say anything for a moment, letting the silence stretch between them. Then, he spoke, his voice softer than usual. "You're not alone in that. We all lose people out here. But the important thing is that we keep going. For them."

Phoenix nodded, blinking back the tears that threatened to fall. Ro had a way of making things seem simple, even when they weren't. She appreciated that about him.

"I'll keep going," she said, her voice firmer now. "I have to."

Ro grinned again, his playful demeanor returning. "Good. Because I'd hate to lose my sparring partner before we've even had a chance to fight."

Phoenix laughed softly, shaking her head. "You're ridiculous."

"That's why you like me," Ro teased, flashing her a wink.

Despite everything, Phoenix found herself smiling again. The weight of her grief lifted for a moment, replaced by the warmth of Ro's lightheartedness. She was glad to have met him, even if he could sometimes be a little too much. His sarcasm was a welcome distraction from the pain beneath the surface.

The silence followed was heavy, settling between them like an unspoken truth. Ro's grin softened, and momentarily, the playfulness in his eyes gave way to something more profound.

"Well, I guess this is where we part ways," he said, his voice quieter now. The jest was gone, leaving only sincerity.

Phoenix's smile faded, replaced by a mix of gratitude and reluctance. "Looks like it," she replied, trying to keep her tone light even as her chest tightened.

Ro shifted his weight as if caught between stepping forward and holding back. "I hope you'll have a good night, Phoenix. And remember, the world's still got its sparks, even in the dark." He glanced at the sky, where the first stars began peering through the twilight.

"I will," she promised, feeling the words anchor her resolve. "You too, Ro."

With a final nod, Ro turned, his steps echoing against the quiet of the settlement as he walked away. Phoenix watched him until he disappeared around the bend, taking that fleeting sense of brightness with him.

As she walked back to the infirmary, the crutches scraping softly against the path, Phoenix's thoughts turned to the past and the present. Her mind drifted to the people she had met here—Serena, Ro, and Jax's family. They had all welcomed her and cared for her without hesitation.

She paused in the middle of the path, looking out toward the heart of the settlement. Phoenix had spent so much of her life trying to protect the people she loved, but it hadn't been enough. And now, she realized, some new people had entered her life—new faces she had started to care about.

Ro's sarcasm and relentless attempts to pull her into conversation had remained constant since her arrival. He reminded her of something she had almost forgotten—how to laugh, banter, and feel like the world wasn't entirely broken.

Then there was Serena, always calm, always focused. Her hands were steady as she tended to Phoenix's leg, but it wasn't just the physical care that had helped Phoenix heal. Serena's quiet words of wisdom, how she seemed to know when to offer comfort and step back, had done more than mend Phoenix's wounds.

And Jax—Phoenix still wasn't sure how to feel about him. He was complex and guarded, but there was no denying he protected those around him. The way he had carried her when she couldn't walk, the way he had shared pieces of her parents' past when no one else could.

Phoenix took a deep breath, the crisp night air filling her lungs. For so long, she had been caught in a cycle of survival—of fighting and fleeing, of losing and grieving. But now, standing here in this peaceful place, she felt something shifting inside her.

It wasn't just about survival anymore. Perhaps it was about living, too.

The thought caught her off guard, but she didn't push it away. She wasn't ready to leave the settlement yet, not with the looming uncertainty. And though part of her still wanted to run and felt the pull of the road and the dangers that lay beyond the walls, another part wanted to stay.

With a renewed sense of purpose, Phoenix continued her slow walk back to the infirmary, her thoughts not on the losses she had endured but on the strength she was starting to reclaim. The night stretched out ahead, calm and quiet, and for the first time in a long while, Phoenix wasn't afraid of what the morning would bring.

The First Stand

"Morning, sunshine," Ro called out, his voice laced with that familiar sarcasm that Phoenix had come to expect from him. "You look like you slept better than usual."

Phoenix rolled her eyes, but her expression showed a hint of amusement. "I guess you could say that."

Ro pushed off the wall, falling into step beside her. "You headed to breakfast? I heard Serena made enough food to feed a small army."

Phoenix nodded, grateful for the light-hearted conversation. "I could use a good meal."

As they walked, Ro glanced at her from the corner of his eye. "You doing okay?" His voice was still casual, but there was an underlying concern there that didn't go unnoticed.

Phoenix hesitated for a moment before nodding. "Yeah. I'm finally starting to feel a little more like myself again."

Ro grinned, though it was softer than usual. "Good. Because you'll need all your strength when we get out of here."

Phoenix raised an eyebrow. "Planning our escape already?"

Ro chuckled. "Something like that. Can't stay cooped up in this place forever, right?"

Phoenix didn't respond immediately, her thoughts drifting as they continued walking. She wasn't ready to leave, but she knew Ro was right. Sooner or later, they would face whatever awaited them outside the settlement's walls.

But for now, she let herself enjoy the moment—the warmth of the sun on her skin, the ease of Ro's company, the scent of breakfast wafting through the air as they neared the hall.

As they entered the main hall, Phoenix spotted Jax sitting with Serena and Elara at a table. His expression was serious, as always, but when he saw Phoenix, his gaze softened slightly. He gave her a small nod, a gesture that, coming from Jax, felt welcome.

Phoenix smiled and made her way over to the table, Ro trailing behind her. As she sat down, Serena placed a plate of food in front of her—a hearty breakfast of eggs, bread, and roasted vegetables. It was simple, but to Phoenix, it felt like a feast.

As the conversation around the table picked up, Phoenix found herself slipping into its rhythm. Ro was his usual sarcastic self, teasing Serena about her cooking while Jax and Elara exchanged quiet words. It was peaceful, a small bubble of normalcy in a world that had been anything but.

But even as she ate and listened, Phoenix couldn't shake the feeling that this peace wouldn't last. There was still so much left unresolved that she had to face. And as much as she wanted to hold on to this moment, she knew it was only temporary.

When breakfast was over, Jax stood, his expression serious once again. "We need to talk," he said, his voice low but firm. "There's something you all need to know."

Phoenix's heart skipped a beat as the weight of his words settled over the table. Whatever it was, she knew it wasn't going to be good. Jax's words hung in the air, heavy with unspoken tension.

Phoenix set her fork down, her appetite fading as she exchanged glances with Ro. He, too, had fallen silent, the easygoing smirk slipping from his face. Whatever Jax had to say, it was clear it wouldn't be a casual conversation.

Serena and Elara straightened in their seats, their expressions shifting into quiet anticipation. They had likely expected this moment, just as much as Phoenix had.

Jax leaned forward, his arms resting on the table as he spoke in a low, controlled tone. "We've had word from one of the scouts. There's been movement outside the settlement—creatures are getting closer."

Phoenix's heart clenched. She had known the peace here was fragile, but hearing that the creatures—the Lost—were near sent a chill down her spine.

"How close?" Serena asked, her voice steady but laced with concern.

"Close enough," Jax replied. "They've been spotted just outside the perimeter. It's only a matter of time before they figure out where we are."

A heavy silence followed his words, the reality of the situation sinking in. The settlement had always been hidden, protected by its isolation and the strength of its people. If the Lost were drawing near, that safety was in jeopardy.

Ro let out a low whistle, his expression hardening. "So, what's the plan? We can't just sit here and wait for them to break down the gates."

Jax nodded, his gaze sweeping over the table. "No, we can't. We need to fortify the perimeter and prepare for the worst. I'm sending out more scouts to keep an eye on things, but we must be ready."

Phoenix felt a knot form in her stomach. She had come here hoping for security, but now it felt like the danger was catching up to them, no matter where they went.

"We've handled the Lost before," Elara said, her voice calm and measured. "We can do it again. But we'll need everyone's help."

Phoenix nodded, her mind already racing with thoughts of what they would need to do. She wasn't fully healed yet, but that didn't mean she couldn't help somehow. She wasn't going to stand by and let the settlement fall.

Jax's gaze turned to her, as if reading her thoughts. "Phoenix, I know you're still recovering, but you've been through more than most of us. If you're willing, we could use your help."

Phoenix swallowed hard, her pulse quickening. She wasn't sure how much help she could be with her injured leg, but the thought of sitting on the sidelines while everyone else fought… it wasn't an option.

"I'll do whatever I can," she said, her voice firm.

Ro leaned back in his chair, crossing his arms. "Same goes for me. I've been itching for something to do anyway."

Serena smiled at Ro's comment but quickly turned her attention back to Jax. "We'll need to gather supplies—medical and otherwise. I'll start organizing with the others."

Jax nodded with approval. "Good. Let's not waste any time. We don't know how long we have before they make their move."

With that, the table broke into quiet discussions, everyone preparing to do their part. The weight of responsibility settled on Phoenix's shoulders, but she welcomed it.

This was something she could control, something she could focus on, rather than the endless grief and uncertainty that had plagued her since Edward's death.

As the others left to begin their tasks, Phoenix remained seated momentarily, gathering her thoughts. Ro, sensing her unease, gave her a reassuring nudge.

"Hey," he said, his voice softer than usual. "We've got this. Don't worry."

Phoenix managed a small smile, grateful for his unwavering confidence, even in the face of danger. "I hope you're right."

"I'm always right," Ro replied, the teasing edge creeping back into his tone. "And besides, I've been waiting for an excuse to test out some of these traps I've been working on."

Phoenix raised an eyebrow. "Traps?"

Ro winked. "You'll see."

Despite everything, Phoenix found herself laughing softly. Ro had a way of cutting through the tension, reminding her they weren't beaten yet.

Together, they stood and headed outside, the crisp morning air filling their lungs. The settlement was already buzzing with activity, people moving with purpose as they prepared for whatever was coming.

Phoenix tightened her grip on the crutches, her mind steeling itself for the challenges ahead. She didn't know what the future held, but one thing was certain: she wasn't going down without a fight.

Phoenix moved carefully through the settlement, leaning on her crutches as she approached the perimeter. She could feel the urgency in the air, the subtle shift in how people moved and spoke. It wasn't panic, but it was close. The quiet determination in everyone's eyes reflected the gravity of the situation.

Ro was already ahead of her, his usual swagger intact, though his expression was a little more serious than usual. He paused at the gate to check one of the ropes he had tied for some new trap he'd set up. Phoenix couldn't help but raise an eyebrow as she watched him work.

"Are you sure this is going to work?" She asked, her tone light, but the question genuine. She still didn't fully understand what Ro had in mind with these so-called traps.

Ro flashed her a grin, though his eyes had an edge of focus. "Trust me, Phoenix. I've been working on these for a while. They're simple but effective. The Lost might be strong, but they're not the smartest creatures out there."

Phoenix nodded, though the image of the Lost—twisted, terrifying beings with no semblance of humanity left—still made her uneasy. It was hard to believe anything could stand against them.

Ro straightened, wiping his hands on his trousers as he turned to face her. "How's the leg?"

"Better than it was," Phoenix said. "Still hurts, but I can move around. That's all that matters right now."

"Good," Ro said, his tone softening. "Because we're going to need all hands on deck for this."

Phoenix shifted her weight on the crutches, glancing at the fortified walls surrounding the settlement. They were strong, built to withstand attacks, but the Lost were relentless. She had seen firsthand what they were capable of and knew the walls wouldn't hold forever if the creatures decided to push through.

"Do you think we'll be able to stop them?" Phoenix asked, her voice quieter now.

Ro was silent for a moment, his gaze following hers to the walls. "I don't know," he admitted. "But I know one thing—we won't go down without a fight. That's for sure."

Phoenix nodded, finding a strange comfort in his words. She had been fighting for so long, and even though she didn't feel ready, something about how Ro and the others approached the situation made her believe they could at least buy themselves some time.

"Let's get moving," Ro said, his usual grin returning. "We've got a lot to do before nightfall."

Phoenix followed him as they moved along the perimeter, joining the others busy reinforcing the gates, checking weapons, and preparing for whatever was coming. She did what she could, offering help where she could manage, even if her leg slowed her down.

The day stretched on, the tension in the air thickening as the sun began to dip lower in the sky. Phoenix's muscles ached from the effort, but she welcomed the distraction. It kept her from thinking too much—from dwelling on what had been lost.

As the light began to fade, Jax called the group together near the center of the settlement. His presence was commanding, as always, and even though his voice was calm, there was no mistaking the urgency in his tone.

"The scouts have confirmed the Lost are close," he said, eyes sweeping over the small crowd. "They'll likely move in once it's dark, so we must be ready. Stay sharp. Stay together. And remember—our strength is in our numbers."

Phoenix felt her heart rate quicken as Jax's words sank in. The danger was real, and it was coming fast.

Ro nudged her gently. "Stick with me," he whispered. "I'll ensure you don't get into too much trouble."

Phoenix shot him a look, her lips curving into a small smile despite the anxiety churning in her stomach. "I think it's the other way around."

Ro chuckled, but his eyes remained serious. "Maybe."

As the group dispersed to take their positions, Phoenix stood near the entrance with Jax and Ro, her mind racing about what was coming. She could feel the weight of the coming battle pressing down on her, but there was also a strange sense of resolve alongside it. She had faced worse before. She had survived.

The wind picked up, carrying with it the faint, distant sounds of movement—unnatural and haunting. The Lost were close.

"Here we go," Ro muttered under his breath, his body tensing as he readied himself.

Phoenix tightened her grip on her crutches, her heart pounding in her chest. Whatever was coming, they would face it together. She wasn't going to let fear win.

But then, a movement. Figures darting between the trees. Something was out there.

Phoenix's blood ran cold. They were here. And they were watching.

"The Lost," Phoenix gasped, trying to catch her breath. "They're here. I saw them."

Jax's face darkened. "How many do you see?"

"I don't know," Phoenix admitted, panic rising in her chest. "At least a few. But I think there are more."

Jax didn't hesitate. He turned to grab his weapon. The Lost were closing in, and if they didn't hold fast, this place—this fragile refuge—could be torn apart instantly.

As they moved through the settlement, Jax called to Ro, his usual light-hearted demeanor replaced by grim determination. ". "We need to get the others armed."
" Ro said, his voice low as he readied his blade

Phoenix watched as Ro's gaze flicked toward her, concern flashing in his eyes.

"You alright?" he asked, though the question was tense.

"I'm fine," Phoenix said, though her voice wavered slightly. "We need to stop them."

Jax nodded in agreement, his face set with grim resolve. "We'll hold them off. But we need to move fast. Ro, gather the others. We can't let them reach the center of the settlement."

Ro gave a quick nod and disappeared into the shadows, briefly leaving Phoenix and Jax alone. The silence stretched between them, heavy with the knowledge of what would happen.

Phoenix swallowed hard, her chest tight. She wasn't ready for this. Not so soon. But she knew there was no other choice.

"I'll fight," she said, her voice firmer now. "I'm not going to let them destroy this place."

Jax glanced at her, his expression unreadable for a moment. Then he gave a curt nod. "We'll fight. Together."

Before Phoenix could respond, a loud snarl echoed through the night, followed by movement—closer this time, faster. The Lost were coming.

Jax's hand went to his weapon, his body tense and ready. "Stay close to me," he said, his voice low and commanding. "And whatever happens, don't stop moving."

Phoenix nodded, her heart pounding in her chest. She took a deep breath, trying to steady herself as the night closed around them.

This was it. The fight had come to the settlement.

And she wasn't going to run this time.

The growls grew louder, more menacing, as if the shadows were closing in on them. Phoenix gripped her crutches tightly, feeling the tension coil inside her like a spring ready to snap.

The soft murmur of the settlement had been replaced by a deadly silence, broken only by the occasional rustle of leaves and the faint clink of weapons being readied.

Suddenly, there was a sharp scream in the distance, and chaos erupted.

"They're inside!" Someone shouted, the voice filled with terror.

Jax cursed under his breath and pulled Phoenix back toward the center of the settlement. "Stay behind me," he barked, eyes scanning the darkness. His hand tightened around the hilt of his weapon, his body tense and ready for the fight.

Before Phoenix could react, one of the Lost burst into the clearing, its pale, twisted form illuminated by the flickering torchlight. Its eyes gleamed with unnatural hunger, its body moving jerkily as it stalked toward them.

Phoenix froze, her heart hammering in her chest as the creature locked eyes with her, its lips curling into a snarl. For a split second, all she could do was stare, her mind reeling with fear and disbelief.

"Phoenix!" Jax's voice cut through the fog of panic, pulling her back to the present. "Get back!"

She stumbled backward, her crutches falling onto the uneven ground as she tried to keep her distance. The creature was fast, too fast, and in an instant, it lunged at her, its claws outstretched. Leaving her crutches behind, she ran, adrenaline taking over.

Jax moved like a blur, intercepting the creature with a powerful swing of his blade. The sound of metal slicing through flesh filled the air as the Lost shrieked in pain, its body collapsing to the ground in a heap. Blood splattered the ground, the acrid scent filling Phoenix's nostrils.

"Stay focused," Jax growled, not taking his eyes off the fallen creature. "There will be more."

More of the Lost appeared from the shadows as if on cue, their twisted forms slithering and leaping toward the settlement with terrifying speed. Screams echoed from every direction as the creatures tore through the perimeter, their claws ripping through anything in their path,

Ro appeared at Jax's side, his sword already slick with blood. "There's more than we thought," he panted, his usual sarcasm replaced by grim urgency. "We're outnumbered.

Jax's jaw tightened. "We hold the line," he said, his voice low and resolute. "We don't let them break through."

Phoenix's heart raced as she watched the chaos unfold around her. The settlement, once so peaceful, was now a battleground. She could see the villagers fighting desperately, trying to hold back the tide of creatures that seemed to pour from the forest in endless waves.

Her mind screamed at her to run, to hide, to get as far away from this madness as possible. But something inside her, something fierce and stubborn, kept her rooted in place.

She couldn't run. Not this time

With trembling hands, Phoenix reached for the small knife Serena had given her earlier. Its weight was unfamiliar but comforting in her grip. It wasn't much, but it was better than nothing. And if she was going to survive this, she had to fight.

Jax turned to her, his eyes narrowing as he saw the knife in her hand. "Phoenix-"

"I can help," she interrupted, her voice shaky but determined. "I'm not going to just stand here.

Jax hesitated for a moment, then nodded. "Stay close to me," he said, his voice gruff. "Don't take any risks."

Phoenix nodded, her heart pounding as she braced for the fight ahead. She didn't know if she was ready for this, if she could face the creatures that had already taken so much from her. But she didn't have a choice.

The Lost were closing in, and there was no turning back.

The next wave of creatures burst into the clearing, their eyes gleaming with bloodlust as they tore through the defenses. Phoenix gripped the knife tighter, her muscles tensing as she prepared for the inevitable clash.

Jax moved first, his blade slicing through the air with deadly precision as he quickly cut down two of the creatures. Ro followed close behind, his sword flashing as he fought to protect the villagers scrambling for cover.

Phoenix watched in awe and terror as they fought. Their movements were fluid and deadly, but she couldn't afford to stay frozen.

A sudden snarl from her left snapped her attention back to the fight, and she turned just in time to see one of the Lost barreling toward her.

Without thinking, she swung the knife, her body moving on pure instinct. The blade caught the creature in the side, and it let out a howl of pain, staggering backward. Phoenix's heart raced as she stared at the blood on her knife, the reality of the fight finally sinking in.

She had to keep going.

Jax and Ro were shouting orders, trying to organize the remaining fighters, but the Lost were relentless. For every creature they killed, two more seemed to take its place, their pale forms swarming through the settlement like a plague.

Phoenix's arms ached, her leg throbbing with each movement, but she refused to stop. She stabbed and slashed at the creatures that came too close, her body trembling with exhaustion and fear. But no matter how hard she fought, the creatures kept coming.

A loud crash echoed through the clearing, and Phoenix's head snapped toward the source of the sound. One of the wooden barricades had collapsed, and the Lost were pouring through the gap, their snarls filling the air as they rushed toward the heart of the settlement.

"We need to fall back!" Ro shouted, his voice barely audible over the sound of battle. "They're breaking through!"

Jax's expression was grim as he surveyed the battlefield, his eyes narrowing. "We hold them here," he growled. "We can't let them reach the center."

Phoenix's chest tightened as she looked at the devastation around her. The settlement was falling. The villagers were scattered, their defenses crumbling under the weight of the assault.

The Lost were winning.

Her breath came in ragged gasps as she gripped the knife tighter, her mind racing. They couldn't hold them off forever. Not like this.

Suddenly, through the chaos, she heard something distant but unmistakable. A low, mournful howl seemed to reverberate through the air, cutting through the noise of the battle like a blade.

Phoenix's heart skipped a beat.

Malakos was here.

(19)

The Weight of Fear

The howl that echoed through the settlement wasn't like the others Phoenix had heard before. This one was different—deeper, colder, carrying a weight that pressed down on the air, thick and suffocating.

The once chaotic growls of the Lost fell silent, replaced by an eerie stillness. It was as if the creatures were waiting, their aggression quelled by something far more potent than their primal hunger.

Phoenix could feel that whatever was coming was closer now. Jax stood beside her, his jaw clenched, eyes locked on the distant tree line. His hand hovered near his weapon, but he didn't move. Ro, who had been light-hearted moments before, had fallen silent, his usual smirk replaced with a grim determination.

"It's him," Phoenix told the others. "Malakos is here."

She swallowed hard, pushing down the unease, clawing at her chest. With Malakos here, that meant Edward was here as well.
Her memory flashed to the moments before everything had gone so horribly wrong. Before she lost him. Before they had merged into one.

Jax's eyes flicked to the tree line again, narrowing.

"Stay close," he muttered. "Things are about to get a lot worse."

Malakos, looming at the edge of the trees, stepped into the faint light cast by the settlement's fires. He moved unnaturally, his hulking form betraying the quiet precision in his steps. His eyes gleamed in the low light, burning with an intelligence that set him apart from the mindless Lost that followed him. The creatures that had once been charging toward the settlement now stood still as if waiting for his command.

"What do we do?" Phoenix asked, her voice barely above a whisper.

Ro's gaze was steady despite the fear she could see behind his eyes. "We split up. You and I head in the opposite direction. Draw him away long enough for the others to escape."

Phoenix swallowed hard, the weight of Ro's plan sinking in. It was dangerous—reckless, but it might be their only chance.

Just then, a loud crack echoed through the trees, followed by the unmistakable sound of branches snapping under the weight of something massive. Phoenix's heart jumped into her throat as she turned toward the sound, her body instinctively recoiling.

Ro acted quickly, pulling Phoenix into the cover of a nearby rock formation and hiding them from view as the monstrous figure of Malakos appeared on the edge of the forest. His eyes glowed in the darkness, scanning the trees with predatory intent.

Phoenix's breath caught in her throat as she watched him. He was massive—much larger than any of the Lost she had seen. His movements were slow and deliberate as if he were savoring the hunt.

Ro leaned close, his breath warm against her ear. "We need to move. Quietly."

They moved carefully, step by step, their backs pressed against the rocky outcrop as they edged further away from Malakos's line of sight. Phoenix's leg screamed in protest with each step, but she pushed through the pain, her focus entirely on getting as far from him as possible.

Malakos's head snapped in their direction, his eyes locking onto Phoenix with terrifying intensity.

"Run!" Ro hissed, grabbing her arm and pulling her forward.

Phoenix's heart raced as they moved deeper into the dense undergrowth, and her body protested with every step. Ro stayed close beside her, guiding her as they navigated the forest's uneven terrain.

The branches snagged at their clothes, and the ground beneath them became slick with damp earth. Phoenix pushed through, her fear of Malakos stronger than her pain. Though Malakos wasn't in sight, she could feel his presence, his dark shadow looming just out of view.

Ro's jaw was tight, scanning the trees ahead. "We need to draw him into a trap. There's a ravine up ahead. If we can lead him there…"

Phoenix followed Ro's gaze, noticing the steep incline a short distance away. It was dangerous, especially with her injured leg, but they didn't have many options left. "You think that'll slow him down?"

"He's big. He won't be able to move as easily as we can." Ro's eyes flicked back to her, his expression grim. "It's our best shot."

Phoenix hesitated, her body screaming for rest, but a low growl behind them spurred her into action. "Let's go," she said, her voice tight with determination.

Ro took the lead, his pace quickening as they neared the ravine. The ground became more uneven, the trees thinning out as they approached the steep drop-off. Phoenix stumbled slightly, slipping on the wet ground, but Ro caught her before she could fall. His grip held her firmly as he helped her regain her balance.

"Careful," he muttered, his voice low but urgent. "We don't have much time."

Phoenix nodded, her breaths coming in ragged gasps as they reached the ravine's edge. It was deeper than she had expected. The ground sloped sharply downward, dotted with jagged rocks and thick underbrush. Ro glanced over the edge before looking back at her, his expression serious.

"We'll go down carefully," he said. "Malakos won't be able to follow us easily. If we can make it to the bottom, we might be able to lose him in the trees."

Phoenix swallowed hard, her fear of Malakos warring with the sheer drop before them. She wasn't sure if her injured leg could take the strain of climbing down, but there was no other choice. Malakos was closing in, and staying put meant certain death.

"Let's do it," she whispered, steeling herself for the descent.

Ro nodded and quickly moved down the incline, using the rocks and roots for support as he made his way down. Phoenix followed, wincing with each movement as her leg screamed in protest, but she pushed the pain aside, focusing only on the task at hand.

The growl from behind grew louder and closer. Phoenix's heart pounded in her ears as she forced herself to move faster, each step bringing her closer to the bottom of the ravine. Ro reached the ground first, his eyes darting back up to check on her as she descended.

"Come on, Phoenix," he called out, his voice tense but encouraging. "You're almost there."

Just as her foot reached solid ground, a massive shadow loomed over the edge of the ravine. Malakos. His glowing eyes burned with an intensity that sent a shiver down Phoenix's spine. He stood at the top of the incline, his hulking figure outlined against the darkening sky. His gaze was locked on hers, and she stood paralyzed in terror.

"Run!" Ro shouted, grabbing Phoenix's arm and pulling her forward as they sprinted deeper into the forest.

Behind them, Malakos let out a furious roar, reverberating through the trees. Phoenix glanced back and saw him step forward, his massive frame straining against the narrow ledge. The ground beneath him crumbled slightly, but he didn't retreat.

"Go, Phoenix!" Ro urged, his grip tightening as they pushed through the thick underbrush.

Phoenix's leg throbbed with every step, the pain almost unbearable, but her fear of Malakos kept her moving. They couldn't stop now—not

when they were so close. The darkness thickened as they ran, the trees
closing in around them. Still, they could hear Malakos's pursuit,
slower now but relentless.

Phoenix and Ro reached the ravine's edge, the steep drop looming
ahead. The descent had been treacherous, but they had made it down.
Their only hope was that Malakos wouldn't be able to follow.

Unfortunately, the heavy, thudding footsteps behind them crushed
any hope of that.

Phoenix's heart hammered in her chest as she glanced back, her breath
catching as Malakos appeared at the top of the incline. His hulking
form was outlined against the darkening sky, his glowing eyes locked
onto her again.

Ro tugged on her arm. "Move! We've got to keep going."

But Malakos was already advancing, his massive frame stepping closer
to the edge of the ravine. The ground beneath his feet crumbled
slightly under his immense weight, but he didn't stop. His gaze never
left Phoenix.

Just as Malakos took another step forward, the ground beneath him
gave way.

The earth shifted, and with a deafening crack, the ledge collapsed
beneath Malakos's feet. His glowing eyes widened as the ground
betrayed him, and with a furious roar, he tumbled over the edge. His
massive form crashed down the ravine, slamming against jagged rocks
as he fell.

The noise of his impact echoed through the forest—a sickening series
of cracks and crashes as his body hit the ground, sending a cloud of
dust and debris up into the air.

Phoenix stood frozen, her body shaking as she stared at the space
where Malakos had disappeared. Her breath caught in her throat, and
part of her hoped it was over, hoping that the fall had been enough.

"Edward!" She yelled, the name tearing from her throat before she could stop herself. The shock of what had just happened, of seeing Malakos, the twisted version of her brother, fall, overwhelmed her. She could barely breathe, her heart pounding in her ears as the reality of it all crashed over her. It was Edward, or what was left of him.

Ro spun her around, gripping her shoulders, forcing her to meet his gaze. "Phoenix, listen to me!" His firm voice cut through the haze of her panic. "That's not your brother anymore. You know that." His words were harsh, but there was a sadness behind them, a quiet understanding of her pain.

Phoenix blinked, tears blurring her vision. She knew he was right, but it didn't stop the ache in her chest. It didn't stop the part of her that still saw Edward and wanted to believe something of him was left in that monstrous form.

"Come on," Ro urged, tugging her away from the edge. "We have to go."

Phoenix nodded numbly, her legs moving instinctively as they retreated deeper into the forest, away from the ravine. Every step felt like a blur, and her mind raced with everything that had just happened. She wanted to believe Malakos was gone, but the dread in her chest told her otherwise.

Behind them, the air grew still. The silence was thick. Then, it came— a furious roar, low and guttural, rising from the bottom of the ravine.

Phoenix's heart sank as she heard it. Malakos wasn't dead. He wasn't even close to being finished.

His voice echoed through the trees, filled with rage and dark promise. "Run while you can, little one. You'll be mine soon enough."

The weight of his words pressed down on her, colder than any fear she had ever felt. Ro tugged her forward again. They were moving as quickly as possible, but the threat echoed behind them, chasing them into the night.

20

Echoes of the Hunt

The forest closed in around them, the trees towering like silent sentinels as Phoenix and Ro moved deeper into the shadows. Each step was a battle—Phoenix's leg throbbed with every uneven footfall, but Ro kept a steady grip on her, guiding her forward, his jaw set in determination.

Phoenix's heart still raced, her mind struggling to process the sound of Malakos's voice echoing through the night. His threat had been more than words—it had felt like a binding promise.

"You'll be mine soon enough."

Phoenix shivered despite the warmth of Ro's arm around her, a cold dread creeping into her bones. She had never heard anything so dark, so filled with malice, and the thought that

Edward was somehow tied to all of it made her stomach churn. The memory of seeing Malakos fall into the ravine played repeatedly in her mind, but the fear remained. He wasn't dead, and she knew he wouldn't stop coming for her.

"We need to keep moving," Ro muttered, his voice low but insistent. He kept his eyes forward, his grip tightening slightly as they navigated the uneven forest floor. "We're not out of this yet."

Phoenix nodded weakly, her breath coming in shallow gasps. She knew he was right, but the exhaustion crept in, her leg screaming in protest. She wasn't sure how much longer she could keep going.

Suddenly, Ro stopped, pulling her to a halt. Phoenix's heart jumped as she glanced around, half-expecting to see Malakos emerging from the darkness. Ro pointed ahead, his voice soft. "Look."

Phoenix could see a faint glow through the trees—flickering firelight from the settlement. Relief washed over her, and she felt a small surge of hope for the first time since the attack. They were close to safety, at least for now.

"We're almost there," Ro said, glancing down at her, his expression softening. "You good to keep going?"

Phoenix nodded, though the pain in her leg was nearly unbearable. "Yeah. I can do this."

Ro gave her a reassuring smile before pulling her forward again, his pace quickening now that they were close to the settlement. As they pushed through the underbrush, the firelight grew brighter, the familiar shapes of the settlement's buildings emerging through the trees.

They crossed the settlement's threshold just as the night fully descended, the forest's eerie silence replaced by the village's murmur. The people here had no idea what had just happened or how close they had come to destruction.

Phoenix stumbled as they reached the center of the settlement, her leg finally giving out beneath her. Ro caught her before hitting the ground, gently lowering her onto a nearby bench.

"Hey," Ro said, crouching beside her, his voice laced with concern. "We made it. You're okay."

Phoenix released a shaky breath, her entire body trembling with exhaustion and adrenaline. "For now," she whispered, her eyes meeting his. "But Malakos will come back."

Ro's expression darkened, but he didn't argue. He knew it, too. "We won't let that happen," he said firmly, though there was a tension in his voice that betrayed his own fear.

Just then, Jax appeared from one of the nearby buildings, his eyes scanning the two of them before he rushed over.

"What happened?" He demanded, his voice tight with worry. "We heard the roar. Is Malakos—"

"He's not dead," Phoenix interrupted, her voice flat. "We lured him into the ravine, but he's still alive. He'll be back."

Jax's jaw clenched, his eyes narrowing as he processed her words. "Then we don't have much time."

Phoenix nodded, her stomach twisting. She knew they couldn't stay here, not with Malakos hunting them. The people in the settlement would be in danger if they remained, and Phoenix wasn't willing to put them at risk. But the thought of leaving, of going back out there, terrified her.

"We can't stay here," Phoenix said, her voice firmer now. "If we do, he'll find us. He'll destroy this place."

Jax sighed, running a hand through his hair. "I know," he muttered. "We'll get you out before dawn. But you'll need to rest before then. Serena's preparing supplies."

Phoenix's heart sank as she looked around at the quiet settlement. The people here had taken her in and helped her heal. And now, because of her, they were in danger.

"I don't want to drag anyone else into this," she whispered, more to herself than anyone else.

Ro knelt before her, his eyes meeting hers with a seriousness that cut through the fear. "You're not dragging us into anything, Phoenix. We're in this together now, whether you like it or not."

Phoenix managed a weak smile, but her chest tightened with emotion. "I don't know what I'd do without you, Ro."

Ro smirked, though his expression softened. "Probably get eaten by a giant monster. But hey, that's what I'm here for."

Despite the weight of everything, Phoenix let out a small laugh, the tension in her shoulders loosening just a bit. Ro always knew how to lighten the darkest moments; now, she was grateful for it.

"We'll get through this," Jax said firmly, standing tall beside them. "But you're right—we can't stay here. We'll leave at dawn."

As Phoenix sat back, exhaustion finally pulling at her, she couldn't help but feel the weight of everything they still had to face. Malakos was out there, hunting them, and she didn't know why.

One thing was sure—they couldn't run forever. Whatever connection she had to Malakos, she had to figure it out and sever it.

As the night deepened, the firelight flickered across Phoenix's face, casting shadows that danced on the walls of the small shelter where she and Ro now sat. Jax had gone to check on the rest of the village, leaving them in a momentary lull.

The silence between them stretched, comfortable but heavy, each lost in its thoughts. Phoenix's leg ached, but the pain wasn't what consumed her now—it was the questions, the uncertainty swirling in her mind.

Every time she closed her eyes, she saw Malakos. She felt his presence as if he were standing beside her, his voice echoing in her head: You'll be mine soon enough.

She shuddered involuntarily.

Ro noticed. He didn't say anything at first; he just watched her, his brow furrowed with concern. Finally, he broke the silence. "Are you okay?" he asked, his voice quiet, lacking its usual teasing edge.

Phoenix didn't respond right away, unsure how to explain her feelings. After a moment, she shook her head. "No," she admitted, her voice barely above a whisper. "I don't think I am."

Ro shifted, leaning forward slightly. "Is it because of what he said? Malakos?"

Phoenix nodded, her hands trembling slightly as she rested them in her lap. "I can feel the connection between Malakos and Edward. I don't know how, but it's there and scares me, Ro."

Ro's eyes softened, and he gently touched her arm, grounding her. "Look, I don't know what's going on with Malakos or Edward, but I know one thing—you're not alone in this. Whatever happens, we'll face it together."

Phoenix bit her lip, trying to hold back the emotions that were threatening to spill over. "I just… I miss him, Ro. I miss Edward so much. And the thought that Malakos has consumed him—" She broke off, unable to finish.

Ro didn't hesitate. He pulled her into a hug, his arms wrapping around her tightly, offering her the kind of comfort only he could. Phoenix leaned into him, closing her eyes as the weight of her emotions finally caught up to her.

"You're not losing yourself to this," Ro whispered, his voice firm. "We'll figure it out. And when we do, we'll end this. You'll get your brother back in one way or another."

Phoenix pulled back slightly, looking up at him with tear-filled eyes. "How can you be so sure?"

Ro's smirk returned just a little, the light dancing in his eyes. "Because I'm always right," he said, his voice filled with quiet confidence. "You'll see."

Phoenix let out a soft laugh, wiping her eyes. "You're impossible."

"Yeah, but you need me," Ro teased gently, his grin widening. "Admit it."

She smiled despite herself. "I suppose I do."

Before either of them could say anything more, Jax returned, his face stern. "Everything's in place," he said, his voice clipped. "Serena's packed the supplies. We leave before first light."

Phoenix nodded, the heaviness of the situation settling back over her. "Where will we go?"

Jax's eyes darkened, a shadow passing over his face. "There's an old outpost deep in the mountains. It's not much, but it's hidden. We'll be safe there, at least for a while."

"Safe," Phoenix repeated softly, the word feeling foreign in her mouth. Could anywhere really be safe with Malakos hunting them?

"We'll make it," Ro said, his voice filled with determination. "We always do."

Phoenix looked between them—Ro's steady presence and Jax's unyielding strength—and felt a flicker of hope despite the fear gnawing at her insides. Maybe they could survive this together.

But even as the thought crossed her mind, she couldn't shake the feeling that Malakos's shadow would follow them, no matter how far they ran.

The quiet after Jax's announcement settled over them like a heavy blanket, stifling the words that lingered on the edge of Phoenix's lips.

Outside the small shelter, the wind howled through the trees, a mournful sound that seemed to echo the storm of emotions swirling inside her. The fire had burned down to embers, its once-warm glow barely illuminating their faces.

Phoenix leaned back against the rough wall of the shelter, her mind spinning. She was grateful for Ro's steady presence beside her and Jax's. But her thoughts kept returning to Malakos—his voice, his eyes, the way he had seemed to see right through her. His threat echoed in her mind, chilling her to the bone: You'll be mine soon enough.

The weight of it pressed on her chest, making it hard to breathe. What did he mean? Why was he so fixated on her? The questions had no answers, and the uncertainty gnawed at her.

Her gaze drifted to Ro, who sat beside her, his eyes focused on the dying fire. His usual sarcasm was gone, replaced by a quiet seriousness she wasn't used to seeing. He had been her rock tonight, pulling her through when everything felt like it was falling apart. She didn't know what she would've done without him.

"Ro," she whispered, her voice barely audible.

He looked at her, his expression softening. "Yeah?"

"I don't know how I'd have made it through tonight without you," she admitted, the vulnerability in her voice surprising even herself. "I'd probably be dead by now if it weren't for you."

Ro's lips quirked into a slight, lopsided grin. "Well, I've always said you'd be lost without me," he said, trying to lighten the mood. But then his expression grew more serious. "But seriously, Phoenix, you're stronger than you think. You would've found a way. You always do."

Phoenix wanted to believe him, but the doubt lingered in her heart. "I don't know," she muttered, her gaze dropping to the floor. "Everything feels different now. With Malakos… with Edward…" Her voice broke slightly at the mention of her brother's name, and she bit her lip, trying to hold back the tears that threatened to spill.

Ro reached out, placing his hand gently over hers. "Hey," he said softly, drawing her attention back to him. "We'll figure this out. I promise. And we'll do it together. You're not alone in this, Phoenix."

His words were comforting, but the knot in her chest didn't ease completely. She nodded, squeezing his hand in silent gratitude.

Standing near the shelter entrance, Jax turned back toward them, his gaze sharp. "We need to get some rest before we leave," he said, his tone leaving no room for argument. It's going to be a long journey."

Phoenix nodded again. She knew he was right, but sleeping seemed impossible with everything weighing on her mind. She leaned her head back against the wall, closing her eyes and trying to focus on the steady rhythm of her breathing, hoping it would calm her racing thoughts.

Beside her, Ro shifted slightly, leaning closer. "You're going to be okay, Phoenix," he murmured, his voice soft but firm. "You've got me, Jax, and Serena. We're not going to let Malakos win."

He smiled faintly, his thumb brushing over her knuckles. "Get some rest, Phen. I'll keep watch."

"Edward," she whispered, the name slipping from her lips before she could stop it. Tears welled in her eyes, the pain of losing him so raw it felt like a fresh wound.

Ro's grip on her hand tightened, grounding her. He leaned in, his voice low and firm but gentle. "That's not him, Phoenix. Whatever Malakos is, it's not Edward anymore."

Phoenix choked back a sob, her heart aching as she nodded weakly. She knew Ro was correct, but the sight of Malakos—the way he had moved and spoken—had shaken her to her core. She wasn't ready to accept the truth yet—not entirely.

"I know," she whispered, her voice cracking, trying to tell herself that.

Ro didn't respond with words. He didn't need to. His hand stayed steady in hers, offering the quiet support she needed as her tears finally fell. The pain of losing Edward, of watching him become something she couldn't recognize, was too much to bear. Ro was there, silently sharing the weight of her grief.

The wind howled outside, but within the shelter, there was a strange sense of peace. Phoenix's tears slowed, her breathing becoming more even as the exhaustion finally won out. She closed her eyes, holding on to the only thing that felt real at that moment—Ro's hand.

By the time Jax stirred from his place near the shelter's entrance, the fire's soft glow had long since faded to embers. Outside, the wind had calmed, and the first faint hints of dawn were creeping through the cracks in the wooden walls. He glanced back at Phoenix and Ro, his brow furrowing slightly as he saw them.

Phoenix was still asleep, her head resting lightly against the wall, her face a picture of calm in the dim light. Beside her, Ro sat slumped against the wall, his head tilted to the side, his breathing steady and even. His hand still held Phoenix's, their fingers loosely intertwined as if they needed that connection even in sleep.

Jax exhaled softly, his usual stern expression softening for a moment before he stepped forward, careful not to make too much noise.

"Phoenix. Ro," he called quietly, his voice gruff but gentle. "It's time."

Ro stirred first, blinking groggily as he slowly lifted his head. His hand instinctively tightened around Phoenix's as he woke. His gaze shifted to Jax, and a sleepy grin tugged at the corner of his lips. "Already? I was just getting comfortable."

Jax huffed quietly. "Comfort's a luxury we don't have right now."

Phoenix stirred at their voices, her brow furrowing as she slowly blinked awake. Her body felt heavy. The lingering soreness in her leg reminded her how much she had pushed herself the day before. She shifted, her eyes falling on Ro, who was still beside her, their hands still linked.

She blinked, a wave of warmth flooding her chest despite the looming reality. She hadn't expected him to stay with her through the night, but somehow, it felt right. Safe, even.

Ro stretched, wincing slightly as his stiff muscles protested. "Didn't mean to fall asleep on the job," he muttered, though there was no regret in his voice. His eyes met Phoenix's, a faint glimmer of mischief returning. "Guess I make a pretty good pillow, huh?"

Phoenix rolled her eyes, a small smile tugging at her lips. "Don't flatter yourself."

Jax cleared his throat, drawing their attention back to the matter at hand. "We need to leave. The longer we wait, the more we risk Malakos coming back. We can't afford to linger."

Phoenix nodded, the seriousness of the situation crashing back down over her like a cold wave. She knew Jax was right. As much as she wanted to stay and recover fully, the thought of Malakos returning to the village sent a chill through her. She couldn't risk endangering these people—Jax's family, the settlement that had shown her kindness.

She pulled herself up with Ro's help, wincing as her leg throbbed. "I'm ready," she said, her voice steady despite the exhaustion weighing her down. "We should go before he finds us again."

Jax nodded, though there was a flicker of hesitation in his eyes as he glanced at her leg. "Serena left you with enough medicine to keep the pain down for a while, but you still need to take it easy. We can't afford you getting worse out there."

"I'll manage," Phoenix replied, her voice firmer than she felt. "We can't stay here."

Ro sighed, his expression softening. "Alright, but don't be a hero if you get too tired. Lean on me. If you need to." He shot her a slight smirk, trying to lighten the mood, though his eyes showed genuine concern.

"Thanks, Ro," she said, squeezing his arm lightly in appreciation.

Jax stepped forward, shouldering a pack as he glanced toward the door. "We'll head out quietly. I've already spoken to Elara. She'll keep the village secure while we're gone."

Phoenix's heart tightened at the thought of leaving Elara and Luka behind. But there was no choice. Malakos was out there, and the village wasn't safe as long as he hunted her.

"Let's move," Jax said, his voice low and determined.

As they quietly gathered their belongings and prepared to leave the settlement, Phoenix's mind churned with everything that had happened and the questions that still hung heavy in the air. What did Malakos want with her? Why did he feel so connected to Edward?

And, more than anything, how much time did they have before he returned?

The forest was shrouded in an eerie stillness as they moved through the trees, their footsteps barely audible over the soft crunch of leaves beneath their feet. The early morning light filtered through the dense canopy, casting long shadows across the path ahead.

Phoenix kept her focus forward, her senses on high alert as they navigated deeper into the wilderness.

Ro stayed close by her side, his presence a constant, reassuring weight against the uncertainty of their surroundings.

Jax led the way, his movements efficient and quiet. His eyes scanned the terrain with the precision of someone who had spent years surviving in hostile environments.

Phoenix's leg still ached with each step, but she forced herself to push through the pain, determined not to slow them down. They had yet to tell how long they had before Malakos returned or how far his influence had spread. The thought sent a cold shiver down her spine.

They walked silently for hours, the tension between them thick. The only sound was the occasional rustle of leaves or distant wildlife calls. Phoenix's mind raced, her thoughts circling back to Malakos and the words he had spoken to her at the ravine.

The connection between him and Edward was undeniable, but the more she thought about it, the less she understood. What did he mean by, "You'll be mine soon enough?"

Her chest tightened with dread, but she shook the thought away, focusing instead on the path ahead.

After a while, Ro broke the silence, his voice low but steady. "So, where exactly are we heading?"

Jax glanced over his shoulder, his eyes briefly meeting Ro's before returning to the path. "There's an outpost a few miles from here, deep in the forest. It's hidden and secure. We can regroup there and figure out our next move."

Phoenix's brow furrowed. "What kind of outpost?"

Jax hesitated for a moment before answering. "It used to be a supply post back when… well before things got bad. Not many people know about it. We'll be safe there for a while."

How he said it and his voice tightened just slightly made Phoenix wonder if he was holding something back. But there was a better time to press for answers. They had enough to worry about without adding more complications to the mix.

They continued in silence, the weight of the unknown pressing down on them with every step. As they neared a small clearing, Phoenix stumbled slightly, her leg giving out beneath her. Ro was at her side instantly, his arm wrapping around her waist to steady her.

"Easy, Phen," he muttered, his tone gentle but firm. "Take it slow."

Phoenix gritted her teeth, frustrated by her own weakness. "I'm fine," she insisted, though the pain in her leg told a different story.

Ro raised an eyebrow, clearly unconvinced. "Sure you are. But maybe let me help you before you end up face-first in the dirt."

Despite herself, Phoenix managed a small smile. "Thanks, Ro."

He smirked, his sarcasm returning in full force. "No problem. Just doing my duty as your personal bodyguard."

Jax slowed his pace, glancing back at them. "We'll take a break up ahead," he said, nodding toward the clearing beyond the trees. "But we can't stay long. We need to keep moving."

Phoenix nodded, grateful for the chance to rest, even if only for a moment. As they stepped into the clearing, the tension in the air eased slightly, and the open space provided a brief respite from the forest's oppressive weight.

She lowered herself onto a fallen log, her body aching with exhaustion. Ro sat beside her, his gaze scanning the treeline as if expecting Malakos to appear at any moment.

"We'll make it through this," Ro said quietly, his voice carrying a note of certainty that Phoenix wasn't sure she shared. "Jax knows what he's doing. We're in good hands."

Phoenix glanced at him, her heart heavy with the weight of everything they had left behind. "I hope you're right," she murmured.

Ro gave her a sidelong look, his usual smirk softening into something more genuine. "Trust me, I am."

The air in the clearing felt heavier the longer they sat, as if the looming danger clung to them, unwilling to let go. Phoenix stretched her leg before her, wincing as she massaged the aching muscles. Every step felt like a battle, and though she hated to admit it, she was grateful for the short break.

Jax crouched on the other side of the clearing, his eyes scanning the perimeter, never fully relaxing. The tension in his body was palpable, his every movement calculated and deliberate. Phoenix knew he wasn't just waiting for Malakos—he was planning, always planning their next move.

She glanced at Ro, who was uncharacteristically quiet beside her. His usual sarcastic remarks were missing, replaced by a somberness she hadn't seen in him before. The weight of the night's events hung over them all like a dark cloud, and even Ro couldn't joke his way through this one.

After a long silence, Ro spoke, his voice low. "What do you think Jax isn't telling us?"

Phoenix looked at him, surprised by the question. She had been wondering the same thing, but hearing Ro say it out loud made her unease feel more real.

"I don't know," she admitted, her voice barely above a whisper. "But I feel he knows more about Malakos than he's letting on."

Ro nodded slowly, his gaze still fixed on Jax. "Yeah. There's something off about all this."

Phoenix's thoughts drifted back to the ravine moment, to how Malakos had spoken to her. Their connection was undeniable, but the why remained a terrifying mystery.

"We'll ask him when we're safe," Phoenix said, her tone firmer than she felt. "Right now, we need to focus on getting to that outpost."

Ro's smirk returned, though it was faint. "Sounds like a plan, Captain."

Before Phoenix could respond, Jax stood and motioned for them to follow. "Let's move."

They pushed themselves up, the brief rest doing little to relieve the exhaustion clinging to their limbs. Phoenix stumbled slightly as they continued their journey, but Ro stayed close, his hand hovering near her in case she needed help.

The further they moved into the forest, the denser it became. The trees grew taller, their twisted branches casting long shadows across the ground. Phoenix couldn't shake the feeling that they were being watched, the hairs on the back of her neck prickling with unease.

Every sound seemed amplified—the rustle of leaves, the snap of twigs underfoot, the distant call of an animal. It was as if the forest held its breath, waiting for something to happen.

Jax suddenly stopped, his hand raised in a silent signal for them to halt. Phoenix's heart skipped a beat as she froze, her breath catching in her throat. The stillness of the forest became suffocating, the silence deafening.

"What is it?" Ro whispered, his voice barely audible.

Jax didn't answer immediately, his eyes scanning the trees around them. After a moment, he motioned for them to move forward again, but his expression was grim.

Phoenix's pulse raced as they continued, her eyes darting around the forest, searching for any sign of movement. The knot of fear in her stomach tightened with each passing moment, and she couldn't shake the feeling that Malakos was still out there, lurking just beyond the edge of their awareness.

Finally, after hours of tense, silent walking, they reached a small rise in the forest floor. Jax gestured for them to stop again, his gaze fixed on something ahead.

Phoenix followed his line of sight, her breath catching as she saw it.

A small, dilapidated structure was nestled into the side of a rocky hill, hidden among the trees—the outpost.

Jax glanced back at them, his expression grim but determined. "This is it," he said quietly. "We'll be safe here for a while."

Phoenix wasn't so sure.

Her breath was uneven as she stood at the base of the small rise, her eyes locked on the weathered structure ahead. The outpost, if it could even be called that, looked like it had been abandoned for decades. The wooden beams were rotting, the stone walls covered in creeping vines, and fallen branches partially blocked the entrance. It didn't exactly scream safety, but they only had a few options.

Ro stepped up beside her, his lips curling into a faint grin. "Looks cozy," he muttered under his breath. "The kind of place where nightmares are made."

Phoenix shot him a look, part of her grateful for his sarcasm, though the other part was too exhausted to respond. Instead, she limped forward, following Jax as he led them closer to the entrance. Her leg ached with every step, the crutches sinking into the soft ground beneath her, but she pressed on.

Jax pushed aside the fallen branches and ducked inside, motioning for them to follow. The interior of the outpost was just as worn down as the outside. The faint light that filtered through the cracks in the walls illuminated a small room with a dusty table in the center, a few broken chairs scattered around, and what looked like a makeshift bed in the corner.

Phoenix limped to the table, her fingers brushing the surface, disturbing a layer of dust.

"How long do you think it's been abandoned?" she asked, her voice hollow in the space.

Jax shrugged, eyes scanning the room as if checking for any threats. "Long enough. It used to be a patrol outpost, back when things were more stable."

"More stable?" Ro raised an eyebrow. "That's not exactly reassuring."

Jax gave him a pointed look. "It'll do for tonight. We need to rest, and we need to figure out our next move."

Phoenix's gaze drifted to the room's far corner, where the shadows seemed to deepen. The cold air crept into her bones, and despite the brief moment of safety, she couldn't shake the sense of foreboding that clung to her like a second skin.

Ro flopped into one of the broken chairs, wincing as the wood creaked under his weight. "So, what now? We sit here and wait for Malakos to come knocking, or are we actually going to talk about why he seems so obsessed with Phoenix?"

Jax's expression darkened, and Phoenix felt her chest tighten. Ro's words hung in the air, thick with tension. She didn't want to talk about Malakos—not now, not ever. But she knew they had to. She needed answers.

Jax's gaze shifted to Phoenix, and for a moment, the silence stretched between them, heavy and oppressive. Then he spoke, his voice low. "There's more to Malakos than any of us realized. He's not just another Lost. He's… different."
Phoenix felt her pulse quicken, dread pooling in her stomach. "What do you mean?"

Jax glanced at Ro before focusing on her. "The connection you feel with him is real. It's because of Edward."

Phoenix's breath caught in her throat, and her hands tightened on the crutches. "Edward?" Her voice was barely a whisper, and the name stung her heart sharply.

Jax nodded grimly. "Whatever Malakos is, he's tied to Edward. I don't know how, but they share something. Something that draws him to you because of Edward."

Phoenix's mind spun, her heart racing. It felt like the ground was slipping out from under her, the weight of Jax's words pressing down on her chest. "But Edward's gone," she said, her voice shaking. "He's gone, Jax. Malakos took him."

"I know," Jax replied, his expression softening. "But I think there's a part of Edward still inside Malakos. And that part of him… it's what keeps drawing Malakos to you."

Phoenix shook her head, the words too heavy to comprehend. "That can't be true. Edward wouldn't—"

"Edward wouldn't hurt you," Jax interrupted, his voice gentle but firm. "But Malakos… he's not Edward. Not anymore. Whatever's left of your brother is trapped inside that thing, and it's dangerous."

Ro leaned forward, his tone more serious than Phoenix had ever heard. "So, what does that mean for us? For her?"

Jax's gaze hardened, and Phoenix felt the weight of his following words before speaking. "It means Malakos won't stop until he has her."

The silence that followed was suffocating, the reality of the situation settling over them like a dark cloud. Phoenix's heart pounded in her chest, her throat tight with fear. She had already lost Edward once, and now, the thought of being dragged into whatever twisted connection Malakos had with him made her stomach churn.

"We can't let that happen," Ro said firmly, breaking the silence. "We won't."

Phoenix nodded, though her body trembled with the weight of it all. She didn't know how to fight something like this—something that was both a part of Edward and yet entirely alien. But she knew she couldn't give in. She had to keep fighting.

"We'll stop him," she whispered, her voice barely audible but filled with determination. "We have to."

Jax nodded, his expression grim but resolute. "We will."

As he spoke, Phoenix couldn't shake the fear that Malakos was always one step closer, lurking in the shadows, waiting for the moment to strike.

The tension in the room was palpable, hanging over them like a thick fog that refused to lift. Phoenix's mind raced, grappling with Jax's words. The connection between Malakos and Edward didn't make sense, but at the same time, it explained everything—how Malakos had spoken to her and how she felt that inescapable pull toward him.

It wasn't just fear; it was something deeper, something far more terrifying.

Phoenix's breath was shaky, and her grip on the crutches tightened until her knuckles turned white. She tried to steady herself, but it was impossible to ignore the growing dread. "So, what do we do now?" she asked, her voice quiet but steady.

Leaning forward with his elbows on his knees, Ro stood up, pacing the small space. His usual sarcasm had faded entirely, replaced by a raw intensity that Phoenix hadn't seen before. "We don't wait for him to come for us, that's for sure."

Jax nodded, his gaze still focused on Phoenix as if weighing his following words carefully. "Ro's right. We need to keep moving. We can't stay in one place for too long, not with Malakos out there. He'll track us down eventually."

Phoenix swallowed hard, her throat tight. She could feel the weight of their situation pressing down on her chest, threatening to suffocate her. But despite the fear gnawing at the edges of her mind, she knew Jax was right. Staying in the outpost was suicide. Malakos would find them eventually, and when he did, they wouldn't stand a chance.

"We'll rest for a few hours," Jax continued, firm but reassuring. "Then we move. The outpost isn't far from a hidden path that leads to the caves. We can use them to our advantage, stay out of sight until we figure out a way to stop him."

Ro stopped pacing, turning to face Jax. His voice edged with frustration.

"So how exactly do we stop him? He's not just some Lost we can take down with a few hits. Malakos is different. He's stronger than anything we've faced."

Phoenix's heart sank at Ro's words, the reality of their situation hitting her like a punch to the gut. They barely survived their last encounter with Malakos because of sheer luck.

How could they possibly hope to defeat him when he was more than a mindless creature? When he was tied to Edward in ways they couldn't even begin to understand?

Jax's expression hardened, his jaw clenching. "We'll figure it out."

Ro let out a humorless laugh, shaking his head. "Great plan, Jax. Real solid."

Phoenix stood there, feeling the pressure of their conversation closing in on her. Ro's sarcasm was his way of dealing with the stress, but she could sense the fear beneath it—fear that mirrored her own. Malakos wasn't just a threat to her; he was a threat to all of them.

But as Ro's words hung in the air, Phoenix realized something. She couldn't let this fear control her. Malakos may have been tied to Edward, but Edward was her brother. There had to be something, some part of him, that could help them.

"I don't know how we'll stop him," Phoenix said softly, cutting through the tension in the room. "But I know one thing—we can't run forever. We have to face him eventually."

Jax nodded, his eyes locking with hers. "You're right."

Ro groaned, running a hand through his hair. "You two really know how to make a guy feel better about his chances of survival, you know that?"

Despite everything, Phoenix managed a small smile. "We're not dead yet, Ro."

"Yeah, thanks for the reminder," Ro shot back, though his tension was laced with an undertone of affection.

Jax stepped toward the door, glancing back at them. "Get some rest while you can. We'll move out soon."

Phoenix nodded, though she knew sleep wouldn't come quickly. As Jax stepped out of the outpost, his figure silhouetted against the dark trees, Phoenix felt Ro's hand on her shoulder, grounding her in the present moment.

"We'll make it through this, Phen," Ro said quietly, his voice steady despite the unease in his eyes. "You're not alone in this."

Phoenix looked up at him, grateful for his presence, even in the face of everything that had happened. "I know," she whispered.

But as Ro squeezed her shoulder and sat back down, Phoenix couldn't shake the feeling that their journey was far from over—and that whatever awaited them next would be even more dangerous than what they had just survived.

The fire crackled softly in the hearth, the dim light casting long shadows across the walls. Phoenix lay back on the cot, her eyes fixed on the ceiling. She tried to close her eyes and let exhaustion take her, but sleep refused to come. In the distance, she could still hear the echo of Malakos's voice, haunting and full of promise.

"You'll be mine soon enough."

The hours seemed to stretch, the fire dwindling to little more than faint embers as Phoenix lay awake, staring into the shadows dancing on the ceiling. Her leg throbbed beneath the blanket, but the ache in her chest was far worse, the weight of Jax's words and Malakos's threat pressing down on her like an anchor.

She tried to keep her breathing steady, to calm her racing thoughts, but the fear gnawed at her, making it impossible to rest. Edward was out there—some part of him, at least, trapped inside the monster that had once been human. And Malakos… Malakos was coming for her.

Ro shifted beside her, his quiet snores a faint comfort in the room's stillness. Phoenix glanced at him, his face softened by sleep, the lines of worry and exhaustion less pronounced. She was grateful for him, for how he had been there for her through all this. He had kept her grounded when she felt like she was slipping into the void. She didn't know how she would have made it this far without him.

But even Ro's presence couldn't chase away the fear that had settled deep in her bones. She could still feel the pull, the strange connection between her and Malakos. It was like a shadow that followed her, always out of reach but lurking in the corners of her mind.

She squeezed her eyes shut, willing herself to sleep, to shut out the creeping thoughts that threatened to swallow her whole. But every time she closed her eyes, she saw Edward's face—his smile, his laughter, the way he had always looked out for her. And then, the image would twist, his face morphing into something darker, something monstrous. Malakos.

Phoenix shivered, pulling the blanket tighter around her. She had to stop thinking like this. She had to focus on the task at hand—surviving, keeping Ro and Jax safe, and finding a way to stop Malakos before it was too late.

Just as she was about to give up on sleep entirely, the door to the outpost creaked open. Phoenix's heart leaped into her throat, her hand instinctively reaching for the weapon beside her. But it was just Jax slipping back inside, his expression grim.

He glanced at her, noticing she was still awake. "You should be resting," he said quietly, his voice barely a whisper in the dark.

Phoenix sat up slowly, wincing as her leg protested the movement. "Couldn't sleep," she admitted, her voice tight with exhaustion.

Jax didn't respond right away. He moved to the corner of the room, checking the small bag he had placed there earlier. Phoenix watched him, the question burning at the back of her mind, but she wasn't sure she wanted the answer.

"Jax," she began, her voice hesitant. "Earlier, when you said Malakos is tied to Edward… what did you mean? How can that be possible?"

Jax stopped his back to her, his shoulders tense. He didn't turn around right away, and for a moment, Phoenix thought he wouldn't answer. But then, he spoke, his voice low and grave.

"Malakos isn't like the others. He's different. And I think it's because of what your father was working on—Project Genesis. Edward was a part of that project, whether he knew it or not."

Phoenix's heart sank, her mind racing. "Project Genesis… I thought that was just about controlling the Lost, keeping them from destroying what was left of the world."

Jax turned then, his eyes dark with something that looked like regret. "It was supposed to be. But your father was always pushing the boundaries, always trying to find a way to reverse the damage that had been done. I don't know the full details, but I do know this: Edward wasn't just a bystander. He was integral to your father's work. And that work… it's what led to Malakos."

Phoenix stared at him, her mind reeling. "How, though? How does that explain what's happening now?"

Jax's jaw clenched, and he looked away as if the truth was too heavy to bear. "I don't have all the answers, Phoenix. But I think when Malakos took Edward, he didn't just kill him. He absorbed and took something from him—his mind and memories. And now, that part of Edward is still inside him, trapped, fueling his obsession with you."

Phoenix's chest tightened, her throat constricting. "So, what? Malakos, is Edward now?"

Jax shook his head, his expression hard. "No. Whatever part of Edward is left it's buried deep. Malakos is something else, something darker. That connection between them is why Malakos won't stop until he has you."

The weight of his words pressed down on Phoenix, her heart pounding in her chest. She didn't want to believe it; she didn't want to accept that the brother she had lost was somehow tied to the creature that was hunting her. But deep down, she knew Jax was right. She had felt it—every time Malakos had looked at her, every time he had spoken her name. It wasn't just a monster stalking her. It was something far more personal.

Phoenix took a shaky breath, her mind whirling with the implications of what Jax had said. "So, what do we do now?"

Jax's expression darkened, his eyes hard as steel. "We find a way to sever that connection. And we stop Malakos, once and for all."

Phoenix sat silently for a long moment, Jax's words reverberating in her mind like an echo she couldn't shake. Sever the connection. Stop Malakos, how? It all felt impossible, like trying to stop an unstoppable force set in motion long before she knew what was happening.

Beside her, Ro stirred, blinking groggily as he woke up. His hand was still wrapped loosely around hers, the warmth of his skin a small comfort in the otherwise suffocating tension surrounding them.

"Morning," he muttered, stretching slightly. He must have noticed the severe expressions on their faces because his usual lightness faded almost instantly. "What's going on?"

Phoenix looked at him, the weight of everything she had learned pressing down on her chest like a boulder. She wanted to protect him from the truth and shield him from the darkness creeping in from every direction, but she knew she couldn't. Not anymore.

"Jax thinks…" She hesitated, her throat tightening. "He thinks that Edward is still… a part of Malakos. That's why he's so drawn to me. Because of my brother."

Ro's eyes darkened, his expression hardening. "Edward?" He ran a hand through his hair, clearly trying to process the weight of the revelation. "So, you're saying Malakos isn't just some creature? He's got a piece of Edward inside him?"

Phoenix nodded slowly. "It's not Edward. Not really. Whatever Malakos is, he took something from him. And now, he's fixated on me."

Ro cursed under his breath, his gaze flicking to Jax. "And you've known this?"

Jax's expression remained unreadable, his shoulders tense. "I suspected it. After what I've seen, it's the only explanation that makes sense."

Ro let out a low breath, shaking his head. "Great. As if we didn't have enough problems already."

Phoenix swallowed hard, her mind racing. The idea that her brother was somehow tied to Malakos made her stomach twist with dread, but it also stirred something else—determination.

She couldn't give up if there was even a chance, a tiny sliver of hope, that Edward was still there. She couldn't let Malakos take everything from her.

She pushed herself to her feet, wincing as her leg protested the movement. "We need to go," she said quietly, her voice steady despite the turmoil inside her. "We can't stay here. Malakos is coming, and we need to be ready."

Jax nodded in agreement, already moving to gather their supplies. "We leave in an hour. The outpost isn't safe anymore."

Ro stood beside Phoenix, his hand resting lightly on her shoulder. "You sure about this? You're not in any shape to be running from monsters."

Phoenix met his gaze, her heart pounding. "I don't have a choice. We don't have a choice. If we stay, we die. If we leave, we might have a chance."

Ro studied her for a moment, then gave a slight, determined nod. "Alright then. Let's get moving."

As they began to prepare for their journey, the weight of what lay ahead settled over Phoenix like a heavy cloak. She knew the road wouldn't be easy, and their danger was more significant than anything they had encountered. But she also learned one thing for sure: she wouldn't let Malakos win.

She had already lost Edward once. She wasn't about to lose herself or the people she cared about to the monster that had taken him.

Phoenix looked at the dilapidated outpost as they packed up their meager belongings. The air was thick with the scent of decay and the chill of looming danger, but there was something else—a faint sense of finality. They wouldn't be coming back here.

"We'll stop him," Ro said quietly, echoing her earlier words as they prepared to leave. "Whatever it takes, Phoenix. We'll stop him."

Phoenix nodded, her resolve hardening as they moved toward the tree line, Malakos's looming presence still pressing down on her. She didn't know what was waiting for them, but she knew one thing: she wouldn't stop fighting.

Not for Edward. Not for herself. Not for the people she still had left.

The outpost walls seemed to close in on Phoenix as Jax's words echoed in her mind. Malakos wasn't just coming for her—he was being drawn to her by whatever twisted connection still existed between him and Edward. The weight of it pressed down on her chest, and no matter how hard she tried, she couldn't shake the growing sense of dread.

She pushed herself up from where she had been sitting, ignoring the sharp pain in her leg. Pacing the small, dimly lit room did little to ease her restless thoughts, but staying still felt impossible. Every time she closed her eyes, she saw Malakos standing at the ravine's edge, his dark, menacing gaze fixed on her. And behind those eyes… Edward.

Ro's voice broke the silence, pulling her from the endless fear and confusion in her mind. "We can't stay here," he said, leaning against the wall, arms crossed. His face was severe, but she could see the concern behind his usual sarcastic bravado. "We've gotta keep moving."

Jax glanced up from where he was sharpening his blade. "He's right. Malakos will find us here eventually. We're sitting ducks."

Phoenix's mind raced. Part of her wanted to run, to put as much distance between them and Malakos as possible. But the other part—still clinging to the hope that Edward was somehow alive inside that monster—made her hesitate.

"I don't know if we can outrun him," she said quietly, her voice barely audible in the thick tension that filled the room.
Ro straightened, his eyes locking with hers. "We don't have a choice, Phen. If we stay here, it's over. We can't take him on—not like this."

Phoenix swallowed hard, her throat dry. Ro was correct, but leaving felt like running from a part of Edward. She hated that the connection had her doubting everything, but Malakos was no ordinary threat, and every part of her knew that facing him now would mean disaster.

Jax stood, his movements deliberate. "We don't need to win a fight. We need to survive. We leave tonight before dawn. If we get further south, we'll be closer to that old supply route—maybe even find reinforcements."

Phoenix's heart pounded in her chest as she nodded. The decision was made, but more was needed to accept.

Ro gave her a reassuring smile, though it didn't reach his eyes. "We'll stick together. We always do." His voice softened, a rare vulnerability slipping through. "And we won't let him get to you, Phoenix. I promise."

Phoenix wanted to believe him. She tried to hold onto the tiny flicker of hope that Ro's words brought, but as she glanced out the narrow window, the forest's dark shadows seemed to whisper otherwise.

"I can feel him," she whispered, almost to herself, her hands trembling slightly as the truth she'd been trying to ignore crept in. "I don't know how… but I can feel him getting closer."

Jax and Ro exchanged a glance, their expressions grim. Neither of them said anything, but the silence spoke volumes.

Phoenix knew that the connection between her and Malakos was more than just a shared history with Edward. It was something darker that bound them together in a way she couldn't fully understand. And every step they took away from the outpost would bring them closer to that inevitable confrontation.

"We leave in an hour," Jax said, his voice low but firm. "Pack light. We'll move fast."

Phoenix nodded, but her mind was lost in her connection with Malakos. She couldn't shake the feeling that he would find her no matter how far they ran.

The hour passed quickly, and Phoenix found herself moving on autopilot as they prepared to leave the outpost. Ro handed her a small pack, his usual smirk absent as he silently checked over his gear. Jax stood near the entrance, his sharp eyes scanning the treeline, the tension radiating from him palpable.

Phoenix slung the pack over her shoulder, its weight unfamiliar but not heavy. Her leg still ached, but the situation's urgency numbed the pain. They couldn't afford to stay here any longer, not with Malakos so close. She couldn't shake the feeling that he'd find her no matter where they went. The thought gnawed at her, an ever-present shadow that refused to fade.

"Ready?" Ro asked, his voice breaking through her thoughts.

She nodded, though, in truth, she wasn't sure she'd ever be ready for what lay ahead. The connection between her and Malakos weighed heavily on her mind, a dark tether that seemed to pulse with every breath she took.

Jax gave a curt nod, motioning for them to follow. "Stay close. We stick to the path I scouted earlier. It'll take us to the caves—it's rough terrain, but it'll buy us time."

Ro moved in beside Phoenix, his presence a quiet comfort as they followed Jax out of the outpost. The forest loomed around them, the thick trees casting long shadows in the dim light of early evening. The path was narrow and overgrown in some places, and the further they went, the more isolated it felt.

The silence pressed down on them, broken only by the occasional rustle of leaves or snap of a twig underfoot. Phoenix's heart pounded in her chest, the weight of Malakos's earlier words hanging over her like a curse: Run while you can, little one.

As they descended deeper into the forest, the trees began to thin, revealing jagged rock formations and steep inclines. Jax led them with an ease that spoke of years of survival, but even he couldn't hide the tension in his steps.

"Malakos knows these woods," Phoenix said quietly, her voice barely above a whisper. "He'll track us."

Ro shot her a glance, his expression unreadable. "Let him try. We've got Jax on our side."

She wanted to believe him, but her pull toward Malakos grew stronger, like a dark thread winding tighter with each step. It wasn't just fear that made her wary—it was something more profound, almost primal. She could feel his presence out there, lurking just beyond the trees, waiting for the right moment to strike.

Jax motioned for them to stop as they reached a rocky incline, his eyes scanning the area ahead. "We'll take a short break here. The caves aren't far, but the terrain will get tougher."

Phoenix leaned against a nearby boulder, her leg throbbing with every heartbeat. Ro sat beside her, his face drawn but determined.

"Hey," Ro said softly, nudging her shoulder. "We've made it this far. We're not giving up now."

Phoenix nodded, though her mind was far from comforted. "Do you think Jax knows more than he's letting on?" She asked, her voice barely audible.

Ro's expression darkened, and he glanced toward Jax, crouched a few feet away, his back to them. "Yeah," he muttered. "But I don't think he's the only one."

Phoenix frowned, her eyes narrowing. "What do you mean?"

Ro hesitated, his gaze meeting hers. "I mean, you're not telling me everything either, Phen. You and Malakos, there's something between you, isn't there?"

Her throat tightened at his words, the weight of the truth pressing down on her. She hadn't meant to keep secrets, but how could she explain her connection to Malakos when she barely understood it herself?

"It's complicated," she whispered, her voice trembling slightly.

Ro's gaze softened. He reached out, gently squeezing her hand. "You don't have to explain right now. Just know that whatever it is, we'll figure it out together. Okay?"

Phoenix nodded, her heart aching at the warmth in his words. She didn't deserve his trust, not when she felt unraveling with every step they took. But Ro's presence steadied her, grounding her in a way she hadn't expected.

Before she could respond, Jax straightened, his eyes locked on something in the distance. His expression was stern, unreadable.

"We need to move," he said, his voice low and urgent. "Now."

Phoenix's pulse quickened as she pushed herself to her feet, the ominous sense of danger prickling at the back of her mind. Whatever Jax had seen—or sensed—was enough to send a fresh wave of fear through her.

They started moving again, faster this time. The terrain grew rockier, the path more treacherous as they neared the entrance to the caves. Phoenix's leg screamed in protest, but she forced herself to keep up, her heart pounding.

Just as they reached the mouth of the cave, a deep, guttural roar echoed through the forest behind them, chilling the air.

Malakos.

Phoenix's blood turned to ice as she glanced over her shoulder, catching a glimpse of the dark figure moving through the trees. He was closer than she'd thought, his massive form cutting through the forest with impressive speed.

"Hurry!" Jax barked, his voice sharp with urgency.

Phoenix and Ro stumbled into the cave, their breaths coming in ragged gasps as the darkness swallowed them whole. The cold, damp air inside the cave was a stark contrast to the oppressive heat of the forest, and for a moment, all Phoenix could hear was the beating of her heart.

Malakos's roar echoed again, this time louder—closer.

"We can't outrun him," Phoenix whispered. "He's too fast."

"We won't have to," Jax said, his tone dark and relentless. "We'll face him here."

The cave was darker than Phoenix had expected, its narrow entrance quickly giving way to a vast, echoing chamber. The jagged walls were cold and damp to the touch, and the air smelled of wet stone and earth. It was the kind of place that swallowed sound, leaving only the quiet drip of water from unseen cracks in the ceiling. Every step Phoenix took echoed, each footfall a reminder of how alone they were in the darkness.

Jax moved ahead, his eyes scanning the walls as if searching for something. Ro stayed close to Phoenix, his hand brushing hers occasionally as they navigated the uneven ground. Phoenix's leg was throbbing again, the pain sharper now in the cold, but she bit her lip and forced herself to keep moving.

Malakos's roar still rang in her ears, louder now in the silence of the cave. He was coming. And even though they had the advantage of the cave's labyrinthine paths, Phoenix couldn't shake the feeling that it wouldn't be enough. Malakos wasn't just a creature. He was something more—something that rocks and walls wouldn't stop.

"We need to find a place to set up a defense," Jax said quietly, his voice bouncing off the stone walls. "He'll be here soon."

Phoenix's heart pounded in her chest. "Jax, are you sure this is a good idea? Facing him here?"

Jax's jaw tightened, and he glanced back at her. "We don't have a choice. He'll track us wherever we go. At least here, we have some control."

Phoenix nodded, though doubt gnawed at the edges of her thoughts. What kind of control could they possibly have against something like Malakos? She knew Jax was right—they couldn't keep running. But standing and facing him felt like a death sentence.

"Come on," Ro said softly, his voice reassuring. "Jax knows what he's doing."

Phoenix looked at Ro, his usual smirk replaced by a calm determination. Despite everything, his presence was steady, and she found herself holding onto that. He had been her rock through all this, and she wasn't sure what she would've done without him.

Jax led them deeper into the cave until they reached a narrow passage that opened into a smaller chamber. The walls were closer here, the ceiling lower, but it was defendable. Jax examined the space, nodding to himself.

"This will do," he muttered, motioning for them to set up. "We can funnel him here. He won't have room to maneuver."

Phoenix leaned against the wall, her leg screaming in protest. She watched as Jax and Ro began to gather rocks and debris, creating makeshift barriers and positions. The air was thick with tension, and despite the cold, sweat clung to Phoenix's skin. Every breath felt heavy, like the weight of what was coming pressed down on her chest. "Ro," Phoenix said quietly, her voice barely above a whisper.

He looked up from where he was stacking rocks, his eyes meeting hers.

"Do you think we can stop him?" Her voice trembled, betraying the fear she was trying so hard to hide.

Ro stood up and walked over to her, his expression softer now.

"Hey," he said, his voice low and reassuring. "We'll figure this out. Together."

Phoenix swallowed hard, nodding. She wanted to believe him. She needed to believe him. But the darkness that had been creeping into her heart ever since they had first encountered Malakos seemed to grow stronger with every moment.

Before she could respond, a low, rumbling growl echoed through the cave.

Phoenix's blood turned to ice.

"He's here," Jax muttered, gripping his weapon tighter.

The sound grew louder, reverberating off the walls, making it impossible to tell where it was coming from. Phoenix's heart raced as her eyes darted around the chamber, searching for any sign of movement.

And then, she saw them—glowing eyes, burning in the darkness.

Malakos.

He moved like a shadow, his massive form blending into the cave's blackness. His glowing eyes locked onto Phoenix, and the world seemed to stand still for a moment.

"You can't hide from me, little one," Malakos's dark and chilling voice echoed.

Phoenix's breath caught in her throat as their connection flared to life again, stronger this time. It was like a tether pulling her toward him, making it impossible to look away.

Jax stepped in front of her, his weapon raised. "You're not getting any closer."

Malakos let out a low chuckle, the sound rumbling through the cave. "You think you can stop me, Jax?"

Ro moved to Phoenix's side, his hand gripping her arm tightly. "We need to move," he whispered, his voice barely audible.

Phoenix nodded, her legs trembling beneath her. They needed to escape, but the connection to Malakos was overwhelming, pulling her toward him like a magnet. She could feel Edward—some part of him— trapped inside that creature, tearing her apart.

"Go!" Jax barked, his voice sharp.

Phoenix forced herself to move, Ro pulling her along as they darted toward the narrow passage on the other side of the chamber. The sound of Malakos's heavy footsteps echoed behind them, growing louder with each passing second.

They ran, the cave's darkness swallowing them as they pushed deeper into the labyrinth of tunnels. Phoenix's breath came in ragged gasps, her leg screaming in pain, but she didn't stop. She couldn't stop. Not now.

Behind them, Malakos's voice echoed through the cave, a dark promise that sent chills down her spine.

"You can run, little one, but you won't escape. You'll be mine soon enough."

Phoenix's heart pounded in her chest, her fear mixing with the burning determination to survive. They had to get out. They had to find a way to stop him.

But deep down, she knew the truth.

This wasn't over. It was only the beginning.

21

Mira's Return

The sound of their ragged breaths echoed against the damp stone walls of the cave. Phoenix pressed her back against the jagged surface, struggling to catch her breath. Every muscle in her leg screamed in pain, but the sharp ache in her chest—the fear gnawing at her insides—was far worse. They had narrowly escaped Malakos, but she knew it wasn't over.

Ro crouched beside her, his face set in grim determination. The light-hearted sarcasm that usually colored his words had vanished, replaced by a seriousness that only made the fear worse.

Jax stood near the entrance of the cave, his weapon drawn, scanning the surrounding darkness for any sign of movement. The low rumble of Malakos's growl still echoed in her ears. His threatening promises still lingered in her mind.

Phoenix shuddered, her heart pounding as she stared at the blackness outside the cave. She could feel the connection, the pull between her and Malakos, growing stronger with every breath she took. It was as if he were standing just beyond the entrance, waiting to claim her.

"We can't stay here long," Jax muttered, his voice low and urgent. "He'll find us."

Phoenix nodded, though her mind was racing. They had nowhere to run. The cave offered temporary refuge, but Malakos was relentless. His presence pressed against the boundaries of the darkness, creeping closer with every second.

Ro glanced at her, his brow furrowed in concern. "How's the leg holding up?"

"Barely," Phoenix admitted, her voice strained.

Ro's hand brushed hers in a small gesture of comfort, but before either of them could say anything more, a rustle in the dark caught their attention. Phoenix's heart leapt into her throat, and her hand instinctively tightened around her weapon. Jax stepped forward, his eyes narrowing as he raised his blade.

A figure emerged from the shadows.

"Mira."

The name slipped from Phoenix's lips before she could fully register what she was seeing. Mira stood before them, her face pale, her clothes torn, and her eyes gleaming with something unreadable. The dim light of the cave cast harsh shadows across her features, but it was unmistakably her.

"Mira?" Ro's voice was laced with disbelief, his hand hovering near his blade. "What the hell are you doing here?"

Mira stepped forward, her movements calm, deliberate. She scanned the group, her face unreadable, her eyes sharp.

"I was tracking you," she said, her voice unsettlingly steady. "Malakos is getting closer. We don't have much time."

Jax's face darkened, his grip tightening on his weapon. "You've got some nerve showing up here after everything."

Phoenix's stomach churned with a mixture of anger and confusion. After all Mira had done—the secrets, the lies—how could she dare to return now? Yet, something in Mira's eyes stopped her from snapping immediately. There was a calm control in the way she stood, as though she had planned this moment all along.

"I didn't come to fight," Mira said, her gaze briefly locking with Phoenix's. "I came to finish this."

"Finish?" Ro echoed, his voice incredulous. "The last time you tried to 'help,' we nearly died."

Mira's eyes flickered with something dark—regret, perhaps, or something far more dangerous—but it vanished as quickly as it appeared. "You weren't ready. None of you were." She turned her gaze back toward the cave entrance. "Now it's time."

Jax let out a low growl, stepping forward. "Why should we trust you now after everything you've done?"

Phoenix's chest tightened as she watched the exchange, raw emotion bubbling inside her. She wanted to scream at Mira, demand answers for everything—especially about Edward—but there was something off, something she couldn't yet place. Mira wasn't pleading for their trust. She was simply stating facts, as if the outcome had already been decided.

Mira's gaze settled on Phoenix, colder now. "Because if you don't, you'll die."

The words fell heavy, like stones sinking into the silence. Phoenix could feel Ro tense beside her, and even Jax seemed momentarily unsure of what to say. They all knew the danger they were facing. Malakos was out there, closing in. And no matter how much they hated it, Mira might be their only chance at survival.

Phoenix swallowed the lump in her throat, her voice shaky as she finally spoke. "What do you know about Malakos?"

Mira's lips twitched into something almost like a smile, but it never reached her eyes. "More than you think."

"What's that supposed to mean?" Jax demanded, stepping closer.

Mira met his gaze with a calm that was unsettling. "He's connected to Edward. That's why he's drawn to you, Phoenix. It's not just about hunting you down. It's deeper than that."

The words hit Phoenix like a punch to the gut. She had suspected it, felt the connection between Malakos and her brother, but hearing it confirmed made the truth all the more unbearable.

Jax's jaw clenched. "How do we stop him?"

Mira's eyes flicked between them, her expression unreadable. "There's a way. But it won't be easy. There's a place, hidden deep in the forest—a place where it all began. The device there can sever the connection between Edward and Malakos."

"The device?" Phoenix repeated, her voice thick with suspicion. "You've known about this the whole time?"

Mira's gaze dropped for a moment, but when she met Phoenix's eyes again, her expression was resolute. "I didn't think it would come to this. I didn't want it to. But now… there's no other choice."

Ro's laugh was bitter. "Convenient, isn't it? You wait until we're cornered to tell us your grand plan."

Mira straightened, her expression hard. "It's the only way."

Phoenix's mind raced. The heart of the forest? A device? It all sounded like some far-off, impossible task. But what choice did they have? She glanced at Ro, who gave a small, reluctant nod.

"Alright," she hesitated, her voice filled with determination despite the fear gnawing at her insides. "We'll follow your plan, Mira. But if this goes wrong, it's on you."

Mira's lips curled into that almost-smile again, her eyes flicking to the dark forest ahead. "Don't worry. It won't go wrong."

Jax stepped forward, his expression still hard, but there was a grudging acceptance in his eyes. "You better not be lying to us, Mira."

"I'm not," she said quietly, though something about her tone made Phoenix's stomach twist.

They were placing their trust—however fragile—in Mira. And the path ahead was filled with danger.

"Let's move," Jax ordered, his voice steely. "We don't have much time."

As they gathered their things and prepared to leave the cave, Phoenix couldn't shake the feeling that things were about to get far more complicated. Mira's return had changed everything, and whatever secrets she was still keeping felt darker, more twisted than before.

They moved quickly, their steps echoing softly against the cave walls. Phoenix kept her eyes forward, her mind racing as she tried to process everything that had happened. Mira's sudden reappearance had thrown everything into chaos.

Part of her wanted to trust Mira—to believe that she had come back to help—but the other part, the part still stinging from the betrayal, couldn't let go of the anger that simmered beneath the surface.

Ro walked beside her, his hand brushing against hers occasionally as they navigated the dark cave passages. The tension between them was palpable, unspoken but heavy. Phoenix could feel Ro's distrust of Mira radiating off him like heat, but he kept his voice low, his steps steady.

Mira led the way, her movements quick and deliberate, as though she knew exactly where they were headed. The flicker of light from Jax's torch danced off the stone walls, casting long shadows that seemed to stretch out and twist with every turn. Phoenix's leg still ached, but she pushed the pain to the back of her mind, focusing on the task at hand.

They hadn't spoken much since leaving the chamber, the silence hanging over them like a suffocating blanket. Phoenix's thoughts were still whirling, her mind racing with questions—questions about Edward, about Malakos, and about Mira's true motives. She wanted to believe that Mira had come back for the right reasons, but after everything they had been through, trust didn't come easily.

As they moved deeper into the forest, the darkness seemed to close in around them, thick and oppressive. Phoenix's skin prickled, and she couldn't shake the feeling that they were walking into something far more dangerous than even Malakos.

As the tension thickened in the clearing, Phoenix's pulse quickened. There was no more running, no more time for doubts. The ancient tree before them, twisted with age and steeped in an aura that sent chills down her spine, loomed like a monument to something dark and powerful. Mira stood close to the pedestal, her eyes cold and calculating, the flicker of something unreadable in their depths.

"Get ready," Jax murmured, his voice low but steady, fingers tightening on the hilt of his weapon.

Ro remained at Phoenix's side, a silent force of support, his presence grounding her as the atmosphere seemed to darken around them. Mira, however, exuded a growing sense of control—almost as if this was exactly where she wanted them to be.

Phoenix's heart was racing, her thoughts swirling with everything that had led to this moment. She couldn't ignore the betrayal that still simmered under the surface, but the reality of Malakos' imminent arrival overshadowed any immediate outburst. They had no other choice but to trust Mira—for now.

Mira knelt beside the pedestal, fingers brushing over its weathered stone surface. "When Malakos steps into this clearing, the device will activate. The energy coursing through it will sever his connection to Edward. It has to be now, before he gets too strong."

The words struck Phoenix like a hammer. The way Mira spoke, there was an unsettling confidence—a control that felt too rehearsed. But there was no time to question it. Malakos was coming.

Jax straightened, his jaw tight. "Let's hope you're right."

Suddenly, a low rumble echoed through the trees—a sound Phoenix knew all too well. Malakos was near. She could feel the connection surging within her, a dark pull that twisted at her insides, growing more intense with every breath.

The forest seemed to hold its breath as Malakos emerged from the shadows, his form towering and monstrous, yet beneath the twisted features, Phoenix could still see traces of Edward—the brother she had tried so hard to protect. His eyes glowed with an unnatural light, and the ground seemed to tremble beneath his steps.

"Phoenix…" Malakos's voice was a guttural snarl, laced with an eerie familiarity that sent shivers down her spine. "You can't stop this."

Phoenix clenched her fists, her heart aching at the sight of him. The connection between them throbbed like a raw wound, but she forced herself to stand firm. "Edward, if you're still in there, fight him. Please."

A flicker of recognition passed through Malakos's eyes, but it was gone in an instant, replaced by the dark, predatory hunger that had consumed him.

Mira's voice rang out, clear and commanding. "Now!"

The ancient tree trembled as the device beneath it came to life, a low hum filling the air. A pulse of energy shot out from the pedestal, striking Malakos square in the chest. He roared in pain, the sound echoing through the clearing as the force of the blast staggered him.

For a moment, hope surged in Phoenix's chest. Maybe this would work. Maybe they could save Edward after all.

But then, something changed.

The energy pulsing from the pedestal began to warp, the air around it crackling with an ominous power. Malakos staggered back, but he didn't fall. Instead, his twisted form seemed to absorb the energy, growing stronger, more solid.

Mira's expression shifted, her eyes narrowing in frustration. She stepped back from the pedestal, her hands trembling. "It should have worked. Why isn't it working?"

Jax cursed under his breath, readying his weapon as Malakos let out another roar, this time not of pain but of triumph.

"Mira!" Phoenix shouted, her voice tinged with panic. "What's happening?"

Mira's eyes darted between Malakos and the device, her face pale. "I don't know. It's not supposed to—"

And then it clicked for Phoenix. Mira's confidence, her insistence that this was the only way to stop Malakos—it had all been part of her plan. But not to save Edward.

It was never about saving Edward.

"You wanted this," Phoenix whispered, the realization dawning on her. "You wanted control over him."

Mira's gaze met Phoenix's, and for a split second, the truth was written clearly in her eyes. But then her expression hardened. "It doesn't matter now. I can still stop him."

But Phoenix knew better. The device had done nothing but strengthen Malakos, feeding his connection to the darkness. And Mira had known it all along.

Malakos let out a bone-chilling laugh, the sound reverberating through the forest. "You think you can control me, Mira? I'm beyond your reach now."

Phoenix stepped forward, her voice shaking with fury. "You used us! You used Edward!"

Mira's expression was unreadable, but there was no denying the truth now. She had manipulated them from the start, driven by a hunger for power that went beyond anything Phoenix could have imagined.

Ro tightened his grip on his weapon, his gaze flicking between Mira and Malakos. "We need to get out of here, Phoenix. This isn't going to end well."

Jax moved closer, his jaw clenched in anger. "We finish this, or we die trying."

Before they could act, Mira made her move.
With a sudden, fluid motion, she stepped toward the pedestal, her hands moving quickly over the device. The energy surrounding the clearing intensified, the air humming with power as the ground beneath them trembled.

"I'll show you what true control looks like," Mira hissed, her voice dripping with malice.

Phoenix's heart pounded in her chest as she realized what Mira was about to do. She wasn't just trying to stop Malakos—she was going to unleash something far worse.

"Stop her!" Ro shouted, lunging toward Mira, but it was too late.

A blinding flash of light erupted from the pedestal, engulfing the clearing in a pulse of raw energy. Phoenix felt the ground shift beneath her feet, her body thrown backward as the force of the blast hit her.

The last thing she saw before darkness consumed her was Mira's face, twisted in triumph, and Malakos, standing tall and unstoppable.

23

Revelations in the Aftermath

Phoenix gasped for breath, the world tilting around her as she struggled to rise. Every part of her body throbbed, the blast's force leaving her bruised and battered.

The once-pristine clearing had become a wasteland of smoke and ruin. A charred remnant of the ancient tree stood in the center, its twisted roots smoking, while the air pulsed with a strange, unsettling energy - something far more sinister than the explosion itself.

"Ro! Jax!" Phoenix's voice cracked as she pulled herself to her knees, her heart pounding in fear. Her vision swam, and she could barely make out their shapes through the haze.

A low groan caught her attention. She turned to see Ro lying a few feet away, coughing and struggling to sit up. His face was streaked with blood and dirt, but he was alive.

"I'm here," Ro rasped, wobbling as he stood and limped toward her. "What the hell just happened?"
Phoenix shook her head, trying to piece together the fragments of memory.

"Mira… she used the device. I don't know what it did, but -"
Her words faltered as she spotted Jax in the distance, near the tree line, clutching his side as he rose. He looked beaten, but he was still standing.

"Mira's gone," Jax growled, his face dark with pain and frustration. "And so is Malakos."

Phoenix's heart dropped. She whipped her gaze to the shattered stone pedestal, now reduced to rubble. Mira and Malakos had vanished. Not dead - she could feel it deep in her bones - but gone. Their presence had been ripped from this place, and an even darker shadow had taken its place.

A cold, crawling sensation wrapped around her spine. They weren't dead. Mira had taken Malakos somewhere else. Somewhere worse.

"We need to figure out what just happened," Phoenix said, her voice tightening with urgency. "This wasn't some last-minute move. Mira planned this. We were nothing but pieces on her board."

Ro wiped blood from his brow, fury flickering in his eyes. "That manipulative -" He stopped short, fists clenching. "So, what do we do now?"

Phoenix stood, testing her leg, the pain still sharp but manageable. She scanned the wreckage, the enormity of everything pressing on her chest. Mira hadn't just escaped. She had escalated everything. And whatever she intended for Malakos, it was only the beginning.

Jax limped over, his expression dark. "Mira always wanted control of Malakos. It was never about survival - it was always about power." He spat blood onto the ground, his jaw tight. "She wants more than that. Something tied to Project Genesis. I should've seen it coming."

Phoenix's mind raced. She could still feel that strange energy - a lingering remnant of whatever Mira had unleashed. She swallowed, her voice shaking. "What does she want with Malakos? What could Project Genesis have to do with this?"
Jax's face hardened, shadows crossing his features. He looked like a man haunted by too many secrets.

"Our father warned me - Mira was always obsessed with control. She'd do anything to command the Lost and the creatures they became. Project Genesis wasn't meant for destruction, it was designed to contain the mutations after the Collapse. But Mira..." He exhaled sharply. "She sees it as her key to reshaping the world."

Phoenix's stomach churned. The threat wasn't just Malakos. Mira's ambitions stretched beyond anything they could have anticipated.

"We can't let her succeed," Phoenix whispered, determination hardening her voice. "If she controls Malakos, if she controls the Lost… it's over."

Ro stepped closer, his face grim. "But how? We don't even know where she went. We're in the dark here."

Jax wiped his lip and nodded. "There's a place… a hidden facility where Mira first got the device. It's tied to Project Genesis. If we can find it, we might have a chance to stop her."

Phoenix locked eyes with Ro. His skepticism was apparent, but beneath it, the weight of the situation couldn't be ignored. They had no choice. "Then we go," she said firmly. We find this facility, and we end this—whatever it takes."

Jax nodded. "It's not far. But we'll need to stay sharp. Mira's not stopping, and Malakos, he will be more dangerous than we've ever seen."

As they turned to leave the ruined clearing, Phoenix felt something shift inside her—a dark flicker, like a shadow pressing against her thoughts. The pull toward Malakos had grown stronger and more distinct. She could still feel Edward, deep within the creature, or what was left of him.

He's still there. Somewhere. Her heart twisted painfully, but she stayed silent. For now, they had to focus. Surviving came first. And as they plunged deeper into the unknown, Phoenix steeled herself. This wasn't over—not by a long shot.

The forest closed around them as they moved further away from the clearing, the trees thicker, the air more oppressive. The silence was suffocating, broken only by the crunch of leaves underfoot and the occasional wind rustle through the gnarled branches. Each step felt heavier from exhaustion and the weight of what lay ahead.

Phoenix's thoughts drifted back to Edward, the brother she had spent so long trying to protect. She had failed him—Malakos had taken him.

Yet, despite the overwhelming sense of loss, she couldn't shake the strange connection she still felt. It was like an invisible thread tied between them, pulling tighter with every step she took.

"Phoenix…"

The voice was faint and distant but unmistakable. She froze, her breath catching in her throat.

Ro stopped beside her, his face tense with worry. "What is it?"

She hesitated, glancing around the darkened forest. "I heard him. I think I heard Edward."

Ro frowned, his hand gripping the hilt of his weapon tighter. "You sure it's not, you know, him?"

Phoenix swallowed hard, her heart pounding in her chest. The voice had been soft and desperate like Edward was calling out to her from somewhere deep within the darkness that had consumed him. But was it real, or was it just another trick?

"I don't know."

Before she could say more, Jax motioned for them to keep moving. "We don't have time to stop. Whatever you're hearing, we'll figure it out at the facility. We need to get there before Mira does something worse."

Phoenix clenched her fists, forcing herself to keep moving, even as Edward's voice echoed in her mind.

"I need you…"

Her heart shattered at the sound of his broken voice. She knew she couldn't trust it—she knew it could be Malakos playing on her emotions. But what if it wasn't? What if Edward was still in there, fighting, begging for her help?

I won't abandon you, Edward. I won't let you go.

She quickened her pace, her resolve hardening. Whatever Mira was planning, whatever she had done to Malakos, Phoenix wouldn't stop until she found a way to save him. She owed Edward that much.

They moved in silence for what felt like hours, the thick canopy overhead blotting out what little moonlight remained. The deeper they went, the colder the air became, and the forest seemed to press in closer, the shadows twisting into unnatural shapes. Every now and then, Phoenix swore she could hear the faint sound of Edward's voice—soft, pleading, and always just out of reach.

Finally, after what seemed like an eternity, Jax stopped, pointing ahead through the trees. "There. The facility."
Phoenix squinted through the darkness, her breath catching as she spotted the faint outline of a structure deep within the woods. It was an ancient building, overgrown with vines and hidden beneath layers of moss and decay. It looked abandoned, but the faint hum of machinery emanating from inside told a different story.

"Stay close," Jax whispered, his voice low and tense. "We don't know what we're walking into."

As they approached the entrance, Phoenix's chest tightened. The pull inside her was stronger now, a deep, unsettling sensation that made her skin prickle. Whatever was inside that facility was tied to Malakos—and to Edward.

Jax pressed his hand against the rusted door, and with a groan, it swung open, revealing a narrow corridor beyond. The air inside was stifling, thick with dust and decay. Faint lights flickered overhead, casting eerie shadows along the walls.

Phoenix swallowed the lump in her throat and stepped inside, her pulse quickening with each step.

Phoenix knew it was only the beginning of whatever awaited them in the depths of that facility.

The facility's narrow corridor stretched ahead, a labyrinth of rusted metal and peeling paint. The walls seemed to close in as they walked, each step echoing in the oppressive silence. Phoenix's breath came in shallow bursts, her heart thudding painfully against her chest. The closer they got to the core of this place, the stronger the pull became—an almost unbearable tug at the center of her being.

"I don't like this," Ro muttered under his breath, his voice barely more than a whisper. "It feels… off."

Phoenix couldn't disagree. Something was deeply wrong with this place, lurking just beneath the surface. It felt alive, almost sentient, watching them with cold, unblinking eyes.

Jax led the way, his movements slow and deliberate as he scanned the hallway ahead. "Stay sharp. Whatever Mira's done, it's not going to be obvious. She's too smart for that."

They moved deeper into the facility, passing doorways that led into darkened rooms filled with broken machinery and scattered debris. Phoenix's nerves were on edge, and every creak of the floor beneath their feet sent a jolt of adrenaline through her veins.

Then, they reached a large chamber.

The room was vast, and the ceiling high above them was lined with rows of malfunctioning lights that flickered sporadically. Strange, translucent pods were scattered across the floor. Many of them cracked open, spilling their contents onto the ground. Phoenix's stomach churned at the sight—remnants of twisted, mutated creatures, long dead but still horrifying in their deformity.

"What the hell happened here?" Ro asked, his eyes wide with shock.

"Project Genesis," Jax muttered, his voice grim. "This happens when you try to play god with nature."

Phoenix swallowed hard, her eyes scanning the room for any movement. The pull inside her chest was unbearable now, like a hook embedded deep in her heart, dragging her forward. She could feel Malakos—feel Edward—somewhere close. But there was something else too, something darker, something dangerous.

"We're close," she whispered, her voice barely audible.

Jax nodded, his gaze sharp. "We need to keep moving. Mira won't be far."

As they moved toward the chamber's far end, the air grew colder, thick with the scent of decay and something more metallic. Phoenix's fingers twitched, her instincts screaming that something was terribly wrong.

Then, out of the corner of her eye, she saw a flash of movement, quick and almost imperceptible, slipping through the shadows at the far end of the room.

"Did you see that?" Phoenix whispered urgently.

Jax nodded, his jaw clenched. "Stay alert."

They moved cautiously, their eyes darting to every corner of the room, but the shadows were thick, obscuring whatever had just darted through them. The tension was suffocating, each breath more difficult than the last as they approached the source of the movement.

Then, the lights flickered and dimmed utterly, plunging the room into darkness.

Phoenix's heart pounded in her chest. She strained her ears, listening for any sound—any movement—but there was nothing but the eerie silence of the facility.

Then, from the darkness, came the whisper.

"Phoenix…"

Her blood ran cold. It was Edward's voice, but something was wrong with it—something distorted, as if it was coming from a great distance or through a broken speaker.

"I'm here," she whispered, her voice shaking. "Edward, I'm here." The silence stretched on for what felt like an eternity. Then, the voice came again, soft and broken.

"Help me…"

Phoenix's breath hitched in her throat. She could feel him—he was so close, but she didn't know if she could trust the voice. Was it Edward? Or was it Malakos using him to lure her in?

"We need to go," Ro whispered, gripping her arm. "Now."

But Phoenix couldn't move. She was frozen, the pull inside her chest stronger than ever, her connection to Edward pulling her deeper into the darkness. She had to find him. She had to save him.

"Phoenix, please…"

The desperation in his voice was undeniable, and before she could stop herself, she took a step toward the voice, toward Edward.

Toward Malakos.

Phoenix's heart raced as she stepped closer, her eyes straining to see through the dim light. The figure slowly turned toward them, and she drew in a sharp breath.

Malakos's hulking form twisted and loomed in the shadows, his eyes glowing with an evil light. Yet beneath the darkness, deep within, Phoenix could feel something—someone—fighting. It wasn't Edward's body standing there—but Edward's mind trapped inside.

She wasn't looking at Malakos anymore. She was searching for her brother, any trace of him she could find.

Malakos's cold, cruel smile spread across his distorted face. His deep and grating voice rumbled from within. "Edward is gone. He belongs to me now."

Phoenix's heart clenched painfully. She knew this truth, but hearing it in Malakos's voice made it unbearable. Edward's body was gone, consumed by Malakos, but his consciousness—his mind—was still trapped inside this monster. She could feel it, a faint presence clawing for freedom. The connection between them hadn't severed; it had only changed.

"I can help you!" Phoenix called out, her voice desperate. "I know you're still in there, Edward. Fight him—fight Malakos!"

For a brief second, Malakos's expression faltered. His eyes flickered, and his cruel grin wavered. It was subtle, but Phoenix saw it—felt it. Edward was fighting. His consciousness was struggling inside Malakos, trying to break free.

"You think he can fight me?" Malakos growled, his voice like ice. "He's weak. His mind is barely a whisper in mine."

Ro stepped forward, his weapon raised. "We're not leaving without him."

Malakos's smile returned sharper than before. "You're too late. I will soon swallow Edward's mind, as his body already was."

Phoenix felt the connection between her and Edward pulse painfully, like a dying ember flickering in the dark. She could still feel him, faint and distant, but there. He wasn't gone yet.

"You're wrong!" Phoenix shouted, stepping forward, her voice fierce. "Edward is still there. I know it. He's still fighting, and I won't let you take him!"

Malakos snarled, but as his body tensed, his glowing eyes flickered again—just for a moment. And in that moment, Phoenix felt him.

Edward. Trapped, buried deep within Malakos's mind, but fighting for control. She could feel his desperation, his pain, and his resolve.

"Phoenix…" Edward's voice whispered in her mind, weak but present. "I'm here…"

Her breath caught in her throat, and tears filled her eyes. Edward's consciousness was still alive, battling against the darkness of Malakos's mind, but she knew time was running out. The longer Edward remained trapped, the harder it would be to save him.

"We need to hurry," Phoenix whispered to Ro, her heart aching. "Edward's still in there, but we're losing him."

Phoenix's heart pounded as the tension in the air thickened. Malakos's twisted form loomed before her, his eyes glowing with that eerie light, but beneath the monstrous exterior, she could still sense Edward's presence—a faint, fragile thread tying them together. She knew they were running out of time.

"We need a plan," Ro whispered, his eyes darting between Malakos and Phoenix. His grip on his weapon tightened, but even he seemed unsure of what they could do.

Phoenix took a shaky breath, her mind racing. Edward was still trapped in Malakos's mind, but how could she free him? There had to be a way to reach him. She had fought through impossible odds before, but this was different—this was her brother, bound to a creature more powerful and terrifying than anything she had ever faced.

"You're going to lose him," Malakos hissed, his voice grating and sharp. He stepped closer, his massive frame casting a long, dark shadow over them. "The longer you wait, the less of Edward remains."

Phoenix's heart clenched. "No," she whispered, her voice shaking but determined. "I'm not losing him."

Without thinking, Phoenix reached out with her mind, focusing on her connection with Edward. It was weak, buried deep within the darkness of Malakos's mind, but it was there. She felt the bond between them pulse, faint but persistent as if Edward were calling out to her, struggling to hold on.

"Edward," she whispered through the link, closing her eyes. "I'm here. You have to fight him. I need you to come back to me."

The air around them seemed to grow heavier, charged with the moment's tension. Ro stood beside her, ready for anything, while Jax remained a few paces behind, his eyes cold and calculating as he watched the interaction unfold.

For a brief moment, the glow in Malakos's eyes flickered. His body jerked slightly, and Phoenix felt the connection between her and Edward grow stronger. She could feel him fighting, pushing against the darkness that threatened to swallow him whole.

"Phoenix…" The voice in her mind was weak with exhaustion and pain, but it was unmistakably Edward.

Phoenix's breath hitched. "You're still there," she whispered, her voice cracking with emotion. "Keep fighting, Edward. Don't let him take you."

But then, with a low growl, Malakos straightened, his face contorted with fury. "Enough!" he roared, his voice echoing through the chamber. The flicker of Edward's consciousness seemed to recede, buried once again beneath Malakos's malevolent force.

Phoenix's hope wavered, but she couldn't let go. She had to keep fighting for him—for Edward.

Malakos advanced toward her, his massive claws gleaming in the dim light. "You think you can save him?" He sneered. "You're just a girl with false hope. Edward belongs to me now."

Ro stepped in front of Phoenix, his weapon raised, ready to defend her at any cost. "We'll see about that," he growled, his voice low and dangerous.

But Phoenix didn't move. She kept her eyes locked on Malakos, reaching deeper into her connection with Edward. There had to be a way to break through the darkness, to bring her brother back, but how? Her mind raced, searching for a solution, even as Malakos closed in.

Just then, a thought sparked in her mind. The facility. The device. Mira had used something to gain control of Malakos, to merge his mind with Edward's. If she could find that device, she could reverse it.

"Ro," she whispered, her voice barely audible, "I think I know how to save him."

Ro glanced at her, his brow furrowing. "What do you mean?"

"There's a device—Mira used it to merge them. If we can find it, we might be able to break the connection to get Edward out of Malakos's mind."

Ro's eyes widened slightly, and he nodded. "Then we need to find it. Fast."

But Malakos was already too close. His massive claws swiped through the air, forcing them to dodge and retreat. The ground shook beneath their feet as the creature bellowed, its voice filled with malice and rage.

"We don't have much time," Phoenix muttered, her eyes darting around the chamber for any sign of the device. "We need to split up— one of us has to distract him while the other finds the device."

Ro didn't hesitate. "I'll handle the distraction. You find that device and get your brother back."

Phoenix nodded, her heart racing as she prepared to run. Ro charged forward, firing his weapon at Malakos, who roared in fury as the shots pinged off his armored hide. It was enough to buy Phoenix a few precious seconds.

She took off, darting toward the chamber's far end, hoping the device would be hidden. As she ran, she could still feel the connection between her and Edward—faint, flickering, but alive. She wasn't too late. Not yet.

But the clock was ticking.

24

Into the Depths

Malakos's enraged roars echoed behind Phoenix as she dashed down the darkened corridor. Every step felt like it was carrying her further away from Edward—and deeper into something unknown.

The shadows in the facility seemed to shift, alive in their silence, as if watching her every move. The pull inside her chest—the link to Edward—burned hotter now, urging her closer to him. How much time did she have before Malakos completely consumed him?

Her breath came in ragged gasps as she turned a sharp corner, stumbling briefly on the debris across the floor.

Ahead, the passageway opened into another vast chamber similar to the one they had just fought in. This one, however, was lined with rows of glowing terminals, each flickering with information Phoenix couldn't yet decipher.

She scanned the room quickly, her heart pounding. The device had to be here. It just had to be.

Behind her, she could still hear the heavy sounds of Malakos fighting Ro. The ground trembled slightly, a clear indication of the intensity of the battle. There was little time.

Phoenix moved toward the chamber's center, eyes darting from one terminal to the next. The blue glow of the screens reflected off the cold metal walls, casting eerie shadows that seemed to stretch out, reaching for her. She swallowed hard and forced herself to focus.

Then, amidst the glow, she saw it. A central console stood out from the others, as it was more extensive and complex. Wires ran from it to the floor, snaking across the room like veins leading to the heart of the facility. On the screen, a diagram of a figure was displayed—two figures, in fact—intertwined. One was human, the other monstrous, like a grotesque shadow of the other.

It was Edward. And Malakos.

"This is it," Phoenix whispered to herself, rushing toward the console. Her fingers hovered over the keys, her mind racing. How do I use this?

She had no time to hesitate. Her hands moved instinctively, tapping at the interface as she searched for anything that could sever the connection between Edward and Malakos.

Come on, come on...

The screen flashed red, and an ominous hum filled the room. Phoenix's heart jumped. Did she trigger something? Was she too late?

A deep, distorted voice echoed from the speakers above. "Intruder detected. Connection stability at risk. Proceed with caution."

Phoenix froze, fear creeping up her spine. The hum grew louder, and the red light on the screen pulsed, synchronized with the beat of her heart. She clenched her fists. She couldn't let this stop her. Not now.

With a deep breath, Phoenix resumed her frantic search, her hands moving faster over the console. She scanned the commands on the screen, her eyes narrowing as she finally found what she was looking for—Severance Protocol.

Her fingers trembled as she selected the Severance Protocol. The screen flickered, and the hum in the room intensified, vibrating through the floor beneath her feet. A small progress bar appeared, slowly filling as the system worked to disconnect the bond between Edward and Malakos.

This was it. This was her chance to save him.

Behind her, the roars of Malakos grew louder. Ro's grunts and the sounds of the struggle echoed down the corridor. She couldn't afford to lose focus—not now.

The progress bar crawled forward, but it felt agonizingly slow. Phoenix clenched her fists, her pulse quickening as a voice—Edward's—whispered in her mind again.

"Phoenix… please…"

Her heart ached at the sound of his desperation. He was still there, fighting, but for how much longer? She glanced over her shoulder, anxiety gnawing at her.

The battle between Ro and Malakos raged on, the creature's fury shaking the facility's walls. Phoenix had to hurry.

The progress bar moved closer to completion but needed to be faster.

Suddenly, the ground shook violently, and Phoenix stumbled, catching herself against the console. A roar—fierce and guttural—echoed through the chamber, and she knew, without turning, that Malakos was coming.

Her time was running out.

The console beeped, and Phoenix's eyes snapped back to the screen. The Severance Protocol was at 90%. Almost there.

"Come on, come on…" she muttered under her breath, her fingers hovering over the controls, ready to act the moment it finished.

Another roar reverberated through the walls, louder and closer this time. Malakos was no longer just a distant threat—he was coming for her. She could feel the air grow heavier, charged with his presence.

93%…

Phoenix's heart pounded in her chest, adrenaline surging through her veins. She could practically feel his malevolent energy approaching like a storm closing in. She had to make this work—sever Edward from this nightmare before Malakos reached her.

The console beeped again.

96%…

Suddenly, the doorway behind her exploded into a shower of sparks and debris as Malakos's massive frame barreled through. His glowing eyes locked onto Phoenix, burning with an intense rage. His twisted, monstrous form filled the entrance, and he let out a roar that shook the ground beneath her feet.

"PHOENIX!" Malakos's deep and unnatural voice boomed through the chamber, reverberating off the metal walls. It was a voice laced with fury and agony.

Phoenix froze, her eyes widening in terror, but her hand still hovered over the console. The bar was nearly complete—just a few more seconds.

"Leave him alone!" She shouted, defiance ringing in her voice. "He's not yours!"

Malakos stepped forward, the floor shaking beneath his weight. His claws extended, gleaming menacingly in the flickering light. "He belongs to me now," the creature growled, his voice filled with cold certainty.

But Phoenix didn't waver. She couldn't. Not when she was so close.

99%…

"Not for long," she whispered.

With a final, resounding beep, the progress bar reached 100%, and the Severance Protocol activated. The lights in the room flickered violently, and the hum that had filled the air abruptly intensified, turning into a high-pitched whine. Phoenix slammed her hand onto the Execute button.

A surge of energy pulsed through the room, centered on Malakos. The creature howled in pain, jerking violently as if struck by an invisible force. His glowing eyes flared, and for the briefest of moments, Phoenix saw something else—Edward. His face flickered within the monstrous form, desperate, reaching.

"Phoenix…" Edward's voice, raw with emotion, pierced through the cacophony.

Phoenix's breath caught in her throat. "Edward!"

But then, just as quickly, the image of Edward vanished, and Malakos roared again—his fury redoubled. The severance had weakened him, but it hadn't fully broken him. He was still in control, still dangerous.

"YOU THINK YOU CAN STOP ME?" Malakos snarled, his voice deeper, darker, and more monstrous than before. He stumbled forward, but his movements were sluggish, unsteady. The severance had worked—partially. The bond was damaged but not completely severed.

Phoenix backed away from the console, her heart racing. She needed to finish this, but she wasn't sure how. Malakos still had Edward, still had control over his brother's mind.

And there was little time.

Before Phoenix could act, Ro came barreling into the room, bloodied but determined, his weapon raised. "Phoenix! Get back!" he shouted, charging toward Malakos with reckless determination.

Phoenix hesitated for a split second, torn between helping Ro and staying by the console. But then Malakos lunged, his massive claws swinging toward Ro with deadly force.

"No!" Phoenix cried out, rushing toward them as the battle between Ro and Malakos intensified again.

Malakos roared, his eyes blazing with fury as he fought against the damage the Severance Protocol had inflicted on him. He was slower now, weaker, but still a formidable threat. Ro ducked and weaved, barely avoiding the creature's strikes.

Phoenix's mind raced, searching for a solution. There had to be another way—to finish what she had started and free Edward once and for all.

And then it hit her.

The console wasn't the only way. If the bond between Edward and Malakos had been damaged but not entirely severed, then maybe— just maybe—she could reach Edward through the connection they still shared. It was risky and could cost her everything, but it was the only chance she had left.

With a deep breath, Phoenix closed her eyes and reached out with her mind, focusing on the bond between her and Edward, which had never fully disappeared. She pushed past the fear, pain, and uncertainty and called out to him.

Edward…

There was nothing but darkness for a moment, a vast, empty void where Edward should have been. But then, faintly, she felt it - him. A flicker of consciousness buried deep within the monstrous presence of Malakos.

Phoenix…

His voice was weak, but it was him. He was still there.

I'm coming for you, Phoenix whispered through the bond. Hold on.

Malakos roared, sensing the intrusion, and lashed out wildly, but Phoenix stood firm. She wasn't backing down. Not now.

Edward, fight him. You're stronger than this.

She felt his hesitation, his fear, but also his determination. And slowly, ever so slowly, the darkness around him began to peel away.

Phoenix's eyes snapped open, filled with a renewed sense of hope. Malakos was weakening. Edward was fighting back.

But the battle wasn't over yet.

(25)

The Confrontation

The chamber trembled as Malakos advanced, his hulking form casting long shadows over the broken, cold metal floor. Phoenix stood near the console, her heart racing, the Severance Protocol still fresh in her mind. It had weakened him, but not enough. Malakos was still tethered to Edward, still dangerous, and she couldn't stop now. Edward was fighting back, but Malakos's grip remained firm.

Behind her, Mira appeared at the far end of the room, her eyes wild with desperation. She wasn't the powerful figure Phoenix had once thought. Now, Mira was cornered, her plans unraveling before her eyes. The flickering lights illuminated her sweat-drenched face, her clothes torn from the chaos of the facility's collapse.

"You did this," Mira spat, her voice low and venomous. You ruined everything!" Her eyes darted between Malakos and Phoenix, realization dawning. You severed the connection. I was so close to controlling him to controlling all of it."

Phoenix didn't answer. She focused on Malakos, feeling Edward's faint consciousness stirring within him.

Mira sneered, pulling out a curved blade from her belt, its edge gleaming in the dim light. "You won't stop me," she hissed, stepping toward Phoenix. "You think you're saving him? You're only delaying the inevitable."

Before Phoenix could respond, Ro lunged forward with a heavy staff he had picked up earlier, his muscles straining as he brought it down toward Mira. She ducked swiftly, spinning around and slicing at him with the blade. He narrowly avoided her strike, his face set with determination.

"Mira, stop!" Ro growled, parrying her next move with his staff. "You've lost. Look around you—this facility is crumbling."

But Mira wasn't listening. Her eyes burned with a crazed desperation as she fought, lashing out with wild ferocity. Phoenix moved out of the way, giving Ro room to handle her, but her gaze kept darting back to Malakos. The monstrous figure still stood, shaking off the effects of the Severance Protocol, watching with eerie calm as Mira fought for her life.

"Why do you fight for him?" Mira snarled at Phoenix, dodging Ro's strike. "You don't understand what Edward is! You never did."

Phoenix's chest tightened, her voice barely more than a whisper. "He's my brother."

Mira's face twisted with fury, and she lunged again, aiming directly at Phoenix. Before she could land a blow, a deep, rumbling growl filled the air.

Malakos moved faster than Phoenix had expected, his monstrous claws striking down between Mira and herself. The ground trembled under his weight as he roared, his eyes burning with hatred. He was no longer interested in toying with them—he was ready to destroy.

Mira staggered back, her eyes wide as she looked up at the creature she had once hoped to control. Fear crept into her expression for the first time, but a twisted grin quickly replaced it. "I made you," she hissed. "You are mine."

Malakos's response was a deep and reverberating snarl, but Phoenix felt a familiar presence beneath that sound. Edward.

She could see the struggle within the creature, Edward's consciousness fighting against Malakos's hold. His pain, his desperation, echoed through their connection, but he was still there. He was still fighting.

Mira's blade gleamed as she held it up defensively. "I can still fix this," she muttered, almost to herself. "I can still control him."

Malakos stepped closer, his massive form towering over her. His claws flexed, the tips sharp and glistening. Phoenix could see the hatred in his eyes—Malakos wouldn't spare her. He wasn't going to listen to her anymore.

"Malakos, no!" Mira shrieked, backing away, her voice cracking as fear overwhelmed her. She slashed wildly with her blade, but Malakos swatted it aside effortlessly. He grabbed her by the arm, lifting her into the air as if she weighed nothing.

Mira screamed, thrashing and kicking as his grip tightened. "You can't do this! I created you!"

Malakos said nothing. His eyes gleamed with cruel satisfaction as he tightened his grip further, crushing the bone beneath his claws. Mira's scream of agony tore through the room, raw and broken.

Phoenix watched, her breath caught in her throat. She had wanted to stop Mira, but this—this was brutal. Mira's suffering was visible on every inch of her face as Malakos squeezed, her body convulsing with pain.

Ro stepped forward, ready to intervene, but Phoenix held him back. "It's over," she whispered, though her voice trembled. "He's going to finish her."

Malakos roared once more, the sound shaking the very foundation of the facility. With one swift motion, he hurled Mira against the wall with a sickening crack. She crumpled to the ground, her body limp, her breath shallow as she tried to crawl away. Blood pooled beneath her, her defiance slipping away with every labored breath.

Still, she reached out, her fingers grasping for something—anything. Her eyes flickered with a desperate need to survive, but it was clear to everyone in the room, especially Phoenix, that Mira had lost. The fight was over.

Malakos loomed over her, his shadow consuming the room. He raised his clawed hand high, the final blow ready to strike.

"Edward," Phoenix called out, her voice breaking through the tension. She needed him to hear her, to stop Malakos before it was too late. "Edward, if you're still in there, you don't have to let this happen."

For a brief second, Malakos hesitated, his glowing eyes flickering, but the bloodlust was too strong. With a swift motion, his claws descended, slashing through Mira in one final, decisive blow. Her body went still, her suffering finally over.

Phoenix flinched at its brutality, her heart sinking. Edward was in there, but Malakos's grip was still too strong. She could feel him slipping away.

Malakos roared again, but this time, it wasn't the roar of triumph—it was the roar of a creature in agony, torn between the darkness and the light. Phoenix could feel the struggle within him, the war raging inside as Edward fought to reclaim control.

As Malakos stood over Mira's lifeless body, Phoenix stepped forward cautiously, her voice soft but determined. "Edward… I know you're still in there. Fight him. Please… fight."

The creature's eyes flickered again, and momentarily, Phoenix thought she saw Edward staring back at her. But then, just as quickly, the darkness returned. Malakos let out a final roar before turning and crashing through the facility's walls, disappearing into the night.

Phoenix collapsed to her knees, her chest heaving as the weight of what had just happened settled over her. Mira was dead, Malakos was still at large, and Edward—her brother—was lost somewhere inside that monster.

Ro knelt beside her, his hand resting on her shoulder.

"We'll get him back," he assured her. His voice was steady, though the exhaustion in his eyes was evident.

Phoenix swallowed hard, nodding though her heart was heavy with doubt. "I won't give up," she whispered. "I won't."

As the dust settled and the room fell into an eerie silence, the weight of their next steps loomed large. Mira's death had closed one chapter, but the battle for Edward's soul was far from over.

Phoenix's fingers dug into the cold metal floor as she remained on her knees, her mind spinning after everything that had just transpired. The air around her felt thick and oppressive like the weight of Malakos's rage and despair still lingered. Her breathing slowed, and for a moment, she allowed herself to close her eyes and breathe, trying to make sense of the whirlwind that had just consumed her life.

Edward is still in there.

The thought repeated over and over in her mind, like a lifeline she clung to, even as the world seemed to spiral out of control around her. Malakos's hulking form was still burned into her mind, and the brief flicker of Edward's consciousness flashed in his eyes, giving her hope. But hope was fragile now - distant and fleeting.

"He's still there," Phoenix whispered, her voice barely audible.

Ro stood silently beside her, his staff leaning against his leg as he wiped a streak of blood from his temple. His breath was ragged, but his focus hadn't wavered. He had seen what Malakos could do, the creature's raw power, and yet there was no sign of surrender in his posture. "We'll get him back, Phoenix," Ro repeated, but even he knew the road ahead would be steep, perhaps impossible.

"We need to go after him." Phoenix's voice cracked slightly as she rose shakily to her feet. Her legs trembled beneath her, the weight of her exhaustion threatening to pull her down again. But she stood firm, squaring her shoulders and brushing dirt and blood off her hands. "We can't let him get away."

Ro raised an eyebrow, concern flickering in his eyes. "Phoenix, we're both exhausted. We barely survived that and Malakos, he's still out there, still dangerous."

"I don't care." Her voice came out sharper than intended, but she meant every word. She turned toward Ro, meeting his gaze with a fierce determination. "I'm not leaving him. I don't care how dangerous Malakos is. Edward is my brother."

Ro exhaled slowly, running a hand through his messy hair. "And I'm with you, Phoenix. I just… I need a moment to think. We don't even know where Malakos has gone, and the facility—" He gestured to the cracked walls and sparking debris around them. "—is on the verge of collapse. We need to regroup."

Phoenix bit her lip, her mind screaming to charge after Malakos immediately, but her body ached with exhaustion, and she knew Ro was correct. They couldn't run after a creature like that without a plan. She turned and looked at Mira's broken body, slumped in the corner of the room, blood pooling around her motionless form. Her fingers still twitched faintly, though her eyes were empty, the glimmer of life snuffed out.

Phoenix stepped toward her, kneeling to examine the shattered remnants of the woman who had once controlled their fate. Mira's face, once so full of arrogance and power, now seemed small and hollow. Phoenix reached out, brushing her fingertips over the blade that had fallen from Mira's grip, now stained with her blood.

In her dying moments, Mira had reached for something more than power. She had tried to survive. But she had lost the very thing she thought she could control.

"You were wrong," Phoenix whispered, her voice soft as she looked at Mira's lifeless face. "You didn't understand Edward. You never did."

Ro approached cautiously, standing behind Phoenix as she rose to her feet once more. "She was consumed by her own ambition. In the end, she didn't care about anyone but herself."

Phoenix nodded, her jaw tight as she turned away from Mira's body. "And now she's gone… but Malakos… Edward… we're not done."

Ro's eyes softened. "I know. And we'll find him. But we can't do it alone." He placed a hand on her shoulder, the weight of his words hanging between them. "We need to think this through."

Phoenix swallowed hard, her eyes scanning the broken facility around them. "Mira knew more about Project Genesis than she let on. There must be something here that can help us understand what we're dealing with."

Ro nodded slowly, understanding her meaning. "You're right. Mira left clues, and this facility—there might be files, records, anything we can use to learn more about what's happened to Edward."

The urgency in Phoenix's chest was growing. Every second felt like an eternity as she imagined Malakos slipping further into the night, Edward's consciousness fighting to hold on. But she knew they couldn't just rush after him mindlessly. They needed answers.

"Let's search the place," Phoenix suggested, her voice steady but tinged with impatience. "We'll gather whatever we can and then go after him."

Ro agreed silently, and together, they moved through the facility's wreckage, their footsteps echoing through the hollow corridors. They passed rooms filled with shattered equipment and broken terminals, the remnants of Mira's grand experiment lying in ruins around them.

Phoenix's heart clenched as she approached a small, intact console in one of the back rooms. The screen flickered faintly, displaying a series of encrypted files. She stepped forward, her hands hovering over the interface. "There's something here…"

Ro stood beside her, his eyes narrowing as he examined the screen. "Can you get it open?"

Phoenix nodded, her fingers working quickly to bypass the encryption. Suddenly, the screen flashed, and a series of images appeared—blueprints, research notes, and, most chillingly, files labeled Subject 001: Edward and Subject 002: Malakos.

Her breath caught in her throat as she clicked on the files. The information was overwhelming—project data on genetic manipulation, brainwave mapping, and mind control. But what struck Phoenix the hardest were the images of Edward as a baby, hooked up to machines, his face pale and expressionless.

"They… they did this to him, Ro," Phoenix whispered, her voice barely audible. "Mira… and whoever else was part of this. They used him for Project Genesis."

Ro's face darkened, his hands clenching into fists. "We must stop this. We have to stop Malakos, and we have to save Edward."

Phoenix nodded, her resolve hardening. She looked at the screen one last time before shutting it down. They had the information they needed—now it was time to act.

She turned to Ro, fire burning in her eyes. "We go after him. Now."

Ro gave a firm nod. "Let's finish this."

As they left the facility behind, the weight of what they had discovered bore down on Phoenix, but her determination never wavered. Edward was still trapped inside Malakos, and she would stop at nothing to save him.

The final battle was coming.

Phoenix's fingers dug into the cold metal floor as she remained on her knees, her mind spinning after everything that had just transpired. The air around her felt thick and oppressive like the weight of Malakos's rage and despair still lingered. Her breathing slowed, and for a moment, she allowed herself to close her eyes and breathe, trying to make sense of the whirlwind that had consumed her life.

Malakos's hulking form was still burned into her mind. She had seen the brief flicker of Edward's consciousness, just a shadow of the brother she once knew. But reality was sinking in fast—Edward was lost, and whatever part of him remained was likely buried too deep to save.

"He's gone," Phoenix whispered to herself, the weight of those words grounding her in the harsh truth. Still, a part of her couldn't fully let go. Not yet. She knew Malakos had to be stopped, no matter what remained of Edward inside him.

Ro stood silently beside her, his staff leaning against his leg as he wiped a streak of blood from his temple. His breath was ragged, but his focus hadn't wavered. He had seen what Malakos could do, witnessed the creature's raw power, and yet there was no sign of surrender in his posture.

"We'll finish this, Phoenix," Ro vowed firmly, though he avoided the notion of saving Edward entirely. They both knew it wasn't likely.

Phoenix rose shakily to her feet. Though exhaustion threatened defeat, she stood firmly, squaring her shoulders and brushing dirt and blood off her hands.

"We can't let Malakos get away."

Ro raised an eyebrow, concern flickering in his eyes. "Phoenix, we're both exhausted. We barely survived that, and Malakos is still out there, still dangerous."

"I know," her voice steadied, less frantic now. "But we can't let him roam free. Whatever's left of Edward, we can't pretend he's the same person. Malakos is our problem now, and we must stop him before he does more damage."

Before Ro could respond, heavy footsteps echoed from the shadows. Jax stepped into the light, his expression tight with exhaustion but his resolve unwavering. His left arm was wrapped with a torn strip of fabric, blood seeping through from a wound he had taken during the battle.

"You're right," Jax agreed, his voice firm but calm. "We need to regroup and plan. Malakos is out there, and he's not done with us. Not by a long shot."

Phoenix turned to Jax, her frustration settling into grim acceptance.

"Edward's gone, isn't he?"

It wasn't a question she needed answered—she already knew. "We have to face the reality that we might be unable to bring him back. But Malakos has to be stopped."

Jax's gaze softened, though his voice remained steady. "I believe you, Phoenix. And you're right. We're no good to anyone if we rush in without thinking. And right now, we're on the edge of collapse ourselves." His eyes flicked to Ro, silently acknowledging the toll the fight had taken on them.

Phoenix bit her lip, her body aching with exhaustion, but her mind knew better than to act impulsively. She turned her attention to the lifeless body of Mira, her broken form crumpled in the corner of the room, blood pooling around her motionless figure.

Jax followed Phoenix's gaze to his sister. His jaw clenched as he stared down at Mira's lifeless face, the anger and pain of betrayal clear in his eyes. For a long moment, he said nothing. He just stood there, fists clenched at his sides, breathing heavily.

Finally, Jax spoke, his voice low and filled with bitterness. "She did this. She thought she could control everything, even Malakos. In the end, she only destroyed herself."

Phoenix nodded, feeling the weight of the moment settle over them. "We can't let her mistakes destroy anyone else. We need to find a way to stop Malakos, and we need to do it fast."

Jax stepped forward, kneeling beside Mira's body. He reached out, not with the tenderness of a brother mourning a sibling, but with the cold finality of someone who had accepted the consequences of her actions.

He pulled a small data chip from the pouch on her belt and examined it.

"This might give us the answers we need," he marveled, standing and holding the chip out to Phoenix. "Whatever plans she had, whatever research she was hiding, it's all on here."

Phoenix took the chip, her fingers trembling slightly as the gravity of their situation settled over her. This could be the key. Mira's obsession with Project Genesis had been the driving force behind everything—the creatures, Malakos, and Edward's transformation. If there was any chance to stop Malakos, it had to be hidden within the secrets Mira had left behind.

Ro approached cautiously, standing beside Phoenix as she pocketed the chip. "We need to find a place to rest and figure this out. We can't keep going like this."

Jax nodded, his eyes hardening as he glanced around the ruined facility. "There's no point in staying here. This place is a tomb now. We'll regroup, find shelter, and plan our next move."

Phoenix knew they couldn't charge after Malakos mindlessly. It wasn't about Edward anymore. This was about stopping a creature that could tear the world apart. She didn't have to like it, but she had to face it.

"Fine," Phoenix relented, her voice quieter than she wanted. "But we don't have much time. Malakos won't wait for us."

Jax gave a firm nod. "Then we'd better move quickly."

As they turned to leave the facility behind, Phoenix cast one last glance at Mira's broken body, her thoughts swirling. This woman had set everything in motion. In the end, she paid the ultimate price for her ambition.

Phoenix wasn't interested in revenge—she was focused on stopping Malakos.

As they exited the facility, the cold night air bit at Phoenix's skin. She could feel the weight of the journey ahead pressing down on her.

Edward might be lost, but she could still end this. The final battle was coming, and Phoenix would be ready.

The cold night air gnawed at Phoenix's skin as she, Ro, and Jax made their way through the remains of the facility. The moon cast long shadows across the desolate landscape, broken only by the faint sounds of wind stirring the debris.

Phoenix's body felt heavier with each step, but her mind was sharp and focused on what lay ahead.

Edward was gone, swallowed by Malakos. Phoenix had to accept that. The flicker of her brother's consciousness she had felt was nothing more than a shadow now—a fading connection. She knew that the real fight wasn't about saving him anymore. It was about stopping the creature that had consumed him, about preventing Malakos from becoming an even more significant threat.

Jax's presence at her side, silent but determined, reminded her of how much they had already lost and how much they still had to fight for. His expression was set in stone, and his eyes scanned the horizon as they moved further from the facility's wreckage.

"We can't keep running on empty," Ro reasoned, breaking the silence. His voice was steady but tinged with weariness. "We need to rest, regroup, and plan this out. We know what we're up against now, and rushing headlong into the dark isn't going to end well for any of us."

Phoenix nodded, her thoughts racing even as her body ached for rest. "There's no saving, Edward, not anymore. But we can stop Malakos. He's not invincible. The Severance Protocol weakened him, and we have Mira's data chip. Whatever she knew, whatever her plan was— there's got to be something in there that we can use."

Jax, who had been silent for most of the journey, finally spoke. His voice was low, edged with the kind of cold rage from betrayal. "We'll use whatever we can find. Mira thought she could control this, but it slipped from her hands. She created the monster, and now it's our job to put it down."

There was no sadness in his words, only resolve. Phoenix could feel the same fire burning inside her, though it was tempered by the reality that the person she was fighting was no longer her brother. The battle to save Edward had passed. Now, they were preparing for war against a creature with nothing to lose.

As they pressed onward, Ro's eyes scanned the landscape, searching for shelter. "There's an old outpost not far from here," he said. "We can regroup there, figure out what's on the chip, and plan our next move."

Phoenix nodded in agreement, her gaze distant. She knew they needed rest, but part of her was already looking ahead—already calculating the steps they would need to take to finish this.

"Do you think he knows?" Phoenix asked, her voice barely more than a whisper.
"Who?" Jax replied, his eyes narrowing.

"Malakos," she clarified. "Do you think he knows that Edward's gone? That he's all that's left?"

Jax considered the question for a moment, his jaw tightening. "If he doesn't know now, he'll figure it out soon enough. And when he does, he'll come after us with everything he has."

Ro glanced at them, his expression hardening. "Then we'll need to be ready. We'll use whatever Mira was planning, whatever she was trying to control—against him. We'll turn her creation into his undoing."

Phoenix clenched her fists, her resolve solidifying with every step they took. "We will stop him. But it won't be for Edward. It'll be for us—for everyone left standing in this broken world."

They walked in silence after that, the weight of their mission settling heavily over them. Phoenix's mind drifted to the data chip in her pocket. The answers they needed were on there, but they would need to be more complex. Whatever they uncovered about Project Genesis and Malakos would be the key to ending this nightmare.

And Phoenix was ready to do whatever it took to finish it.

As they neared the outpost, its weathered structure coming into view against the pale moonlight, Phoenix allowed herself a moment of quiet before the storm. The final battle was coming, and this time, there was no room for hesitation or doubt.
Malakos would fall.

25

The End of the Beginning

The air hung thick with tension as Phoenix, Jax, and Ro stepped away from the ruined facility. Each step felt heavy, like wading through an unseen force that sought to pull them back deeper into the chaos they had just escaped. The forest ahead seemed darker than before, the shadows clinging to the trees, whispering with malice.

Phoenix felt the weight of her decisions pressing down on her shoulders as the wind cut across her face. She hadn't let herself fully accept the truth until now. Edward—her Edward—was no longer who he had been. Malakos had taken him, and worse, Edward had let it happen. A hollow ache filled her chest as she replayed his words in her mind.

I've accepted it.

It was more than just a loss. It was betrayal, and Phoenix didn't know how to reconcile that. She had spent so long fighting for him, believing that somehow, somewhere, he would return. Now she realized that wasn't possible. Edward had chosen his side.

Beside her, Jax walked in silence, his face hardened by the events of the last hours. His eyes flickered toward her occasionally, but he didn't speak. They all knew what was coming, even if none of them had the strength to say it yet. Malakos had to be stopped. Edward had to be stopped.

Ro brought up the rear, his grip on the heavy staff firm, his eyes scanning the darkened woods for any sign of movement. Something was unnerving about the silence around them, the way the wind barely stirred, the way the creatures of the night seemed to have vanished.

They came to a halt near a clearing, and Phoenix knelt beside a large stone, her hands shaking as she pulled out the data chip Jax had taken from Mira. This was their only chance now—this piece of information held the key to understanding what they were truly up against—Project Genesis, the Oblivion fail-safe. It was all connected, and they needed to know exactly how.

Jax stood over her, his Shadow long and menacing in the faint moonlight.

"What's on that chip could be the only way we take Malakos down," he said quietly, though the steel in his voice was unmistakable. "It's also what Mira was hiding from all of us. Whatever she was planning, she knew it would lead us here."

Phoenix glanced up at him, her expression unreadable. "You're not wrong. Mira knew the stakes. She thought she could control everything, even Malakos. Now we have to clean up the mess she left behind."

Jax's jaw tightened as he knelt beside her. "The fail-safe. Do you think it can stop him?"

Phoenix hesitated, turning the chip over in her hands. "It's supposed to wipe out the mutations and everything connected to Project Genesis. But that includes Edward." Her voice faltered slightly, but she forced herself to stay composed. "If we use it..."

"We'll lose him." Ro's voice cut through the air like a blade.

Phoenix's fingers clenched around the chip. She didn't want to say it, didn't want to accept it. But deep down, she knew it was the only way. Edward was gone. What was left of him was tied to Malakos in a way that she couldn't undo.

Jax's eyes softened for a brief moment, his voice low. "Phoenix, we don't have to do this. We could try—"

"No," Phoenix interrupted, her voice firm now. She met Jax's gaze, her expression hardened by the weight of what she had finally accepted. "We don't try anything. We stop him."

Jax straightened, a flicker of understanding passing between them. He nodded, his voice steady. "Then we use the fail-safe."

Ro moved closer, his face grim. "But that still doesn't explain the Shadow. If Malakos is connected to Edward, what role does the Shadow play? Why is he using Edward?"

Phoenix stood, her eyes narrowing as she looked toward the darkness beyond the clearing. "The Shadow has been manipulating everything from the beginning. He used Mira. He used Edward. Now he's using Malakos to achieve something bigger."

"What could be bigger than controlling Malakos?" Jax asked, his voice tinged with frustration.

Phoenix stared into the shadows, her mind racing. "Power. Control. The Shadow isn't interested in just stopping the mutations. He wants to control them, harness them. And with Malakos under his command, he'll be unstoppable."

A chill ran through her as she spoke, the enormity of what they were facing finally hitting her full force. This wasn't just about saving Edward. It wasn't even just about stopping Malakos. This was about stopping something far more insidious that could reshape the world as they knew it.

She swallowed hard, her voice barely a whisper. "We have to stop them both."

Jax placed a hand on her shoulder, his grip firm. "We will."

Phoenix nodded, though the fear gnawed at her from the inside. They were walking into a war they hadn't fully prepared for. And worst of all, they would have to face Edward—not as her brother, but as the weapon of the Shadow.

"We move at dawn," Jax said, stepping back. "Rest up while you can. We're going to need everything we've got."

The cold of the night bit at Phoenix's skin, but she barely felt it. Kneeling on the ground, her thoughts swirled like the ash still rising from their dying fire. Malakos's presence still weighed heavily on her chest, and the flicker of Edward's consciousness, however brief, was fading from her mind. That fleeting moment when she thought he might still be fighting—it now felt like an illusion, a shadow cast by her desperation.

Maybe Edward was gone. Maybe he had been for longer than she wanted to admit.

She exhaled slowly, her breath clouding in the cold night air. The weight of the truth settled over her like a lead blanket. She had been clinging to the hope that her brother could be saved, but the cracks in that hope were growing. The Edward she knew was slipping away—if he wasn't lost completely.

"He's still there," Phoenix whispered to herself, though the conviction in her voice had all but disappeared.

Ro, leaning against a nearby tree, remained silent. His eyes met hers briefly, and in that look, Phoenix saw the same uncertainty she felt reflected back at her. He hadn't voiced it outright, but even Ro knew they were chasing a ghost. Edward might not want to be saved.

Phoenix pulled herself to her feet, brushing dirt from her hands. Her body ached from exhaustion, and the fight they had barely survived, but the ache in her chest was worse. She could feel the grief settling in—the realization that she might have lost her brother long before they had set foot in that facility.

Jax emerged from the darkness, his face drawn and tired, his injured arm hanging stiffly at his side. He didn't speak immediately, but his gaze fell on Phoenix, his sharp eyes catching the subtle shift in her demeanor.

"You're starting to understand, aren't you?" Jax's voice was low, but there was no judgment in it. He had already accepted that Mira was beyond redemption, that her lust for power had consumed her entirely. He had warned Phoenix about Edward, but now it seemed like she was finally coming to terms with the grim truth.

Phoenix nodded slightly, her voice barely audible. "I saw him for a moment, Jax. But I think I was wrong. Maybe he doesn't want to be saved. Maybe he… can't be."

Jax's expression softened, though he remained stoic. "You've always been stronger than you realize, Phoenix. This fight—it's not about whether Edward can be saved anymore. We're facing something much bigger. Something that has nothing to do with what we want."

Phoenix's jaw tightened, her mind racing back to the twisted look in Malakos's eyes. Edward was part of something darker now, bigger than both. And whatever it was, it was beyond her reach. She wasn't going to chase after her brother anymore, hoping to pull him out of the darkness.

She wasn't here to save Edward anymore. She was here to stop whatever Malakos—and whatever force was behind him—was planning.

"I'm not giving up on him," Phoenix said finally, though her voice was sharper now. "But I know what we're dealing with. Malakos has him, and maybe, he wants it that way."

Jax nodded, a grim understanding passing between them. "If that's true, then we'll have to face him as he is—not who he was."

Ro stirred from his spot by the fire, rubbing his temples before pushing himself up. "Malakos won't stop. He's not just out there roaming. Whatever this Project Genesis was, it set something into motion. We need to figure out what."

Phoenix's eyes shifted to the chip Jax had given her. Mira's plans, her obsessions, were locked inside it. Whatever Project Genesis was meant to be, the answer lay within the secrets she had left behind.

"We'll find out what they've done," Phoenix said, her resolve hardening. "We'll discover why Edward was part of it, why Malakos exists, and what the Shadow wants. If that means we must face Edward along the way, so be it."

Jax stood, his movements stiff from the wound on his side. "We'll need to rest before we go after him. The Shadow isn't some random threat. It's orchestrating all of this."

Phoenix's eyes flickered with recognition. The Shadow. Mira had mentioned it briefly, a presence she seemed to fear even though she was ruthless in her own right. But now, more than ever, Phoenix could feel it. A dark force is looming just beyond the edges of their understanding, pulling the strings.

The Shadow wasn't finished with them.

Ro picked up his staff and gave a grim nod. "We need to be ready. Because if the Shadow's pulling Malakos's strings, then it's already planned its next move."

Phoenix's heart tightened, but her resolve didn't waver. "Then we don't just stop Malakos. We stop the Shadow. Whatever it takes."

The fire had burned to ashes, the darkness creeping in around them. But Phoenix no longer felt the weight of uncertainty dragging her down. She wasn't chasing after her brother anymore, clinging to an impossible dream.

She was preparing for war.

The next morning arrived slowly, with the first rays of sunlight struggling to break through the heavy clouds overhead. Phoenix sat quietly, the dying embers of their fire crackling softly at her feet. The night had been long, filled with restless thoughts and the growing realization that the battle ahead would demand more of her than she had ever imagined.

Jax and Ro stirred nearby, gathering their things in silence. The three of them shared a quiet understanding now—there was no longer any illusion of saving Edward. They were moving toward a confrontation none truly knew how to prepare for. Whatever Edward had become, whatever Malakos was, it was bigger than anything they'd faced before.

Phoenix's fingers brushed against the small chip in her pocket containing Mira's secrets. Answers, perhaps, but not salvation. Its weight felt heavier with each passing moment.

"We need to move quickly," Jax said, breaking the silence. His voice was firm, but beneath the coldness, there was an edge of urgency. "If Malakos and the Shadow are tied to Project Genesis, we don't have time to waste."

Phoenix nodded, her face set in grim determination. "Let's get somewhere safe, and we'll see what's on this chip. It might give us the advantage we need."

Ro stood, tightening his gear around his waist, but his eyes were distant. "I've been thinking," he said slowly. "If the Shadow is controlling all of this, do you think it's possible we're part of its plan too?"

The question lingered in the air, dark and unsettling. Phoenix had wondered the same thing, but hearing it aloud made it feel more real. Had they been manipulated from the start? Was everything—Mira, Malakos, Edward—part of some larger scheme they couldn't even see yet?

Jax narrowed his eyes, glancing at the horizon. "We won't know until we get more answers. But one thing's certain: the Shadow isn't just watching us. It's waiting for something."

They set out shortly after, moving swiftly through the forest, the air cold and sharp. Phoenix's mind churned as they walked, but her thoughts always circled back to Edward. She hadn't spoken much about him since the night before, but the conflict still gnawed at her.

She wanted to stop Malakos, but deep down, she wasn't sure if she could bring herself to face her brother in that twisted form.

The terrain grew rougher as they moved deeper into the woods, and after several hours of travel, they came upon an abandoned outpost nestled between jagged cliffs. The structure was old, its metal walls rusted and covered in vines, but it provided enough shelter to give them time to regroup.

Once inside, Phoenix wasted no time. She pulled out the chip and slid it into a small terminal they'd found in the corner of the outpost. The screen flickered, and for a moment, she worried the chip had been damaged during the battle. But then, files began to appear—encrypted documents, recordings, research logs. Everything Mira had been hiding.

Phoenix's heart pounded as she opened the first file, the words blurring slightly before coming into focus:

"Subject 001: Genesis Core – Edward."

Her breath caught as she scrolled down, revealing detailed schematics of the experiments they'd run on Edward as a child. The project hadn't just been about controlling mutations—it had been about creating something entirely new that could wield the power of the creatures and bend them to their will.

Her hands trembled as she continued reading. Mira had been desperate to control the creatures, yes, but she had also been desperate to control Edward. He was the key, the centerpiece of Project Genesis. Malakos was the weapon, and the results of those experiments went wrong.

"They used him," Phoenix whispered, her voice cracking slightly. "They used Edward to create Malakos."

Jax stepped forward, scanning the screen. "They wanted more than control. They wanted power. Complete dominance over the creatures, the mutations, everything. Edward wasn't just a subject. He was their prototype."

Phoenix felt her stomach churn. This wasn't just about Edward being taken over by Malakos—he had been designed for this from the beginning. Project Genesis had never been about saving the world. It had been about bending it to someone's will.

Ro's voice broke through her thoughts. "Look at this," he said, pointing to a final line of text at the bottom of the screen.

"All subjects await final command from the Master."

Phoenix's blood ran cold. The Master—the Shadow. Whatever had been controlling Mira or lurking behind all of this was still out there, waiting for the right moment to strike.

Suddenly, the room seemed darker, the air heavier with an unseen presence. Phoenix's heart pounded, and she turned toward Jax and Ro, her voice barely a whisper. "The Shadow. It's not just controlling the creatures. It's controlling everything. Including Edward."

Jax's jaw tightened. "Then we're not just dealing with Malakos. We're dealing with something much bigger."

Ro glanced at the screen, his face pale. "The final command. What does that mean? What's the Shadow waiting for?"

Phoenix didn't have an answer. All she knew was that whatever was coming was far worse than anything they'd faced.

The outpost seemed to creak and groan, as if the walls were reacting to the revelation. Then, as if on cue, the lights in the room flickered, casting long shadows against the walls. Phoenix's pulse quickened, and her eyes darted to the entrance of the outpost.

She could feel it for a moment—a presence, dark and evil, watching them. The Shadow was near.

"We need to move," Jax said sharply, grabbing his gear. "With the Shadow this close, we can't stay here."

But before anyone could act, the temperature in the room dropped suddenly, the air turning icy. Phoenix froze, her breath catching as a deep, rumbling voice echoed through the room.

"You've come far, Phoenix."

Her blood ran cold.

The voice wasn't just coming from the shadows—it was inside her head, creeping through her thoughts like a virus. She turned slowly, her eyes wide with fear, as she searched the room for the source. But there was nothing—just darkness.

"You've come to find him," the voice whispered, a dark chuckle following. "But you won't save him. Edward is already mine."

Phoenix's knees nearly buckled as the weight of the voice pressed down on her. She had expected the Shadow to be powerful, but this— this was something beyond anything she had imagined.

Jax and Ro stood still, their eyes wide as they heard the voice as well, but it was Phoenix the Shadow had chosen to speak to.

"You should stop fighting, Phoenix," the voice continued, cold and emotionless. "He's already where he belongs. Soon, he will lead them all."

Phoenix's heart raced, her mind spinning. "What do you mean?"

The Shadow laughed again, the sound reverberating through her skull. "You'll see soon enough. When the time comes, Edward will stand at my side. He was always meant for greatness. You—on the other hand—are just a distraction."

The room plunged into deeper darkness, the weight of the Shadow's words settling over them like a suffocating fog. Phoenix's mind raced, every thought colliding with the next.

Edward was leading them with the Shadow?

Before she could process the horror, the presence vanished, leaving only an eerie silence in its wake.

Phoenix's heart pounded in the deafening silence that followed the Shadow's departure. The oppressive weight of its presence was gone, but the chill it left behind remained, sinking into her bones. She felt sick, her mind racing through the implications of what the Shadow had just revealed.

Jax stepped forward, his face ashen, but his eyes filled with determination. "We're not waiting for it to come to us," he said, his voice low but fierce. "Whatever the Shadow has planned, we need to stop it. Now."

Ro nodded, though his face was pale, his usual confidence shaken by the encounter. "We're in over our heads here," he muttered, glancing at Phoenix. "But we can't let this thing win."

Phoenix tried to steady her breathing, pushing away the icy fear that clung to her. She wanted to scream, break something, and rail against the impossible situation they found themselves in, but that wasn't an option. Not anymore. The stakes had just become unimaginably higher.

"We find Malakos," Phoenix said, her voice steadier than she felt. "We end this."

Jax's eyes hardened. "And the Shadow?"

Phoenix's jaw tightened. "We figure that out as we go. But if what it said is true…"

She trailed off, the reality sinking in. Edward wasn't just a victim of this anymore. He was becoming something more. Something worse. And if the Shadow truly led him, then the fight was no longer just about saving her brother. It was about stopping him.

Jax exchanged a glance with Ro, both understanding the grim reality they were about to face. Phoenix wasn't naïve enough to think Edward could be separated from Malakos anymore. That hope had shattered long ago. But the thought of facing him—of possibly having to fight him—was something she wasn't ready to confront. Not yet.

"We need to move fast," Jax said, pulling Phoenix from her thoughts. "If the Shadow knows we're coming, it won't give us much time to prepare."

Ro nodded, his eyes narrowing with resolve. "We'll have to hit hard and fast. No second chances."

Phoenix stood, gathering her gear and swallowing the lump in her throat. There was no room for hesitation anymore. They were heading into the unknown; whatever lay ahead, she would face it head-on for Edward. For the world, he was being pulled into.

They left the outpost, the sun hanging low in the sky, casting long shadows over the forest as they moved deeper into enemy territory. Every step felt like a countdown, each breath a reminder of how close they were to something far beyond their understanding.

It didn't take long for the first sign of the Shadow's growing influence to appear.

The forest around them began to change. The trees twisted unnaturally, their branches contorting into strange, angular shapes that made Phoenix's skin crawl. The air grew colder, a dark energy pulsing in the atmosphere. It was as if the very land was reacting to the presence of the Shadow, warping under its influence.

Jax tightened his grip on his blade, his eyes scanning the twisted landscape. "We're close. The Shadow's reach is spreading."

Phoenix felt it, too—the pull of something dark and ancient, drawing them closer with every step. It wasn't just the land that was changing. She could feel a deep, almost magnetic connection pulling her forward, the same connection she had felt with Edward in the past. Only now, it was twisted, corrupted by the Shadow's influence.

Her pulse quickened as they pressed on, the forest growing darker, the trees thicker. As they broke through the edge of the forest, they saw it.

In the distance, silhouetted against the darkening sky, stood an ancient structure—massive and imposing. Its spires reached toward the heavens, jagged and angular, casting long shadows across the ground. The air around it crackled with dark energy, the same oppressive force they had felt in the outpost, only now concentrated, focused on this place.

"The Shadow's lair," Jax said grimly, his voice low.

Phoenix's heart pounded as she stared at the structure. This was it. The final confrontation.

They approached cautiously, the tension thickening with every step. As they neared the entrance, the massive stone doors loomed, sealed tightly. Phoenix felt the familiar pull in her chest, the same connection she had always felt with Edward. Now, it was different. Stronger. Darker.

"He's inside," she whispered fearfully.

Jax nodded, his face hard with determination. "Then we go in together."

Phoenix took a deep breath, her heart racing. There was no turning back now. With a nod from Jax, they pushed open the heavy doors and stepped inside.

The interior was cold and dark, lit only by the faint glow of strange, pulsing orbs embedded in the walls. The air was thick with tension, every breath heavy with the weight of the darkness surrounding them.

The oppressive energy grew stronger as they moved deeper into the structure, pressing down on them like a physical force. Phoenix could feel it in her bones, the dark presence of the Shadow lurking just out of sight, waiting for them.

Without warning, a deep, rumbling voice echoed through the chamber, sending chills down Phoenix's spine.

"You've come, Phoenix."

The Shadow's voice filled the air, surrounding them and penetrating their thoughts. Phoenix's heart raced as she gripped her weapon tighter, her knuckles white.

"You've come to witness the birth of something greater. Your brother has chosen his path. Now, so must you."

The words sent a jolt of fear through her, but Phoenix pushed it down, refusing to let the Shadow control her. She stepped forward, her voice steady despite the terror swirling inside her. "Where's Edward?"

The Shadow's laugh echoed through the chamber, cold and cruel. "He's already here, Phoenix. He's been with me all along. But you have yet to understand."

As the words faded, the darkness in the chamber began to shift, twisting and contorting until a figure emerged from the shadows. Phoenix's heart stopped.

It was Edward—or at least, what remained of him.

His form was twisted, consumed by the power of Malakos. His eyes glowed with the same eerie light, his body now a fusion of man and monster. Behind the monstrous exterior, Phoenix could still see her brother, the one she had fought so hard to save.

"Edward..." She whispered pleadingly, her voice heavy with emotion.

He stepped forward, the ground shaking beneath his feet. There was something different in his gaze now—something that made Phoenix's blood run cold.

He wasn't fighting the Shadow anymore.

Edward's monstrous form shifted as he stepped fully into the light. His once broken and twisted body was now whole again, though grotesquely enhanced by the power of Malakos. His features had merged into a terrifying fusion of man and beast. His eyes, no longer flickering with the inner conflict that had once hinted at his former self, now burned with a cold, calculated determination.

The Shadow's dark energy swirled around him as if reconstituted him, granting him a new form of dark sovereignty. He stood tall and powerful—no longer the brother Phoenix remembered, but something far more dangerous.

Ro gripped his weapon tightly, his eyes narrowing as he took a defensive step forward. Standing beside Phoenix, Jax tensed, his hand hovering over the blade at his side, prepared for whatever was about to unfold.

Phoenix was frozen. She stared at the creature before her, her heart aching at the sight of Edward—whole again but twisted into something entirely different. The connection she had once felt with him was now tainted, drowned in the power of the Shadow.

Edward's voice came, deep and reverberating through the chamber, sending a chill down Phoenix's spine. It was his voice, but there was something darker, more controlled.

"I'm not broken anymore, Phoenix. I'm not trapped inside Malakos. I am Malakos."

"Edward… no." She could barely find the words, hurt by what he was saying.

Edward's face twisted into a cruel smile, and his monstrous hand flexed, the sharp claws glinting in the faint light.

"You still don't understand, do you?" He continued, his voice steady and cold. "I was never meant to be saved, Phoenix. This was always the plan."

Ro's voice broke through the tense silence. "What are you talking about?" He demanded, stepping forward with his staff raised.

Edward's eyes shifted to Ro, the smirk never leaving his face.

"You're all so small," he said, his tone dripping with contempt. "I've seen the truth, Ro. The Shadow has shown me everything. The world is broken, and I—we—will fix it."

Jax's voice was sharp as a blade, cutting through the rising tension. "By doing what? By becoming this? What has the Shadow promised you?"

Edward's smile faltered briefly before returning darker and more evil. "Power. Control. Everything I was meant to be. You can either be part of the new order or be swept away with the rest of the broken world."

Phoenix's hands trembled, but not from fear—rage was boiling beneath her skin this time.
"So this is it? You've just given up everything? Your family, your humanity, everything we fought for?"

Edward's gaze finally locked onto Phoenix's, the flicker of recognition there before the darkness swallowed it.

"Family?" He echoed, mocking her. "You never understood Phoenix. The Shadow showed me what I was meant to become. I am the future. Malakos was always the key."

Her heart clenched painfully, but the truth began to solidify in her mind. Edward was gone. He had chosen this path—he wasn't trapped anymore. He wasn't under the influence of some dark force. He was the dark force.

"I know what you're feeling, Phoenix," Edward continued, stepping closer. "But this is the only way. The world needs more than heroes—it needs rulers."

Phoenix's breath caught in her throat. The brother she had spent so long trying to protect, the one she had fought so hard to save, was now standing before her as her enemy.

"You're wrong, Edward," she whispered, her voice raw with emotion. "This isn't who you are. This isn't who you were meant to be."

Edward's expression darkened, and for a brief moment, something like anger flashed across his face. "Who I was meant to be? You have no idea, Phoenix. You were always too blind to see the truth."

Jax stepped forward, his voice filled with barely - contained fury. "So, what now, Edward? You'll follow the Shadow, enslave the world, and what—destroy anyone who stands in your way?"

Edward's smile returned, cold and unfeeling. "Not destroy… control. This world will bend to our will, or it will crumble. It's that simple."

Phoenix's mind raced. The Shadow had done this—twisted her brother into something unrecognizable. But as much as she wanted to believe that the Shadow had manipulated him, she could see it in Edward's eyes: he had made this choice. He had embraced the darkness.

"There's still time to turn back," Phoenix said, her voice steadier now, though the pain in her chest was almost unbearable. "You don't have to do this."

Edward's laugh was sharp and cruel. "Turn back? There's no going back, Phoenix. This is who I am now. I choose this."

A heavy silence settled over the chamber as Phoenix realized that her brother—her real brother—was gone. The Edward she once knew was buried deep within the monster standing before her, willingly controlled by Malakos and guided by the Shadow's influence.

Jax's hand tightened around his blade, his voice quiet but firm. "We stop him, Phoenix. Whatever it takes."

Phoenix nodded, the weight of her decision heavy in her chest. She had come this far, fought so hard to save Edward, but now… now she had to face the harsh reality that there was no saving him—not from this, not from the darkness he had chosen.

Edward stepped back, his monstrous form towering over them. "This is your last chance," he said, his voice low and dangerous. "Join us, or be destroyed."

Phoenix clenched her fists, her gaze never leaving his. "We won't let you do this. Not to the world. Not to us."

The ground trembled beneath them as Edward's expression hardened, his eyes glowing viciously. "Then you'll die like the rest."

The ground beneath them quaked as Edward, now in full control of Malakos's body and power, raised one clawed hand toward the ceiling. The shadows twisted around him, swirling in a terrifying display of the dark force he commanded.

The air crackled with malevolent energy as if the very world was bending to his will. Phoenix, Ro, and Jax braced themselves, feeling the oppressive weight of the darkness pressing down on them.

"I gave you a choice," Edward said, his voice no longer carrying any hint of warmth. It was cold, final, and full of contempt. "Now, you'll witness what true power looks like."

Before they could react, a loud sound filled the room—like the roar of the earth itself splitting apart. The walls trembled violently, cracks spider-webbing through the structure as debris began to fall. The shadows surrounding Edward coalesced into solid, black tendrils, spreading out like roots, burrowing into the ground, feeding on the chaos he was creating.

Jax darted forward, his blade drawn, the resolve clear in his eyes. He had made his decision. "We're not letting you destroy everything!" he shouted, charging toward Edward.

Before he could get close, one of the shadowy tendrils lashed out with lightning speed, striking Jax hard and sending him flying across the room. He crashed into the far wall with a sickening thud, crumpling to the ground in a heap.

"Jax!" Phoenix screamed, her voice raw with fear. She started toward him, but Ro grabbed her arm, pulling her back.

"Stay focused, Phoenix," Ro urged, though his voice was thick with worry. "Jax knew the risks."

Her heart pounded painfully as she stared at her fallen ally. Jax had sacrificed himself for this—he had known what would happen, but that didn't make it any easier. Her pulse hammered in her ears, the world narrowing to the brutal reality in front of her. But Ro was right. She had to stay focused. There was no time for hesitation.

Edward's monstrous form loomed before them, and Phoenix's gaze hardened. This wasn't just about saving the world anymore—it was about stopping her brother from becoming the monster he had chosen to be.

"You won't win," Phoenix called out, her voice steady though every nerve in her body screamed with exhaustion. "Not like this."

Edward's eyes locked onto hers, glowing with that same cruel light.

"Win?" He echoed, his tone mocking. "I've already won, Phoenix. This world is mine to reshape, and you… you're just another casualty."

Ro stepped forward, his staff ready. "Not if we have anything to say about it."

Edward's laugh was low, dark, and chilling. "You still don't understand, do you?" He raised his hands, and the shadows twisted more violently as if reacting to his will. "This world has been broken for far too long. The Shadow has shown me what it needs. Control. Power. Order. I will fix it."

The room continued to shake, the very foundation of the facility crumbling as the shadows reached higher, cracking through the ceiling as if trying to pull the sky down itself. Phoenix's heart pounded, but her focus remained locked on Edward.

"No," she said quietly, her voice unwavering. "You're not fixing anything. You're just tearing it all down."

Edward's expression darkened, the glow in his eyes intensifying. "Then you'll die with the rest of them."

Without warning, Edward lashed out again, the shadowy tendrils whipping toward Phoenix and Ro with deadly precision. Ro spun his staff with lightning speed, blocking the first attack, but the force of the strike sent him staggering back. Phoenix ducked just in time as another tendril slammed into the ground she had been standing, leaving a deep gouge on the metal floor.

They couldn't keep dodging forever. The room was collapsing around them, and Edward's power grew with every second. Phoenix's mind raced—there had to be a way to stop him, to sever his connection to the Shadow before everything was lost.

"Ro, we need to hit him hard," she called out, breathless but determined. "We need to take him down now."

Ro nodded, his face set with grim determination. "We'll need to distract him long enough to do that. If we can separate him from the Shadow's power, he'll be vulnerable."

Phoenix's heart raced as she weighed their options. It was a long shot, but it was their only plan. If they could disrupt the connection, even for a moment, they might be able to bring Edward down. She knew the risks—if they failed, there would be no coming back from this.

Before they could act, however, a low, rumbling voice echoed through the chamber—a voice that didn't belong to Edward. It was deeper, darker, and far more ancient.

"Enough, Edward."

The very air seemed to freeze as the words reverberated through the room. The shadows around Edward twisted violently, writhing in response to the voice. Phoenix's blood ran cold as she turned her gaze toward the source of the voice.

And there, emerging from the swirling darkness, was the Shadow.

Its form was indistinct, a mass of darkness given shape and presence, its eyes glowing with an unnatural, predatory light. It towered over them, far larger than Edward or Malakos, a being of pure malice.

The very sight of it sent a shiver down Phoenix's spine. This force had twisted Edward, the entity that had turned him into what he was now.

The Shadow's eyes locked onto Edward, its voice a deep, rolling thunder that seemed to come from the depths of the earth itself. "You have done well, my child. Now you are ready."

Edward's monstrous form seemed to stiffen, his gaze shifting from Phoenix to the Shadow. There was no fear in his eyes—only something darker. Something willing.

"Ready for what?" Phoenix whispered, her voice barely audible as the full weight of the situation settled over her.

The Shadow's smile was cold, calculating. "For your ascension."

Before Phoenix could react, the shadows around Edward pulsed violently, enveloping him in their dark embrace. His form seemed to shift, to expand, as if the Shadow was merging with him, feeding him more power than he had ever known.

Edward's dark and twisted voice echoed through the chamber, but there was no longer any hesitation or conflict. He was fully, completely one with Malakos now.

"I told you," Edward said, his voice low and dangerous. "I'm not broken anymore. I am what I was always meant to be."

Phoenix's breath caught in her throat as she realized the horrifying truth. Edward wasn't being controlled anymore. He had chosen this. He had embraced the Shadow; now, there was no turning back.

Ro stepped closer to Phoenix, his voice urgent. "We need to leave. Now."

Phoenix couldn't move. Her eyes were locked on Edward, on the creature her brother had become. The Shadow had given him everything—power, control, dominance—and he had accepted it willingly.

The Shadow's form loomed over them, its presence suffocating and unyielding. Edward—no longer torn between two identities—stood taller, his monstrous frame now more refined, controlled, and terrifying. The tendrils of darkness swirled around him, tethered to the Shadow's essence but now fully embraced by Edward's will. He had become something else entirely, something far more dangerous than Malakos alone.

Phoenix's heart hammered in her chest, the weight of the revelation pressing down on her like a vice. She had thought Malakos was the monster, but now she saw the truth. Edward had become the darkness, willingly stepping into the role the Shadow had prepared for him.

"Phoenix, we have to move!" Ro's voice cut through the thick tension, pulling her out of her spiraling thoughts.

Phoenix turned to look at Ro, then at Jax, who was still motionless against the far wall. Her body screamed at her to run, to flee from the overwhelming power before her, but her mind was stuck—frozen by the sight of her brother standing so far from the person he used to be.

Edward's eyes met hers, glowing with a sinister gleam, and for a moment, she thought she saw a flicker of recognition, something almost human buried beneath the dark power that radiated from him. It was gone as quickly as it had appeared, replaced by a chilling indifference.

"I am no longer just Edward," he said, his voice low and vibrating with the weight of his transformation. I am Malakos. I am the future."

The Shadow shifted behind him, its voice rumbling like an earthquake. "The world will bow, or it will burn. You will lead them, Edward. Show them what it means to wield true power."

Phoenix clenched her fists, every muscle in her body trembling with the enormity of the moment.

"This isn't you, Edward," she whispered, but the words felt hollow even as they left her lips.

She could feel the finality of it, the understanding that the brother she had known was gone. Malakos had taken him; now, with the Shadow, he was something else entirely—something she couldn't save.

But Edward's twisted smile only deepened. "No, Phoenix. This is who I've always been. You were just too blind to see it."

The room shook violently, as if the facility itself was reacting to Edward's newfound power. The tendrils of Shadow lashed out again, breaking through walls and floors and destabilizing everything around them. The building groaned, cracks forming in the ceiling, raining debris down on them.

Ro grabbed Phoenix by the arm, pulling her toward the exit. "Phoenix, now! We have to go!"

Jax stirred, groaning as he pushed himself off the ground. He was battered and bloodied, but the fierce determination in his eyes hadn't waned.

"Get out of here," he said through gritted teeth. "I'll hold him off."

"No!" Phoenix shouted, turning toward him. "You can't—"

"I can," Jax interrupted, his voice hard, leaving no room for argument. "I won't let him destroy everything. You two need to find a way to stop this, and that starts with getting out of here alive."

Edward took a step forward, his gaze locked on Jax. The darkness swirled around him with renewed intensity.

"You can't stop me, Jax," he said, almost lazily. "You're just prolonging the inevitable."

Jax's grip tightened around his blade, the defiance in his eyes burning brighter. "I've fought harder monsters than you, Edward. I'm not scared of you."

Phoenix's heart broke at the sight. She knew Jax was buying them time, and every fiber of her being wanted to stay and fight alongside him. But she knew, deep down, that staying would mean certain death—for all of them.

With one last agonizing glance at Jax, Phoenix allowed Ro to pull her toward the crumbling exit. The facility shook as they ran, debris crashing down around them as the structure threatened to collapse at any moment.

As they reached the facility's shattered threshold, Phoenix paused, turning back to see Jax standing alone against Edward and the Shadow. The immense power swirling around them dwarfed his figure, but his resolve remained unshaken.

"Jax!" Phoenix shouted, her voice barely audible over the roar of destruction.

Jax didn't look back; his focus was entirely on Edward. "Go!" he shouted. "I'll find you."

But Phoenix knew the truth. Jax wasn't planning on finding them. He was sacrificing himself, buying them whatever precious time he could to escape the nightmare that Edward had become.

The facility groaned, metal twisting and screeching as the Shadow's power tore through its foundation. Edward's dark form stood at the center of the chaos, a storm of shadow tendrils swirling around him as if the world itself was bending to his will. Jax, standing alone, his blade raised in defiance, looked impossibly small against the oncoming wave of darkness.

Phoenix stumbled forward, her eyes locked on Jax, knowing this was it. His final stand. She tried to call out, but her voice caught in her throat, the words dying on her lips. There was no saving him now. The bitter truth settled over her like a weight she could barely carry. He was giving them a chance - one last, fleeting chance to escape.

"Phoenix, we have to go!" Ro's voice was raw and urgent, pulling her back to the moment, to the danger closing in around them.

But as Phoenix turned to flee with Ro, she stole one last glance at Jax, standing resolute as Edward, now fully Malakos, advanced toward him. For a heartbeat, their eyes met, and in Jax's gaze, Phoenix saw no fear—only grim acceptance.

Then the Shadow moved.

Tendrils of dark energy lashed out, crashing into the walls and ceiling, ripping the facility apart. The ground trembled as the power of the Shadow surged, its force overwhelming and unstoppable.

Phoenix and Ro sprinted through the collapsing hallways, debris crashing around them as they fought to escape. The sound of destruction roared in their ears, but the silence behind them - the absence of Jax's final cry - tore at Phoenix's heart.

The exit loomed ahead, a jagged opening into the night. They burst through it, stumbling into the cold air, gasping for breath. But as they turned, the facility exploded, engulfed in a wave of Shadow and fire.

A sickening crash echoed through the valley as the facility caved in on itself, consumed by the Shadow's destruction. And then, as the dust settled, silence. Only the faint crackle of distant flames broke the eerie stillness.

Phoenix fell to her knees as the weight of Jax's sacrifice hit her like a blow. He was gone. The man who had fought for them and stood defiant in the face of the impossible had given his life to buy them time. And now, Edward—no, Malakos—was all that remained.

Ro knelt beside her, his hand on her shoulder, silent, but his eyes were filled with the same loss she felt.

The night shifted suddenly as the darkness around them thickened. A cold wind whipped through the air, carrying a familiar and dreadful presence.

Edward.

Phoenix's head snapped up, her heart racing as she saw him. His form was no longer bound by flesh - he was a shadow, a dark, ethereal figure, his once-human body now twisted and melded with the power of the Shadow. Tendrils of black energy radiated from him, like an extension of his very being, swaying and twisting as if alive.

His voice was low, distorted, almost unrecognizable. "You should have joined us, Phoenix."

Phoenix stood slowly, her legs weak beneath her, but her resolve hardening. She stared at the shadowy figure before her, refusing to look away. "I will never join you, Edward."

A dark chuckle escaped from him, and the tendrils of Shadow shifted, reaching out toward her. One of them brushed against her arm, and she flinched, but it was too late. The tendril left a small black mark on her skin, cold and seeping into her flesh like poison.

She gasped, feeling the darkness crawl beneath her skin, but she fought to keep her expression hard and unyielding.

"You're marked now," Edward said, his voice dripping with malice. "The Shadow has touched you. You'll never escape it, no matter how far you run."

Phoenix's hand instinctively moved to the mark, her fingers brushing the cold black tendril etched into her skin. She gritted her teeth. "You've lost, Edward."

Edward's smile widened, his eyes gleaming with dark amusement. "No, Phoenix. I haven't lost anything. You've only delayed the inevitable."

The ground beneath them trembled again, but it wasn't the facility crumbling this time. It was something else—something far deeper, darker. Phoenix could feel a pull, a slow, steady drawing toward the Shadow, toward Edward's new form.

"You don't understand, do you?" Edward's voice was condescending. "I am not the one who needs to be saved. I have embraced what I am and was always meant to be. The Shadow doesn't corrupt—it reveals. And now, Phoenix, you are a part of it. You'll carry that mark, and one day, you will understand. You'll see the truth."

Phoenix shook her head, her heart pounding in her chest. "You're wrong."

"Am I?" Edward's form flickered, and at that moment, his eyes— glowing with dark power—locked onto hers. "You've lost everything already, Phoenix. Jax. Mira. Soon, Ro will fall, too. And when you stand alone, when the weight of your choices bears down on you, you'll regret not joining us. You'll regret fighting the inevitable."

Phoenix's jaw clenched, her fists tightening. "I won't fall. I'll fight you until my last breath."

Edward's shadowy form swayed, and the tendrils of darkness around him seemed to pulse with a life of their own. "Perhaps. But know this, Phoenix—one day, you will beg for the power I now possess. You will beg to join me."

He turned slightly, his form shifting, ready to disappear into the night. But before he left, he spoke one last time, his voice a twisted echo of the brother she had once known.

"I am Malakos now, Phoenix. And the world will bow to me. When it does, you will too."

With that, Edward vanished into the shadows, leaving Phoenix and Ro alone in the destruction's aftermath. The cold night air wrapped around them, the silence almost unbearable.

Phoenix touched the black mark on her arm, a shiver running through her. The mark burned a constant reminder of Edward's warning—of the Shadow's reach.

Ro moved closer, his voice low and steady. "We'll stop him, Phoenix. Whatever it takes."

Phoenix nodded, but inside, a seed of doubt had taken root. Edward was gone—truly gone. In his place was a monster far more dangerous than she could have imagined.

As they stood there, staring into the darkness where Edward had disappeared, Phoenix couldn't shake the feeling that this was only the beginning.

The Shadow had claimed Edward.

And now, it had its sights set on her.

Preview of Book 2

Chapter 1: *The Edge of Oblivion*

Edward no longer knew where he was—if this place could even be called a place. His body, now Malakos's, stood at the edge of reality, in a dimension that defied all understanding. Shadows curled around him, formless, shifting, alive. The ground beneath his feet wasn't solid nor liquid, but something in between, pulsating with an eerie glow. The air—if it was air—felt thick and cold, like breathing through a suffocating fog. He had no sense of time here. Hours, days, even years could have passed without his knowing. The only constant was the presence of the master.

The Shadow.

It loomed somewhere in the distance, always watching, always waiting. Edward could feel it, like a great weight pressing down on his mind. Malakos's memories pulsed within him, fragments of ancient pain and rage clawing at the edges of his thoughts, but Edward fought to stay in control. He wasn't ready to let go—not yet.

"You are no longer who you were," the Shadow's voice echoed through the void, a soundless whisper that filled Edward's mind. "Malakos is you now. You are power. You are rebirth."

Edward clenched his fists, feeling the strange strength in his new form. He was no longer the boy he had once been. His mind battled the darkness and malevolence that came with Malakos's body, but every moment that passed in this place wore him down. He could feel himself slipping, memories of Phoenix, Ro, and the world he knew fading like whispers in the wind.

The master's realm twisted and shifted around him, an eternal landscape of chaos where no horizon existed and no path led anywhere. The Shadow moved closer, its presence oppressive, but Edward didn't flinch. Deep inside, the part of him that was still Edward refused to submit.

"I am more than you think," Edward whispered into the void, his voice swallowed by the endless dark....

www.ingramcontent.com/pod-product-compliance
Lightning Source LLC
Chambersburg PA
CBHW032008310726
48972CB00002B/320